ADORATION
& AFFLICTION
Novellas and Short Stories

Also by Robert Scott Leyse

Novels

Tease and Dare: Angie and Ella's Summer of Delirium
Attraction and Repulsion
Self-Murder

Collections

Playgrounds and Battlegrounds: Four Novellas

Novellas from the above collection are
available separately as eBooks:

Excitation and Oblivion, or Kaleidoscopic San Juan
Playgrounds and Battlegrounds
Idleness and Unrest
Nighttime Euphoria and the Field of Reeds,
or One Can Get Away with What One Dares

ADORATION & AFFLICTION
Novellas and Short Stories

Robert Scott Leyse

ShatterColors Press
New York, New York

Cover star: Angie Esther Ella Leyse
Photo of Angie: Robert Henry Leyse
Other photography + cover design: Robert Scott Leyse
Photo of RSL: Don Robin

"Penelope Prim" and "The Urban Primeval" are released individually as eBooks.

ISBN 979-8-9985093-0-8

Library of Congress Control Number: 2025908744

First Edition

Contents

Abrupt Awakening

It can be said that at present our heroine, Nicoletta Bajari, is a much doted upon only child of a prominent family who's led a highly sheltered life, never had occasion to deal with overmuch stress. It can also be said that many people, regardless of how sheltered, are capable of being extremely feisty, resourceful, and courageous when faced with serious adversity for the first time.

So let us proceed by asking: is it Nicoletta's fault that, at sixteen years of age, she's a beauty many considerably older men, despite cautionary inner voices, can't help but follow about with their eyes, lingeringly stare at? Her fault the said men can't help but be drawn to her bright brown eyes that both pierce and caress whatever they gaze upon, can flare up or soften at a mood's notice, generally display an intriguing mix of sweetness and mockery, modesty and pride? Her fault the perpetual interplay of emotion on her face—now delighted, now pouting—now dreamy, now alert—now shy, now haughty—grips these men to such a degree they can't help but cast her in leading roles in fantasies that frighten them, particularly as they've never attached such fantasies to an adolescent? Her fault she's far more than the sum total of her physical attributes? Yes, disregard the abundant waves of pitch black hair, perfectly proportioned oval of her visage, flawless lily-white complexion; disregard her lissome curves, yoga-augmented musculature—nonchalant grace, feline poise, sensually mellifluent voice: many girls possess the same and, while certainly not lacking admirers, aren't close to being in Nicoletta's league. What sets Nicoletta apart? It's the pronounced tone of yearning, outright hunger, that pervades the lineaments of her beauty—the electric restlessness gleaming in her eyes, surging under her skin, animating her movements, charging the air about her. Magnetism's an understatement—Nicoletta's energy is a rip current.

So Nicoletta's older admirers are held in check by her age (and her family's status in the community surely also encourages restraint), even if they're occasionally sorely tempted to approach her—it's too easy to overlook she's legally a child due to her precocity and charisma—setting rooms alight the moment she enters them, seeming to bend the light in her direction, lend crispness to the air. Except that one very married, rotund, double-chinned, puffy-cheeked, mid-fortyish Edmund Sloffor of under average height, while generally pusillanimous, finds himself under the influence of increasing lack of restraint with regard to Nicoletta. Whether it's on account of his essential weakness of character or outright stupidity or because he's never actively pursued a woman (having been marked for marriage early on by his wife, a woman who values stability, predictability, and calling the shots above all else): who can pinpoint why Sloffor's increasingly unable to comprehend what constitutes acceptable behavior when confronted by Nicoletta's beauty?

So let us proceed further by asking: is it Nicoletta's fault that on a Friday night at one of her parents' gatherings—to which the so-called movers and shakers of her coastal California hometown come to see and be seen, network and solidify business connections, propose and follow up on deals—Sloffor, having imbibed overmuch single malt, becomes nothing short of fixated upon her, watching for every flicker of her aquamarine dress as she flits from room to room, socializing with all? Her fault he becomes despondent when she disappears upstairs, off-limits to guests, for over half an hour? Her fault she chances to glance in Sloffor's general direction shortly after she reappears—passes an unsteady hand across her forehead, flings her hair behind her shoulders, takes deep breaths, her face flushed? Her fault Sloffor mistakes her glance and hair-fling and deep breathing for an invitation—assumes her flush is a blush in his favor—when, in fact, she's become nauseous as a consequence of having smoked half a cigar, pilfered from a coat pocket in the guest-closet, on the third-floor terrace? Her fault that, when she exits the party to fortify herself with fresh air in the backyard's rose gardens, Sloffor follows convinced she's expecting him to do so? Her fault that, after she's seated on a bench a couple dozen yards from the house—hyperventilating to flush her lungs—he supposes she's joyously anticipating his arrival, preparing herself? Her fault he embraces her from behind, fingers her breasts, slobbers on her neck, intones, "Thank you! Thank you!" in a tremulous voice?

Nothing has prepared Nicoletta for being groped and slobbered upon by a man nearly three decades her senior, but she remains self-possessed; or perhaps it's more accurate to state she's too dumbfounded to be upset, half disbelieving what's transpiring. The first thought to occur to her is that the family dog, an affectionate English Setter, is licking her neck; the second thought to occur to her, upon hearing Sloffor's words, is that dogs don't speak; then she hears herself exclaim "Eeeeewww!"—springs to her feet, whips about. Sloffor stumbles towards her, strikes the bench with his thighs as if blind to it, barely manages to two-handedly seize it's back in time to avoid falling forwards; then he's stammering, flailing desperation in his eyes, "I'm sorry if I...I didn't mean to surprise you...sorry I made you jump. I should've said I...that I was here for you...I'm sorry if I...please understand!"

Vaguely recognizing Sloffor, an individual she's paid little mind and likely addressed with less than two dozen words (such being perfunctory greetings at the above-mentioned gatherings), Nicoletta's disgust knows no bounds, becomes self-defense on the physiological level, in the sense that she stops him dead in his tracks with a glance of fury she feels surge into her eyes from the pit of her stomach, coiled tautness of her muscles, rigidity of her spine—a glance that energizes every inch of her body, propels her into an emotionally heightened distance—distance from which she watches the features of Sloffor's face fall apart, collapse—cheeks turn to quivering jelly, eyes drown in scampering erratic light. Truth to tell, Nicoletta has no clear idea what to do, but she *is* aware of measuring herself against Sloffor and finding him considerably weaker. Following a few moments of paralyzing him with her eyes, she simply turns away and unhurriedly saunters to the house—his panicked intonation of "I didn't try to, I'm sorry I...that I didn't tell you that...please...please let me explain...please!" reaching in her ears as if from a great distance, originating from an alternate reality—a dislocated dream.

Upon reaching her house, though, Nicoletta's trembling, unsteady in her stride—faced with a, so to speak, blank white wall of numbness, as she's never experienced before. It's as if the air's become an all-seeing eye, privy to every nuance of her frame of mind; and she's not sure how others might manage to discern something's amiss and pity her, but is tight in her throat—feeling smothered, her skin heating—as if it's occurring, the faces of the guests blurred, voices indistinct, and so finds herself dashing up the rear foyer's stairs to her bedroom on the second floor. Once there, she flings herself on her bed, where she's soon writhing on her back, involuntarily reviewing what's occurred—cringing at the thought of Sloffor's clumsy lips and fumbling fingers and stinking breath. "My God!" she exclaims aloud, fighting off the impulse to cry—shaking to her bones, assailed by disorientation and fear.

In the garden the shock of the intrusion—presence of the offender and necessity of fending him off—had endowed Nicoletta with energetic composure, focused emotional strength. She'd stared Sloffor into confusion as if on automatic pilot—instinctively, with next to no thinking involved. Now that the immediate threat's gone the inner unity it brought about dissipates, leaving her alone with the horror of the incident—alone with an oppressive sense of helplessness, as in not being safe within her own home—the idea that if her home's no longer a safe place, safe places don't exist.

But then Nicoletta's just as suddenly infuriated, informing herself it's unthinkable, and humiliating, to allow herself to be afraid on account of a sickening slob—unthinkable to allow Sloffor to walk away free and clear. How dare he drool upon and paw her, revolt her to the core of her being. She *must* recover the inner unity and strength she experienced when staring him down, use it to rise above the abuse she's endured—*must* dispel her uneasiness, quiet the noise in her nerves, strike back! And then a means of retaliation occurs to her and she springs from the bed—rapidly paces about, mixing in twirls and high kicks, to flush the shakiness from her limbs. But quick! Sloffor might be dim-witted and delusional, but he's surely disinclined to linger at the party. Just five more minutes of frenetic exercise—cartwheels, running in place, jumping jacks—and physical-exertion-engendered euphoria will rout doubt, lend courage to intent, transform hesitation into action. Sure enough, within ten minutes Nicoletta's splashing her face in the adjoining bathroom's sink, waiting for her audible breathing to subside; then she's exiting

5

her bedroom, descending the stairs, saying to herself, "I hope it's not too late!"

Nicoletta's plan of retaliation unfolds as follows: upon rejoining the party, she locates Sloffor's wife (A loquacious woman of amiable mien, attired in a silver ankle-length black-fringed dress, with a veritable helmet of hair—dyed ochre—held in place by an abundance of pins; taller than and not as filled-out as her husband, even if her hips are noticeably wider than her shoulders.), joins the cluster of people of which she's a part, and engages her in conversation; at first, chats of inconsequentialities such as the fluctuations of the weather, variety of quality discounted merchandise at a local department store, having a taste for seafood, large salads, and tropical fruit—all the while adopting an increasingly affectionate manner. Nicoletta absolutely *must* make a friend of Sloffor's wife, establish a dependable means of bedeviling the lout who's slobbered on her neck, touched her with repulsive hands. Necessity lends a tone of ingenuousness to Nicoletta's manner—the blitheness of her voice, inclination to laughing lilts in her enunciation, distracts from whatever stress and irritation might be involuntarily revealed via her flashing glances about the room, as she seeks to locate Sloffor, wonders where he's gone. Why doesn't the creep show himself? Why can't he enter the room, freeze in panic at the sight of her chatting with his wife, helplessly stare as worry devours his features, knifes his guts?

After being carefree and giggly in the wife's company for a spell—all but clinging to her with wide delighted eyes—Nicoletta redirects. Suddenly grasping one of the wife's hands with both of hers, squeezing with urgency, she assumes a look of perplexity and, following a few seconds of nervous hesitation, inquires in a quavering voice, "Can I tell you something?" Then, before the wife can respond, she blurts out, "A boy at school is bothering me and won't stop! He thinks it's funny but it's not! He throws paper clips and other stuff in my hair, pulls my sweater from behind, and dumps pencil shavings on my lap! He also lifts up my dress partway and says he wants to lift it all the way, and says more bad things, like what he wants to do with me after school!" Uneasily glancing at the floor in apparent embarrassment, Nicoletta chokes back the beginning of a sob and asks what should be done.

Pleased to hear the wife state in no uncertain terms that the boy needs to be reported to the school authorities and disciplined, Nicoletta gazes gratefully into her eyes, affectionately caresses her hand, says, "I haven't done anything to him—try to stay out of his way—so why does he act like that? I don't like to report people, but he's picking on me and it's scary!" The wife responds by saying that making others afraid is unpardonable and anyone who does so must be stood up to and deserves no sympathy; that Nicoletta owes it to herself and others to bring the boy's behavior to the attention of the authorities, and should do so without delay; that, at the very least, the boy's parents should be notified and an official warning issued—a warning which, if not heeded, will result in immediate suspension. Nicoletta's very comforted by these words, indeed, and more so by the looks of outrage which accompany them. Indications are the wife will make her spouse wish he was never born if notified of his conduct in the garden.

Nicoletta has no intention of notifying the wife or anyone else of her spouse's conduct. Not that she doubts for an instant she'd easily convince all present of the truth, move them to blistering anger—cause Sloffor a great deal of grief—with a detailed presentation of the facts accompanied by a liberal amount of trembling and tears. She knows Sloffor would quickly crumble in the face of the accusation and give himself away. She ascertained the feebleness of his will while staring him down following his offense. But Nicoletta's pride revolts at the prospect of being regarded as a victim and pitied—sympathy, particularly the condescension that often accompanies it, is poison to her. Also, by keeping the matter to herself she remains in charge of redressing the wrong which has been done her, meting out the amount of punishment she deems fit. It's up to her to personally see to it she can continue to hold her head high—counting upon others to do so will invariably backfire, in the sense that she'll be at the mercy of debilitating feelings of dependency. Not to mention that if word gets out among her peers, is spread about her school, she might lose something of her top-tier social status, perhaps become the subject of unflattering jokes—or, worse, start receiving unwanted attention from emboldened boys. There's never been a meddlesome boy at school, the majority of them being in awe of her, and she wants to keep it that way—she *must* keep it that way. All the same, though, Nicoletta's experienced a vivid shock and is suddenly outside the safe place where she's spent her life, under the influence of emotions no sixteen year old girl should have to deal with—recoiling at the persistent recollection of Sloffor's hands on her, livid with indignation, and also feeling vulnerable and uneasy, and also playacting her heart out while remaining focused upon her plan of retaliation. Because feelings of vulnerability *must* be defeated, *cannot* carry the day: the promise Nicoletta's made to herself is that when she's finished with Sloffor he's going to want to crawl into a corner, stay in it forever. So Nicoletta continues to cling to the wife while periodically scanning the room for Sloffor's presence. Eventually he'll show himself, right? He can't avoid his wife, right? And when Sloffor shows himself Nicoletta will turn away from the wife for long enough to strike terror into him with a razor-sharp glare and evil smile: he'll be bedeviling himself all night with highly unpleasant speculations, fearing the worst—no one's going to victimize her without regretting it a thousand times over, living in hell.

But Sloffor, afraid to reenter the house, sends the valet to inform his wife he's indisposed and waiting in the car. When the valet delivers this message Nicoletta tightens and twitches in every muscle, flushes and turns ashen of face—heat whipping up and down her spine, breathing becoming rapid and shallow. Apprehensive her face might be about to betray her, reveal her true intentions, Nicoletta covers her mouth and feigns a cough, turns to the wall. Gritting her teeth, clenching and unclenching her hands, shaking her head and slapping one of her cheeks, she succeeds in masking outward indications of outrage. Within thirty seconds she's facing the wife again, saying, "Sorry, Mrs. Sloffor, I had a tickle in my throat—I didn't mean to be so dramatic about it. Anyway, it's gone now." The wife, smiling warmly and patting Nicoletta's shoulder, assures her no apology's needed and asks if she's sure she's fine and if there's anything she can do. Nicoletta, bringing a charming pout to her face, answers by saying, "I'm fine except for one thing. I wish you didn't have to leave already but understand why. I'm sorry Mr. Sloffor isn't feeling well and hope he gets better soon. Please give him my best wishes." The wife, hugging Nicoletta goodnight, assures her that she will.

As Nicoletta watches the wife make her goodbye rounds, circle about the room, shortness of breath seizes her again, along with pronounced trembling: she visualizes her enemy escaping scot-free—visualizes a look of smugness overspreading his face—and understands she'll suffer on account of failing to make him suffer; understands she won't be able to sleep, enjoy a moment of ease, on account of deflected vengeance. Already, hints of the misery to which she'll be subject are assailing her nerves—the brightly illuminated spacious living room, filled with festive people, feels small and dark and gloomy—the air dense, oppressive, smothering—walls advancing towards her, boxing her in. Then, after perhaps a minute of anguish that seems like an hour, a solution pops into Nicoletta's head, seemingly of its own accord, and she instantly acts upon it. Scampering to the coat check, she obtains the wife's coat and purse and brings them to her; instead of handing the wife the purse, though, she insists upon carrying it herself and accompanying her to the car—insists upon it with an adorable smile, adding, "I want to be of use!"

A few minutes later, as Nicoletta steps outside with the wife, she's hit upon a means of instilling terror in Sloffor without alerting the wife. Continuing to act the part of charmingly enthusiastic youngster, she asks the wife if the car near the fountain midway down the driveway (where the valet parks the cars of guests ready to depart) is hers. Once the wife affirms it is, Nicoletta races towards it quick as she can, shouting over her shoulder, "I'll get the door for you, Mrs. Sloffor!"

Upon reaching the car, noting Sloffor's slumped in the passenger seat, Nicoletta, in what seems to her a swift unbroken blur—as if someone else is performing her actions and she's along for the ride—yanks open the door on the driver's side, thrusts her head halfway in, glares at her enemy, hisses, "You're in big trouble!" As when staring him down in the garden she feels herself surge into the special electric unity within herself and her perceptions seem to slow down: she's watching his face blanch, shoulders jerk, hands shake, eyes flail as if from the other side of a thick pane of glass; at the same time a mix of anger, apprehension, excitement, and relief surges in her breast, all but robs her of breath, although she's outwardly as calm and immobile as a statue. But quick! The wife's halfway to the car: time to erase the venom from face, realign with an innocent demeanor, put on blitheness! Nicoletta turns from the door, steps to the car's rear, is shortly leaning against it at the taillight while observing a nearby palm's rhythmically swaying fronds, silently counting, *one one-thousand, two one-thousand, three one-thousand,* measuring the wife's approach from the corner of her eye. Once the wife's within a few feet, Nicoletta steps to her with a smile of admiration, thanks her for the advice concerning the boy at school, loudly declares, "I guess I *do* have to report him!" Nicoletta's standing close enough to the open driver's door to feel Sloffor recoil, exhale as if smacked in the back—his fear's emanating from the car, acting upon her like a drug—streaming contentment through her veins, redoubling her confidence and courage, sweeping her towards a place where daring's richly rewarded. Therefore, before Nicoletta's half aware of what she's doing, she turns about and leans inside the door again, says, "Get well soon, Mr. Sloffor!" in the sweetest tone imaginable with the most hostile eyes imaginable. Then she's standing upright again, facing the wife with an angelic expression. "Silly me, I still have your really cute purse!" she giggles, handing it to the wife, pecking her goodbye on the cheek. "It was nice talking to you, Mrs. Sloffor, and thanks again for your help—get home safe," she concludes, affectionately clasping her hand a last time before turning towards the house.

When the wife lowers herself into the driver's seat Nicoletta hears her exclaim, "Oh, my God! Honey, you're so pale! Are you running a fev...?" before the door shuts, renders her voice inaudible. Soon thereafter, as Nicoletta watches the taillights of Sloffor's car recede, she says aloud, "Sweet dreams, creep!" Then she's circling around the house to the guesthouse in back to play with Byron, the aforementioned English Setter. Byron's been placed in the guesthouse because some people at the gathering are either uncomfortable around dogs or allergic to them, and also because he's fond of snatching unguarded hors d'oeuvres.

Soon as Nicoletta steps within the guesthouse Byron's all over her, as if he's been deprived of her company for weeks—dashing in circles about her, placing his paws on her chest, licking her hands. "Here, sweetie!" she calls, racing to the bedroom, leaping onto the bed and bouncing up and down, her hair flying every which way. Byron, fairly crazed with excitement, likewise leaps onto the bed and they bounce together—soon Nicoletta's laughing uncontrollably, crying out for joy—what welcome respite from all she's endured tonight. Then she's kneeling on the mattress, hugging Byron close, covering him with caresses, as he licks her face. "Cooping you up's a crime!" she declares, stroking him behind the ears, gazing into his eyes. "This is your home too and the anti-dog people can leave if they don't like it!" So saying, she scampers to the door, is soon outside with Byron, he sprinting hither and thither, frequently circling back to her with a look of expectation, his tail wildly swishing. She doesn't disappoint him. Crossing to the tennis court, she obtains a tennis ball, throws it across the yard. Byron—already anticipating and heading in the ball's direction before it exits her hand—dashes after it as if possessed, quickly bringing it to her and dropping it at her feet. She throws it again and he's off again—his effortless speed and agility, fluidity of motion, bringing elation to her heart.

Playing with Byron whisks Nicoletta apart from the emotional disarray she's endured; but it could also be said she's racing inside herself to stay a step ahead of said disarray, keep it at bay. She's extremely intelligent and headstrong—adept at discerning pretense, tough to intimidate—but she's *still* a sixteen year old girl, lovingly indulged by protective parents, who's been violated by an adult, endeavoring to regain her bearings. Never mind the adult in question's a gutless dimwit she's by no means afraid of. The fact remains Sloffor's robbed Nicoletta of the undisturbed ease of mind she's always known, shattered the illusion of unassailable security, and she needs to deal with it. Soon she's dashing about as well, only pausing to pick up the ball when Byron drops it and toss it anew, becoming frenzied and dizzy, relishing such.

About twenty minutes into their game Nicoletta throws the ball after spinning about, her aim off, and it soars over the hedge separating the lawn from the rose gardens and rolls under the bench where Sloffor groped her, halted by its curly-cue ground-hugging grillwork in back, and Byron's unable to seize it. Hearing him address her with his worry-bark, indicating he needs assistance, Nicoletta dashes around the hedge. It's not until she's near enough to perceive the bright green ball under the bench that she realizes she's returned to the location of the assault and starts, slowing to a half-jog; then, annoyed at her hesitation, she races to the bench with a vengeance, intending to throw the ball back on open lawn. But she finds herself laughing, twirling about, kneeling low and jumping high, Bryon accompanying her with leaps. Finally, thoroughly winded, she sits at the spot where Sloffor foisted himself upon her, Byron instantly at her side.

"Good dog, you brought me back here," Nicoletta says, hugging Byron. "It's my backyard, I can't be afraid of any of it! And if you hadn't been locked up because some idiots are afraid of nice dogs you would've been here to tear the creep to pieces if he tried anything! You sure would, sweetie darling!" Following a couple minutes of recovering from her exertions—happy windedness, semi-dazedness—Nicoletta finds herself reviewing what transpired when she dashed ahead of Sloffor's wife to confront him at his car. She'd only planned to do the first part—the "You're in trouble!" part. That she'd added on a part two while Sloffor's wife was mere feet away—poked her head inside the car again, wished him a speedy recovery with honey in her voice while stabbing him dead with her eyes... How thrilling to surprise herself thus, do something advance thinking would've cautioned against! How intoxicating to unexpectedly become disconnected from thought, act solely on impulse! Who knew she'd be capable of playacting to such a degree—being in two opposite emotional places at once, tormenting her assailant while being a perfect sweetheart in the eyes of his wife? Nicoletta's never been called upon to act in such a way before and can't help but congratulate herself. "The slob picked on the wrong girl!" she declares to Byron, he immediately licking her hands.

Soothed by Byron's presence, springtime ocean breeze, and her beautiful backyard—the row of palms, gently swaying and rustling, marking the garden's left boundary—crescent-shaped beds of white and red and pink roses radiating one after the other, overflowing with scent—sweep of the lawn beyond the hedge to her right—all splashed with moonlight's silver tinge—Nicoletta removes her shoes and lies on her back on the grass at the base of the bench, Byron shortly curled up beside her.

Approximately an hour later she's ascending the stairs to her bedroom with Byron, again reflecting upon her victory. "Who knows?" she addresses Byron after she's entered her room and shut the door. "The slob might start running a fever for real, instead of only looking like he is! And he won't be coming here again—he's banned! I had to settle the score and I think I did!" Observing herself in the sliding closet door's full-length mirror, she spins about twice, kicks high, and pumps a fist.

After showering and climbing into bed, Byron asleep on his doggie bed nearby, Nicoletta lies awake repeatedly reliving the sequence of abuse, stare-down, escape, onset of trembling, res-olution to punish, success at doing so. More than once she, upon reaching the end of the sequence, slams her fist into the mattress and hisses, "That's what scums get!" or a variation thereof. As the night advances, however, she finds herself dwelling far more on the abuse than anything else—eventually unable to see beyond the fumbling fingers, drooling lips, fetid breath, slobbery voice.

"No! No! No!" she cries while twisting with fury, punching and biting the pillows, kicking the blankets. "Go away!" she yells almost loud enough to be heard outside her room as Sloffor's face looms in her mind's eye and his rheumy eyes stare at her, cling to her as if seeking to infect her with their sickly light. "No!" Icy hot stings race up and down her spine, spread throughout her—tighten her face, immobilize her limbs, stifle her breath.

Regardless of how much Nicoletta's pride revolts against admitting it, that man—the groper—the *thing*—has robbed her of a carefree night, stolen her happiness. If she can't sit on a bench in her own backyard without having to guard against violation where can she? Damn him, insipid, oafish, cowardly, less than half-man that he is! To think that such a creature's stolen precious unconcern from her, compelled her to endure mental and emotional strain, afflicted her with blazing nerves, actual physical agony; stolen thoughts of what to wear to the beach on Sunday from her, replaced them with suffocating rage! Clearly, it was premature for her to assume the score's been settled, balance restored—it hasn't, not by a long shot. Clearly, she must resume the fight, hit Sloffor harder, if she's to regain her life, pass a peaceful night.

Nicoletta resolves that for every night she sleeplessly suffers, she'll make Sloffor suffer tenfold. But how is she to flay him as he deserves, poison his waking hours and destroy his sleep, ensure he's tormented by thoughts of worst-case scenarios—thoughts of what she *might* do next? How is she to make him cower like a rat that's been clawed by a cat, his fear unbounded? She has to get around the fact she's barely over sixteen, bridge the gap between the teenage and adult world; has to or she'll know no quietude—never be able to look at herself in the mirror without feeling inferior, ashamed. Reacquiring her confidence, sense of being safe and secure and in control of her destiny, is a *ne-*

cessity—there's *no* alternative. And so Nicoletta's thoughts are soon overrun with possible courses of action, all either virtually impossible to implement or insufficient: for over an hour she fears she'll fail to hit upon a viable plan, writhe on hot coals all night. But then, just as her distress becomes almost unendurably acute, a viable plan spontaneously crystallizes, as if by magic, and relative ease of mind is her reward. Necessity truly is the mother of invention.

Nicoletta manages to sleep, albeit periodically awakening to find herself entangled in the blankets, wet with sweat—her rage has subsided but impatience stands in the way of uninterrupted sleep. For now, Sloffor's been transformed from a tormentor into a target: thoughts of the abuse he's subjected her to have been replaced by thoughts of what she's going to do to shatter his life.

As to how Nicoletta goes about shattering Sloffor's life, restoring balance to her self-esteem, she rises at nine thirty and, after letting Byron out, phones Sloffor's number. The wife answers and Nicoletta, putting on more of the eager young person concern, asks if her husband's feeling better. The wife replies that his condition's worsened and he's weak, achy, running a fever. After an exclamation of horror, and bringing added tenderness into her voice, Nicoletta asks if he's been given tea, ginger, and echinacea—if he has enough blankets—if he's eating chicken soup; in short, spares no effort in further coming across as the sweet altruistic helper. The wife, in a tone of marveling admiration, thanks Nicoletta for her concern and assures her he's being well taken care of. Nicoletta then says she doesn't want to be a burden on the phone and keep the wife from tending to her husband and asks her to tell him he's in her prayers. Upon hanging up, Nicoletta paces about her room while picturing, with a scowling smile, the amount of fear she's certain will blanch her enemy's face when the wife conveys her message. "Sure thing, Mr.

Sloffor," she says aloud, "you're in my prayers—I didn't lie about *that*! I pray trepidation eats you alive!"

We hasten to add Nicoletta's phone call is preliminary preparation for the execution of her plan, not the plan proper: its primary purpose is to establish that Sloffor's home, as well as discover what he's doing. She's hardly inclined to settle for middling secondhand retaliation, having a message delivered by a third party. And, for that matter, how does she know Sloffor will receive her message? If he's sleeping the wife won't wake him to communicate it and could easily forget to do so later. Unexpectedly, the thought that Sloffor might not receive her message or know she's called, even though she has far more in store for him, begins to bother Nicoletta. "The creep might be sleeping like a baby when he ought to be scared enough to want to crawl under the bed!" she winces with indignation; and then she's picturing Sloffor sound asleep, with a look of smugness on his face; and then she's again feeling his hands on her breasts and lips on her neck—smelling his malodorous mouth, hearing his revolting voice speak words of gratitude, "Did the thing really say *thank you*?" she hisses as hot needle nerves sting her—as her throat contracts and she gasps for breath. Suddenly she fears her plan of retaliation might slip away from her and envisions the chance of remaining a victim, being everlastingly lashed by self-loathing. "That's *not* going to happen! I'm going to get him and get him good!" she almost screams as she advances to the bathroom, intent on calming herself with a shower.

Once Nicoletta's in the shower she runs the water hot for a couple minutes, then cold for a couple more, then hot again, continuing to alternate, while stretching—slow dancing—in an effort to approach some semblance of equilibrium. To no avail: the second she starts lathering herself she imagines Sloffor's hands are upon her instead. "Really?" she chides herself. "I'm doing a

What if my hands were his? thing? Unbelievable!" she concludes with a yell, dashing the bar of soap to the tiles—only to have it ricochet about, strike her shin. "Jesus Christ!" she yells again as the walls close in on her and the shower stall reels. "I'll kill him!" she cries as she slaps the stall door open. Then she's at the sink, splashing her face and chest with frigid water: raising her eyes, she meets her gaze in the mirror, and declares, "I'm not close to finished with him! He's not going to put me through a bad night, not going to put me through *this*—make me hate so much it hurts—without finding out what hell's *really* like! He's not going to make this girl cry! Not going to make this girl crawl into a corner and wilt!"

Upon exiting the bathroom Nicoletta dries herself, her hands trembling. Then she dresses in the manner she and her girlfriends call the "innocent look"—ponytails her hair with a lavender ribbon, applies a smidgen of eyeshadow and coat of lipstick, both pale pink—puts on a pleated knee-length ivory skirt with lavender lace fringe, a lavender blouse, white pumps with lavender bows on top—as tension continues to tighten her muscles. Then she descends to the kitchen, eats a grapefruit and bowl of yogurt in a mechanical manner without tasting a bite. Unease is gnawing at her, which annoys her: she has no business being uncertain as to whether she'll be able to execute the plan she's concocted, especially when it's as if her life depends upon doing so. How calm herself, gather resolve? She returns to her room, removes her shoes and skirt, leaps onto the bed, bounces up and down on hands and knees, pummels the pillows with her fists. "I'm going to get there! I *have* to get there!" she vows, referring to the variety of euphoria, fired-up spaciness, engendered by frenetic physical activity. Then she springs from the bed, flings herself into eye-high kicks and jumping jacks; then she's running in place, twirling about, doing the twist, punching at the air; then she's on the floor, executing crunches while hissing through her teeth.

"All right," Nicoletta says after nearly half an hour of exercise, "no more dallying!" She's worked up a sweat and her blouse is moist in places, as well as rumpled, but she doesn't care. She's reached the state she needs to be in, is humming inside—aglow with exertion, smooth in her nerves. Seizing her phone, she calls a nearby restaurant, places an order for chicken soup, says she'll pick it up. Then she puts her skirt and shoes on again, exits her room, grabs the keys of the least used car from a coat hook in the study, and drives to the restaurant regardless of the fact she's unlicensed to drive, only in possession of a learner's permit. As stated, the primary purpose of Nicoletta's call to the Sloffor residence was to establish he's at home and how he's preoccupied—it's fortuitous that he's bedridden.

Less than an hour later Nicoletta's on her enemy's doorstep with the chicken soup. We'd like to state she's calm and composed, steadfast and icy of will, but such isn't wholly true. Granted, she's unwaveringly dedicated to executing her plan—knows what needs to be done and knows she'll do it—but there's also scatteredness in her nerves, chilliness in her bones. She'll be entering her enemy's home, attacking him on his private property, and there's also the unfortunate extent to which she'll be lying to the wife, who's a very likeable person, genuinely sweet. Also, she's never been in Sloffor's house and knows nothing of its layout: it's far from guaranteed she'll be able to arrange to be alone with him, give him what he has coming to him. But, again, she absolutely *cannot* turn back and seek to balance matters at another time and place—she'd assuredly endure hell on earth if she did. So she squares her shoulders, draws a deep breath, counts off one-two-three, instructs herself, "Just do it!" and knocks.

Following a couple agonizingly suspenseful minutes (during which Nicoletta begins to fear the Sloffor's are no longer home) the wife, in an apron and with cake mix on one of her hands, opens the door and Nicoletta launches into her act. Mustering a face that's beaming with pride and enthusiasm, she gushes, "I've brought Mr. Sloffor some chicken soup! Can I take it to him? I have napkins and utensils and everything! I'd like to surprise him, if that's OK! He won't be expecting a gift from little me! He's your husband so I'd like for him to like me!" The wife, touched by Nicoletta's kindness, responds, "Of course you can take the soup to him, dear. What an angel you are," and begins to accompany her towards the stairs. "Well, I know it's silly," Nicoletta hastens to say, "but I'd really like to surprise him, although... But I completely understand, Mrs. Sloffor, if you'd rather come along, since he's not feeling well."; then, afraid she might be overdoing it, starting to arouse suspicion (Never mind such isn't the case.), she adds, "Oh, I don't believe it... I'm sorry, I should've checked—they forgot to put in a spoon! Mr. Sloffor can't eat his soup without a spoon! I'm sorry, I tried to do it right, I should've checked, I..." She trails off with a look of wounded confusion, casts her eyes at the floor as if in shame. The wife, unable to resist hugging Nicoletta, albeit careful to hold her cake mix coated hand away, assures her she's already done much more than she'd have a right to expect of anyone and it's not her fault, but the restaurant's. Then, patting Nicoletta on the shoulder, the wife says she's more than welcome to go on ahead and surprise her husband, adding he's in the first room on the left upstairs and she'll be there in a few minutes with a spoon, after she cleans up. "Thank you so much, Mrs. Sloffor!" Nicoletta says, briefly grasping her hand. "I like doing things for nice people! It's good soup!"

"I'm sure it's *very* good soup," the wife smiles; then, turning towards the kitchen with a wink, "See you in a bit."

Nicoletta, steeling herself against the inner trembling which has been present throughout her performance, approaches the stairs. Her legs are quivering and self-consciousness is increasing, so she finds herself dashing to the top of the stairs quick as she can in an effort to avoid being overwhelmed; then she's vigorously shaking herself for a few seconds, inhaling deeply, to further counter tension. "OK! I've come this far—time to end it!" she says to herself. Without further hesitation, she strides into the first room on the left, aware of heat flushing and tingling her face.

Sloffor's turned to the far wall with his back to Nicoletta, snoring loudly—she's decidedly dizzy but it's dizziness bred of eagerness to carry out her plan—there's also an element of surreality, as in she could never have imagined she'd be doing such a thing. But she soon gathers herself, apprehension fading into the background. "Perfect, it's all arranged for me—he won't see it coming!" is the thought that springs into her head. "He came at me from behind, let him have a sample! Let the worm squirm like he's never squirmed before!" A moment later she's beside the bed, removing the lid from the soup, noting the container's kept it warm—feeling its heat waft over her fingers. But, just as she's about to douse Sloffor with the soup, she pauses. A new idea, more satisfying than that of giving him a soup bath, occurs to her at the sight of his exposed arm. Quickly and quietly setting the soup on the nightstand, she seizes his arm, yanks it to her mouth, hisses, "I'm capable of anything!" and bites him hard. Sloffor yells, rolls onto his back, flops about with flailing arms, sputters incoherently. Nicoletta sees the eyes widen and recoil in the pasty folds of the face; sees the face wince and jerk in disbelieving fear; sees the thin dry yellowish lips part, hears more sputtering burst from the contorted mouth; then hears herself repeat, "Capable of anything!" as she dashes the soup onto Sloffor's chest.

Nicoletta, turning away from the bed just as the wife enters with a look of alarm and wonder, hears herself shout, "He spilled his soup!" and walks past the wife without looking at her as the room's walls seem to close in on her, air seems to hiss. But she senses, via agitation in the air, as if some of the space behind her is shattering apart, the wife's frantic dash to the bed—feels her erupt with consternation—hears her exclaim, "What on earth? Honey, what's happened? Nicoletta—Nicoletta! Please don't go!"

Nicoletta, who originally had no intention of revealing the reason for her actions, as she doesn't want Sloffor's assault to be public information (As noted, she loathes the idea of being paraded as a victim, pitied.), suddenly realizes it might be a good idea; otherwise, Sloffor will be in a position to lie and say *he's* been the victim of an unprovoked attack. Plus, Nicoletta's feeling ashamed of herself on the wife's account. The wife's a genuinely kind hearted person who's entitled to an explanation—she ought to be informed what sort of man her husband is, not to mention she'll be extremely distressed if she feels a teenager's played her in order to gain entrance to her home and attack her husband. As matters stand at this moment, the wife's a victim on account of Nicoletta's actions, and would be justified in feeling Nicoletta's a coldhearted monster. So Nicoletta halts at the doorway, wheels about, points at the quaking figure on the bed, shouts, "Tell her what you did to me in my backyard at the party! Tell her how you came up behind me and did those sick things! Tell her where you touched me and slobbered on me! Tell her the *real* reason you had to leave early and don't feel well! And you'd better tell her the truth, sicko, or I'm coming back with my dad!"; then, turning to the wife and lowering her voice, "Mrs. Sloffor, you're *way* too

22

nice to be stuck with this animal. Make him tell you what he did. I hope you know I like you and that I'm sorry I used you to get to him—I didn't know any other way, I was in hell. Now I'm leaving—I have to leave. " Nicoletta dashes down the stairs and exits the house.

During the drive home Nicoletta's so giddy, as if semi-floating outside her body, she needs to pull off the road twice to gather herself, focus her gaze; while driving she's instructing herself to be extra careful on account of the way elation's toying with her attention span, literally distorting vision; far from exceeding the speed limit, she avoids reaching it. It's as if she's leapt from a cold cage into a warm swiftly flowing stream—gone is the sense of being crammed into a space too small for her feelings to fit—and she's flush with this freedom, tears of relief soaking her cheeks. She can't stop twisting and bouncing on the car seat—she keeps turning the music, Middle Eastern dance-trance, louder—she's liberated her hair from its ponytail, swishing it in the crosswinds whipping through the windows. Not that her drive home's unadulterated sweetness and light: uneasiness periodically stirs in the background, as in that she had no choice but to strike back at Sloffor but the means by which she did so, in retrospect, is frightening—it's no small matter for anyone, let alone a heretofore sheltered sixteen year old, to bluff their way into someone's home and attack them. "It seems I really am capable of anything and I'm not sure that's good," she reflects at one point, referring to the unpremeditated biting of Sloffor's arm. "What if a letter opener was on the nightstand? Would I have stabbed him?" But then something of pride, as well as a trace of wicked delight, creeps into this thought. "I'm not a victim anymore!" she says aloud. "Let Sloffor try and lie his way out of it and get me in trouble—I dare him! I hope he's stupid enough to try it because he'll lose! I'm an unleashed wildcat, yeah, and he'll lose big time! I'm not afraid of anything anymore!" she concludes with a shout, slapping the roof of the car. Emotionally it's as if she's racing ahead of the car—tilting towards the sky, soaring into the sun.

Nicoletta's return home doesn't conclude as seamlessly as she wishes, even if it's naive to suppose her parents wouldn't notice her unannounced absence and the missing car. Once she's near the garage her parents emerge from the house, looking very worried and none too pleased. Spoiled she may be, but sneaking out with the car before earning a license isn't a stunt her parents are willing to overlook, particularly as it's a question of her safety. Nicoletta, who's never been inclined to withhold information from her parents, has already decided to inform them of Sloffor's behavior at brunch (As she's put the fear of God into him and it's unlikely she'll be viewed as helpless, she feels it's acceptable for others to know what he did.), but now she's compelled to do so on the spot. Out the entire story comes on the driveway, including needing to rectify the situation without assistance. "You get it, don't you?" she concludes. "I had to show myself I could fight back without anyone's help and not cry about it—I don't want pity, pity's sick! Sloffor's not a human—he's a pathetic worm and I couldn't stand for anyone to think it's safe to mess with me. I had to prove to myself on my own that anyone who assaults me will regret it a thousand times over! No one's *ever* going to see a target on my back, assume I'm a scared pushover, fair game! I couldn't sleep last night—last night was a nightmare! He had to pay for that! Sorry for taking the car—it's the first and last time."

It would be impossible to exaggerate the horror of Nicoletta's parents when told of Sloffor's actions. They hug their daughter tight, caress and kiss her and dispense comforting words, praise her for her courage, albeit with gentle reminders that they're a family and family's stick together, and she could've told them straight off—they would've had Sloffor arrested when he was on the premises. In short, there's a great deal of fallout following Nicoletta's revelation and it's wholly in her favor. The story of Sloffor's offense and her retaliation spreads like wildfire among her family's friends and acquaintances, adults and children alike, and subsequently to a great deal of the town. At school Nicoletta, already popular, acquires something of unassailable celebrity status and, far from being a victim in anyone's eyes, is regarded with unqualified respect. Although often requested to recount her doings at Sloffor's house, she always declines, saying, "It's over and done, let it go away and die," while knowing full well it isn't going to die anytime soon. She doesn't need to be told that the more she avoids describing the events of that morning the more they'll be embellished by others, and she's already heard some amusing versions. She's particularly fond of the one in which she sets Sloffor's bed on fire, and also of the one in which she leaps onto the bed and stomps on his legs, kicks him in the face.

As for Sloffor, he neither remains in the town nor in his marriage. Charges, at Nicoletta's request, aren't brought against him because she wants nothing to do with courtroom tedium or the time investment, but her parents ensure he's crucified in the court of public opinion. On Monday he gives notice to his employer and shortly disappears, his wife remaining behind. Nicoletta, fairly on a mission, tells people his wife is a sweet person who isn't to blame in any way and to be nice to her. She also calls the wife to offer her friendship, which is gratefully accepted and offered in return. They speak for over two hours and meet for tea thereafter.

Nicoletta's sleeping soundly again—no longer at the mercy of post-assault unrest, even if she'll never forget the groping hands and slobbering lips and reeking breath. It occasionally occurs to her she could hire a private investigator to obtain Sloffor's new phone number and call him, yell "I'm capable of anything!" and hang up (Given what she's already done, he'd surely fear the worst was yet to come.), but such would be flogging a dead horse—Sloffor's life is in ruins. Besides, she has her own life to live, needs to welcome the future instead of dwelling on the past. From an emotional do or die standpoint, Nicoletta's finished with Sloffor.

It's not our intention to imply Sloffor hasn't irreversibly altered the course of Nicoletta's life—robbed her of emotional virginity, compelled her to join the adult world ahead of schedule. He violated her in her backyard, shattered assumptions of safety—brought about sensations of helplessness and vulnerability, inflamed her veins with revulsion and outrage—stung her to the core of her being, forced her to thirst for revenge—and she literally tasted of blood when biting his arm: such experiences can't fail to profoundly influence a sixteen year old girl. Nicoletta's been abruptly yanked from girlhood—her familiar world of innocence is gone forever. The fact she's not only successfully dealt with Sloffor's intrusion but that it's turned out to be a journey of self-discovery—put her in touch with the amount of inner resilience at her disposal, strength of her will—doesn't mean it's going to cease haunting her. She's emerged from the experience stronger but newfound strength is girlhood's undoing. She's never going to surrender to romance-novel-inspired wonderment, daydream about being swept off her feet by prince charming, again.

Sure, Nicoletta pursues the same activities as previously with her friends—credit card sprees in stores and restaurants downtown, surfing and sunbathing and beach volleyball, splashing for hours in the waves—dress-up marathons, makeup contests, hairstyle experimentation at all-weekend slumber parties—but there's a different tone to these activities now. Overnight, she's become the serious one—the one undisputed leader—the one whose opinion counts most—the one who's unable to entirely manage to be carefree. She's no longer able to squeal with delight, behave as if it's a mesmerizing experience, when trying on a new pair of shoes.

Among the changes Nicoletta undergoes is that she, so to speak, inwardly unites with—matures into—her beauty. Girlhood's been chased away and so has susceptibility to awkwardness and hesitation—the shock of Sloffor's intrusion and necessity of rising above it has aroused Nicoletta physically as well as emotionally. Her movements—manner of walking, maintaining a stride—or of simply cocking her head, flicking her hair, tapping on a tabletop—have become more sure of themselves, acquired a firmly rooted center of gravity—radiate effortlessness, unflappability. Her facial expressions, regardless of how commonplace the situation—frowning at an automatic door that's taking too long to open, pouting because a hair ribbon's come undone, smiling because it's her turn at the parallel bars in gym class—have become more vivid, seamlessly swift in their transformations, and there's a pronounced quality of inscrutability about them—an indefinable sub-expression, tone of unattainability. Men are starting to feel uncomfortably transparent when she glances at them.

Nicoletta's awakening to her potential—becoming aware of having greater emotional resources than she imagined possible, acquiring the finesse of a woman several years older—whether she wants to or not. Suddenly she finds herself endowed with new orientation, greater perspective, regarding the opposite sex. Suddenly she's able to enter a classroom, or crowded lecture hall, and feel herself unfold to its furthest corners, project her energy—feel the glances of the boys dance over her curves. Suddenly she's not only able to discern, via their glances, which of the boys possess more inner drive than the others—more depth of emotion, range of need, than the others—but able to negotiate the glances. Suddenly she's adept at moving the boys about the room according to where she casts her gaze, compelling them to place themselves in her line of vision, put on airs—compelling them to approach her, then acting baffled at the attention, declining invitations without needing to speak. Not only has Nicoletta mastered the art of providing encouragement without committing herself, giving the boys anything tangible to cling to—such that they're unable to categorize her as a flirt—this ability's appeared fully formed.

Nicoletta's feelings concerning unforeseen subsurface connection with the opposite sex are mixed. There's pride in her newfound ability to influence men, as in, "Who knew it could happen so fast, be this easy? Crazy it's happening because a creep molested me!" There's also something of being in possession of a new toy, as in, "Let's see how many guys I can move over to the wall I'm looking at, get to fidget, unsure what to do." But there's also an element of regret, as in feeling too much is happening too soon—innocence and naivety's just plain fun when all's said and done, wonderment's a gift. It's occurred to her she might never know another moment of unadulterated peace for the rest of her life. She understands that if she has an open channel to the feelings of the men it also means they have an open channel to her, in the sense they'll constantly be intruding on her attention. She's confident of ability to dictate behavioral boundaries—determine who, if anyone, will be allowed to cross over to her—but also finds the situation invasive, because she'll henceforth need to trouble to be aware of the boundaries and monitor them. All told, Nicoletta's undergone an irreversible transformation and she has no choice but to accept it and adapt—girlhood's rosy bubble has burst.

As the weeks advance Nicoletta does indeed adapt—so much so there are moments when she wonders if Sloffor did her a favor, in the ironic gratitude sense. Of course Sloffor's a disgusting creep deserving of everlasting misery, but perhaps he's been useful. Previous to Sloffor's abuse Nicoletta never knew she had it in her to, however justifiably, hunt a man down in his home and sink her teeth into his arm—she's still thrilled, surprised, proud, deliciously scared when bringing it to mind. She's tasted of far stronger sensations and emotions on account of Sloffor's abuse than she otherwise would have—she's tasted of authentic extreme behavior, ordinariness rendered a dream. Nicoletta's experienced what it is to become laser-fixated, unswayable—guided by courage that brooks no opposition, has a life of its own outside rationality.

Such is the expansion of Nicoletta's emotional boundaries—vaguely unsettling, predominately enthralling—that she's commenced dropping hints to an older man because she finds the boys at school shallow, predictable, immature, fumbling. She's aware of the statutory rape law and detests it—considers it unfair, discriminatory, is dead-set on circumventing it. Why should she be subject to the same restrictions as girls who are less experienced and mature, unable to make informed decisions, simply because she falls within the same age range? Age is relative. By what right do distant authorities seek to prevent a precocious girl from pursuing experiences her precocity entitles her to?—by what right do they presume to take care of her when she's able to take care of herself?—by what right do they arbitrarily assign an age to those they deem in need of protection, without accounting for personality differences, varying levels of intelligence and independence? There are classes at school for students who are ahead of the learning curve. Why aren't there laws for students who are ahead of the emotional curve?—why must she be lumped among the inexperienced, subject to like restriction?

The man in question owns the restaurant where Nicoletta obtained the soup with which Sloffor was doused. She's been a customer for several years, it being located near her home, and the two of them habitually banter—innocently, absent of flirtation, as in he inquiring after her school day, or providing helpful information—where the secret beaches are, how to add nutritional density to salads with herbs, why yoga's the best exercise, why Sugar Bowl's his favorite ski resort. She's overheard him recounting his adventures, both youthful and present, to others—among other things, he's a licensed pilot and regularly books flight time at the local airport and enjoys banking turns such that the plane's wings are perpendicular to the ground, or flipping it completely upside down—he's courageous, handsome, entertaining, quick-witted, imperturbable, unpretentious. She's observed him chatting up adult women—seen the light ignite in their eyes, noted their admiration and nervous delight. He's the man for her and she's going to show him she's the girl for him, do him proud. She'll be discreet, not tell a soul. Should they be discovered she'll deny everything, acknowledge nothing—she'll never cooperate with meddlesome busybodies who attempt to enforce the statutory rape law. She *must* convince him she's trustworthy, considers said law her enemy—she *will* convince him! Nicoletta lies awake nights thinking of many things and uppermost among them is the necessity of being educated in the ways of love by this man and being a good student and rewarding him with all the energy and gratitude at her disposal—she's always felt obligated to see to it her teachers haven't wasted their time.

Sloffor may have placed Nicoletta on this path of self-discovery, inadvertently revealed an enthralling new world to her, but she'll naturally always wish living death on him, curse him to high heaven. She's still capable of tensing with rage, even if fleetingly, at the recollection of his clumsy hands and repulsive kiss and foul breath—she's going to obliterate that recollection, purge herself of Sloffor, once and for all. She's sure her chosen one can put Sloffor to flight forever and is starting to toss and turn through the night again, even if the tossing and turning's of the thrillingly hopeful variety. She can't stop yearning for the moment when her chosen one's embracing her and his kisses dispense serenity, security, delight. "In a twisted way Sloffor was my practice run," she observes to herself on a Saturday morning, as she readies herself to visit her chosen one's restaurant—launch her campaign, do her best to reach an understanding with him. "Hitting back at Sloffor awakened courage I didn't know was in me and now I can do the right thing with courage, use it to go after love. I'm going to catch and love a man who's able to appreciate me—he's going to show me how to make him feel like he owns the world and I'm going to do it and he's going to make me feel like I own the world too. So help me God, I'm going to be the luckiest and happiest girl I know!" And, with that, she mists herself with eucalyptus oil, slips on scarlet heels, pins a rose to her hair.

The Red Light (Bearings Blurred)

Saturday, December 19, 2015

I glance about disbelieving at my new abode—the faded yellow walls of this windowless cell, peeling paint exposing cement's leaden hues. Nothing of nature's here—all is cement, metal, porcelain, plastic. Nothing invites the eye—all is stark, filthy, dismal, claustrophobic. The rusted bed-frame and box-spring, creaking and squealing at my slightest movement—foam pad mattress, malodorous with innumerable stains—interminable drip-drip of the cracked sink's ancient faucet.

The closest anything in this cell comes to being of nature is this notebook in which I'm scrawling these words, its pages comprised of pulp extracted from once-living trees. Seems I requested pen and notebook and was immediately provided with them, doubtless because it keeps me preoccupied, reduces the likelihood I'll misbehave, require greater monitoring. Why am I bothering with a journal in this hope-annihilating place? I'm seeking to comprehend what's happened to me!

Incarceration? Me? I blink my eyes, slap my cheeks, endeavor to jar myself awake from what I feel must be a case-of-mistaken-identity nightmare. Alas, the peeling paint isn't going anywhere—my unclean abode continues to press in upon, mock me!

Yesterday afternoon I was still a model citizen, without so much as a parking ticket on my record. Today... I can't bear to think about it! Nevertheless, I must force myself to understand—I *have* to understand how I've come to be here.

When I awakened on Tuesday I was still my familiar self. Tuesday? A mere four days ago by the calendar, an infinity ago in terms of alteration of my circumstances. I can't believe what overcame me—I never knew such monstrosities lay concealed within me. Or was it that...? Well, I've never been inclined to superstition—never given credence to an invisible world, the possibility of spiritual interference, personality-manipulation, outside human comprehension; but now I can't help but feel my present situation could be explained as... Listen: it was as if a bored demon, flitting through the air and encountering me at random and having nothing better to do, slipped into my thought-stream, took possession of my will, pitilessly led me to my doom.

Tuesday... It was a windy Manhattan evening, I was strolling home from work as always, heading north on 3rd Avenue's east side, approaching 53rd Street; a limousine was idling at the curb, its rear door wide open... Why did I glance inside it as I passed by? There wasn't overt curiosity involved; I swear I didn't gaze within that open door with any more interest than I was gazing about in general—at buildings, traffic, other pedestrians, objects on the sidewalk. I glanced inside the limousine because it was there: I wish to God I'd never done so!

I seek to account for my reaction to what I glimpsed within the limousine, ascertain if there was anything unusual earlier in the day that could've precipitated it, predisposed me—whether I was stressed, hadn't eaten enough or lacked sleep—whether worry was stealthily gnawing at me, remaining just outside notice of conscious thought: I come up empty! I sincerely believe I was as balanced as I've ever been before gazing into that open door. I cannot, try as I might, account for my reaction. I swear I've never been inclined to spontaneous emotional extremes, perceptual exaggeration—swear it's the first time I've undergone instantaneous panic-inundated disorientation.

There was no warning: the moment I gazed within the limousine's open door fiery knives of nerves knotted my chest, suppressed breathing, forced me to a dead stop. The sight that unnerved me? A beautiful woman was on the back seat; bright red light, originating from within the car, was flowing up her legs and the pleats of her skirt onto her chest and throat and cheeks—twisting in the cascading curls of her hair, streaming from the top of her head to her shoulders and down her sleeveless arms to her tapered fingers. All else vanished from awareness; the whole of my perceptible world was the red light as it writhed upon the reclining beauty's features. Sensation of the sidewalk below my feet vanished: was I standing on a cliff's crumbling edge? Vertigo, nausea, fear! Was I about to faint—fall from the cliff, tumble to an untimely demise? I ask: why did it occur to me—for no viable reason, with no supporting evidence—that the woman wasn't relaxing but injured? Why did the red light whisper, *I'm blood, sticky blood! Blood born of hatred, violence, murder!*? Why was I gasping for breath, clutching my chest? I recall abruptly wheeling about, running erratically—recall startled alarmed glances, passersby stepping away to avoid colliding.

Upon arriving home I topped off a tumbler with rum and emptied it so rapidly, hardly pausing to breathe, it blazed in my throat, then did so twice again—me, who's ordinarily disinclined to drink, primarily keep liquor on hand for guests! But I wished to place a state of intoxication, erect a wall of oblivion, between myself and consciousness of the red woman, extinguish recollection of having glimpsed her.

I fell on my bed fully dressed, fitfully twisted about for what seemed most of the night, inner heat unrelenting, finally dozed off. The alarm hadn't been set and I overslept my wake-up time, failed to report to work—I've *never* missed work, had a single sick day. I enjoy my work, pride myself on being a conscientious employee, no rebellious inclinations; and yet when I awakened over three hours late on Wednesday it didn't once occur to me to contact my employer.

I remained indoors shivering, dread unabatedly attacking my very bones: it was as if the walls were observing me with hostile intent—as if the air was charged with menace—as if all of existence was rewriting sanity's rules, whipping me towards undisclosed terrifying behavior, stripping me of the ability to rationalize and resist.

Sunday, December 20, 2015

Dare I hope to gaze upon the sky again? Will I dwell in this cell for the remainder of my existence? Hopefully I won't exist for much longer! So, again, why trouble with this journal? Call it my confession. Perhaps I need to write of what's befallen me before I'm able to unreservedly surrender to death? Perhaps existence demands an accounting concerning my lapse into evil before it will allow me to permanently close my eyes? It *has* occurred to me I'm writing in order to pass into the next world with as whole of a soul as I'm able to obtain—there's no one to hear my confession, so it's on paper. As for absolution... Oh, I've no hope of such! But I do wish to *attempt* to embrace serenity, even if the idea's utterly delusional and I'm undeserving of the tiniest bit!

Or do I write with the idea of my journal being discovered after my death, determined to be of value and published as a cautionary tale? I'd like to think I'm not that naive! Who in this dreary institution would take the trouble to care if my journal has value? In the minds of the authorities this journal will likely be thought of as having made their jobs easier by distracting me, reducing need for supervision, and that'll be all. This journal isn't much more likely to see the light of day than it's likely I'll see the sky again, feel sunlight's warmth on my skin.

But to resume narration of events: I remain indoors on Thursday, still avoiding contact with my employer. I turn off my phone, don't turn on my computer—dread the prospect of hearing familiar voices, reading emails, being online, without comprehending why. Such behavior's out of character. As mentioned, I've always been a dependable employee. As hasn't been mentioned, I enjoy yoga classes, concerts, dinner dates, beaches, and especially dancing, salsa and merengue—I've had a great deal of fun with amazing women. Alas, such things are a lost world now! All my attention and energy's devoted to *not* remembering what I saw in the back of the limousine! Out-of-character behavior's suddenly the norm: I devour unhealthy food, seek to eat myself into a stupor; I steadily imbibe liquor, afraid of abandoning the state of intoxication I've been in since Tuesday evening (I *do* turn on my phone to arrange food and liquor deliveries, such being my sole interaction with the outside world.); I watch TV so as to further smother mental activity. While awake I somewhat succeed at blotting the red woman out of mind—not so when I sleep: she returns to me, scary vividly, in dreams.

Yes, the red woman attacks me in my sleep—dreams obey their own rules, mock waking consciousness, push back with a vengeance, gleefully parade their power and influence, twist the knife! I see the red woman on the back seat of the limousine again, bathed in the blood light—freeze on the sidewalk again, every muscle afire. Again it occurs to me she's not reclining in comfort but that she's injured, unable to sit upright, move. Has she fainted due to copious bleeding, hidden wounds? Is she in shock, paralyzed? Has her neck been broken? Is she outright dead? Who's abused her, and why? How could horrors be unleashed upon such a beauty? Dread rips through my nerves during these dream-sequences, coils my muscles tight: I'm repeatedly jolted awake, massaging very real cramps from my calves and toes, hissing through my teeth! Who says dreams are airy concoctions separate from flesh and blood, incapable of inducing physical distress? These dreams strain sinews and joints to the degree it's as if my bones are about to be wrenched from their sockets, and I'm grinding teeth until my jaws ache! Some dreams are a steady scream, and I'd give anything to be unaware of the fact. Undisturbed sleep's a *gift* I'll never take for granted again.

Sleep may be solace for others—not for me. Sleep's my greatest enemy! Waking-consciousness is maneuverable: unwanted impressions, terrifying thoughts, may be shoved into the background via willed forgetfulness, alcohol consumption, pursuit of mindless distraction. Dream-consciousness is its own master, deaf to all entreaties to spare me: it stares at circumstances straight on—nothing's able to divert its attention. Soon as I dare shut my eyes, or am forced to do so by mortal necessity, I'm forced to once again watch the red light flow over the supine woman's curves, caress her face—again suppose her a victim of violence, cringe in every muscle, blaze in the deepest pits of my nerves—again awaken drenched in icy sweat while silently screaming—again reach for... Well, reach for what—how calm myself?

Wednesday and Thursday I'm interrogating myself, as in: "Why this haunting? Why is the sight of a woman reclining in the back of a limousine inundating me with terror? Why has injury, outrage, violence, homicide entered the picture? Why am I skittish, starting at shadows, insomnia-racked—physically drained, weak and aching, headaches (which I've *never* had before) coming and going? Why is my conscience stinging me as if I've committed a heinous crime when I'm a law-abiding citizen? Absolutely insane! I have nothing to hold against myself, conceal from anyone. Yet the comfortable life I've always known has evaporated simply because I glanced inside a car! I'm spending every waking moment vainly seeking to avoid mentally revisiting the chance sighting of a woman! It's a variety of nefarious psychological quicksand: the more I struggle the deeper I sink!

"Curse that limousine! Why was it idling there, its back door open, inviting me to look within? Why was the woman slumped on the seat, as still as if dead? What's happening? It's some sort of twisted love-at-first-sight experience, that's what! Is love always flowery? Nay! Falling in love at first sight frequently borders on slavery! Not everyone's overjoyed at being uprooted from their customary life, compelled to become close to an utter stranger without seeming to have any say in the matter. I balk at the notion, but apparently I'm undergoing an obsession-at-first-sight experience! And if love isn't always rosy, how much less so is obsession! This obsession's invading my subconscious, upending my personality, burying me in apprehension and gloom!"

Monday, December 21, 2015

I accept this cell as my due, realize it's my only option as long as I remain among the living. Incarceration spares me the agony of endeavoring to police myself while knowing it would be wasted effort. Any man who, by failing to be aware of the horrors that lurk within him, exposes himself to the chance of being waylaid by a destructive obsession isn't fit to be among people. If this journal is discovered and read... You, then, who are reading it *ought* to make it available to the world: if but one person, treading precariously close to the precipice I plunged from, is spared my fate on account of being cautioned by these words then the scrawling of them will have saved at least two lives.

The lesson I'm offering is: "The manner in which a hard-working law-abiding individual was caught off-guard—introduced to dark aspects of himself he was unaware of, seized by a horrific obsession—and compelled to commit an unforgivable crime: within seventy-two hours he became a justifiably despised denizen of a dismal cell."

I resume with Friday afternoon: terrified of sleeping due to dreams that recreate every detail of my sighting of the red woman, mercilessly add on vivid depictions of assault and homicide, I've succeeded far too well in remaining awake. In the past fifty or so hours I've obtained a handful of brief catnaps' worth of slumber at most and I'm only mortal—enduring sleep deprivation for over two days while hounded from within's a surefire recipe for instability, erosion of ability to direct one's actions. Was there a boundary between wakefulness and sleep?

It was irresponsible of me to suppose it possible to suppress the bad dreams—one's dreams will be heard, whether one sleeps or not. If one's dreams are dissuaded from flourishing in their natural habitat of slumber they've no option but to invade the waking state, surely as water seeks its own level. My dreams were increasingly displacing waking consciousness, acquiring possession of my will and body.

Waking consciousness? Ha! What use is waking consciousness—preoccupation with a career, living up to society's expectations—if it blinds one to harrowing impulses that secretly bide their time in one's depths? Waking consciousness is a presumption that belongs to my former life, previous to Tuesday evening on 3rd Avenue—nothing but the illusion of supposing it possible to know oneself, a veil of lies. By Friday afternoon I could no longer comprehend what it is to have a career—such is how swiftly the devouring obsession forced me onto an alternate future's path. All was transpiring in an insomnious daze.

Friday evening I switch on my phone for the first time since placing multiple delivery orders Wednesday morning, seemingly centuries ago. As I speak the overhead lamp flares from muted yellow to piercing silver-white, shimmers up and down the walls, hot shivers seizing me—suddenly my voice no longer belongs to me, my words are being enunciated by a *someone else*—I'm as wary as if alone in a forest with a randomly encountered stray dog, troubled by said dog's demeanor.

At some point I'm advancing to the front door as if guided by volition not mine—thence into the hallway, descending in an elevator, strolling through a lobby, reaching the sidewalk—I climb into a limousine at the curb, instruct the driver to proceed to the northeast corner of 53rd and 3rd. It's not until we arrive at 53rd and 3rd and I spot a woman with long wavy red hair in a sleeveless pleated dress near the lamppost that I recall having booked an escort as well as the limousine. The limousine halts alongside the woman—my hand's shaking as I reach for the window-button, press it: when the window descends I'm gazing into the eyes of she who's become an all-consuming obsession, the extent of my world, from the moment I glimpsed her in red light.

What pops into my thoughts as I open the right rear door—the door corresponding to the open one on Tuesday—and step onto the sidewalk to greet the woman is I *must* place her at ease, be unforcedly tactful and considerate, avoid jitteriness of gesture, tremulousness of voice. In my former life—my life before seventy-two hours ago—I was known as a man who knows how to treat a lady; and good manners appear to still be within my purview as I grasp the woman's hand, assist her within the car, politely request she recline on the seat, stretch out her legs and cross her ankles, in the manner of the woman on Tuesday. Then I'm seated alongside her, turning on a flashlight with a red bulb, placing it on the floor—addressing her quizzical look by explaining a past love had a red lamp in her bedroom and I exist to relive the memories. I have no recollection of where I obtained the red bulb flashlight, nor can I account for my ability to provide the woman with an adequate explanation as to why I've brought it along—the more so because it sits well with her, she smiling warmly and clasping my hand, stating in a sweet hushed tone, "I understand." Again, it's as if I'm hovering in the distance—everything's taking place as if I'm miraculously managing to recollect how to conduct myself properly, adhering to an ingrained behavioral blueprint, relying on the emotional equivalent of muscle memory.

I inform the driver to drive about aimlessly and the car enters traffic—the woman's reclining on the seat beside me, bathed in the flashlight's red. The air within the car loses clarity, turns blurred, warped, convoluted, alternately convex and concave—overwarm, humid, clinging. I only see the red light sliding up the woman's legs onto her belly and chest and face, spreading into her hair, writhing in its waves of curls, following them downwards in contrary motion to her shoulders—spinning into the air, pressing against my eyes—soon I'm unable to discern where the edges of one object end and those of another begin. Is the woman aware tension's coiling tight inside me, accumulating—that scattered nerves, stinging electric jabs, are depriving me of the ability to orient myself in space? I periodically whip my gaze outside the limousine's back window, seek relief from claustrophobia—the dense air, sweat-inducing heat—but no relief's forthcoming: the city flings its building fronts and brightness back at me, eliminates distance and perspective, there's nowhere for my gaze to travel. Can the woman sense panic stirring in my breast, hissing in my ears—my vision blurring further, hands twitching? Will she become alarmed, call out to the driver—request he pull over, let her out? *Will she abandon me?*

Something's shoving at, pounding, my chest. Am I reeling sideways and forward, grasping at air, seeking to seize anything solid, orient myself via touch? I hear rapid belabored breathing: am I hyperventilating—what's whipping bursts of heat over my face? I only see vague jerky shadow-outlines amidst fuzzy red brightness: where's the woman? Where am I? My extremities are tingling! I'm seeking to scream, without understanding why, but unable to move my lips.

Ah, now I hear a scream—the air's tightening, reverberating, seeming to splinter apart! Am I the one screaming? Something's battering my cheeks, clawing: *what*? A long slender object's piercing the red light's haze—I'm glimpsing silver flashes, metallic glints! Hair spilling, arms flailing! Has a knee struck my stomach? What...? God! It's the woman who's screaming! It's her nails scratching my cheeks, neck, arms! It's a knife that's glinting, zigzagging wildly! My fingers are warm, wet, sticky! The woman's screams flutter, weaken, fade; her nails cease to scratch, arms fall away. "Oh, no! It's blood!" she yells, delivering a well-aimed kick to my solar plexus.

A gruff yell, originating from the car's front, reaches my ears—I believe I pitch forward, fall to my knees, roll—a side of my body, and shoulder in particular, erupts with pain: has the car abruptly stopped? A door opens—rough hands seize me, yank violently, drag me outside—I'm face down with a weight on my back, aware of city pavement's motor-oil-and-vomit stench—voices stridently jabber nearby.

Rapid-fire glimpses of the life I once led—friends, career, recreational activities, travel, love of beaches, my home—are whirling down a dark gaping funnel in the center of my head.

I'm watching blackness smother my field of vision, falling into dreamless sleep.

Tuesday, December 22, 2015

Ha! Instead of solving the riddle of my undoing with this journal, I've only relived it—only succeeded in racing out through in-doors that lead to less hope! The more questions I ask the fewer replies I receive!

I've already declared my unworthiness to continue breathing—overcoming despair's never been my intent, I'm not deluded in that department. As for understanding how my undoing could happen, assuming such understanding's achievable, I no longer care. What's the advantage of understanding when it's powerless to restore radiance to the red woman's face, grace to her manner, raise her from the dead? Nothing will spare me from the unmitigated hell life's become! She was a nice woman earning a living, did nothing to warrant encountering a client enslaved by a terrible obsession due to weakness of will. No amount of jotting in journals will prevent the red woman's demise from saturating my waking hours with dread and desolation, unremittingly grinding my conscience. Meaning this is my final journal entry. Midnight's arrived (something I know due to the bell announcing the third shift changing of guards) on what will be my last day alive.

I've refused all assistance, offered no excuses, made it clear sympathy's poisonous to me—conversations are torture. No defense attorney's slickly argued mitigating circumstances—as in my previous lack of a criminal record, unblemished life—character references, employment records accessed to show glowing reviews, people at the animal shelter affirming I was a well-regarded volunteer—will make dwelling in my present memory-whirl, where thoughts are sharp blades ceaselessly stabbing, bearable. Nothing society could devise would be more dreadful than my present state of existence—my frame of mind's my very own special echo chamber of agony, from which the only avenue of escape's death. What I most dread is continuing to be alone with myself, with nothing but bleak walls to stare at, blank paper to fill.

I've been informed I'll be relocated to a state-of-the-art clinic, per investigation and examination results—incredibly, I've received apologies, which I absolutely do not comprehend. People are puzzled by my insistence at remaining here, disinclination to acknowledge comforting words. But how could relocation to less nightmarish quarters be something I desire, when each time I shut my eyes I see a beautiful woman thrashing in her blood's red, feel agony as of thousands of hot needles jabbed into every square inch of my skin? I routinely grind my back into the concrete floor, stare into the blank white ceiling's unyielding void. I'll shortly join the red woman, reside where she resides—never gaze upon comeliness in death throes again.

The plumbing is ancient, rusted, brittle: it was easy to break the pipe under the sink with a kick, wrench its top portion from the porcelain, muffling the noise by wrapping a blanket about the pipe. I've sharpened the pipe's edge, scraped it against the concrete floor between my legs with the blanket spread over my lap. The pipe's sharp as a knife.

These are my final words: before the first-shift bell sounds I'll be pressing my back to one of these walls and cutting my wrists, ridding myself of the demon—the obsession, unshakeable image of the red woman—that invaded my personality, robbed me of well-being and comfort and sanity, flung me into this hell. I'll slip free of awareness forever while watching my blood's red flow over

44

my hands, paint the floor, as the red woman screams, flails for her life, for the final time.

Friday, January 1, 2016

Miraculous! I'm still of this world, happy even, demons dispersed—life's obviously willing to play pranks. I'm in a new facility, my room sunlight-drenched—two high wide windows, curtains parted.

Blessed be, I'm too giddy to continue! This is all for today.

Sunday, January 3, 2016

My circumstances haven't merely changed, they've reversed themselves. I'm continuing this journal on a laptop, previous entries scanned onto it—have awakened to the fact I was preyed upon and unhinged by delusion. It's not strictly true that life played a prank on me—I played a sanity-straining prank on myself. On the one hand my life *was* hanging in the balance, inner disturbance all too desperation-engendering—sleep deprivation, disorientation, panic very real—and on the other hand it was entirely based on fantasy. I needed a nudge.

I was spared slashed wrists—rescued. Turns out I was never in a prison. I was in a holding facility, its dilapidated state a consequence of city budget reallocation. (It's scheduled for demolition, a brighter facility nearing completion a half mile away.) Minimum security's why I was given a notebook and pen, and why people who weren't guards were speaking to me every day. I blotted out everything positive, raved about deserving death, and the people who weren't guards were perplexed and concerned, secretly monitoring me—a pinpoint camera was in a corner of the ceiling without my knowledge, privacy laws disallowing it from including the sink, as the toilet was adjacent.

I was prevented from harming myself—not only did I kick the door multiple times in advance of preparing for my demise, I sat against the wall opposite the door's one-way viewing window, attendants able to raise its shade, peer within. It appears I also turned my planned demise into something of a ritual—removed my shirt, waved the sharpened pipe in figure-eight motion. Suffice to say attendants entered and wrested the pipe from me, sedated me. When I awakened I was *here*: facing third-floor windows, the tops of swaying evergreens outside, sky bright.

I'm curious: was there authentic intention of cutting myself, or was I subconsciously playacting in front of myself—chasing dramatic extremity due to boredom? Of course kicking the door would alert people, summon observers—seems I was deceiving myself.

There's a great deal to clarify to anyone reading this, as well as to myself—I'm piecing sequences together, seeking to make sense of them. My initial location, the dismal cell, was never a final destination. It wasn't clear if charges would be pressed, which would determine where I'd be transferred. Mental disturbance had been officially certified, but I was nonviolent—a mumbling somnambulist when apprehended, dazed but cooperative. The woman in the limousine had *not* been physically harmed, but lasting emotional trauma was a possibility.

Charges were pending—the escort service woman didn't immediately know what to make of my behavior. In the limousine she was alarmed for good reason—the visuals were terrifying. A waved knife—red liquid on her face and neck, streaming down her arms, soaking her dress. She had every reason to scream, and the driver had every reason to believe her in urgent need of rescue. (The driver was courageous and capable, selflessly sprang to action, for which I'm very grateful—better for my behavior to be halted sooner than later.)

But the knife was rubber—harmless floppy rubber with thick blunt edges, incapable of cutting. Wild how I was able to blot the fact it was rubber from the forefront of consciousness, fixate on what didn't exist. How close did I come to wholeheartedly believing I'd stabbed the woman, spilled blood? I've no idea. And the blood wasn't blood—it was coconut milk and red dye, whipped up in a blender. I had a thermos-full, sucked it into my mouth and spat it out, poured some around—lots resembled blood-spatter. Mind you, I don't recollect these details, they've been related to me. The limousine's interior was dark, shaded glass blocking Manhattan's lights, my flashlight's red light the sole illumination aside from thin lines of muted amber framing the floor, doubtless to assist inebriated customers in orienting themselves.

Upon reflection, the woman concluded it was a client indulging in roleplay, unusual and extreme but harmless once the air cleared, and waived her right to press charges—she regretted screaming, but pointed out the proceedings were suggesting a terrible outcome, and I couldn't agree more. Disturbing visuals for sure—a waved knife she couldn't know was rubber, gooey warm red liquid spilling all over! She's stated her imagination raced ahead of comprehension, led her to sense phantom physical pain—she marveled afterwards there wasn't a scratch on her. I'm extraordinarily fortunate the woman's bearing me no ill will—she's mentioned that, frightening theatrics notwithstanding, I was well-mannered. She's gorgeous, spirited, kindly, classy—I noted such despite being thoroughly disoriented, hallucinating without hallucinogens.

Tuesday, January 5, 2016

My world's altering for the better beyond imagining—the woman's name is Cynthia and she's an angel. She's visited, is helping me overcome memory-gaps, solve the puzzle of my behavior. I was waylaid by obsession without warning, my imagination enslaved, delusion shoving reality aside and scaring me to death, but thankfully inner directives of which I was unaware arrested me from indulging in atrocity. Cynthia's a seasoned professional, has dealt with creeps that compensate for inadequacy with rudeness, verbal or physical abuse—she's self-defense-trained, which explains the kick to my solar-plexus. (Oh, I definitely deserved *that*, we've laughed about it.)

Cynthia was undecided concerning my doings until a couple days afterwards, once initial recoil receded. She'd ascertained there wasn't a blemish on her body—recalled my caresses went down easy, were curiously engaging, pleasantly teasing. (In her words, "rising to the top from under my skin and that's rare.") At one point I was lifting her hemline to her waist, licking her thighs while shining the red light on her—she found it cute until I brandished the knife. She couldn't know the knife was rubber, even if no wounds were forthcoming, and I had no idea either, was haunted and in hell afterwards. I agree that I should remain here until distinction between imagination and actuality's sorted out. I've no history of erratic or illegal behavior, seek serenity.

In the same way that holding a seashell to my ear seems to echo infinitely, suggest unchartable depths, the sight of the woman in red light in the limousine on December 15 lifted my fancy towards infinitely receding horizons—wild how I was insomnious for days, speculating concerning daimonic possession, with no previous susceptibility to such. My accustomed world and values, reputation for punctuality and conscientiousness, instantly vanished. I didn't willfully avoid the office, neglect to contact my employer—defiance wasn't in the picture. Defiance presumes an opposing force—I was utterly oblivious.

Wednesday, January 6, 2016

Cynthia held my fate in her hands—could've ensured a criminal record dogged me for the rest of my days, barred me from resuming my smiled-upon-by-society life, and chose not to, blessed be. Cynthia's continuing to visit—her voice and gaze energize and motivate me, sunlight delights in flowing over her complexion and contours almost as much as I delight in aligning with her moods. She's not only willing to recollect the manner in which we met, help me understand the difference between what I thought I was doing and actually was doing, she relishes doing so—our delight in one another's growing by leaps and bounds, we're able to read one another from across the room.

Cynthia told me: "Sure, you came at me from *way* outside left field, and I feared you were authentically totally nuts. But you were also a gentleman, which confused me in the nicest way, titillated me subliminally! Sure, the theatrics flung me headlong into fear, made me scream, want to be anywhere but there—it's not every day I'm being stabbed with a rubber knife by a man spitting fake blood, and I'm unaware it's a game! I want to play again. When I *know* the knife and blood's fake it'll be turn-me-inside-out-tickle-me-crazy, and don't forget the red flashlight, and when you were licking me and looking at me like you were in a separate universe, no rules in that universe! Games that suggest bad things without being bad are unusually cathartic."

So my rubber-knife-fake-blood episode, following discussion and joking, has been recast as a game Cynthia and I can't wait to repeat, added motivation for us to work towards effecting my release. I told her: "I have no clue how I could've become *that* obsessed with playing a game I'd never played before, and without knowing it was a game! The self-deception factor, not knowing it was a game while playing the game, given what the game consisted of, truly transported me to unsuspected places, ripped boundaries away. Claustrophobia, smothering gloom, and terror at the time, but now you're in my life, and... OK, during the dreadful days leading up to when you joined me in the limousine I was cursing my fate during the rare intervals when I was capable of reason, but the new verdict is fate munificently smiled upon me. The convoluted frightening path I negotiated to reach you's just... Well, enough of attempting to figure it out, sweetheart!"

So I played the rubber-knife-fake-blood game in public without informing anyone, including myself, it was a game; and I won't be informing anyone other than Cynthia I was unaware it was a game, as such would likely complicate my diagnosis, further call my sanity into question. The limousine driver was justified in restraining me until the police arrived. Then I'm arrested for the first time, placed in a transitional facility pending Cynthia's decision whether to press charges. Not many people can say they've gotten away with publicly enacting murder fantasies with complete strangers, springing the game on them with no advance information or warning—the game sprang at me as much as it spang at Cynthia, alarmed her and the driver. (Admittedly, this is a slight amount of gloating, but I by no means advise anyone to attempt to get away with such a thing, as it's highly unlikely it'll turn out well, my fortunate outcome's nearly outside belief.) My arrest has been invalidated, I'm officially a victim of legal misunderstanding, qualify for state-funded therapy—indulgence in lieu of incarceration. And the limousine company has been reimbursed via a cleaning fee charged to my credit card—my mess mild compared to drunks throwing up.

Apparently I've also gotten away with enacting a suicide fantasy, since I'm now persuaded I had no guts-deep intention of cutting myself—I kicked the door multiple times, then fiddled about, postponed follow-through, until I was dragged out of there. When I say I've gotten away with enacting a suicide fantasy I mean the extent to which I convinced myself I was going to slash myself without, so to speak, being emotionally able to do so—I didn't intentionally fool anyone, fake an emergency, because I was fooling myself at every turn. Wild how thoroughly I immersed myself in despondency and dread, even altered the feel of myself in my skin, the air heavy and dense, pressing in on me, and I'm overjoyed there *was* a subconscious urge to emerge. All of which, admittedly, begs the question: is fantasy still capable of destructively possessing me? I've no wish to con the people entrusted with my care. I want to believe I'm no longer a danger to myself.

Friday, January 8, 2016

I'm in "The Program" in a state-of-the-art facility upstate, encouraged to wander its extensive grounds, many pathways cut through the snow—spending time in nature is part of "the cure." Well-to-do people routinely hold fundraisers for this facility, visit for photo ops, social media adulation—it's a must for politicians. I was initially amazed I'd been selected to be here, wondering what I'd done to be worthy of such good fortune—seems my suicide-theatrics were the deciding factor, go figure. One's subconscious is an uncharted ocean: is it possible I got wind of this *posh* facility at some point in the past, perhaps via mention in the press, and concocted a suicide-routine to gain access? Well,

I have ample leisure to overthink my situation, invent new ways to deceive myself, or wonder if I'm deceiving myself! Who knows to what degree one's able to subconsciously alter one's fate? What I most hope for is to cease wondering *how* the sight of the red woman in the car seemingly a lifetime ago gripped me to the exclusion of all else—cease fretting about my future, escape speculation's self-contradicting whirl. But it's awe-inspiring that I've wound up here! Truth to tell, it's a soothing vacation. Predictability's out the window.

Consultations with social workers and/or psychiatrists occur every Monday, Tuesday, and Thursday—they're earnest well-meaning compassionate people, I'm at ease with them while also feeling I need to be careful what I say—sessions are recorded. Fellow residents laugh about telling the social workers what they want to hear, acting vulnerable, in need of continuous therapy, lest they be deemed fit for release, expected to obtain employment—they're far savvier than the social workers give them credit for and know it. One of my new friends said our situation is "rich people's way of not feeling guilty about being rich." The majority receive monthly government stipends, and some are free to wander outside the grounds in town during designated hours. They've advised me how to prolong my stay indefinitely, what lies and routines work best, congratulated me on being here, and I'm truly touched. What most interests me is obtaining permission to visit the town outside facility grounds, meet Cynthia without supervision, but I won't complain if permission's denied. After all, this facility's not a "psychiatric hospital," it's a "retreat." I'm treading water for now.

Sunday, January 10, 2016

My evaluation's in progress, official status pending—I'm going all-out to not merely appear balanced but authentically be so, and Cynthia's participation's invaluable. It speaks volumes when the person one was initially accused of traumatizing is lobbying for one's release, arriving well ahead of time *every* visitation day. Perhaps I would've considered being fussed over in a facility that resembles a spa to be manna from heaven, license to relax worry-free for months, even years, were it not for Cynthia—what I most desire is freedom to be alone with her, spend nights with her. No assurances I'll be discharged from the facility, or authorized to venture outside its grounds, anytime soon. It's easier to fake needing therapy than convince people one's overcome the need.

The facility staff's not merely compassionate and caring, clearly happy with their work, the possibility of dalliance has been hinted at. One of the nurses, abundant of chest and squirmy-graceful in manner and stride, eyes bright, always smiling, often brushes against me, clasps my arm, calls me "Sweetie." OK, I hope she doesn't go to the hell-hath-no-fury place, turn on me because Cynthia's the only one I hunger for. There's no substitute for Cynthia, she's flowing through my veins—attraction's untamable. All cats are *not* equally grey in the dark—some cats blind one to others, positively *glow*, if one's lucky.

Cynthia's an escort in the strictly-defined sense, as in she's hired to be seen and conversed with and that's all, which some clients, including myself, fail to realize. Would I be bothered if Cynthia was an escort in name only, a hooker in fact? As the situation's nonexistent, I'll never need to know. Cynthia electrifies me, delights my fancy, as no other. The very tone of her gaze, gestures, posture, voice... Miraculous!

Cynthia visits in conservative attire—people *do* judge books by their covers, particularly staff at psychiatric facilities that are designated as "retreats." I'm not permitted to have a phone or Internet access, but Cynthia's permitted to show me selfies on her phone; and she's not in conservative attire in any of them—she's nerve-twistingly luscious in all of them, her dark locks spilling freely and athleticism and flexibility on display, and my imagination's on overdrive and I can't wait to get out of here, lingeringly kiss and undress her, hit heights of bliss the Gods will surely envy. We attempted under-the-table touching, were cautioned—floor-level cameras exposed us—and won't attempt it again. This facility might resemble a spa more often than not on the surface, but surveillance is omnipresent and repeated rule-breaking's not tolerated, relocation to less indulgent places isn't merely a threat. It's a privilege to be here and the governing body knows it—ingratitude's unforgiveable.

I've no intention of being cautioned again, am going all out to appear grateful and, hey, I'm *inordinately* grateful, no playacting on that score—Cynthia and I are in love! We're behaving like priest and nun during her visits, refraining from so much as clasping hands—exemplary behavior's the sole path to possibility of release.

Thursday, January 14, 2016

I've convinced the doctors my behavior in the limousine was an ill-thought-out game, silliness my rationale, which regretfully didn't pan out as planned—I'd intended to inform Cynthia of the roleplay parameters and props, but was sleep-deprived, inexcusably forgot—I'm not seeking to minimize the oversight, avoid the truth. Cynthia's vouched for me, apologized for overreacting; and I've stated her reaction was more than warranted, myself alone to blame. As for my suicide attempt... Such was additional fantasy-enactment, a game I played purely out of boredom, and I'm mortified people believed it to be real. Crying wolf's disgraceful, I'm very sorry I did so, and it's my responsibility to police myself, ensure it never happens again.

As it's New York State, there are generous legal allowances relevant to my case—some states might mandate observation of me for months—and I'll do right by New York's laws, religiously obey them to the letter henceforth. Although I'll stress anew that without Cynthia's testimony, petitions to administration, it's possible my discharge would be delayed for a long time. Evidently I was verifiably unstable—mumbling to myself, gaze unfocused, gesticulating at things not there—when arrested. Questions were put to me and I didn't appear to comprehend a word. No sobriety test was administered for the worst of reasons.

I dare not forget what possessed me on Tuesday, December 15! Sure, I've survived the red woman episode, and well enough to convincingly spin it when dealing with doctors, but the fact remains I *was* thoroughly disoriented, dreaming invading waking states, scared to my bones. Perhaps the red woman episode was bred of accumulated impatience with predictability, hunger to tear comfortable foundations from under myself, extend boundaries and possibility—perhaps to merely ascertain what I could get away with. As to the extent of what I'm able get away with, the jury's still out. I doubt I'll ever know to what extent I was subconsciously policing myself, or seriously endangering myself.

Cynthia and I invented a version of the events that led to her panic and my arrest and my reaction to being arrested in about five minutes during one of her visits. To wit: we've known each other since April, 2014, enjoy roleplay games, are ashamed our miscommunication involved others. I stupidly neglected to inform her the knife was rubber, blood fake! We were sleep-deprived and frazzled, hadn't seen each other for months—there was unfortunately unanticipated readjustment to one another in the mix, baffling to us now. As a law-abiding citizen I was traumatized, propelled to an unreal nightmarish place, when arrested—to my mind I was playing the equivalent of a Halloween game with a dear friend, then I'm abruptly handcuffed for the first time in my life. Sleep-derivation and, admittedly, alcohol consumption flung me into questionable behavior and paranoia, especially as the night began as an innocent, albeit naive, wish to have fun with a new game. Plus the limousine driver immobilized me before law enforcement arrived, without legal authorization. I've been told suing the limousine company's an option, and my takeaway is I'm free to lie with impunity in order to be discharged from here—reality's relative.

Inventing our version of events, anticipating and countering disbelief, isn't straightforward. There's the fact I called Cynthia's agency, booked time with her, instead of meeting her on her time—a matter of record. Solution: Cynthia had committed to being on call at her agency and is a conscientious employee, so the only way for us to meet was for me to book time with her—she'd reimburse me her share of the fee but her agency would take it's cut, fair enough. Cynthia believed we were going to act out a taking-her-to-prom fantasy, as we'd done before, but I didn't pin a corsage to her dress or ask if her dad wanted me dead or inquire about a curfew, as customary, and she was unsure what we were doing.

Social workers have heard all manner of explanations as to why so-and-so behaved in such a manner in given circumstances—my explanations were greeted with professional detachment, dispassionately entered into the record. Clinically speaking, roleplay equals "means of sustaining a healthy relationship." Or so I've been informed.

I stated to a social worker, "Misunderstandings regretfully occur, the fault's mine for failing to clarify boundaries, place Cynthia at ease—shame on me for bringing panic to her. But here's the miracle: we've reevaluated our friendship, wish to be in a relationship—she's my girlfriend now, our support for one another unwavering. My dream's to be given the opportunity to live an exemplary life with Cynthia, do right by our love. I've been consistently responsible in the past, it's on record—have held my job since March 26, 2012, been entrusted to supervise myself, received glowing reviews. Please verify."

As a significant person involved in my recovery, Cynthia's been present during two of my sessions with social workers. She's stated: "It's crazy what's happened between me and Bobby! We're apart for a few months, he calls me, then reserves me through my agency because my agency would've been upset had I wanted the night off after signing on—reliability's essential, flightiness raises red flags, bumps me down the availability list. Then Bobby's semi-raving, as if he doesn't know it's me even though I know he knows it's me. Again, we hadn't seen each other for months, both of us busy and just one of those things, and I don't understand how we could partially behave as if we're strangers, but we did. Love isn't always a bed of roses, but I firmly believe love's the best we can aspire to, and we're dedicated. Please release Bobby, I'll look after him and he will look after me—there's a family plan."

I'm not presuming our version of events will weather clinical analysis, be accepted by the distant administration people, result in my discharge. My world revolves around Cynthia's visits—she's the beginning and end of hope and aspiration.

Sunday, March 28, 2016

Last entry, via laptop on a Torrecilla Baja beach not far east of San Juan, Puerto Rico—my circumstances have outstripped boldest hope on all levels, including the life I led *before* spotting the woman in red light in the limousine, temporarily veering off on the strangest of tangents. Happiness eliminates need to maintain a journal, account for myself, so after today I'm done. Turns out I didn't quit my job—my employer was contacted through official channels, informed I'd suffered an "emotional episode." What people tend to overlook regarding bureaucracy is that its impersonality can work in one's favor: emotion's not a consideration, it's solely a formula, and if one falls within the formula's parameters one receives benefits. Details were withheld from my employer on legal grounds, particularly as I wasn't accused of a crime. Employees routinely take medical leave and my situation, regardless of optimum physical health, robust vital signs, qualified—no employer dares challenge a professionally certified "emotional episode." Following renewed contact with my employer administration praised my "resiliency," so I seized the opportunity to request authorization to work 100% remotely, which was granted. True, there was institutional pressure involved in the granting of my request, as New York State had pre-approved my medical leave at the upstate facility's request, but I'm also an employee the agency wishes to retain. I'm adept at an essential task the majority either don't comprehend or care not to, and am proud to be one of perhaps five people authorized to work remotely.

Elysium's an isolated Puerto Rico beach with Cynthia alongside me. Less than a mile away are crowded beaches, people competing for towel-space—on this beach three people are meandering about the upper shore a distance away, no one else in sight. Seems the expanse of razor-sharp lava between this beach and the crowded ones, absence of sandy shoreline, is enough to stop the majority from traveling further east of San Juan, arriving here. Incomparably gorgeous unfrequented spots are often not too distant from crowded ones—it's simply a matter of orientation. Falling under the spell of the woman in the limousine's red light in far-off, as if a lifetime ago, December, becoming obsessed for no explainable reason—despite stabbing distress—was a Godsend, as it's led to Cynthia and I falling in love, having this beach to ourselves.

We're in Puerto Rico for nine more days, I'll be showing Cynthia why Puerto Rico's my favorite island—beaches, rainforests, mountains, expansive views; and where high surf sings in lava-caves, and the flamboyant-framed roads, and white herons raiding garbage bins (A higher class of bird picks through trash in Puerto Rico!); and where tarpon accelerate in the shallows, riffle the sea's surface, seize sardine treats—where roadside vendors offer coconuts, conch, octopus, pinchos; and the dance floors under the stars, and... Well, I could go on and on describing wondrous Puerto Rico, but what's truly wondrous is I'm also looking forward to returning home with Cynthia. She'll turn Manhattan otherworldly, saturate every streetcorner and block with joy—simply going grocery shopping with her will be magical.

Seven pelicans are gliding on the breeze, scanning for fish—intermittingly folding their wings against their bodies to counter wind-resistance, dive in flashes of speed—they're hitting the sea's shimmering surface with hardly a splash.

Penelope Prim

Chapter I

I imagine every man who appreciates gorgeous women, lives for enthralling conquests, has encountered a Penelope Prim—a woman who, apparently ill at ease on account of being conspicuously well-endowed, downplays her attributes by exclusively presenting herself in conservative attire. Penelope was both the most stunning woman at the firm—the firm a world-renowned midtown Manhattan law firm—and the woman who was least inclined to parade her beauty: she behaved as if her beauty didn't exist. Aside from having highly appealing curves, none disproportionate to the others and throwing the balance off, she measured in at five feet eleven inches tall, weighed in at a size eight, clocked in at thirty-two years, had a face of stop-and-stare-at radiance of complexion and symmetry of line. Penelope's customary demeanor, noted by many admiring, if resigned to defeat, men was that of inviolable placidity—as if nothing short of a meteor striking the city, if that, could compel her to abandon it. She also possessed the finest head of soft-textured pitch-black hair any woman could wish for.

Penelope's hair was never seen in freefall: she imprisoned it in a bun, nary a wisp escaping, and its length could only be deduced.

According to the bun's size, the tightness of which couldn't wholly rein in her hair's abundance, it might easily reach her lower back. Occasionally her frumpy dresses—high necklines, mid-shin hems, long sleeves, cut from heavy cotton or wool, of dull colors, often beige—would fail to deprive observers of a glimpse of her figure's glories, as when a strong wind on the sidewalk pinned the fabric to her body. Very infrequently, and only if the thermometer hit the nineties, she'd wear a knee-length pleated skirt, always a dark color, and blouse—invariably a pale gray or off-white blouse which, if viewed from the side when adequate light was behind it, would acquire enough transparency to allow a reasonably accurate assessment of the proportions of her midriff and breasts. Several men, on account of these rare displays, had noted that Penelope, although of voluptuous build with an ample bosom, was possessed of a trim waistline and very fit and toned. Penelope's blouses caused one man to observe there was a portion of her personality, be it ever so slight, that couldn't resist being mildly exhibitionistic a half dozen times a year—an observation that was enthusiastically, even if wryly, embraced by most of those to whom it was conveyed.

Enter Stuart, a man of thirty-seven years recently hired by the corporate department, where Penelope works and is highly valued, assigned to high-profile deals. Shortly after setting eyes on Penelope Stuart declared he wouldn't know a moment's peace until she became his; and he was aware he shouldn't declare such publicly, he'd never done so before, been that reckless, but didn't care—if anything, he felt public declaration would oblige him to deliver. According to him she was a woman who, despite contrary appearances, endured sleepless nights on account of feverish yearnings and desired above all to indulge them. He didn't feel there was a small portion of her personality that occasionally semi-consciously played at being exhibitionistic with a

61

backlit-blouse maneuver—not for him such naivete. He insisted she was a thoroughgoing tease, dropping veiled sex-signals: she was simply waiting for a man capable of deciphering them, overwhelming her. She was putting on a chastity-act, he said, in order to keep the uninitiated at bay, avoid being pointlessly pestered. The man capable of decoding her secret sex-language, approaching her without annoying her, blundering into clumsiness or presumptuousness, would be treated to sensual rapture few imagine possible. Penelope was love-hungry but her hunger wouldn't settle for anything less than soul-altering delirium. She'd never shortchange her instincts, bow to social pressure—as in acquire a boyfriend solely to parade him—for the sake of halting speculation concerning her relationship-status, amazement she was not only apparently uninvolved but unconcerned. She didn't care a whit about broadening her social circle via a relationship, placing others at ease concerning her isolation. Yes, he'd stress, the notion Penelope was prudish was laughable: she thirsted to surrender to the sort of all-consuming, potentially disruptive, desire convention frowns upon and such was the key to her reserve. The outright fierceness of her reserve indicated presence of an ardent and daring disposition, necessitating she exert herself to keep it out of open view; lack of overt evidence of desire betrayed desire that scorned anything run-of-the-mill. In short, Stuart would conclude, Penelope harbored preferences the likes of which would make seasoned streetwalkers blush, was thirsting to explore them with a worthy man. When a group of men, rolling their eyes, opined he was succumbing to wishful thinking, projecting qualities onto Penelope that suited his fancy and ignored her prudish tendencies, Stuart shrugged his shoulders and smiled, saying, "Thanks for leaving the field to me."

"How can you say," Stuart would argue, "that Penelope doesn't dress sexy? Her dresses fit snugly enough and when she's walking in front of me in the hall her behind undulates under the material—all that rippling sensuality, fluid flexibility, muscle tone. I can feel electricity radiate from her hips—sense the untapped hunger of a healthy woman in her prime, a sure darling of nature, of boundless energy and determination alike. Penelope's hunger may be hibernating, but it wants to awaken and run wild, uninhibited as the waves of a storm-tossed sea. You could say the general appearance of her wardrobe's conservative—that the colors aren't come-hither colors, as with scarlet or violet—that the material's never smooth or fluffy, as with silk or cashmere—that there's never an eye-grabbing pattern, as with swirly stripes or polka dots or roses on black—that there's never any pattern whatsoever, only solids—that her legs are never bare and her tights are never barely there, always either thick or dark or both—but I say the more conservative Penelope dresses the more her lusciousness is set in relief, heightened through contrast. Penelope's adept at understatement: the more she conceals herself the more one thirsts for her to reveal herself. Penelope well knows what she's doing, even if perhaps subconsciously. Plus you're overlooking the obvious: Penelope *only* wears dresses. Not for her those inane pantsuits—bane of every man's existence. Pantsuits are a disgrace and hail women who shun them. Is there another woman at the office who never wears pants? No! That alone's a dead giveaway. What sort of woman only wears dresses? A woman who enjoys subtle self-stimulation, sensation of her legs rubbing together, caressing each other from calves to you-know-where. How can you be blind to that? One thing's certain: no woman who looks like Penelope and has her energy and attracts dozens of lingering glances a day could be indifferent to frolic, it's a law of nature. She has abundance of aptitude for frolic, doesn't matter that she's disinclined to admit it, and I'm going to do her the favor of making her fully aware of it, enough that she'll not only want to admit it but revel in it—scream it from the rooftops."

"Penelope was on the cafeteria terrace, in the sun," Stuart said one afternoon. "Her legs were crossed and the wind was toying with the hem of her dress, fluttering it over the knee of her top leg onto her thigh, steadily moving it upwards; she didn't appear to be concerned about it and wasn't correcting it—proof of what I've been saying from the get-go, that she's as much of a flirt as any other woman. Bright women always know where their hemline's situated and what's being revealed—if they ignore such things, it's by intent. They're pleased by eye-caresses, reveling in the desire they inspire: it's as essential to them as breathing. The sun was passing through Penelope's blouse, rendering it very see-through, allowing me to admire the way her breasts swelled in her brassiere's cups, motion of each inhaled and exhaled breath; and her belly's firmness, silkiness—what a pillow to lie my head on! She was chatting with two women, both first-year associates—talking with her hands, squeezing her legs together—squirming in the chair, alternately leaning forward and sitting back: a showcase of the energy and grace of her movements—her animal vitality. Now I know, for a fact, Penelope's not only skilled in bed but has a fair amount of experience. She's as good as whispered her secret to me and I'll do her the honor of following up. What a honey she is!"

Inside of a month Stuart was assigned to work with Penelope on a major deal. (According to rumor the assigning partner had started a betting pool among the partners, the idea being to come closest to the date at which Stuart might succeed in bedding Penelope. In the event of no success on Stuart's part the money would be donated to Save the Children. Also, the fact it might be impossible to determine when, or if, Stuart succeeded was assumed to be part of the risk. But such was only a rumor. The more plausible reason was that Stuart was eminently qualified to assist on the deal.) The deal required Stuart and Penelope to frequently work side-by-side: it was essential they function efficiently in the face of ever-changing and often mind-boggling, or downright capricious, client direction, and they swiftly settled into doing so, found it easy to work together. As the deal progressed Stuart plainly saw Penelope enjoyed his company: her eyes brightened and voice acquired tender nuances when they met in the morning, discussed the day's agenda; always was she cheerful and smiling when he was near; never did they miss lunching together, an event she referred to as their "little vacation." At her suggestion they temporarily abandoned their offices, open-endedly booked a conference room, encamped themselves therein: much non-work-related conversing was indulged in and their eighty-plus-hour weeks were a version of heaven as far as Stuart was concerned, as enthralling as surfing high SoCal swells at dawn.

During their conversations Penelope revealed things that Stuart felt she hadn't revealed to anyone else. As in she hailed from the small town of Kewaunee on Lake Michigan's shore directly east of Green Bay—as in she grew up ice skating, cross country skiing, ice fishing, deer hunting, snowmobiling, and relished polar bear plunges—as in she was the girl without a date at the prom, but not caring, enjoying the experience nevertheless—as in it was her love of opera, which she first heard on the Texaco Metropolitan Opera broadcasts, that brought her to New York, led her to select Barnard and Fordham Law—as in she'd attended over two dozen Metropolitan and City Opera performances annually after enrolling at Barnard—as in she'd dressed as Carmen, Manon, and Tosca for Halloween parties as a girl, gotten into a knock-down-drag-out fight with a girl in middle school because the girl made fun of her costume and the opera—as in she'd thrown punch in the girl's face and they'd wound up entangled on the floor—as in she shredded the girl's Queen Victoria get-up, pulled her hair and clawed and punched her and made her scream until yanked away—as in she was proud of it, taunted the girl afterwards, dared her to badmouth the opera again.

Stuart, for his part, revealed much to Penelope that he was generally disinclined to reveal, finding it effortless to trust her. Never was there worry she'd judge and categorize him, fail to comprehend. The end result of exchanged confidences was Stuart began to feel affection for Penelope that caught him unawares, spawned unforeseen confusion, it having little in common with physical attraction. He'd catch himself feeling ashamed of sneaking glances at her, savoring her beauty, longing to embrace and caress her: how could he be thinking such thoughts about his dear friend, who'd entrusted him with many secrets and been entrusted in turn? Was he violating her trust? How would she feel if she knew he was thinking such thoughts? He frequently found himself questioning his intentions, wondering if he was a bad person, while unable to abandon them: no other woman had divided him against himself in such a manner. It wasn't that he'd never felt protective towards a woman, he had many times, but he'd never allowed such feelings to muddle and delay a potential conquest. "All's fair in love," was his guiding light, conscience had never introduced complications.

Stuart and Penelope took to frequently touching each other, in friendly casual fashion—light shoulder taps, brief caresses of the backs of hands, playful rib-pokes: the touching was something of punctuation during spirited conversations, as well as support during problematic intervals of the deal, when they had good reason to believe the client was gratuitously being a nuisance, taking advantage of the fact millions were involved. Gossipy observers, noting the easy manner in which they touched one another, began to speculate as to whether they were sharing a bed. Stuart, vaguely aware of such speculations, was embarrassed, as they only reinforced how far he was from making them come true. To Stuart's dismay there was an invisible barrier between himself and Penelope—a barrier he could neither account for nor work up the courage to seek to openly breach. They'd become very close, effortlessly read one another's moods, completed one another's thoughts—relished sharing inside jokes, having secrets from the rest of the firm, but it was as if they were close in the manner of brother and sister. Cruel trick of fate! Stuart had been given a golden opportunity to get to know Penelope and was making the most of it, but the more he knew about her—not merely factual details, but dispositional tendencies, nuances of facial expression and glance, very tone of her gestures—the further he seemed to be from spending a night with her, and he had no idea what he was doing wrong. Which isn't to suggest he'd abandoned hope: every moment spent in Penelope's company lifted vivid to unsuspected heights, he'd never been so eager to see a woman again after parting ways. Despite himself, and even while making fun of himself, he'd countdown during toss-and-turn nights until arrival at the office the next morning. He couldn't stop imagining frolic with Penelope, refused to accept such might be out of reach. He'd catch himself thinking, "The chase in and of itself's so absorbing it could be an end in itself! But no! Aspiration's only intoxicating to the extent it's likely to yield results! Penelope's a dear friend, but... Jesus, she's a wellspring of energy and euphoria and hungering to clasp her close is *not* betrayal!"

One evening Stuart, having joined one of his best friends—Henry—for dinner, found himself compelled to admit his lack of progress with Penelope, Henry having been apprised of the chase from the start. "I don't know how she does it," Stuart began, wringing a hand. "I've always been able to tell straightaway if a woman's inclined to hook up, able to walk away if she isn't, but I still can't tell with Penelope, and it would be psychic suicide, pardon the melodrama, to walk away. I've never needed to get anywhere near as close to a woman as I am to Penelope before she indicated beyond a doubt if she was inclined to hook up. So much for priding myself on rapid assessment. Sex was my motive but now I'm unsure, in unfamiliar territory. I not even sure what I'm enjoying or not enjoying—unfamiliar territory's a kick one moment, a knife in my nerves the next. How does Penelope remain inscrutable as far as frolic goes? I'm accustomed to rapid transparency, can't tell if it's yea or nay! We trade anecdotes, share idiosyncrasies, have loads of fun while working under pressure often with little sleep, carefully scrutinizing entangled legalese, ensuring the client isn't victimized by loopholes. I know the modulations of Penelope's voice, changes of her expressions, tones of her posture—way she has of cocking her head, pursing lips, arching eyebrows, focusing her glance. I've never been as close to a woman as I am to Penelope, yet closeness is also illusory since I still have no idea if she'll ever want to kiss and cuddle; and yet I'm unable to abandon hope. (Maybe I've said that?) Never do we mention relationships—the subject's tacitly understood to be taboo. Never have we spent time together apart from company time, not one conversation—it's tacitly understood we'll be going separate ways. Just crazy how everything's crystal clear between us except for how she feels about extracurricular activities, never vaguely hinting. We bond like there's no tomorrow when we're busy legal bees, then it's gone."

"You're telling me you've done *nothing* with Penelope outside of work?" Henry asked, eyes widening. "I'm *very* amazed."

"Pathetic but true," Stuart responded, "and don't ask me to explain how I can be so close to her and faraway at the same time.

She's able to keep me at a distance while being extraordinarily kind. She says goodbye every night in ways that prevent me from suggesting we go for a drink, never ceasing to be sweet. She hasn't, by so much as an involuntary blush or trembling hand, given me reason to hope I'll ever be more than a friend, nor has she hinted I ought to forget about being more than a friend—I didn't know a woman could keep me in perpetual suspense. Either Penelope's the most guarded, fearful, shy woman on record when it comes to frolic or it hasn't occurred to her to think of me in that light. Perhaps we're *too* close—perhaps friendship's a blockade. Makes me think of what a guy in college said: 'He who befriends a girl will never bed her.' Of course that's imbecilic and he was a pompous dolt who was mean to girls, due to insecurity, and now trapped in a bad marriage, getting his just deserts and aging badly, but I'm starting to wonder if there's a grain of truth in it, goes to show what a nut I'm becoming. It's not as if Penelope's married; and I'm ninety-nine percent sure there's no boyfriend, since there's never been the slightest hint of a relationship. I don't see how she could hide such a thing for so long, and why would she trouble to do so if she hasn't expressed any desire to go out with me? Yet I debate the issue constantly, while knowing it's stupid to do so. My head's scrambled chaos of hair-splitting, over-analysis, self-contradiction—constantly doubling back to points of departure."

"But why fuss about absence of blushes, watch for trembling hands?" Henry frowned. "Who cares if there's a boyfriend? So what if Penelope's inscrutable? Do you want to sleep with her or do you want to drive yourself nuts trying to solve puzzles that might not exist? Why not ignore her after-work goodbyes and ask her out, be forthright? Why flail in vagueness, analyze everything to death, get scrambled? I don't believe you're bottling everything up instead of coming out with it! Debating the issue of a boyfriend? I'm so amazed you admitted that I'm not sure I heard correctly. The Stuart I know *never* mopes and lingers, wallows in analysis, if a female declines to be shown a good time. He swiftly moves on. Plenty of fish in the sea, and all cats grey in the dark, are clichés but like many clichés are surprisingly on point. Has it occurred to you Penelope's waiting for you to ask her out, baffled you don't? Keep it up for too long and she'll start to wonder if you're attracted to women. You'll become her valued *confidant*."

"Good point about not coming out with it," Stuart responded, momentarily smiling. "I've told myself the situation's insane and I ought to end it, kill the confusion. But I can't do so, there's suddenly a great deal at stake. I've never feared rejection—if one woman isn't interested, I approach others—yeah, many fish in the sea and all cats are grey and a cashier at the supermarket can bring elevation as well as dozens of others. I've never troubled to prefer one woman over others so long as basic requirements of cuteness, fitness, verve are met but Penelope's slipped under my skin, itching in my nerves, the sole fixation of my thoughts. My world's hanging in the balance and don't ask me to explain. I'm being painfully careful, dare not ask her outright—lay it all on the line at once. I'd say I'm chasing her from the inside out—seeking to emotionally align, tug on her subconscious strings, set the stage for nature to hopefully take its course. I'm not being so subtle because I want to, but because I don't see an alternative. Actually I don't know what I'm doing half the time! It's like I'm on autopilot and the autopilot's forcing me to tread water, wait with baited breath. Think I enjoy treading water? Think I enjoy wallowing in analysis, dwelling on what a given look in Penelope's eyes may or may not have meant, whether the tone of her voice at some point in a conversation indicated she's weakening on my account? Think I enjoy being paralyzed by conflicting interpretations of every inconsequential little detail?

Hell no! It's as inane as it's robbing me of sleep! But at the same time—and here's some fodder for mocking yours truly, I lob it over the middle of the plate—I've never felt more electrifyingly alive. Each new day's a wild waking dream, shot through with hope and aspiration and vividness of sensation that drives me half insane. Bloody hell! If only Penelope would drop her cloak of inscrutability—give me something substantial to seize upon, sustain myself with—for one measly second, before I completely lose my mind! Sometimes I feel I'm trapped in a nasty alternate Sisyphean reality, labor yielding nothing."

"Well, that's revealing," Henry observed. "Seems you can't decide if you're enjoying the experience or not. And the only alternate reality I see is your crazy exaggeration of what boils down to indications of healthy lust that's being denied for no good reason. Since desire's unfulfilled, you might as well talk about being electrified and hopeful and suppose you're living in magic-land, right? And I'm not mocking you for it—only amazed that you, of all people, are erecting a fantasy world to compensate for failing to bed *one* female, instead of acting sensibly and replacing her with someone less reserved. As for Penelope's inscrutability, maybe the explanation's staring you in the face. Maybe the only mystery is there isn't any mystery aside from the one you're projecting onto her. Has it occurred to you Penelope's quite simply frigid and you're looking for responsiveness that'll never be there? It would explain why you can't read her, why she isn't behaving like a regular woman, why there's no hint of yes or no. Think of the drab nun-like stuff she wears—cumbersome dresses, her mania for bundling up her hair. She doesn't want to come off as good-looking and maybe that's because she can't think of a reason why she should."

"I'm not sure what you mean by Penelope not wanting to come off as good-looking," Stuart countered. "Does it make any difference if she does or not, since nothing changes the fact she's just about the most ravishing dish in town? Think she's oblivious of being gorgeous or thinks she can change that or would want to? I defy you to state Penelope doesn't scream the sort of beauty the vast majority of women can't come close to equaling, even if she's wearing a gunny sack!"

"Hey, I only said she doesn't seem to want to be a dish, not that she isn't one—no one in their right mind would deny she's crazy gorgeous," Henry protested, mirth suffusing his expression. "I know you're dying to have a knight-in-shining-armor moment and rush to your lady's defense, but don't willfully misinterpret me so you can. Far be it from me to..."

"As for your truly loony theory," Stuart interrupted, gazing at Henry with disbelief, "I can assure you Penelope isn't frigid. If I didn't know you as well as I do I'd think you were slandering a woman simply because you don't understand her, as losers are wont to do. But I know you'd never lower yourself to that and are trying to be helpful. But now I'm worried about you: Penelope's so the opposite of frigid it doesn't speak well of your judgment and, since you're not hiding that you're looking for a wife and want to start a family, you should be careful who you wind up with. I'd advise reevaluating your powers of observation before getting hitched, lest you find yourself in divorce court before the first child arrives. Saying Penelope's frigid is like saying Puerto Rico's bound in permafrost! There's such an aura of electric sensuality hovering about her—so much magnetic restlessness within her! If only she'd allow herself to trust it!" Stuart nearly shouted, slamming his fist on the table; then, after taking a deep breath, "But it's as if Penelope's willfully denying her inherent disposition. I don't understand how such a healthy, energetic, bright woman can emotionally asphyxiate herself, ape a nun's reserve. I don't see how it's possible—it defies all natural laws.

Penelope's warm-hearted, and there's a playful side to her. We laugh and joke all day—there's a mischievous side to her. But there's always that distance between us, with Penelope not once abandoning her reserve as far as intimacy's concerned-—not giving me a single reason to entertain, or not entertain, hopes of hooking up. Somehow she's radiating sex-energy and denying sex-energy at the same time. And I'm not saying I'm going to be the one she favors, but she has to favor someone. But, again, there's zero evidence of a boyfriend and it's as if nature's laws are out the window. And it's not like I can give up on her, start fresh with someone else. There's no one else to start with—no other woman's come close to affecting me like Penelope. She's invaded my bloodstream—is outright haunting me—and I've no choice but to see it through. Nothing will persuade me I've already reached the end with Penelope, that there's no revelation in the works—that she won't eventually drop the act, either accidentally or by intent, and reveal herself to be the sensual firestorm of a woman I know she is."

"You've contradicted yourself again," Henry smiled. "First you say you might not be the one Penelope favors, then you say she's going to turn into a sensual firestorm for you. Which way is it going to go? Are you going to be her chosen one or not? Will you finally savor sweet victory or are the spoils going to someone else? Will all the crazy drama pay off or be a dead-end? Will Penelope kiss you or take someone else to that heaven? Will you be electric following a night of bliss with Penelope or cursing that another's claiming that distinction?"

"Right, good fun," Stuart answered, smiling in turn. "I'm aware my predicament's comical, sometimes laugh about it myself—I wouldn't believe it possible to be so off-balance because of a woman if it wasn't twisting in my guts, affirming its reality every day, and laughing about it makes it easier to endure. But

I'll clarify anyway: what I meant by Penelope revealing herself is I'm positive there *will* come a time when she owns up to being a woman with flesh and blood needs and the implication is that when she does I'll finally have a tangible reason to hope we'll be getting together, but I'm by no means presuming we will, such would be insulting and tacky. I've got to get her to cast the nun's habit aside, drop the act—solving her puzzle's the only pathway to peace of mind. But enough talk, it doesn't do any good, change the situation. There are other women out there—gorgeous women, uninhibited women, sweet and giving women, all amazing—and it makes no difference, because I can't run to them for relief, a rollicking healthy good time! *That's* how insane I am! I've become a monk because *one* woman won't stop pretending to be a nun!"

Chapter II

Nearly a month and a half has passed since Stuart commenced working on the deal with Penelope. He's no closer to solving her riddle—still hasn't a clue as to where he stands, potential relationship-wise—and is afraid of becoming noticeably unhinged. It's beside the point such fear's a product of his increasingly excitable and fertile imagination and that in the minds of his coworkers he's harmlessly infatuated, they only amazed he hasn't turned his attention to a willing woman, of which—incidentally—there are several at the firm: he's beginning to believe he may soon be unable to remain even-keeled in Penelope's presence—prevent telltale facial expressions and ill-thought-out words from alerting her to his heart's discord, enough that she'll ask to work with others. Far from coming closer to acquiring the courage to reveal his feelings, Stuart's grown more wary of doing so: he feels there's too great a chance she'll greet such a revelation with horror, view it as a violation of trust. Because they've been working together for weeks, have shared so much of their life-histories, he's afraid she'll feel betrayed, accuse him of lying to her via omission. Should he reveal his feelings will she not wonder how long he's harbored them, demand to know? And once he tells her, because he'd *never* sidestep a direct question, might she not wonder how much he's confided to her is the truth, as well as question his motives? Might she not wonder if their friendship's tainted by self-interest, or an outright sham, cold-hearted playacting solely in the interest of sex? Such is Stuart's uneasiness in this regard he feels it's possible she'd never speak to him again.

It's a frigid Friday mid-February and, as the firm's awaiting client comments before documents can be updated, Stuart and Penelope are free to leave before six o'clock—a rare occasion, even if they're on call for likely weekend work. As customary, they cheek-peck each other goodbye. Stuart, at a departure's approach, finds himself preparing for their cheek-peck—seeking to conceal self-consciousness, and also be as affectionate as possible without overstepping friendship's boundaries. He realizes it's ridiculous to hope cheek-pecks will inspire more urgent feelings than friendship, cause Penelope to communicate she'd rather not part ways, but can't stop hoping for precisely that. Physically speaking, it's as close as he gets to Penelope and the touch of her lips on his cheeks enables him to extrapolate the situation—imagine pulling her close, kissing and caressing for all he's worth. There's guilt in the mix—one's not supposed to hunger to bed a friend, sometimes he feels like a deceiver. He's never needed to give much thought to the notion of a boundary between friendship with a woman and urges to bed her—occasionally feels he's regressed to schoolboy emotions, indulging in doomed-to-unfulfillment fantasies involving a sweet teacher.

But he's nevertheless helpless to stop imaginatively making the most of their goodnight cheek-pecks, thirsting for spontaneous combustion—picturing Penelope naked, feeling her curves in his hands, unabashedly falling into her gaze. But he doesn't find their cheek-peck remotely pleasant on this occasion: the fact Penelope doesn't depart from her composure, is as kind and considerate and sexually distant as a sister as always, stings him as never before—makes him feel empty, abandoned, alone—cast into cold indifferent streets with nowhere to go, nothing to do.

Manhattan's hum and light, ordinarily uplifting, is smothered in gloom, for some reason suggests heaps of dirty socks (Who can account for out-of-the-blue sensory impressions?), during Stuart's stroll home. His Midtown West one-bedroom, sizable and well-illuminated, seems to have shrunk—it's walls are crowding him, the less-illuminated corners disproportionately noticeable, invading open air's brighter space, compounding depression. His habitual meal of sockeye salmon and salad, ordinarily pounced upon, is about as savory as sawdust and he's barely able to choke down a dozen bites. He's neither able to endure being unoccupied nor find anything to preoccupy himself with. Anything he turns his attention to makes him wish to cease thinking at the same time it prods him into thinking about what to do next in order to settle down. Checking texts multiplies desolation, because every text Penelope's ever sent is work-related; perusing social media leads him to feel cut off from all of existence, because Penelope's not reciprocating his affection; executing yoga postures leads him to feel separated from his body, because he's too upset to sense changes in his muscles. The walls continue to crowd, light continues to fade. Unable to endure remaining indoors, being hammered inward on himself, tormented by his imagination (going so far as to fear onset of a seizure even though his annual physicals are near-perfect), Stuart bolts from his apartment.

Close to nine o'clock Stuart's approaching Lincoln Center on Columbus Avenue's west side, heading north, when a limousine erratically darts across the avenue, abruptly stops at the curb. A rear door's flung open so roughly it bounces back on its hinges, slams shut—muffled yelling's detectable. He's within a dozen yards when the door opens again and a woman in an ankle-length mink emerges, annoyance evident in the hard tone of her stride and gesticulations. A foot, belonging to the person who's annoyed her, appears on the pavement below the door and Stuart hears the woman shout, "Don't come out, creep! Keep your disgusting hands away! Stay in there or you'll regret it!" as she kicks at the door. Having struck the door at an angle, instead of straight on, and failed to close it, the woman raises her foot to kick it again but changes her mind, instead electing to remove the mink coat, gather it in both hands, shake it at the person in the backseat. "This is what I think of your bribes, creep!" she shrieks before walking to the front of the limousine, dropping the mink in the gutter, stomping on it.

It's then that the woman's identity, as she's illuminated by the limousine's headlights, becomes clear and Stuart's chest all but leaps into his throat: the woman's Penelope! Instantly he's racing forward to shield her from whatever unpleasantries the individual in the limousine might resort to; but she, unaware of his presence, takes care of that herself. "Get out of here before I tear your eyes out!" she yells as she returns to the open door, raking her fingers, spread and arched like an attacking cat's claws, through the air; then, placing her foot squarely against the door, she slams it shut with her leg. The limousine lurches forward a few feet, pauses. "Get out of here!" Penelope repeats, marching towards the limousine while scanning the sidewalk, apparently searching for something to throw at it. "You don't want to find out how crazy I can get!" The limousine accelerates, drives past Stuart.

Stuart's soon at Penelope's side, grasping one of her hands with both of his, rapidly saying, "Penelope, it's me...whateve r I can do...how can I help?" She's too absorbed in her state of excitement to recognize him at first: her eyes are glazed and glassy; she's breathing so quickly it's a hiss; she's enveloped in an aura of antagonism; she keeps twisting her head every which way, glancing about wildly, as if expecting the limousine to reappear. Stuart's never seen Penelope in such a state: he's appalled, amazed, fearful, and also—curiously enough—vaguely pleased. "Penelope, it's me," he repeats. "Your friend...Stuart! Anything I can do, I'll take you to your door. Do you want to go home?"

"Stuart!" Penelope exclaims, appearing scared—flinging her eyes at the pavement and flushing, antagonism instantly gone from her body language. "Dear friend, I'd give anything for you not to see me like this...hardly my finest moment, riled up, dolled up like a slut," she says quietly, raising apologetic eyes. "But yes, I'd appreciate it, sweet of you...always the gentleman, kinder than I deserve, so considerate...I'd like to go home and get out of this stuff." Only now does Stuart realize Penelope's attired in a manner the opposite of reserved. She's in a backless and sleeveless skin-tight lavender one-piece, with a hemline above mid-thigh and neckline nearly at mid-breast, tops of her black lace brassiere's cups visible. Open-toed heels, a chiffon scarf, and her eyeliner match the hue of her dress; her legs are sheathed in seamed black stockings, scarlet lipstick's upon her lips, abundant silver bangles upon her wrists. But what's most extraordinary is that her hair's no longer confined in its customary bun: a magnificent cascade of black curls is tumbling nearly to her waist, swishing in the breeze.

Urgency doesn't permit Stuart to be more than fleetingly astonished at the reversal in Penelope's mode of dress: his mindset's that of someone rendering assistance at the scene of an accident and he doesn't hesitate to remove his down jacket, hold it out to her. "No, Stuart," Penelope half-whispers, intonation quavering. "I'm to blame for this absurd...this unbecoming direction...my irresponsibility. I don't want you chilled because I'm a blind woman tonight, tramping around in atrocious stuff. I have no business...any business involving you in my abandonment of judgment. Please keep your coat and stay warm."

Stuart's response is to wordlessly step behind Penelope, open his jacket, coax her arms into the sleeves and lift it to her shoulders, free entrapped waves of hair. As her hair crackles in his fingers—as he watches it unfurl and writhe when he releases it—he's aware of gasping, tingling; but, again on account of urgency, doesn't permit himself to savor the situation. Then he's hailing a cab, assisting Penelope therein, seated alongside her, providing the driver with her Upper East Side address. For most of the trip Penelope silently stares straight ahead, head immobile; at the same time she's two-handedly clasping Stuart's forearm, unintentionally digging with her nails as she squeezes tight and releases according to agitation's ebb and flow. At one point she folds herself into a ball—raises her knees to chin, heels on the seat's edge; then, slapping at her shoes, glaring at them derisively—and also, strange to tell, in fear—she mutters, "Ghastly things," and slams her feet back on the floor. Then she's blankly staring again, her head vibrating, wobbling: Stuart can sense tension winding into tight knots within her—sense she's shuddering, fighting to suppress emotion. As for the shoes, they're sleek, stylish, expensive and Stuart has an idea why she dislikes them: they're doubtless another "bribe," like the mink coat.

Once the cab's at Penelope's building she appears to regain her composure—smilingly faces Stuart on the sidewalk, grasps his hand with steady glance and touch, says, "Thank you, Stuart," in her familiar sisterly tone, voice measured and melodious. "I'm glad we're friends and you understand dates don't always go as planned, and flagrant bribery, slinging about of wealth, can't make it better. We all have our fiascoes, don't we? I've had a doozy but the bad feelings are going away—I'm breathing easier, calming down. Sleep beckons."

"Dates can be chancy, who knows who's misrepresented themselves and who hasn't, lying's too common," Stuart responds. "Not easy to accurately size someone up before committing to a date and sometimes too late to bail. I have more dating-fiascoes under my belt than I care to recall, happens to everyone. It's no one's fault if a date winds up being unpleasant, or overreaches, or is a loon. What's important is you're feeling better. The shock's wearing off, will soon be as insubstantial as incidental ghost-feelings temporary bad dreams can stir up." While speaking Stuart's marveling at how quickly, considering her distress minutes ago, Penelope's recovered her even-keeled self. Aside from her uncharacteristic attire, she's the familiar Penelope of equanimity of demeanor: the unflappably good-humored and gracious Penelope, elusive by virtue of her very politeness—separated from him by an invisible wall. But he's also wondering if she's playacting serenity, seeking to forestall him from gaining further access to her secret life.

"Feeling worlds better," Penelope says, squeezing Stuart's hand and then releasing. "Some stress, but it's over. Sorry you had to see the stress." He's about to tell her an apology's unnecessary when she, disinclined to dwell upon her misadventure, hastily adds, "I believe this is yours, kind Sir!" and removes his jacket, circles around him and slips it up his arms onto his shoulders, makes it snug at his neck, as he did with her. Then, as if fearful of lingering, she swiftly embraces him, cheek-pecks him goodnight, turns towards her building. As she hurriedly approaches the entrance she smilingly calls over her shoulder, "Well, there's a good chance we'll be working tomorrow!"

"Am ready for it," Stuart responds in an involuntarily crestfallen manner, his voice perhaps dying in the wind before reaching Penelope. As he watches her step through the automatic door into her building's lobby he catches himself becoming disappointed she's become calm so quickly. He'd intended to accompany her upstairs, do whatever he could to help her overcome her distress, and also realizes he was eager to discover more details concerning her veiled activities. From concern for Penelope's well-being, heartfelt as it is, he passes to regretting the loss of an opportunity to come closer to solving her riddle. What does it matter if he's been thoroughly confirmed in the accuracy of his instincts regarding Penelope life outside work if she's going to revert to her reserve? She's leading a double life to an extent exceeding his suspicions but acting as if the limousine episode never happened.

In short, Stuart feels short-changed and is reluctant to leave. As he watches Penelope advance to the elevators in the back of the lobby, push the button, wait for one to arrive he yearns to go after her, and... And what? Admit he's been hoping to get to know her outside of work, explore the possibilities of a relationship, since first glimpsing her? Make a forthright declaration? Highly inappropriate, given the situation. Approaching her concerning matters of the heart after she's been disorientated by a date gone sour, possibly disposed to grasp at straws she'd ordinarily avoid, would be little better than taking advantage of a woman who's blind drunk. But as Stuart pursues this train of thought he finds himself admiring the fluid muscles of Penelope's hips and legs as she restively shifts her weight from one foot to the other, impatient for an elevator to arrive. He's never seen her in revealing clothes and is, for the first time tonight, allowing himself to relish the sight. He's imprinting her attributes upon his mind's eye, making a lasting picture: it's of little consequence that she has her back to him most of the time, only occasionally turning slightly in either direction. She's a veritable hallucination of loveliness, equally earthy and ethereal. Electric sensuality glides about the symmetry of her curves—suggestion of familiarity with fervor approaching delirium, trancelike states, somehow radiates from the tone of her stance and gestures. The very light in the lobby collects about her, as if delighting in her at once svelte and voluptuous figure. Stuart feels Penelope's energy is rippling through the lobby to the sidewalk, lapping against him in gentle yet insistent waves, slipping into his bloodstream: when he arches his back, tightens his muscles, such delicious waves of tingles course throughout him it's as if he's uniting with her energy, embracing her subsurfacely, being swept towards a realm where nothing annoying occurs. Penelope's hair is a miracle of abundance—raven black softness swishing loose and wild, seizing the light, bending it into restless silver streamlets. And the radiance of her skin! Stuart suddenly realizes he's never seen Penelope's exposed skin before, apart from that of her face, throat, hands; realizes he's never seen her proportions clearly delineated head to toe. Now he's a starving man before a sumptuous feast, so overwhelmed with his good fortune he's unsure where to begin—glancing up and down Penelope's arms and about her back and up and down her legs, as made possible by her sleeveless and backless high-hemlined dress, unable to stop seeking to take in all of her at once; and while aware how preposterous it is that she's concealed herself for so long, not so much as exposed a forearm, for a reason he isn't close to comprehending. Then it hits him: he *needs* to speak to Penelope, has no choice! He *must* cast qualms aside, seize this opportunity to exploit her vulnerability, before she's able to revert to inaccessibility, re-erect the invisible wall. He's waited weeks for such an opportunity and who knows if there will be another anytime soon?

Once Stuart realizes he can't allow Penelope to vanish before speaking to her—realizes he'll assuredly endure hell on earth if he doesn't—he feels he's able to read something of her frame of mind. Is it true she feels his eyes admiring her from behind, as women often do, and is warming to them?—that, although uneasiness accompanies interest, the latter's gaining the upper hand?—that her body language is losing its hurriedness, communicating curiosity and hope? Has she ceased to shift from foot to foot, become close to motionless, on his account? Is she tensing with anticipation, radiating an invitation, smiling inside? When she adjusted her hair just now, flicked it from the side of her face that was briefly half-turned towards him, was it a flirtatious gesture—a come-hither gesture? Does she likewise wish to prolong this chance meeting, make use of the surprise element to strip away additional layers of veils? Does she likewise feel it would be a shame for matters to revert to how they've always been, continue to never socialize outside the office? Does she likewise desire to eliminate the invisible wall? Or is he perceiving what he wants to perceive, dreaming up an encouraging imaginary situation, so he'll be more relaxed, better able to say the right things and place Penelope at ease, dispose her to wanting him to come upstairs? Stuart's well aware of lacking clear answers to these questions! At any rate, the questions whisk by in the amount of time it takes him to stroll into the lobby. Because there's one thing of which Stuart's *very* certain: he's no more able to stop himself from speaking to Penelope than he is to stop himself from breathing.

When Stuart's about three yards from Penelope she, alerted by his advancing blurred reflection on the elevators' brass doors, abruptly spins about and faces him. Despite the swiftness and determination, air of challenge, of the movement her expression's startled, as if scampering to hide under her skin. Her cheeks are trembling, ashen; her eyes are unfocused and worried, wobbly silver flecks in them; she's glancing at the floor, to the sides, at the ceiling, into the vacant air—at everything except him. She seems to want to turn away, bolt—her body's half-straining in the direction of flight—while too emotionally flooded to do so. Stuart barely has time to be alarmed, stop dead in his tracks, before Penelope lunges forward, casts herself into his arms with a smothered cry, grips him tight; then, shaking profusely and shifting her weight to counter it, she says in a quavering voice, "I can't take it—I might go mad!" Pausing for a couple seconds, widening her eyes and whipping her glance about as if to confirm no one's near, she lowers her voice to a whisper he can barely hear and continues, "I feel like I'm splitting down the middle—like there are two parts of me, each fighting and trying to defeat the other! I feel like..." Trailing off, she lifts her eyes to his imploringly, clutches tighter, emits a tortured moan.

"Fighting with yourself, Penelope?" Stuart asks tenderly, steadying her in his arms, awareness of his surroundings fading—the lobby's becoming bright gray fog. "But why? You're so strong, the most centered and healthiest person I know. I understand tonight didn't go as planned, that a man who isn't a man took you by surprise, but that's not a reason to blame yourself or war with yourself. It'll pass, Penelope, believe me, and... I'm here to help, will do whatever I can...anything, just tell me what you need." Thoughts of gaining admittance to Penelope's secret life have vanished: dispelling her distress is paramount. She's clearly more troubled by her date-gone-sour than she cared to admit at first. She's temporarily lost her balance, it's his *responsibility* to assist her in recovering it. But Penelope's quivering body as she clings to him, and that he's grasping the exposed skin of her shoulders and back, is unavoidably informing Stuart of what he's hungered after for so long. This *is* their first embrace, so how can he not be vividly affected? It's not how he imagined their first embrace would be—a far cry from an embrace brought about by loving desire—but there's no escaping the fact she's clinging to him; that, in a convoluted manner, his dreams are coming true. But he can't allow such sensations to gain the upper hand, blind him, in Penelope's moment of need. Perhaps at some point she'll embrace him in clarity of mind, affection and delight, but that time isn't now. He must stay strong for her, will himself to disregard her stirring vibrations, tough as such is.

"God, Stuart!" Penelope exclaims, casting her gaze into the air behind him, blanching as if perceiving a ghost. "I'm trapped in dark tunnels, don't see ways out!" She yanks herself from his embrace and spins about, slams both palms against an elevator door, shaking and sobbing. Then, stifling her sobs as swiftly as they appeared, she faces him again, grasps his shoulders at arms-length, seeks his eyes. "Help me," she says in a tone that's a mix of pleading, insistence, misery which rends his heart, chills his spine. "I need a friend, someone who won't be scared...someone smart, who won't think I'm too...too out on the brink. A good friend, who..." She trails off, tears welling.

"Let's go upstairs," Stuart responds, reaching to caress Penelope's shoulders but somewhat clumsily clutching instead, too astonished to be wholly aware of what he's doing. He's entertaining the notion someone else is speaking his words while perfectly aware such is ridiculous; he's seeking to sort out conflicting emotions—particularly fear, the last thing he expected to experience on Penelope's account. "Sitting down, having some water, shaking out the nerves, figuring out what went wrong and how to stop it from happening again...making sure that guy doesn't bother you again. You'll be yourself in no time, I won't leave until you're laughing about the bad date. Like, that bad dates aren't worth worrying about, happens to all of us—people misrepresent themselves, shamelessly lie, it's usually impossible know what's true in advance."

"Thank you, Stuart!" she exclaims, hugging him tight again. "Embarrassing to think I could fall for a creep's lies, but I totally did, hook, line, and sinker with expectation—not hiding it from you! But I don't want to burden you with my bad decisions, involve you."

"Inconceivable that you could burden me in any way, Penelope. You're self-reliant and strong to the bone and I'm humbled and honored you feel I can make a difference, lift you free of negativity."

"Well, maybe self-reliant but sometimes too compliant and then upset about being compliant, my tendencies in a nutshell. How escape a nefarious self-divided personality? But, yes, let's go upstairs. *(She gestures at the elevators.)* I'm becoming a spectacle, it's a gossipy world. Neighbors I don't know have seen me like this and who knows who they know, even if I don't care, although I probably *ought* to—caring's barometric, I *want* to care." She's referring to the three people who gingerly circled around them, boarded the last elevator.

"The Penelope I know's flawlessly barometric, much admired—only an utter loser could spread negative gossip about you, their problem. Your bad date's fresh so it's tougher to see past it, but you soon *will*. A glass of water and relaxation, simple things go a long way towards restoring balance...amazing how effective they are."

Stuart and Penelope are silent during ascent to the twenty-first floor and barely stir, backs pressed to the wall opposite the elevator's door, she tremblingly clasping his arm. For reasons Stuart's unable to articulate, he dares not turn towards her, seek her eyes. At one point, though, his eyes involuntarily meet hers on the door's polished brass: she appears to be gazing at him intently, with something of criticism and doubt, perhaps mild hostility. Before he can confirm if he's reading her expression correctly, the overhead light's reflected glare obscuring interpretation, Penelope averts her eyes, grips his arm tighter.

Chapter III

"This way," Penelope says somewhat tersely once they exit the elevator, releasing Stuart's arm and swiftly darting to the left: her abruptness of manner is such that it occurs to him she's having second thoughts regarding his presence, perhaps close to announcing she's made a mistake and would rather be alone. Coming to a stop at the apartment—21C—that's one removed from the end of the hall on its left, she turns to him with a vague air of irritation, extracts keys from her purse, tosses the latter at the door's base. Upon opening the door she shoves it hard enough for it to bang against the entryway's wall, kicks her purse inside, curtly gestures for him to enter. What's going on? Penelope's bidding him enter her home without appearing to want him anywhere near it. She's acting as if she's inviting him in because she wants to argue, even if he can't imagine why. How long until she informs him to get lost? Nevertheless, Stuart enters, Penelope prodding him forward with taps at his back, slamming the door shut. By the time he turns to face her, ascertain if she's angry, they're in the living room. It's then he perceives she's breathing audibly and rapidly enough for it to approach hyperventilation—she's deathly pale, gritting her teeth, white-knucklingly clenching her hands, head shaking—he's so alarmed his legs are wobbling. Penelope's clearly been through far more than a date-gone-sour in any ordinary sense—behaving as if something harrowing occurred, laboring to maintain semblance of self-possession, and he needs to gather himself, be courageous for her. Gesturing towards a long couch, liberally supplied with fluffy decorative pillows, he suggests, "Penelope, you should lie on the couch. I'll get water or make a smoothie, whatever you need. Just tell me where things are, I'll bring them to you. I promise I won't leave until you're calm."

"Calm? How can I be calm?" Penelope shrieks, jerking her arms at the ceiling, her eyes incredulous; then, in the space of about two seconds, she stomps up him, seizes his wrists and squeezes, continues speaking in a strained voice of erratically alternating volume. "How be calm if I'm torn in two by opposing impulses? If a fight's constantly brewing in me, nerves waiting to burst the dam? Calmness is a fantasy—self-dividedness doesn't calm down! I live in dread of the fight, intervals when nagging urges gather, kick up a stress-storm—they shatter me and I'm a fish washed up on a beach, suffocating! Why do you think I dress plainly, keep my cursed body covered, wear drab shoes and everything else? It's to keep men, and therefore also the insane part of me, at bay! All I want to do is hold down a job, be busy with duty, so as to quiet dangerous urges and live an approxi-mation of a secure life! But the longer I go without surrendering to the unrest that devils me the more nastily it erupts! Let me tell you something about earlier on, after I came home from work. Did I even know what I was doing when I called that man? Oh, I know him, all right, met him last month at a club I had no business being at! He's someone who wants me to be a slut—who's no good for me—who wants to ignite the bad things in me and burn me to the ground! A suffocating dream, that's what it was when I called him! I was in a nightmare daze starting from when I found his number in a drawer, since those numbers are *never* on my phone! It's when my peripheral vision gets dark and fuzzy—when smudged panes of glass separate my sight from everything around me! Nearby objects seem like they're far away and make me feel alone; faraway objects rush at me in swarms and crowd and compress me; and then I'm not me anymore! I'm no more in control of my direction than fallen leaves in a storm and someday I might be blown into a fire! Don't you believe me?"

Stuart's aware he's likely unable to conceal his astonishment, but doesn't feel he's indicated he disbelieves Penelope. He believes her implicitly, even if he could've never imagined her hidden life would be half as vivid as she's describing, or that it's dangerous for her. "Penelope, it's me," he says softly, endeavoring to caress her hands. "You know me—I'd never doubt you. I only want to help in any way I can. I believe everything you've said and will do whatev..."

"Look at this, then—here's proof!" she breaks in with a yell, having made up her mind he needs further convincing; then she's two-handedly leading him by the wrist into her bedroom, stopping in front of the closet, sliding its door open with a bang. "Take a look at this, then you'll believe me!" she resumes, parting the clothes on the front rod to expose those on the rod behind. "Guess what? It's not the wardrobe of a respectable woman!" she announces, seizing several dresses and throwing them on the floor. "They're all very revealing, I can tell you that! Hemlines up to my ass and necklines down to my tits and a real tight fit! And there's leather and fur and all the slut lingerie ever made! I'm two people—shameless hussy and uptight priss! After a sex-binge I spend weeks not allowing anyone to think I've ever been laid! One day an ice maiden, the next a trollop in heat—that's the story of my life! I'm two personalities, one hell-bent on ruining the other!" Seizing her cheeks with thumbs and forefingers, Penelope pulls them in opposite directions, meeting Stuart's eyes for the first time since entering the bedroom. "Don't you get it?" she asks. "This is what's going on inside me! This is what I deal with every hour every day! This is my personality war!" Exhaling with a hiss, she glares at him as if he's insulted her.

It's as if Stuart's followed a path into a forest, expecting to be soothed by verdant quietude, and found it to be overpopulated by prowling predators—panic doesn't begin to describe what's jolting his nerves. The fact that Penelope's glaring at him, in itself, chills him to the bone, not only because she's doing so as if he's against her but because she's never come close to doing such a thing before—never been anything but cheerful, supportive, kind—and there's nothing rational about it. He was convinced she was concealing part of herself and persisted in this conviction for weeks, refusing to believe she was the prude she made herself out to be; he ignored those, and they were legion, who laughed at him for clinging to this conviction; he was determined to bring her hidden places into the open, reap the rewards; but did he imagine she'd scare him? Did he imagine Penelope's secrets included susceptibility to frightening extremes of emotion and action? Did he imagine introduction to the secret Penelope would involve apprehension of danger, as in she's sometimes knocked about by distorted interpretations of reality, dueling with phantasms? Her eyes are communicating instability, and unwarranted hostility in particular, as he's never seen before: it's almost as if she feels he's responsible for her inner war. He understands their friendship's forever altered; understands not knowing her secrets made the innocent aspect of their friendship possible—can't help but wonder if she'll regret having revealed her hidden side, wind up disliking him for knowing too much.

Which isn't to imply concern for her well-being isn't uppermost in his thoughts—she's divided against herself, afraid and hurting. This business of denying healthy desires then hating herself after finally indulging them makes no sense: he'll do whatever he can to put a stop to this pointless war, bring peace to her heart. It isn't what he anticipated doing from the moment he glimpsed her—he foresaw having a good time, if only she'd cast the nun act aside, own up to her ardent disposition. But helping her overcome self-conflict exceeds anticipation, if only because it's as unexpected as challenging. What's a good time, after all, compared with his contrasting reactions as he faces Penelope's glare? She's revealed herself to be a troubled angel, in thrall to impulses that unbalance, outright threaten, her, and he's going to brave hell and highwater to bring lasting serenity to her gaze. "Penelope," he says tenderly, gently grasping her hands. "You're an amazing woman, bright and strong, and it tears me apart to see you this way. Please tell me what I can do, anything at all. I'm at your service, won't hesitate to..."

Penelope isn't listening: casting her eyes at the ceiling as if it's caught fire, she cuts Stuart off—cries, "My God!," while tearing her hands from his grasp; then, rapidly wheeling about and crossing to the other side of the room, she sits on the floor, removes her shoes and throws them at the wall, shouting, "I hate those shoes—hate everything I'm wearing! Nothing good's ever happened when I'm in this stuff! If I'm in this stuff it means my bad side's beating on the good!"; then, springing to her feet and returning to the closet, seizing more dresses, throwing them at those on the floor, she resumes, "This stuff will be my death! I try to stay sane and resist—sometimes I go for weeks without reaching for this stuff! But the bad urges never rest—always needling, wearing me down, waiting for me to weaken! My head reels, thoughts get unfocused, eyesight fuzzy—I feel faint and excited at the same time—my body races a hundred heartbeats a second—I pace like a maniac and sleeping's impossible! I try to stay away from the back of this closet, forget it's here, but it keeps yanking at me, chasing comforting things away, ruining my life! I get crazy here—*look*!" she shrieks and, with that, yanks her hemline to her waist with one hand, points between her legs with the other. "Tickles drive me insane and I just don't care anymore! I give up and go with it and, anyway, there's no choice!" Flicking her hem back into place, she stomps up to Stuart, wraps her arms around him, squeezes with all her strength. She's shaking, hyperventilating, digging her nails into his back.

Stuart's giddy verging on vertigo, the room a silvery blur, as Penelope places her palms on his cheeks, treats him to the very sort of hungering look he's fantasied about for seemingly an infinity, heatedly whispers, "Love me!," crushes her mouth against his. They're kissing as if there won't be another dawn and he's reaching up Penelope's dress in back, her hair swishing, belly pulsing, a leg wound about his. How smooth, soft, strong, electric her thighs are when he slips his hands inside the tops of her stockings and caresses, squeezes! Penelope's hugging him as if endeavoring to slip under his skin—he's periodically readjusting his footing, lest they lose their balance, fall to the floor.

Shortly thereafter Stuart and Penelope are undressed on the queen-sized bed, comforter and sheets flung to the floor. She's below him with legs wrapped about his waist, by turns softly bite-kissing his cheeks and sucking his neck insistently and licking his face while clutching the back of his head—whispering sweetly, her words emotion-slurred. Her breasts swell against his chest as her thighs rhythmically tighten and relax; the scents of her hair and body and perfume, suggestive of a kaleidoscope of delights the more delightful for being impossible to pin down, are worlds unto themselves; her wide dark smiling eyes periodically blaze with silvery emphasis, swirling tingles up his spine. Stuart's never waited so long to bed a woman, had anticipation build dizzyingly high; never had fantasy flip to actuality so spontaneously and vividly it's as if he's acquired a fresh set of senses. When he kisses Penelope such leaping elation overtakes him it's as if he's become impervious to death. It's not until sunrise splays across the windows, flings orange-gold across the bed, that exhaustion overtakes them.

Chapter IV

Shortly past noon, Stuart and Penelope seemingly having forgotten they're on call for work that could easily materialize, neither having turned their phone on (A first for each, as they're proud of being conscientious.), he awakens to find her on hands and knees, taut in every muscle like a cat poised to pounce, gazing at him intently, eyes alight with astonishment and hunger. Her body language—aura of readiness, lust, shock—is as good as a command, whereupon he's reaching for her shoulders, happily saying, "Come here, you!" But she yanks herself away in alarm, scrambles out of reach. "No!" she winces, flatly contradicting what he's read in her eyes and manner. "I can't!" she continues, scooting further away. "Men *never* understand!"

"Understand?" he asks softly, becoming uneasy. "What's to understand besides that I adore you, want to make you happy?"

Penelope's quivering on the bed's edge, her hands clenched in fists, elbows digging into ribs, struggling to steady herself, feet on the floor. "You don't understand!" she shrieks, slamming palms on the mattress, whipping her head about, glaring. "I tried to tell you—I did tell you—I have no business being with a man! There are things in me that can't be stirred up! Men stir me up, I can't be with them! I told you that!"

"I didn't hear you say that, Penelope," he responds, not moving an inch. "I heard you say some men are the wrong ones. If I..."

"If you what?" Penelope cuts in, half-spitting the words. "I took you to my closet, showed you bad things..." Trailing off with a faraway aspect to her gaze, she appears to be sifting through recollection; then, apparently locating what she's searching for, she slams her palms on the mattress again, shouts, "You shouldn't have flirted, looked at me like you've been doing! Yeah, that's right—don't look surprised! I know you've been entertaining ideas! The stuff in your head's never been a secret! I've been onto you from early on, let that be understood! And I've kept you at arm's length, as you know! The moment you brought me home you should've turned around and gone to *your* home! Let me inform you of something: *all* men are the wrong man, including *you*! Wake up, why don't you, and go home and leave me be!" She's frantically gesticulating towards the door, eyes ablaze and glazed.

But wasn't I invited to stay? Stuart asks himself, feeling a need to affirm the truth even though he's aware of it, whereupon a rapid-fire sequence of pictures of the manner in which Penelope flung herself at him in front of the closet—clasped him, intoned *Love me!*, kissed him—flashes into his head. Yes, regardless of what Penelope's saying, she didn't want him to leave—he *was* invited to stay, if not with words then with action. He's on solid ground, Penelope's mistaken! He's searching for a response, seeking to point out he was invited to stay without appearing to contradict her, but doesn't find the words. He's aware contradicting an angry woman, especially one as willful as she's revealed herself to be, is the height of idiocy and no amount of tact will suffice. He's rising to his knees, walking on them towards her.

"I told you not to touch me!" Penelope shrieks, yanking herself further away, still on the bed's edge; then, switching to pleading, her expression softening—intonation and countenance altering as swiftly as sunlight dancing on waves rushing ashore, "Please, Stuart, I'm asking as a friend, I can't...can't be who you want me to be or even try to be that person."; then, in a whispery distant, as if half-absorbed in waking dreams, manner, "No...not such things, not again, I don't think...things have happened before, I'm not fit for..."; then, shouting again, recoiling as if ghosts are approaching, "I *told* you being with a man was bad for me and bad for the man too! Why did you stay after I told you *that*? Why did you kiss and arouse me, awaken feelings that *need* to be left alone? I'm not making stuff up! Some feelings are malicious sprites and dangerous, should *never* be conjured forth, meddled with, lest they get enraged and fade the daylight, smother me! Why for God's sake...?" She trails off trembling, collapses on the mattress, curls into a ball.

Stuart's never felt more powerless: afraid to speak and afraid to touch, as either will likely increase Penelope's distress, he's little better than paralyzed—an unwilling witness of her misery. He can't see beyond the bed, Penelope's shaking body, and it's as if her sobbing's louder than thunder cracking the sky. What's to be done? There's the obvious risk of further upsetting her but how can he remain idle? Just because she's resisting assistance doesn't mean she isn't in need of it. He says very quietly, "Penelope, I'm your friend and will never do anything you don't want me to do, presume to choose what's best for you without your blessing. But as your friend I can't just sit here twiddling my thumbs while you're not feeling well. Sorry, but I can't. There must be something I can do. What do you want me to do?"

Turning to face Stuart with a scowl, Penelope hisses "You mean you *still* don't understand?" in a manner that causes a picture of a cornered cat, fangs bared and claws spread, to leap into his head, along with the idea she might be on the point of springing at him, such that he's involuntarily bracing for an attack, flinching. He's about to respond when she yells, "Shush! I don't want to hear it! Either stay or go, I don't care! All men are dead to me so I don't care what any do or say, especially *you*!" and leaps to her feet, stomping about the room erratically—flailing her arms, incoherently muttering, emitting smothered cries—as if half of her truly is warring with the other.

The sight of Penelope entangled in inner turmoil, apparently oblivious of his presence—the sounds she's making, unlike any he's heard a woman make before—the swipes of her arms, as if she's fending off imaginary creatures, living in a hallucinated world: Stuart's so alarmed it's as if his chest's on fire. But he also can't help but be thrilled at the sight of her: there she is, without a stitch of clothing on, repeatedly whipping her long dark tresses away from her face as noon sunlight glides over her curves—such unblemished alabaster skin, symmetrical lines of muscle tone—no part of her body's out of sync with the whole; and such fiery eyes, inexhaustible energy! The contrast of her hair's black waves with the ivory of her face and shoulders and back, simple in itself, twists delicious buoyancy into his blood, makes him feel as if he has limitless emotional resources and stamina—as if boredom's ceased to exist, wonder drenching all, expansiveness beckoning. The woman he's longed for, dreamed about, lost ease of mind on account of for what seems like years is here before him, in all her glory—of course he can't help but relish her beauty despite his fear and dismay. And, besides, this is Penelope, for God's sake! She's always been just about the most centered person in existence—unflappably serene, cheerful. So surely she'll soon be that person again. And she *did* say either stay or go, which means she isn't asking him to leave: it might be her roundabout way of asking him to stay without compromising her pride. She might very well be expecting him to read between the lines and come to her aid. He will snatch her from the demons' clutches, restore her to her balanced self! He *will* dispel the darkness in her eyes, make things right between them! He must make things right between them, because his sanity depends on it! He's in love with Penelope in full measure, he sees it clearly now—it's no passing fancy, whimsical wish to solve a mystery. He's in love with her with all the emotional upheaval and psychic realignment and toughness and responsibility love demands. He's finally spent a night with her and understands that, rewarding past relationships notwithstanding, he's never been in love before. What he previously believed was love is a pale reflection of what he's experiencing.

Penelope, aware of the touch of Stuart's eyes (She's not so absorbed in self-conflict that she can't feel his gaze slip under her skin.), comes to a stop, falls silent aside from out-of-breath breathing, and faces him, chest heaving; looking at him very seriously, she swallows hard—seeks to silence her breathing—and says in a worried, almost motherly, tone, "Stuart, you don't know what you're doing—the things you're kicking into motion in me aren't nice."; then, exhaling in exasperation and slashing at the air with an arm, she yells, "Stop looking at me! I'm not an amusement park for your eyes! I'm not someone who should be excited! Damn my body! Damn it to hell!" Turning away, she advances to the dresses she threw on the floor the night before, derisively kicks them towards the closet. "See—see what my body's good for!" she resumes. "It's only good for wearing these atrocious things and exciting men! And the excitement of men's poison, sickness, fever that tears me from everything that's good, puts me in a dreadful place! Let me tell you something: I'm never lonelier and more miserable than when I'm with a man! Men can't do anything for me, except make me feel caged and crazy! When I'm with a man all I want to do is scream! Why won't you understand? But then you *can't* understand, can you? You're just like the others! You *can't* understand!" Dropping her arms to her sides in a gesture of futility and moving further away, she sinks to the floor—is soon fitfully twisting from side to side on her back, clutching her temples with shaking hands, staring at the ceiling as if it's about to collapse. She appears to be oblivious of Stuart's presence again.

Stuart's head may be informing him he'll likely increase Penelope's distress if he ventures to comfort her but his heart's brushing that information aside: she's hurting and he needs to bring an end to it. He must prove to her he's her friend first and foremost—it's his responsibility to demonstrate he's different than those who make her feel lonely and miserable—he *will* obtain her trust, ease her into being at peace with herself. But no sooner is he at the bed's edge, lowering his feet to the floor, than Penelope's eyes ignite, scatter and flail, with absolute terror and she, with a cat's swift agility, flips onto her stomach, raises herself to her knees, presses her palms against the air between them. "Please don't, Stuart!" she implores. "Please, leave me be, I'm begging you! You still don't understand, I...I'm so sorry, Stuart, but... A man's affection, desire, touch! It blazes nastily under my skin and disorders me beyond endurance and makes me want to die! Just die!"

Stuart freezes, feels as if he's being pinned against the air: beautiful Penelope's before him, there's nothing he wants more than to assure her of his unquestioning devotion, do anything he can to put the pain and dread in her eyes to flight, make her smile, but she won't allow it—it's revolting to her. She's right: he isn't close to comprehending why.

Perceiving Stuart's ceased to approach, Penelope flings her gaze at the floor, takes deep breaths while rolling her shoulders forward; then, lifting her eyes to him again, says in a tremulous voice, in which tenderness isn't lacking, "I know you've fallen for me, Stuart, you poor dear—the worse for you and, believe it, hell for me. I wish it were otherwise—wish I could be with a good man. At the very least I wish you had a better woman to fall for, as you deserve."; then, raising her voice a notch while unseeingly staring into the air above his head, "Don't you see I shouldn't be—can't be—stirred up? Don't you see I can't answer for myself in a man's arms? A man's touch makes me feel slammed against a wall, restricts and smothers me, and I turn into a bad person! I get crazy and mean and hate myself for it! I'm not a good woman, Stuart, you need to realize that!"; then, announcing as she brings her hands to her throat, "Sometimes I want to strangle myself."

Stuart starts in Penelope's direction again, but checks himself: his wish to soothe her encounters aversion and fear, she frenetically flailing her hands in the air between them. It's agony to wish to help and be prevented from doing so; especially, it's agony to hear her state she's contemplated doing violence to herself: it's as if the room's on fire and Penelope's fainted and he's chained to the bedframe, unable to carry her to safety. All the same, though, since she's mentioned self-harm, he starts paying particular attention to her hands—where they're located, what they're preoccupied with: she must not be allowed to use them against herself. Noting Stuart's gaze, Penelope crawls to the dresses on the floor. "Stop looking at me!" she screams, heaping the dresses in her lap, draping them over her shoulders, wrapping them around her waist. "I don't want to be looked at! I hate the looking! I told you that!"

"Penelope," Stuart says gently, extending his hands palms-up. "I'm your friend, will do anything to help, only want to..."

"Hush!" she breaks in with a shriek, wringing her hands again, slapping at the air, tears welling into her eyes. Moments later she's wiping the wetness from her cheeks with the backs of her fingers, lips trembling and gaze wobbling. "Stuart, I pity you, am so sorry," she says, lowering her voice to a half-whisper. "I can't change who I am, it's not in my power, I'm weak. You've fallen for a bad woman—a haunted woman—a cursed woman! There's a bottomless pit in me that wants to swallow me! There's an undertow in me, direction I don't want to go in but can't stop going in! There's unfriendly energy in me that wants to undo anything that supports security, see to it I'm helpless and afraid *all* the time! When men pursue me horizons vanish and hope dies, it's like my feelings are imprisoned in gloomy tunnels...like they're being invaded by cruel things—things cruel to me and the man! There's no compromise and I might crack up someday! The specter of murder-suicide haunts me! I'm telling you it shadows me when I'm with a man! Sometimes I think I could shoot a man then shoot myself!"

Did she really say what I think she said? Stuart asks himself, by way of hoping he's misheard. But it's indisputable what Penelope said: she clearly enunciated the words and looks the part. Her expression's strained, distant, as if she's stranded in a perilous frame of mind; her eyes are unfocused, scattered; she's sitting still but her muscles are so taut it's as if they're seeking to rip themselves from her bones; she's shivering as if the room's freezing even though the heat's turned on high. She keeps erratically whipping her glance about and shuddering, as if shrinking from urges to do something rash or dangerous or outright deadly, and Stuart can't help but wonder if a gun's nearby, picture her lunging for it. Any second now! Any second now he might need to wrest a gun from Penelope's grasp, subdue her! Has emotion really become so volatile it's as if the very air's distended and blurred due to an electric charge? Is Penelope really under the influence of suicidal urges—murderous urges? Is she the same woman he's fallen for? Do her inclinations still belong to her? Who, *or what*, is inhabiting Penelope?

"I told you your Penelope's bad!" he hears her say in a tortured mournful tone. "Murder-suicide, a twin killing, bad girl and poor boy dead in bed! Now you know! And now get out!" Raising herself on her knees and lifting her head high, the dresses she draped over herself sliding off her and rendering her naked again, she screams, "I swear I'll bash my head into the floor if you don't get out of here!"

Stuart's at Penelope's side in a second, gently but firmly pulling her onto her back, holding her in place. "Why do you want to hurt yourself?" he cries incredulously. "Everyone thinks highly of you, looks up to you—you have a good job, wonderful place to live—you're beautiful and kind. And stop berating your beauty, it's extraordinary, draws people to you before they know how sweet you are—you inspire with kindness and intelligence—are a shining light, positive and beneficent. You keep telling me I don't understand and I agree, am utterly baffled. Why are you inventing enemies, allowing phantoms to devil you, hounding yourself? If you don't want to be with men, fine; if you don't want to be with me, fine; if you want to be left alone, fine: that's your right. But stop taking it out on yourself! You have worlds to live for and I don't understand why you, of all people, are speaking about throwing it away!"; then, lowering his voice, inquiring in gentle tones, "Is there a gun, Penelope? Where's the gun? Please tell me if there's a gun, Penelope." He's straddling her, careful to avoid doing so with his full weight, while pinning her wrists to the carpet, gazing into her troubled eyes, dreading the chance she really does have a gun.

"You don't want to find out!" she yells, twitching against his hold, eyes blazing. "Here, listen a wee bit: the last man who restrained me like this didn't walk without bending forwards for days! Better not let me get a good kick in, I'll whack you where it counts! The legs you admire will propel my foot straight to the target! Better hope I don't get my hands on it, I'll tear it off!" She's gazing between his legs none too kindly, still seeking to escape; but then her eyes suddenly soften, her tone kind, "Sorry, Stuart, I...I'm not a good person, I told you that, this is proof. I don't want to be putting you through this, don't want... I liked being friends with you and am...I just..." Her voice faltering, she closes tearing eyes and ceases to resist, becomes absolutely limp.

"Penelope," Stuart hastens to say, emboldened by her apology, "you're not hurting yourself as long as I'm around, OK? I won't allow it and you're not going to allow it either, understand? We're going to get you some compassionate professional help, OK? I'll see you through this, do whatever I need to do. We'll get you some help and all will be well. You'll see you're a sweet person and that life's yours for the taking—you're entitled to enjoyment and happiness, as are all good-hearted bright people. You're a sweetheart through and through."

"Help?" she scoffs, opening her eyes. "What help do you propose? What reaches inside a person, makes bad directions disappear, turns devilment into fluff? Am I your pity-party mission, personal experiment? Think you can push buttons in my feelings, automatically make me the happiest person on earth, as if I'm a programable robot, virtual toy? You snap your fingers and Poof! the poor woman's problems are gone and she's delirious with joy? Right, poor piteous Penelope! Your special project, good deed, reason to puff yourself up, parade pride, as if you've climbed K2 or conquered a country! *Pathetic!*" Her eyes are glaring like light on steel. Then he hears her announce with real menace, "Didn't I tell you to keep your eyes and hands off me?" as she rakes her nails down his right forearm, he having released her wrists. "Get off me and get out of here or I'll scream loud enough for the neighbors to call the cops! I'm counting to three."

Not doubting Penelope will follow through, Stuart places a palm over her mouth, whereupon she screams so vehemently his hand's inundated with heat and vibrations shoot up his arm, even though volume's muffled; nor does she cease seeking to claw him, glowering with wishing-him-dead eyes—he scoots forward, pins her arms with his knees, careful to avoid injuring her—as the carpet's a couple inches deep, he's immobilizing her against a soft surface. While restraining her Stuart's wondering when, or if, her mania will end—he's never been plunged into tumult such that nothing seems wholly real and he's as if entrapped in an oppressive dream. What, indeed, is real? How could sweet serene Penelope be raging thus, mentioning guns, mental collapse? Has he ever felt this mentally and emotionally taxed? Then he's aware of speaking in a firm even voice, grateful he's able to do so: "Sorry, Penelope, but you're staying on your back, where you can't harm yourself, until you're calm. I don't want to be doing this, it's the last thing I want, but... Well, I'd be a terrible friend if I released you while you're threatening to harm yourself! Shame on me if I did."

"Think I haven't been through this a zillion times, one big yawn by now?" she mocks, having yanked her arms from under Stuart's knees, wrenched his hand from her mouth (As he's never pinned or placed a hand over a woman's mouth before, is apprehensive of applying overmuch force, escape's easy for her.); then, becoming stock still, radiating rage, "Think you're the first I've tussled with, so *incredibly* special? Think poor Penelope's going to off herself because of you? Pah! Once you're gone I'll be fine and dandy—just *leave*! Oh, and I won't be screaming for help like a baby, that was a lie—you can't sit on me all day. I'm not a wisp of a woman and am in shape and riled-up people are *strong*, so I'll outlast you and be on my feet before you want me to. Wake up and go while you can, before you're in *way* over your head."

Momentarily drifting outside strife, seemingly deaf to Penelope's warning, Stuart finds himself marveling at the force of will in her eyes. Her eyes are unlike any he's gazed into before: it's as if he's on the cusp of admittance to unsuspected emotional riches, deathless as storm-tossed surf rushing ashore—as if he need look no further for fulfillment of every dream he's had. Penelope's eyes are as dazzling as the sky on clear moonless nights on eastern Sierra mountaintops, away from civilization's obstructing lights, and likewise birth marvelous inner expansiveness. But Stuart isn't allowed to marvel for above ten seconds, as another slash of Penelope's nails, at his midriff and drawing blood, jolts him. "Don't know why you would do that, Penelope," he says, gritting his teeth, steeling himself against the sting—seizing her wrists again. "I can't leave, it wouldn't be right when you're..."

"When I'm *what*?" she interrupts acerbically; but then she smiles, playfully squirms, blithely says, "Ooooo, very nice! Pin me, sweetie—I'm fair game, surrender's the best fun!" No sooner is Stuart wondering why Penelope's become compliant or if it's real, relaxing his hold predominantly on account of wishful thinking, than she strikes him below his left shoulder from behind with a knee. As he pitches forward onto his hands, just managing to avoid tumbling sideways, she spins from under him, rights herself to hands and knees, scampers towards the closet, flinging the dresses on the floor in front of it behind her, one of them wrapping around his neck. Whirling to confront him, she raises a cautionary hand, says matter-of-factly, "I won't be held down and domineered, Stuart. Try it again and you'll regret it, first and last time I tell you. And kindly refrain from speaking—you need to listen."

"Peachy," Stuart snaps, succumbing to annoyance as he unwraps the dress from his neck, wads it up, throws it over Penelope's head, "You speak, I listen... Just *perfect*! Now, please, you listen: I don't budge until you *prove* you won't hurt yourself, I don't care how many tantrums you toss—how many times you fake niceness, then whack me."

"Do please explain," Penelope sneers, "why I'm obliged to prove anything to you! Where do you come off presuming I owe explanations when I'm in *my* home and you won't go! I don't care if you think I'm in a bad way, too excited for my own good—it's none of your business! My life's mine, not yours! Men and their icky clinging fake-concerned ways make me *sick*! Men getting pompous, casting themselves in roles of chivalrous knight, supposing they're protecting me when *they're* the problem! I'm so weary of it! I'm weary of you, and if you don't get out of here... Listen carefully," she lowers her voice, speaking slowly, her words dripping with venom, "now that I have requested that you exit my home and you have refused to do so you are officially a trespasser in the eyes of the law. If you do not exit my home immediately I will call the police and inform them you assaulted me in my place of residence."; then, her voice rising to a scream again, "Out, do you hear! How many times do I need to tell you? No verbiage about conscience, no verbiage about what's right, no verbiage about poor pitiful me, just get out! Out, or you *will* have a mad woman on your hands and I won't be able to answer for myself! You're an unwanted trespassing stalking intruder, harassing and persecuting me, and I'll act fittingly! You don't know how violent I can be! There's a demon in me and you'll be a target!"; then, absolutely glaring at him, "Why aren't you gone? For Christ's sake! What does it take?" And with that she leaps to her feet, throws shoes.

Stuart's already on his feet—exiting the bedroom clothes in hand, swiftly dressing in the living room. He's aware of objects being thrown, fabric being torn, furniture being kicked, cries rending the air, and pictures of guns and knives and mayhem burst into his head. Penelope's words *There's a demon in me and you'll be a target!* continue to singe his ears as he approaches the front door. Then he's in her building's hall, the walls of which appear to be converging ahead of him. Then he's in the elevator, surrounded by gleaming brass—sharply clashing bright angles, his very thoughts splintering into shattered patterns devoid of sense. Then he's on a sidewalk, glancing about like one who's been jolted from a harrowing dream, endeavoring to orient himself.

Chapter V

Less than ten minutes after stepping outside Stuart's panic is dissipating in the open spaces of the Upper East Side streets—the wind's cold gusts, simple act of briskly walking—and he's berating himself for leaving Penelope alone. "She was trying every which way to be rid of me, get me to lose my nerve, crumble," he begins. "When one approach didn't work, she tried another—a matter of stringing tactics together, playing the odds, pushing random buttons, calling my bluff any which way. That bit about me being a trespasser and calling the cops, then her frenzy—she absolutely unleashed herself, was wrecking her room as if it belonged to someone she detested, wailing like a banshee. Highly unnerving, I've never been in a like situation, but that's no excuse. How could I fall for it—be that weak, get scared, lose sight of the big picture, tear out of there? Supremely pusillanimous to abandon the woman I love—yes, love!—when she might need me the most, never mind her denials! I don't believe I bolted, it's as if I was under a spell! Penelope's eyes flared—the air became hot, suffocating—the room itself was suddenly hostility-saturated, wanting me gone! How did she do that?"

What's to be done? Should he retrace his steps to Penelope's building, phone 911, state she's suicidal, wait for emergency personnel to arrive? Surely, she is a danger to herself and needs intervention. But such would be futile—she'd readily revert to outward serenity, come across as enviably balanced. The moment emergency personnel announced themselves she'd blithely call out, "Just a moment, please!" or something similar, after which she'd open the door with a questioning smile—be exemplarily self-possessed in conservative dress, as at the office. She'd calmly look straight at him in their presence, announce she's mystified why he summoned them. She'd add that she's touched by his concern but that he's misread the situation. She'd cheerfully bid everyone, including him, good day and dispense well-wishes and shut the door, never ceasing to be polite: the emergency personnel would swallow her act hook, line, and sinker and he'd have no choice but to accompany them out of her building. He'd only succeed in annoying the emergency personnel, who understandably don't take kindly to people crying wolf, and further annoying Penelope and, more to the point, she'd still be alone and at war with herself—still be a danger to herself.

Stuart's randomly walking, only distantly aware of and not caring in what direction he's headed, while absorbed in recollections of last night and this morning and afternoon—seeing Penelope flip between tears, anger, iciness, pleading—between haughtiness, apologies, whimpering, humility, blank staring—seeing her facial expressions and body language repeatedly race through the dark emotional spectrum, from dismay to despair to rage to terror to indications of authentic instability, utter abandonment of rationality—hearing her speak, in tones by turns tremulous and scared and stern and challenging, of being a bad person, unfit for love—especially, hearing her declare in a frightful hurried whisper: Sometimes I think I could shoot a man then shoot myself!

After at least forty minutes of wandering Upper East Side streets, seldom cognizant of his precise whereabouts despite knowing the area well, having lived there for over four years in the past, Stuart's seated on a rock outcropping in Central Park. A gently descending expanse of winter-withered grass is before him, blurring in afternoon's shimmering golden light—brightness vivid enough to distort apprehension of space and distance; nor is he able to detect the fluctuations and chill of the breeze. Penelope's the sole occupant of his attention and he's ceased to dwell exclusively upon her emotional imbalance and dramatics, mentions of murder-suicide. He's recalling her radiant presence, electric caresses—touch of her trembling fingers, silk soft skin, cast of her aroused gaze, slide of lamplight about her curves, ability to be utterly abandoned, her little girl giggles—hungry for more of what he felt while clasping her close. A kaleidoscopic swirl of impressions and pictures of the bliss he experienced with Penelope, miracle of her fairly flinging herself at him, is taunting him—plunging him into such loneliness and desolation, empty expanses of need, it's as if existence itself is spurning him. His body's his enemy—desire-flayed, stung by hunger impossible to sate. He can't run or hide from blazing blood! Penelope's the only woman able to quench the blaze but he's deathly afraid the door's been slammed shut, has no idea if he'll see her again. He believes she *may* have yelled, "I can't be in the office again, must quit a job I love, because of tonight's cursed chance meeting, nasty turn of fate—don't want you looking at me sideways, pitying me, spreading stuff! Rumor-mongering and pity's *sick*!" But maybe she said no such thing.

"I lost my nerve because of things Penelope said while un-hinged?" Stuart hisses at one point. "I allowed her disturbance to speak for her, assumed it was conveying heartfelt feelings, mistook disorder for carefully measured words?—allowed it to paralyze me with panic, rob me of clarity and courage, chase me away? What a shoddy reason to run! She was fantasizing about suicide—dying with a lover—and babbling about danger and demons, all while excessively manic and certainly not wholly aware of what she was saying, less likely believing it, and I fled like a weak-willed half-man who wilts at a hint of conflict. I'm ashamed to be me—don't know how I can face myself in the mirror, won't blame the mirror if it refuses to hold my reflection, spits it into the void. How could I run from the *one* person who holds the key to my well-being? How could I forget the moments when her eyes were trained upon me trustingly, sharing their wonder and hope and hunger and daring and courage?—when they blazed with desire as immeasurable as the night sky, illu-minated me from the inside out, had me joyfully gasping for breath, thankful beyond measure to be alive? How could I forget the moments when the amount of emotion she was under the sway of infused her beauty with added depths of mystery, that I've never discerned in a woman before, and it was understood I could safely express myself as I've never done, liberated from questions, judgment, taboo?—when it was as if she'd gifted me with a frame of mind uncontaminated by the status quo, im-mune to dogma, impossible to tame? Have I experienced such freedom before? No! Penelope lives on the edge of a precipice that's inside her, intermingled with her very blood, and loving her is like plunging headlong over that precipice without hitting bottom: have I experienced a hint of such rejuvenating vertigo with anyone else, imagined such could be possible? No! Before Penelope did I embrace a woman whose transports carried me outside my familiar world, suggested the possibility of a greatly intensified, dizzyingly engrossing, manner of living? No! Has any other woman led me to believe it's possible to be reincarnated without dying—reborn via love? No! Penelope speaks of living with frightful impulses, wrestling with the temptation of death, and I'm here without her, feeling death would be preferable. For God's sake, she's shown me I had no idea what life is, revised my versions of reality! My former life's an embarrassment, empty distraction via pseudo-desire, and I've stupidly thrown away the chance to trade it for a far more enthralling life and now I seem to have no life at all. But that can change—it *has* to change! Just because I was an imbecile and coward doesn't mean I have to keep on being one. Who's to say knowing Penelope ends now and I stay here by myself, away from her magic? Knowing Penelope *must* continue, lest I be smothered in perpetual desolation, claustrophobia slamming in. A brief taste of bliss in her embrace, then gone? No! One and done is *worse* than if I'd never spent a night with Penelope, known the surge."

It's eleven degrees below freezing and Stuart's indifferent to such. Gloves are in his pocket and he leaves them there, and leaves his coat unbuttoned. Springing to his feet and heading east, he continues addressing himself: "I'm alone after spending the night with Penelope, basking in life-altering sensations, lush rebirth? Insane! I've lived and breathed Penelope ever since setting eyes on her, undergone a personality overhaul for the better by getting to know her. She's the sweetest, most considerate, woman imaginable and a dear friend, first and foremost, and I need to gather myself, go help. She's alone in her apartment, distraught and in need, so enough of moping in the park like a pusillanimous dolt who's undeserving of her regard. Penelope's an oasis of wildness in a domesticated world—so refulgent, beautiful!—and the last thing she should be is hurting. The only thing that matters is being with Penelope and calming her, until she's her happy serene self again. She will not drive me away again—I will show her I'm unafraid to be by her side during her strident episodes, prepared to do my best to shield her from herself. I will be the man she needs me to be."

Within five minutes Stuart's exited Central Park. He's strolling through the Upper East Side again but it's as alien to him as Antarctica, visual distortions abounding. He's as if sur-rounded by panes of glass upon which the sunlight blurs, scatters, glares—sometimes there's just enough discernable outline, de-tection of motion, for him to avoid bumping into fellow pedes-trians. A couple times he's on the point of running his fingers along building fronts to confirm he's on the safer side of the side-walk, away from curb and traffic, but then shakes his head, clears his vision, laughs. Is it nuts to suppose he's so overwrought he needs his hands to assist him with not wandering into the street? He's partially pleased such could be the case—is decidedly under the influence of perception-altering emotion, intoxicated with-out substance-assistance. "I'm the luckiest man alive," he informs himself while observing his reflection in a window, watching it sharpen and fade in sunlight's glimmering dance. "I'm so charged with the need to trade my old life for a better one in Penelope's arms it's not only rewiring my senses but enabling adjustment without fear—disorientation's an indication I'm smashing op-pressive boundaries, illusions I formerly held dear. I'm already stronger—on my way to obtaining authentic freedom, absent regret of leaving anything behind. Overnight, the business of having a lucrative secure career, adding to my investment port-folio without overmuch effort, owning an apartment that accu-mulates value by leaps and bounds, has become distant, hollow, farcical—it's no more meaningful than litter clattering in breeze. What previously dispensed comfort is revealed to be parasitical artifice, prettified imprisonment, false faith, and is therefore unable to continue blinding and binding me—barring me from obtaining what I never knew I needed to obtain. Darling Penelope's gifted me with the ability to bid delusion begone.

"And what about running into Penelope last night, finally catching her dressed in a manner that flaunts her beauty, and in the grip of heated emotion, as wild as I *knew* lurked underneath her carefully cultivated stoic exterior? If that wasn't a preordained event there's no difference between black and white. An event of that nature had to occur, right? Wasn't it absolutely *necessary* that my gut intuition be confirmed, considering I was becoming unhinged and something had to give? Being repeatedly repelled by Penelope's puritan-act, unable to cross the distance between us no matter how desperately I tried, was unsustainable. It's wonderful how fate weaves it's way! Is it farfetched to suggest all-consuming attraction's able to bring about events that confirm one's instincts, end the agony of suspense, justify the said attraction? Farfetched to suggest the closeness and camaraderie Penelope and I enjoyed at work birthed subconscious communication-from-a-distance abilities, enabled our nerves to send signals from blocks away, arranged for us to run into each other when she was without her mask? Farfetched to insist my most treasured dreams—ones I've been, at best, barely conscious of—have materialized, become flesh, in the person of Penelope? Farfetched to insist buried aspects of my hunger have been lifted into the light of day, so that I may finally recognize and indulge them, achieve fulfillment that would otherwise elude me? Certainly I've seen unlimited possibility reflected in Penelope's eyes! It's as if the primal life-force has retained its purity in Penelope—as if an untamed elemental spirit from ages ago inhabits her—as if she's a throwback to a vanished time of unbounded emotion, unsullied by civilization. But why seek to pin Penelope down? Urges to analyze belong to my world previous to last night, when everything had to be explained, nothing taken on faith, and I need to shed those urges along with all else that hinders approaching heaven on earth. All that matters is Penelope and the new world she's revealed, self-deception she's done away with, barriers she's knocked down. It's almost as if my body's boundaries are dissolving and I'm becoming one with the bright sunlight of this beautiful day—as if my blood's surge is uniting with the sky's expanses—the rooftops suddenly seem near enough to touch. But why am I in the streets when I ought to be returning to Penelope, keeping her safe? Oh, and bathing in the life-sustaining light of her eyes! Her eyes by turns sweet and alarmed and disturbed and angry and worried and hopeful and serene and loving, reflecting her storm-tossed depths, nurturing wildness. Yesterday's another life—the life of the person I no longer am—and today I'll live with Penelope as never before."

Chapter VI

By the time Stuart arrives at Penelope's building he's feeling as if he's adrift alongside his body, watching it walk and listening to it talk as if it belongs to someone else. When he enters the lobby the man behind the desk appears to be outside normal speech's audible range, even though he's about four feet away. When Stuart addresses the man at unwarranted volume he's unaware of the latter's startled reaction, unconcealed wariness, has no idea why he's being asked to repeat what he just said; and that he's managed to comprehend the man's words seems nigh miraculous to him. Then Stuart's heeding the man's request and, although his words are on the mark, he's neither wholly aware of which ones he employs nor that he's still speaking louder than need be. As Stuart watches the man reach for the intercom phone and press a button, listens to him inform Penelope a guest has arrived, it occurs to him the man's a wax replica of a human that's acquired animation. Stuart neither detects the man's worried tone nor that he's drawing out the conversation, going so far as to ask Penelope if she's sure she's disposed to receive anyone: what's primarily occupying his attention are the flickering patterns of sunlight on the marble floor. Then a voice from behind the desk enables Stuart to comprehend he may proceed and he commences strolling to the elevators without the slightest turn of his head in the voice's direction, acknowledgment of having heard.

Then Stuart's in an elevator, all but blinded by the overhead lamp ricocheting flaring brightness between its brass walls—seemingly blurring the boundary between solidity and space. Only the numbers of each floor, briefly illuminated in red in ascending order as he rises, are discernable in the golden haze. When the elevator opens he's momentarily facing a mirror on the hallway's wall: there's an enrapt—some might say cat's-eyes-aglow-in-the-dark—aspect to his gaze.

Then Stuart's facing Penelope's door, watching its pale blue warp and glow, shift between convex and concave, in the florescent lights, the tubes of which are directly above—watching the doorbell-button fade in and out of focus, alternately appear larger and smaller, as he lifts a forefinger towards it. But the door's yanked open before he rings the bell: Penelope's before him and sensory distortion's gone—sharply delineated depth-perception's restored. She's wearing a semi-transparent scarlet nightie, plunging of neckline and mid-thigh high of hem, with a white rose in fluffed freefalling hair—radiant of face, smiling benevolently, hopeful anticipation in her eyes—vermillion-lipstick-slicked lips open, tongue slowly circling about them.

"Stuart sweetie, I'm *very* happy—what took you so long to come back to me? I was missing you *insanely* right away, positively flailing! Please come inside." She steps backwards, enabling him to enter—soon as he crosses the threshold playfully shoves the door shut behind him, not troubling to lock it. "And off with this please, kind Sir, I want to see you!" she giggles, removing his coat and embracing him.

Stuart's never undergone such an abrupt shift in orientation, from extreme sensory exaggeration to solid grounding in clarity, before. Penelope's urgent, warm, elated—her stomach and chest stirringly pulsing as he runs his fingers over her neck and face, joins his lips to hers, she sweetly warbling. She's not driven by disturbance and desperation, as when she jerkily grabbed him last night, kissed him as if involuntarily, but kissing him as ardently and tenderly as he could wish, joy evident in the undulations of her lips and tongue. She's not racing inside herself to escape stinging recollection of an infuriating experience, being knocked about by strident reverberations and resentment and rage, but jubilantly embracing a positive experience in serenity of mind. She's wrapping an arm around Stuart's neck, curling a leg about both of his, breathing deeply, stimulating his ears with feather-soft caresses, her hair swishing, as he clasps her closer. His increasingly unbearable nerve-flaying insomnia-fueling fixation's finally bearing fruit—fate's intervened to spare him. Penelope's beaming bliss—there's no reason for Stuart to dread banishment to loneliness, desolation.

"Penelope, have I told you you're my favorite person," Stuart says, gingerly interrupting their kissing, taking a step back while grasping her forearms, looking her up and down with inordinate delight, she having unwound her leg from about him, released his neck.

"You're my favorite person for all my life, Stuart," she responds, freeing her forearms, seizing his hands and squeezing such that sparkles radiate up his spine. "I was painting my toenails when the doorman rang *(She glances at her toes, wiggles them.),* clearly getting pretty for you. But it's a mystery how something told me you'd be coming back to me, especially since I was so beastly. Sorry for being beastly but I wasn't surprised when the doorman announced you, just turned into a *huge* smile of thankfulness! Sorry my toenails aren't done, I *squealed* when I knew you were coming up and abandoned them. You're the first who's come back to me, and the first I've *wanted* to come back! Just imagine."

"Being here's surpassing wildest imagination, Penelope—been waiting a long time for attraction to bend me to its will, even if I was unaware—when I first set eyes on you I became aware."

"Stuart!" she gushes. "Come into my bedroom once more, no bad drama—shame on me for being an indecisive weakling earlier!" She's two-handedly tugging his left wrist, soon turning her back to him and tugging from her hip, advancing while smiling over her shoulder.

Stuart couldn't be more elated. Penelope regrets her antics of earlier—he refused to succumb and be pounded under, returned to her despite the extent of his bewilderment and panic. He's assuredly performed the labors of Hercules on Penelope's behalf, in the sustained-inner-psychological-shock sense—bombardment-of-his-identity sense—and she's rewarding him, unabashedly parading herself as he's yearned for and lost sleep over for weeks—her swishing voluptuous symmetry near-hallucinatory under her nightie's semi-transparency, and lavender's in the air. In her own leap of faith Penelope hoped he'd return, prepared for his arrival, has taken special care: she's not making a secret of it, neither acting coy nor affecting surprise. She's offering herself to him, all smiles and radiance and jubilation, with no wish for him to endure further tribulation. This is the Penelope he always knew was hiding behind the curtain of conservative clothing, and her avoidance of remotest allusion to sexual attraction to anyone—the Penelope who vastly exceeds everything he could've hoped for in a woman.

Chapter VII

Three or so hours later they're side by side on the bed's edge, feet on the floor—wrapped in a down comforter and otherwise unclothed, toasty warm although the windows are open wide, wintry wind whooshing, parted pale olive drapery rippling. Penelope's leg, slung across Stuart's lap, is stimulatingly jiggling—she and he are dancing while seated—bouncing up and down, shimmying their shoulders, arms wrapped around each other—suddenly fall onto the mattress laughing.

"Woo hoo!" Penelope exclaims a couple minutes later, framing Stuart's face with her fingers, they facing one another on their knees on the mattress, lightly bouncing. She's gazing at him as if he's as essential to her well-being as she is to his, and he's never been closer to believing in undying bliss. "We're birds of a feather, joined at the hip," she mirthfully continues, twisting to tap a hip against his. "Never been able to trust a man, Stuart, but I can trust you—you've been tinkering in my subconscious, messing with magnetism, for weeks and I didn't know for sure until today. What a luscious eye-opener, my inner building blocks beneficially rearranged, and with courage in the picture! *(She licks her lips, arches her back and swishes her hair.)* There's a fantasy dear to my heart, my dear, and I feel safe in sharing, you'll be the first I've told."

"I couldn't be more honored, Penelope," Stuart responds, two-handedly grasping her waist, holding her at arm's length to better gaze upon her. Emboldened by the benevolence in her eyes, he says, "Penelope, the second I saw you I was smitten to my core, but scared to ask you out, the signs weren't there, plus I didn't want to jeopardize our amazing working relationship, client lunacy considerably easier to deal with. Last night's chance meeting spins into today's undreamed of..."

"Yes yes yes!" Penelope cuts in, pulling him close. "Chance lives on a razor's edge, can whip positive or negative or not deign to appear, and never underestimate the value of shock, we could easily still be orbiting each other, scared to cross our distance. I was *mortified* when you caught me with the creep, stomping the mink, yelling I wanted him dead! I supposed maybe you'd want nothing to do with me ever after. I was blurting secrets, couldn't be quiet, and you didn't flinch, no reoil, no judgement, your balance supremely priceless. I *love* you for that."

"Penelope, I've spent seemingly an infinity of charged sleepless hours thinking of you, hoping we'd get to know each other outside work, last night's encounter was a heaven-sent miracle, I *love* you for letting me come back to you today. We've never dared stray from..."

"Never dared stray from professional decorum," she gleefully interrupts, "and look at us *now*!"; then, noting Stuart's about to speak, she places a finger on his lips, intones, "Shsssss, sweetie. I'd like to tell you it's a mystery to me why I've publicly acted the virgin for seemingly forever, rejected relationships. Maybe it's that my amazing dad died early in my life, at ninety-four and a half years. I was born when he was seventy-four, my mother forty-two—raised by two wilder-than-any-others parents, jumping off Door County rock walls into Lake Michigan, climbing Kilimanjaro, visiting Antarctica, sailing from San Juan to Sanibel Island when dad was eighty-five, we three alone on the boat. So my fantasy's to... OK, imagine we're surrendering to the next world's pull, fearlessly greeting imminent death, as when my dad, after a heart attack and fully active until the heart attack, hiking Sun Valley's hills, bid me and my mother farewell in full clarity of mind in the hospital, assuring us of his undying love. Then he's preparing for departure, inspired—requesting we please back away slightly from the bed—he's *radiantly* aligning with the next world's pull, one needs to be there to understand, no description comes close—dad embracing the next life while still in this life, earthly attachments slipping away. We were privileged to have front row seats, obtain an inkling of what lies beyond and why it isn't to be feared, dad's parting gift. So approaching the experience of passing over to the next world in serenity of mind's my driving fantasy. You're the first person I've told."

"Penelope, your dad's the ultimate success story in the eyes of life, blue ribbons on every level—lived a long happy eventful life then departed on *his* terms, which I feel's exceptionally rare, although I've admittedly been totally spoiled and don't really know, since I haven't lost anyone near and dear, my grandparents are still feisty. I can only hope to greet the next world half as courageously as your dad."

"We the living are too easily deluded by an extremely fleeting situation, unable to comprehend that when the end's approaching it alters priority and revises courage, lifts us to heights outside regularly acknowledged perception," Penelope smiles; then, upon exiting the bed and facing Stuart, motioning for him to follow with her fingers, their vermillion nails aglow in sunset's light, her co-op facing west, "Please come over and take a look, I'll prove I'm not playing—there's no sideshow here, no fakery and empty speculation, posturing."

"Would never imagine you'd be content to do anything halfway, Penelope—it's not in your nature, another reason why I..."

"Well then, over here, pretty please, and thank you," she breaks in, leading him to the opposite right corner, an alcove revealed as she pulls aside a floor-length veil on a ceiling track. Assorted weapons are arranged on a circular beveled glass table—carving knives, an ice pick and meat cleaver, phillips and flathead screwdrivers, a pearl-handled revolver and twenty-two caliber rifle. "OK, so maybe it's fantasy-overkill (and the rifle's an antique passed down from my great grandfather)," she says, gripping his shoulders and squeezing, eyes brightening, rubbing a calf up and down the outside of his right leg, "but I want to approximate—no, *experience*—the state of surrender as the next world beckons, because there's more to life than life on earth. Dad was joking about his demise before leaving us, just amazing."

"Fantasy's one thing, overmuch enactment might be..."

"Right, I'm a *weird* girl," she breaks in again, "haunted by where the boundary between earthly life and passage beyond blurs, when the two commence seeming to share qualities, not appear wholly opposite. The chance death's continued sentience on a different plane with different properties, as in death could be illusion, intrigues and tempts me—I adore being bewildered, prodded towards experimentation. To what degree will we approach death's threshold, passage to the next world? Do we dare seek to sample of the next world? Oh, but I absolutely *relish* life! And, yes, I'm *constantly* contradicting myself, don't really know who I am when it comes right down to it, and there's freedom in that, as in when spreading my arms towards lightning during thunderstorms on this building's roof, metal railing on all sides. Well, just babbling, sorry! But rest assured I'm wide open for you, Stuart, for any direction you choose, no hesitation and hopefully no boundaries, I won't recoil."

They've knelt to the carpet, Penelope's hair swishing at Stuart's cheeks, flowing about his shoulders, as she caresses with

120

soothing-as-a-fluttering-breeze fingers—seconds later they're lying on the carpet, kissing and intertwining. Thrilling to Penelope's shivering grip and writhings, soft cooing, though he is, Stuart can't help wondering about the weapons. Are they always on the alcove's table, or did she place them there in anticipation of his arrival? They're aesthetically arranged in a circle bisected by the rifle. There's an amber bulb in the alcove's lamp, lending a golden sheen to the weapons—no one could build an altar, create an aura of mystery and menace, with greater care. The contrast between the weapons and Penelope's gentleness, soft lush voice, is tough to make sense of. Inclusion of common screw drivers lends a doubly sinister air to the knives, ice pick, cleaver, guns.

"Stuart, no one I've known professionally has seen me carrying on like last night, suspected I have such inclinations," Penelope says, gazing deep into his eyes. "I've been terrified of being discovered but am at ease with you, never supposed such possible with a man. That I screamed like I did, said inexcusably horrid things last night and this morning, chased you away—my dearest friend!—makes me very ashamed, and I couldn't be more blissful you came back, animated by faith and courage I didn't deserve. If I was testing you it was despite myself, although... OK, I confess to suspecting you wouldn't tolerate it, hoping you wouldn't. Why was idiotic drama with you in the picture at all, considering how close we are? Shame on me! You touch me as no man before—instead of turning irritated I want more, so washing-over-me wonderful, hope you don't mind I'm strange. I don't know why I'm strange with intimacy when mom and dad were infinitely loving and supportive, adventures happening thick and fast. I was college-prepped as very few, homeschooled on sailboats and at Kilimanjaro base camp." She's kneading his shoulders, pulsing against him, shutting her eyes.

"Penelope," Stuart responds, "no chance do I achieve what I feel's my potential, experience wildness as life's meant to provide, uncontaminated by civilization-perpetrated self-censorship, without you and I've never felt this way about anyone else. Thank you for making my fondest wish come true—you're opposite of strange."

"I just *desire* you!" she gushes, clasping him tighter. "Didn't know I could feel this way about a man without being inwardly attacked, splintered and stung. Last night at Lincoln Center I was *petrified* when you encountered me, and here we're... Well, I just *know* we can go in my fantasy's direction, as I've never dared—I'm in safe hands, protected! How far will we proceed before warning bells sound and yank us from the threshold, return us to regular reality, assuming they do? It's scary exciting that thoroughly engrossing experiences can fool one into believing life's inextinguishable, lead one to recklessly court danger. To what degree will fantasy and actuality become indistinguishable, fear taking a backseat, no hindrance to progression? I've been prodded towards that edge a number of times, always wondering... Stuart, your skin's a dip in soothing tropical waters, it's like I could fall forever without hitting bottom while holding you. Sunset's outside—hitting the windows, spreading over them, beckoning! Drunkenly uplifting."

Stuart's as euphoric as when locked into a wave's sweet spot while surfing, snapping upright on the board, uniting with ocean's surge. Has Penelope not clarified she wishes to be in his life for the remainder of their lives, 'til death do they part? She's inhaling deeply—tense, gathering her core, beaming energy, enthrallingly flooding his bloodstream. "Honey, I couldn't be more thrilled to ride along with you—chase elevation, fling myself into your fantasies. The mere fact of calling you 'honey,' after waiting forever, is otherworldly.

"Mmmmm, honey," Penelope coos, her gaze flaring with beneficence, she kissing and rubbing against him as if seeking to unite with his depths. Is he aware she's reaching over her head, grasping the revolver? Does he detect the gun's click as she cocks it?—glint of its pearl handle's iridescence as it approaches his head? Does it occur to him to wonder if the gun's loaded, danger shoving fantasy aside?

The Rooms I Will Not Enter

E stella was vivacious and playful. Even following a double shift, when by all rights she should've been exhausted, she was radiant and laughing, eager for fun—regardless of the time of day or in what manner she'd exerted herself or how little sleep she'd had, her presence heightened the atmosphere. We lived in an early twentieth century two-story oceanfront house in a small town on the northern California coast, the Pacific's soothing surf perpetually audible. I'd been gifted with the deed to the house, mortgage-free, by an aunt who'd relocated to Spain. I worked as a bartender at the hotel, the only one in town, where Estella worked as a cocktail waitress. Between us we easily covered the property taxes, insurance, and other expenses involved in maintaining the house—lived very comfortably, routinely surfing up and down the coast, occasionally flying to Hawaii. Before meeting Estella I'd intended to sell the house and use the proceeds to establish myself in Manhattan. But I'd fallen in love with Estella—the proverbial love at first sight—shortly after arrival in town and chosen to keep the house and remain in town when she made it crystal clear she returned my affection. Once Estella and I fell in love Manhattan ceased to exist.

Estella was nearly six feet tall and had a cheerful head of light brown hair, vaguely red if indoor light slanted sideways upon it. She was a curvy size six, athletic with a hint of voluptuousness.

She seemed to have stepped from 1930s and 40s movies; her hair was styled in the manner and the blouses and skirts she preferred suggested likewise. She was innately graceful, like a cat. In the many pictures I have of Estella there's the same flawless poise, impossible to define; even in the pictures where she's being silly—making faces, sticking out her tongue, striking awkward postures—her poise is there: arresting otherness, sensual and earthy yet somehow also elsewhere. But what was most unforgettable was Estella's visage and piercing eyes. To paraphrase Poe, "There's nothing gut-punchingly beautiful that lacks an element of strangeness in its composition," and the oval of Estella's face was an example—Estella's face that I caressed and kissed, endlessly doted upon, when she was among the living, we cuddling each night.

For my darling Estella passed over to the next world a month ago. She became noticeably ill early last autumn. Pancreatic cancer was the diagnosis, no hope of remission. I'll forgo describing the devastation of this discovery. I'll likewise forgo describing the hospice program I set up in our home and the naive hopes I entertained that she'd recover and we'd be happy again. Nor will I dwell upon the days and nights spent languishing at her side as she lay in bed. Estella died in February, six days after her thirtieth birthday.

Seventy-two hours previous to death Estella was able to sit upright and speak of happier times and smile, even laugh. (She never pitied herself; never despaired; never cried: such things were for me, sentenced to life without her, to do.) She died on a Thursday after midnight following nearly a day of delirious ramblings in English and German, the latter her native tongue. She died in my arms, I speaking to her for hours after the light departed from her eyes. I had to be pulled away, stunned and disbelieving, by two nurses so the funeral home director could place Estella on the stretcher, wheel her from the house.

But I'll forgo further description of that ghastly night. Nor will I linger upon the wake, when I was staring disbelieving at Estella's empty shell of a body—unable to accept that her eyes would never open again, enliven my life, stir me euphoric, with their beneficent light again. Estella is dead and has been buried. I no longer work as a bartender or socialize and am alone in the house, subsisting on money saved. I'll be selling the house and will depart, never to return. But I'm unable to depart at this time. I need to confront, and endure, what has happened to Estella. I need to mourn here. I'll know when it's time to leave.

Estella is dead and the house has changed. Formerly all of its rooms were drenched in delight. Now many rooms have declared themselves off-limits, due to the searing memories of lost joy they conjure forth. Should I dare enter these rooms adverse reaction's physical as well as emotional: I shiver and shudder as if naked outside on a windy frigid night; the very walls bleed dread, rush at me and shrink peripheral vision, buzz at my temples, pound at my heart, burden breathing. I bolt from those rooms as if from a conflagration's advancing flames.

Our bedroom's by far the most difficult to enter, a minefield of memories slashing to the bone. I've attempted to enter our bedroom multiple times, gather precious mementos of our life together, pack them for shipment to a less emotionally-charged locale, where I might be comforted by them instead of wrung inside out by them. Soon as I cross the threshold dark veils appear, twist and wind from corner to corner, dim the light. In vain do I stare out the picture window, seek to expand field of vision: the veils press closer in greater profusion, further smother field of vision. Although the room's cheerfully wallpapered and decorated, well-illuminated by windows on two walls (I only attempt entry in bright sunlight), the air acquires cavernous depths, emanates gloom: all's as if glimpsed through thick gray glass. Then comes the hollowness—acrid, icy. It's as if I'm falling into inner chasms, my stomach's pit swallowing me, nerves ground into sputtering dying sparks. The dark veils hiss, it's as if they're winding against me—I feel as if I'm screaming, although no sound escapes my throat. Thus far I've been whipped from our bedroom before allowed to open a dresser drawer or look in our closet, gather a memento—anything I touch turns hot in my hand, anything I focus my gaze upon burns my eyes. There are pictures of Estella and I surfing—of us embracing on Oahu's north shore—of us seated side by side on the bar of the hotel where we worked—of us rapt and laughing at Land's End in my hometown—of us rolling in meadows of springtime wildflowers—and I'm unable to look at any for above a second without being stung to the bone.

The house has divided itself into areas I'm allowed to be in and areas that I'm not. The first floor, excepting the add-on room that replaced the front porch, belongs to me. In other words, I'm permitted to be in the kitchen, dining room, living room, and downstairs bathroom without suffering unendurable attacks of grief. The second floor's far more restrictive: I'm permitted to walk the hallway and enter one room, the guestroom with the balcony facing the sea. I dare not so much as glance at the closed doors of the other two bedrooms and upstairs bathroom: it's only by rapidly striding past them, endeavoring to pretend they aren't there, that I escape hints of what I'll suffer if I enter them.

Estella's loss has imposed a routine. I awaken evenings in the upstairs guestroom with every discernable portion of my body seemingly saturated with loneliness, desolation, dread—it's as if there's an empty inner space, on the cellular level, that I must fill. No lingering in bed's possible and I'm instantly on my feet, after which I switch on music and turn it up loud—aside from the fact music's comforting in its own right, uninhibitedly flowing through and expanding the atmosphere, it enables my attention to wrap itself around something besides distress. Next I turn on every light in my areas of the house, upstairs and downstairs; then I hastily shower, eat, brush my teeth, viewing these activities as annoyances forced upon me by maintenance of health and hygiene; then I brew a pot of tea and return with it to the guestroom, where I stand before the easel and canvas in its center, a bright light directly overhead, and resume work on a painting, music continuing to blare. I've never been as fixated on my painting, nor produced work I'm as proud of. But I don't credit myself for my newfound discipline, marked improvement. I simply have no choice—painting's the only activity that mitigates pain. I paint because I *must* do so, and wield the brush with greater skill because I *must* do so: while painting it's as if I'm racing to stay a step ahead of awareness of the utter blackness of my life, especially flashbacks of Estella's last week alive, when she was wilting to such a degree I could no longer lie to myself, believe she'd recover.

I'm painting the scene in front of me, facing the wide open balcony door—the room's illumination gives way to the night sky and Pacific's surf outside the door. It could be a doorway on death, as in passing from light into dark, but there's positivity in the painting: stars crowd the sky, muted harbor lights flicker on the waves—the world outside's as beautiful as it's potentially threatening. I feel the open door's more of a window on wonder and mystery than a window on darkness and danger. Indoors is warm, well-lit, comforting but expansiveness beckons—unknown experiences await under the stars. Estella would want me to have these experiences, live my life in wonder while never forgetting her. As mentioned, I've never painted in this manner before, where it's a lifeline to sanity, means of keeping searing grief at bay. The open door also allows the ocean breeze, salt-tinged and occasionally misty, to flow about the room in steady rhythm, as of breaking waves, and the heat's turned on high: cold will be hugging my legs while heat's streaming over my back and then the two will switch places. I'm physically engaged with the world outside the door while painting.

As long as I'm conjuring forth form and harmony with colors and lines on the canvas, recollections of Estella politely approach and remain at a bearable distance; she keeps me company instead of overwhelming me with despair at loss of her company; a stream of vivid pictures of our life together soothe instead of stinging—I'm permitted to be grateful for having known Estella, appreciate the joy she brought to me, instead of being stabbed by her demise. I paint all night until around noon the next day, only pausing to eat, brew fresh pots of tea, visit the bathroom, and these distractions are taken care of quickly—pausing from painting's dangerous, from a vulnerability-to-attacks-of-grief perspective. Even when I mix paint, am no longer actively engaged with the canvas, memories of Estella acquire an unpleasant edge, sheen of darkness and gloom, threaten to immobilize me. When I complete one painting I begin more—always the same scene, but done in different styles, accentuating different features. As the scene outside the door changes according to the weather and hour, several paintings are in progress simultaneously—others are of dawn breaking, or of full daylight, or of steady rain, thereby ensuring I'm constantly occupied. I feel the theme of the series—tension between indoor security and outdoor mystery—the uncertainty of security and lure of mystery—is inexhaustible. When I lie down to sleep for six or so hours after painting for hours—gazing into distances outside the door for hours—it's as if the empty space within me has been filled, grief softened. When I reawaken in the evening the dread and emptiness are there again and the cycle repeats.

Unfortunately the above-described routine doesn't reliably remain within manageable timeframes, since I'm often too electrified from painting to sleep. Too frazzled and unfocused to paint satisfactorily and too aflame inside to sleep, I'm left with no refuge and become easy prey for the despair I've been holding at bay—the fact my darling Estella's gone forever is soon gripping my chest in a vise, grinding my nerves. The room's suddenly suffocating, its furthest corners rushing at me, forcing me to flee to the living room downstairs, where two large picture windows afford views of the lush yard. Relief's not forthcoming—flight to the living room's a desperation-impulse I can't help surrendering to. I wind up curled up on the floor, unseeingly staring into blindingly bright air, erratically breathing, half-wishing for death. It's when I'm emotionally stranded, in dire need of distraction, that I'm compelled to enter the rooms which have declared themselves off-limits. I do not do so because I wish to multiply distress; I do so because I feel distress cannot possibly be multiplied and I've nothing to lose; I do so because it's a means of squarely facing off with my sorrow, in the hope sorrow will eventually subside. Mostly I do so because it's a means of repeatedly shocking, eventually exhausting, myself. I enter the forbidden rooms over and over, remain within them as long as I'm able, race from one to another, never ceasing to move—I do so until I'm thoroughly drained, collapse. Instead of falling asleep I blackout.

Four days ago, after painting for nearly twenty hours, lifting expressiveness to unsuspected heights, coming as near to enjoyment as I have since Estella's departure, I found my reward was inflamed nerves that wouldn't allow me to stand still, much less sleep. I attempted to resume painting but was too agitated to focus—the colors blurred, ran together—were swallowed in brightness, it being a sun-blasted day. There was no outlet for accumulating energy—no dodging the despair nipping at my heels. The dam of my grief burst, loss of Estella as good as singeing and pummeling every cell of my body—with a cry I flung my-self face-down on the bed, sobbing uncontrollably, arms folded over my head. When, I wondered, would the pain subside, and would I be able to sustain sanity until it did? Would the pain *ever* subside? Would I emerge from the loss of Estella with my life? It was then that I resolved to enter our bedroom, without advance mental preparation—I was neither informing myself I had nothing to lose nor that it would be beneficial to face grief head-on: blind panic whipped me into the hall.

Within seconds I was yanking our bedroom's door open. (Our bedroom's adjacent the guestroom where I'm allowed to sleep and paint, I've no idea how or why matters have fallen into place thus: grief lays down the law and I obey.) Upon entering I rashly advanced to the foot of our bed, observed its rumpled blankets, unchanged since Estella was moved to the hospice-pro-vided bed in the add-on front-room downstairs—immediately recoiled as if punched in the chest. Upon wheeling about I found I was staring straight at Estella's vanity table, something I hadn't dared do since her death. I envisioned her applying makeup and fixing her hair there, a semi-transparent scarlet and black night-ie hugging her curves, as bliss-inducing a sight as any I'll ever know—was stepping forward as if she was actually present, arms outspread to hug her. Instants later the desperation and futility of the gesture became obvious—Estella was gone, never to return! *Why? For the love of God, why?* I shrieked as reminders of what I'd lost had me clutching the back of my neck, unsteady and wobbling on my feet. It was as if invisible arms roughly shoved me out of our bedroom.

I don't recall descending the stairs. What I recall is that the vision of Estella seated at the vanity table, smilingly combing her hair, eyes alight with love, followed me to the living room, continued to rend my heart. I could only sit shuddering on the white carpet, jaws clenched, teeth grinding. Although I saw on the wall-clock that barely five minutes here—two minutes there—another five minutes here—had passed, it seemed as if I'd been on the carpet for hours. Any alteration of positioning of my head caused all within the room to haphazardly bend and shift, as if reflected on rippling water. The air was heated, humid, dense, stifling, dimensions of the room pressing in on me—nerves further flaring, rushing towards the center of my chest—it was as if I was being repeatedly flung against electrified inner walls.

No! I yelled, springing to my feet, pacing swiftly in tight circles, jumping up and down, swatting the ceiling with my palms. But attempts to dissipate unease via physical exertion only stoked excitement. Where could I run, hide? How escape memories of a lost, desperately missed and longed for, loved one? When the love of one's life comes calling via recollection after her death, advertises joys never to be had again, the breadth of existence becomes a chasm into which one's falling.

I remember slumping to the carpet as if physically wounded, rolling quivering onto my back, arms and legs splayed. I was staring at the ceiling's stark white—the ceiling was becoming indistinguishable from the space of air between it and myself—appeared to be descending, about to crush me—I was being pounded into the floor by fear, muscles spasmodic! Then all was glaring blinding white and sharp hissing, an amount of terror that waking awareness was unable to withstand.

My next recollection, following an interval of oblivion, is of Estella framing my face with her fingers, smiling into my eyes, speaking to me in mellifluous tones: it had been far too long

132

since I'd tingled in response to her touch! We were cuddling in bed: what euphoria to glance about our bedroom, lovingly decorated by her, while in her arms—Estella's hair swishing over my face, neck, shoulders, shimmering under my skin. Our lips joined in a kiss, tongues undulating: how starved I'd been for our kisses! We'd always poured our souls into our kisses—obliterated day-to-day cares, imparted safety and security, with our kisses—united with life's wellsprings with our kisses. Sensations I'd once been blessed with every day, bliss easy to come by, reawakened. Again, I inhabited a delight-scintillated realm, was dizzy with rapture the Gods would envy—the loving regard darting back and forth between Estella and I, her magical healing energy, was vivid enough for me to believe I was surging into the sky. We wished to rejoice in one another for uninterrupted days but couldn't elude human limitation: exhaustion overtook us and we slipped into sleep.

When my eyes opened at what was likely the next day's dawn I was uncertain if I still dreamed. Red-orange was upon the eastern windows, but who's to say it was sunrise occurring in the waking state? It was physical discomfort—fact my right ankle was trapped under my left thigh, aggravated by the weight—that eventually notified me I wasn't dreaming. Upon sitting upright I became aware the usual emptiness, loneliness, and desolation that greeted me upon awakening wasn't there. For the first time since diagnosis of Estella's illness I felt I was a whole man again, relishing a new day, thrilling to life. Estella had paid me a visit after so long away, so how could I not be inundated with joy?

I was disinclined to dwell upon the fact Estella's visit had occurred during dreaming. Estella was dead and buried, but she'd miraculously returned to bestow serenity, so why undercut well-being by reminding myself I'd never gaze upon her in the waking state?—never caress her with flesh and blood hands, hear her voice reverberate in real air?

Positive emotions were upwelling, trembling me, in a manner I'd resigned myself to never experiencing again. For the first time in seemingly years I was eager to be outside—went for a day-long stroll on the beach, delighting in the surf's rhythm, salt-air's touch. I snow-angeled on the sand, dug my toes into the sand, splashed my chest with the sand, grateful I was able to be grateful for the giddy gift of life. Estella's beauty was in my mind's eye, keeping me company, throughout—her visage radiant with love's munificent light.

I ran around and danced and did headstands (sand softening my falls) and yelled on an isolated area of the beach (only accessible via an overgrown path on steep grade) until nightfall, returned home deliciously spent, no inflamed nerves needling me, easily fell into deep sleep. It wasn't until I awakened predawn that the emptiness reappeared, as if Estella's dream-visitation hadn't happened—bereavement cutting me to the bone again, fear of losing my grip on reason looming. Had I truly believed I'd arrived at self-salvation, was at last able to live without grief hobbling me? Nothing but fleeting self-deception!

Illusion's veil fell away and I was again inconsolable in the house I'd shared with Estella, surrounded by dread-inundated shadows at the slightest thought of entering the forbidden rooms. My beloved's dream-visitation had replaced misery with faith, hope, and joy—made me feel loved, safe, and whole—but the spell was broken. *Estella must continue to visit and love and nurture me!* I yelled aloud at one point, facing myself in a mirror, agonizingly uncertain if I'd be thus blessed.

Nearly a fortnight's passed since Estella's dream-visitation. Now an utter stranger to what passes for pride in the non-grief-distorted world, I've approached relatives for an allowance, which has been granted, and abandoned all hope of emerging from mourning and leaving this town. Estella visited me once, I'm determined she shall do so again. I solely exist for when my anguish becomes pronounced enough to once more summon Estella from the shadows—I need to gaze upon her, hear her voice, hold her close and kiss her. I don't care what horrors of emptiness and dread I must endure—how long I must wait. I'm remaining in this house until I'm blessed with another night of Estella's love.

It's said Paradise is girded about by swords. I'll willingly brave all manner of swords for another night with Estella—will enter our bedroom, remain there shaking until the black veils appear, smother vision, my chest constricting, breathing labored, suffocation grinding—will court insomnia, foster sensory and emotional disorientation, strain reason and sanity—will stoke panic, sear myself to my bones—will watch the white ceiling pitilessly descend, engulf and blind me—nerves flaring and stinging, shoving me towards blacking out. Surely my undying love will bring Estella back, however incorporeally, to the land of the living and reunite me, however temporally, with untold joy.

Those who accuse me of avoiding the responsibility of reindoctrinating myself into society—of living in an irrecoverable past, existing in a limbo state—of being no different than a drug addict endlessly craving doses of illusory bliss—I say to them: love as I have and lose that love as I have before presuming to judge me.

Only imbeciles think beauty's only skin-deep. Being in a relationship with Estella intensified sensation, the very feel of myself in my skin—ordinarily mundane tasks, as of grocery shopping or taking the car in for an oil change, became near hallucinatory.

The light in Estella's eyes, symmetry of her visage, tone of her posture, energy radiating from the softness of her voice, slightest curl of a finger... All is soul-twistingly *beautiful*! Estella's irreplaceable and I *won't* be moving on!

It's past midnight—gusts are rattling the windows—I've been awake for at least two days. I'm unable to sleep, the walls of our house are slamming in on me, dread flaring. I'm going to do my utmost to further unnerve and shock myself, travel to the blinding white light place, by entering our bedroom, sorting through drawers I haven't opened since Estella's passing, walking into our closet and staring at the clothes she'll never wear again—touching them, stroking them. Will I succeed in spending another night with my beloved in life-sustaining dreams?

Surveillance

Right on schedule: the spike-topped wrought iron gate has slid to the left and clanged against the ivy-cloaked granite pillar, allowing your chauffeur driven Rolls to exit your estate. I arrived fifteen minutes ago and parked a few yards further down on this winding street, which allows me sufficient view of your driveway through the gnarled branches of this interposing oak. Naturally, I am going to follow you, keep track of your every movement during every second of at least the next twenty-four hours. And, my, but how I do adore your personalized license plates—Lydia is such a beautiful name.

Within another fifteen minutes we are well within the city limits—so uplifting it is to take this shortcut through neglected neighborhoods, pass empty shells of stripped cars and fire-gutted buildings, sidewalks glittering with broken glass. And the scenery does have a tendency to change abruptly, with very little warning, doesn't it? Thus we are now surrounded by well-maintained nineteenth century mansions—all of them so safe and secure behind massive walls fitted with razor wire and cameras, patrolled by security guards. But, no, we do not remain here. We pass on.

A few settings later your car pulls to the curb. And the street is somehow without character, what one might deem suspiciously plain. It could be located anywhere. Just an inconspicuous row of necessity stores—clothing, hardware, drug, shoe repair, grocery. But, then, appearances are not to be trusted, are they? Who would suspect, Lydia dear, why you have really come here, who could ever know why you have just descended that set of cellar-destined steps?

Oh no, there is no need to follow you down them. There is, you see, no other exit and, after all, I know your habits so well. I know that your wrists and ankles will wear wide studded black leather bracelets, that they will be affixed to gold plated hooks in the floor and ceiling, that you now and then need to feel that whip and turn inside out and scream. Is it that those riches of yours now and then make everything seem too easy, give you the unpleasant impression of all too effortlessly skimming over the surface of life? Do you need a point of contact with reality? Do you need to compensate for your comfort by feeling pain and humiliation, desperation and dread?

I also know the precise hour at which you will reappear, know that you will be relaxed and self-possessed, almost religiously serene. Yes, it is so pleasant to feel balanced—nothing like being restored to one's foundations, brought back down to earth. And Lydia: I even know where you will instruct your chauffeur to drive you next.

Sure enough, now that night is falling and the neon is beginning to stand out, glow vivid emerald and red, you are standing on the busy sidewalk of Broadway, brushing back your long ebony hair. And how effortlessly you stand out from the crowd—what a remarkably beautiful face you have, how perfect is your poise and posture, self-assured the slightest twist of your hand or flick of a finger—how commandingly you glance about. Yes, indeed, a very impressive femme fatale exterior, all of the *I dare you!* mannerisms down pat. In other words, just the type of invitation I find impossible to ignore.

You begin to walk and I am never far from you, twice step on the streetlight-cast shadow of your ankle-length sable coat. In the same way that you are vaguely conscious of your shadow you seem to be vaguely conscious of me, distantly aware of the brooding young man who now and then pauses to scan his surroundings, several times crosses to the other side of the street only to cross right back. Seems to be searching for something, doesn't he? Seems a trifle overwrought and excitable, impatient of everything in sight.

And what a coincidence that you have chosen my favorite nightclub, one with obsidian tabletops, crimson lighting, an excellent stage show. You take a seat at a table near the front right corner of the stage, order your usual brandy Manhattan, and light a Gold. On the stage a supple slender semi-famous woman is wrapping the microphone cord about herself while straddling the stand, shoving it back and forth, singing a possible hit. Her orange hair blazes in the blue-white beam of the spotlight and her thighs flash like lightning through the waist-high slits in her indigo-black dress.

But I do not notice her for long, do I Lydia? I find your performance inspires far more compelling fantasies, infinitely stronger desires. I love the way you wind your necklace about your fingers, how its rosy beads gleam like savagely clear eyes, seem to laugh. I can sense the coiled energy within you—grow so warm at its touch, tingle inside. And, yes, rest assured that you will soon sense my presence in a similar manner—your skin is going to flush and twitch and sparkle in response to the ice crystal whirl of my nerves.

How disturbingly gorgeous you are, Lydia! I want to meet you in a back alley, press you hard against a cold wet wall. I want to rip your dress into ribbons, scatter it about. I want you maddened, to feel your fingernails scratching my cheeks. I want

139

to see your sweat-glistened body writhing, your face drowning in excitement and shock. I want your mouth all over me, to see nothing but and drown in the vermillion of your lips. I want to get to the bottom of your detachment, shatter your sophistication, cut you with glass. Already I can hear you panting and squealing, feel your undulations and contractions inundating me with electric bursts. We are writhing at the base of the wall and my hands are numb from striking the pavement, excitement blurring perception of pain. I am only aware of the river of thought-suspending emotion we have become—almost as if the veil that society casts over existence, wild nature, is being torn aside, revealing the mystery on its other side.

Oh yes, Lydia, I am now seated opposite you at your table, have suddenly appeared from out of the dim light of the club. You cannot suspect how long I have watched you, how self-assured I am. True, on the surface I am playful and joking, all laughs and lighthearted charm. But then, you are a perceptive woman, aren't you, Lydia? You cannot help but detect the tension and hunger and apprehension which churns below the surface of my manner, agitates for relief.

It is with my suffering that I ensnare you, Lydia—with my inner turmoil that I fascinate and subdue. Your inquisitiveness drowns in my depths and that is why you are so anxious to please. You feel superior to people you are able to categorize but pain is bottomless and that is why you will never know me. Yes, Lydia, I know you well.

I do not have a personality in the usual sense, am not psychologically constrained according to convention. So who am I? Simply a collection of masks, playacted roles. And I am highly versatile—get to the bottom of one role and I will switch to another, play it so thoroughly that before long you will believe I could not possibly have been anyone else, that the previous version of me was invented by your imagination. And that appeals to you, doesn't it, Lydia? You adore an absorbing game of psychological hide and seek.

Already I am stroking your thighs and toying with the tops of your stockings, tickling your neck and ear with my tongue, suggesting we leave. And you agree, don't you, Lydia? How could you not?

And how pleasingly blinding is the swirl of the neon and the slash of the headlights outside, how nice to be in the midst of a crisply darting breeze. And your eyes also dart, don't they Lydia? You are a trifle uneasy, wondering about our destination. But why bother? You know as well as I that you cannot help but come, that the strongest part of you is the one which lead you to leave the club in the first place—the same part which leads you to the whip.

We stroll down a garbage-littered alley, up a set of dusty narrow steps, through a rusty-hinged door. Yet the room itself is quite sumptuous, decorated in the highest style. Yes, in the same way that the outer shell of an oyster conceals a pearl this beat up building conceals such a room. Simply never can trust exteriors, never can know.

All of the walls are mirrors and a dusky indigo light flows from several glowing disks on the ceiling, adds density to the air. You slip off your coat and toss it towards the base of the window, stand in the center of the room in an iridescent crimson dress. And how expertly you remove it—such smooth nimble gestures, a graceful frenzy of manner which twists my nerves from their pathways, fills me with as-if-drug-induced warmth. And, yes, I would like to assist you: nothing like the sensation of slowly peeling your stockings down your thighs, as strong as they are sleek and soft. And how rhythmically the curtains undulate behind you, how thick and supple and downy they are.

Why don't you tear them from the rods and use them as veils, perform a dance? No need to worry about privacy—the windows are painted black. That's right, twist and wind below the lights as they illuminate the rippling symmetry of your immaculate body—mesmerize me with a symphony of movement, inundate me with rapt appreciation, make me *need* to lose my tongue in your mouth.

Such luscious wet ruby lips! They taste like mashed pomegranates and brandy, are so responsive and warm. And those gasps and squeals and excitement-slurred whisperings of yours! They send ice crystals up and down my spine, have my vision blurred. Such confusion! Tremulous fingers are winding the dark waves of your hair about them—do they belong to you or me? And I am looking into a pair of deliriously silvered eyes—mine in the mirror at the head of the bed or yours upon your face? And what has happened to the sense of touch? Why is it that I seem to be simultaneously sinking into warm mud at a spa and floating above the bed in mist-saturated air?

And why, Lydia, does such panic seize me? Why is it that one moment I want to slam your head into one of the mirrors, that the next I want to be so worshipful and indulgent and kind? Why do I at one and the same time want to cut you with a knife and lick you tenderly, crush your skull and give you every comfort on earth? Why do I both love and loathe? Is it because you mirror me so perfectly, because every time I look into your eyes I see myself staring back? Is it because part of me wants to leap from a building, be guillotined?

And one of us is screaming. Who is it? Is it I who stuffs the sable sleeve into your mouth or you who stuffs it into mine?

Dream Displacement, or Love from the Grave

I.

L ife in Manhattan had become claustrophobic, suffocating. The lack of refuge from prying eyes, save within the walls of my dismal apartment, had commenced to rub my nerves raw, relegate me to an unremitting state of skittish pent-upness. The unrelieved stress of never being left to myself (not even in my apartment, actually: the woman to my right would rap on the wall at the slightest sound that issued from my activities, including speaking on the phone; the man below would bang on his ceiling, by way of informing me he could hear my footfalls; the couple who lived directly across from me in the building behind mine tirelessly argued at high volume, windows open, particularly at night) had affected me on a physical level: my hands seldom stopped shaking; my joints, particularly at my knees, ached, throbbed; my lower back was a minefield of muscle spasms, inflammation; a strained expression was stamped upon my face. For the first time in my life I thought of sleep as relief from conscious awareness instead of a waste of time, and dreaded awakening. Slumber became a battlefield.

My apartment was on the second floor in the back of a moldering tenement building over a century old. Sunlight vainly struggled to force its way into the narrow space between my building and the one behind it; even had I ventured to raise the blinds, expose myself to the view of the endlessly bickering couple, barely a hint of daylight would have reached me: it was little better than perpetually dark outside and I lived exclusively in artificial illumination. But I didn't live alone: hardly a day went by that I didn't encounter several of the spiders, representing at least a dozen species, that spun dense webs under my bed and in the corners; mice were often heard rustling in the kitchen, below the bathroom sink, behind walls; cockroaches proliferated and nothing killed them. The grimy walls of peeling paint absorbed the light, saturated the air with dimness regardless of how many lamps I turned on; the ancient steam radiators unabatedly hissed and sputtered in winter, even though the rooms were rarely warm; come summer there was no respite from heat and humidity and I was constantly sticky with sweat, it impossible to run air conditioners without blowing the basement fuses, shutting down the building's power for hours. Pipes would burst in the walls, spread water over the floor, soak the footfall-obsessed man's apartment below, incite him into paroxysms of rage. Homeless people would invade the basement, fiddle with the building's heating-dials, overload the steam radiators, birth waterfalls on every floor.

My neighbors were prying, neurotic, resentful, hateful; but they weren't united against me: they disliked each other and themselves as much as they disliked me. They lived for complaining, spreading slander, hoarding spite, stockpiling grudges. Instead of killing themselves outright, they immersed themselves in death-in-life.

I had to escape that building! My neighbors were mostly far older than me, and age hadn't endowed them with wisdom—they were case studies in how *not* to live. Sad and scary that they'd wound up frustrated, hateful—their negative frames of mind were literally seeping through the walls, affecting me—I was afraid of being pulled in, blinded to joy. I'd always been healthy and fit, and still ate nutritious unprocessed food, exercised regularly, but was nevertheless wasting away, beginning to feel feeble: such is the nefarious ability of sustained gloom, piled-on stress, to undermine health. A quiet cheery apartment, flooded with sunlight, on a high floor of an uptown high rise would surely reverse my spirits. But the ground had, as it were, been yanked from under me: I lacked the will to rally myself, switch professions, seek the income that would make such an apartment possible. In dread I considered the possibility of having become infected with too much inertia, debilitated by depression, to extricate myself from the tenement building. Is it possible to be undermined by the thoroughgoing bleakness of a place, rendered incapable of shaking off its clinging influence, bolting?—as if the very walls are able to creep under one's skin, smother one's better instincts? How many high-spirited individuals, newly arrived in town and only able to afford a dwelling such as mine, had found such a dwelling erasing recollection of uplifting emotions, ensnaring them in frustration and hopelessness—out-and-out imprisoning them?

I wasn't going to be a casualty of that building, age prematurely, waste precious time listening for, wincing in irritation at, noises outside my door—wasn't going to drown in pettiness, emanations of misery—wasn't going be swindled out of my better instincts, lose my love of fun. But the more I informed myself it was *necessary* to leave the more a tone of paralysis and indifference—frightful indifference, as of being separated from the very flow of my blood—froze me in my tracks. Again, it was as if debilitation was drip-dripping from the walls—as if erosion of well-being, stagnation of the soul, pervaded the air.

But there *had* to be an avenue of escape from negativity's sway! What was I supposed to do, kill myself before hopelessness infected me to such a degree I was robbed of the ability to follow through? Above all, I dreaded becoming a death-in-life person, floundering forever within dim walls—surely freedom was still obtainable.

II.

I'd like to take credit for extricating myself from the smothering building but honesty disallows me from doing so. An event occurred that had nothing to do with the any amount of foresight, planning, or exertion on my part. Blind intervention of chance tossed a rope into the stagnant water in which I was drowning, enabled me to climb ashore.

A distant relative passed away and, being without siblings or progeny, left the bulk of his estate, including a house, to my parents. I was asked if I'd be interested in traveling to the remote coastal town in Maine where the house was located, arranging with a realtor for it to be shown, and receiving sixty percent of the sale price. I agreed without hesitation, tears of gratitude and joy streaming down my cheeks.

My good-cheer and vigor, too long buried, was reborn with a vengeance—overnight I was immune to my surroundings. I not only enjoyed the transition interval during which I was mailing my belongings to the Maine address, I intentionally prolonged it: because the door of my cage had been flung open, it was fun to linger within it for a spell, knowing freedom was assured—the contrast was emotionally *and* physically instructive.

Cast of mind's infinitely influential—I was laughing at the apartment that had previously oppressed me.

I'll own up to having fantasized for months about retaliating against the nitpicking pestering nosy neighbors, resolving to play pranks galore should I be assured of escaping the building, bettering my circumstances. So there I was in the perfect position to turn all faucets on high and stopper the drains, plus clog the toilet and flush it multiple times, drench the creep below; and to leave a CD playing at maximum volume on repeat on a cheap CD player, my windows open wide; and to squeeze quick-drying glue into the door locks of the extra hateful. But I found I was too happy and healthy to bother—the building and neighbors were already half unreal to me, fading fast. When one's free and clear why trouble to look backwards, arrest forward motion?

I'd arrived in Manhattan to experience whatever my sheltered suburban upbringing had denied me, although I was by no means sure of what I'd been denied or expected to accomplish, simply following newfound hunger for the unfamiliar—impatience had yielded inadequate preparation, imprisonment in a dismal place. But I'd learned a valuable lesson, as in that one's future can flip upside down and surprise one for the better or worse at any time—fate's as fickle as the wind.

For reasons I couldn't fully clarify I didn't feel suburban living suited me going forward, even though I'd been blessed with childhood bliss in California's suburbs—skied the Sierras in winter, surfed and boogie boarded in summer—diving lessons, skinny-dipping with girls in their swimming pools, neighborhood bazaars under the stars. But I *was* suddenly eager to flip opposite of Manhattan, relocate to a wilderness town. A sojourn in the country, I reasoned, would purge my emotions of the wrong directions with which they'd become burdened. I'd surrender to the forests and sea, trust nature to restore me to centeredness of purpose. I'd reflect upon the mistakes I'd made and learn from them, train myself to recognize my weaknesses, be better prepared to counter them. I'd regather myself for a renewed attempt to settle in the city I was still persuaded I belonged in—no more dispiritedness, depression, claustrophobia—no more spiders, cockroaches, spiteful neighbors.

III.

I arrived at the seaside town late January, hours after eight inches of snow fell. I hadn't troubled to inquire concerning the particulars of the deceased relative's property—call it a consequence of being intoxicated by good fortune, afforded the luxury of devil-may-care. I'd assumed it was a run-of-the-mill house next door to other run-of-the-mill houses on third-of-an acre lots—imagine my surprise upon discovering it was a mansion with a wide Doric-column-framed porch, decks encircling the first and second floors, firm iron bones supporting brick and wood, sixteen bedrooms, eleven bathrooms—the most opulent residence in the county. The property surrounding the mansion was slightly over thirty-seven acres, its eastern boundary ending where the Atlantic Ocean began—I was marveling at the vicissitudes of fate, nearly swooning for joy! Wild how swiftly I'd been carried from a dark cramped noisy vermin-infested hovel into an enormous sun-drenched mansion!

From an emotional perspective I'd had next to no privacy for endless months, come close to forgetting privacy existed—misery seems to last far longer than its calendar interval. So instead of immediately arranging to sell the mansion, losing my opportunity to be left alone for a spell, I resolved to wait until late summer at the earliest, subsisting on the modest stipend provided by my family—the miraculous windfall of peace and privacy wasn't to be squandered. What paradise to have the mansion to myself for months, without the need to earn a living, answer to anyone. I'd owe no one a second of my time, be free to wander from room to room and saunter about the shoreline with only my thoughts for company. I'd read the books I'd brought along, idle in an agreeable daydream daze, often forget what day of the week it is. Absolutely insane that I'd been sidelined for so long—wound up in an ambition-killing tenement apartment—but fate was favoring me now.

My first two months in the mansion were, indeed, paradise: aimless wandering about the forested property and rocky shoreline, my favorite spot a pocket of sand, slightly over six yards wide, nestled between high jagged rocks—many sunsets spent there watching surf turn scarlet and gold, greet the sand with roiling silver foam—occasionally treated to northern lights, emerald flushing to indigo and deep purple and vice versa—surging, pulsing; and night after night of unbridled imagination-life until dawn and beyond—nights and days I count among the most euphoric of my life. Contact with others consisted solely of brief exchanges while purchasing necessities. I avoided places people gathered, neither eating in restaurants nor attending events. I politely sidestepped overtures on the part of neighbors, stating the love of my life had dumped me and I needed to deal with it alone (about the only excuse, I've found, that deflects accusations of unsociability and snobbishness, forestalls resentment). Thus there was no one to provide a counterpoint to my imaginings, drag me out of rapt fantasizing, expose me to the confines of customary existence. My friends were the authors of the books I read, dependably inspiring waking dreaming.

To casual observers I was leading an uneventful life: doing nothing but read books, seldom venturing outside the property, each day outwardly unvarying. But I was electric with intimations of the possibility of uniting with the representations of my imagination, becoming a self-sustaining world of wonder unto myself—I relished the contrast between others' impression of my life (apparent in the glances, bordering on pity, I'd receive when in town) and the incandescence I was experiencing. Always, did a larger-than-life cityscape form the background of my fancies—cityscape of mist-shrouded streets above which cloud-high buildings towered; of labyrinthine basement nightspots, familiar only to the initiated, where beautiful women unabashedly prowled and abundant thrills surpassed euphoria; of unfrequented alleyways where secret trysts took place and forbidden love-rituals flourished. Outwardly my days were unvarying but inwardly each day was a fresh kaleidoscope of breath-stealing imagery, parade of sensory stimulation—ongoing effort to intensify existence, welcome unfettered emotion. I was aglow with gratitude from the moment of greeting a new day to the moment of bidding it adieu and couldn't wait to greet the next day and indulge in waking dreams anew, and my dreams while asleep were as soothing as mellifluous lullabies.

I loved to read of love: stirrings-at-first-sight tales, courtship-and-conquest tales, rapt-anticipation tales, delirious-consummation tales. Any narrative that dealt with single-minded pursuit of a spirited beauty, as if the protagonist's sanity depended upon success. The stages of becoming enthralled, arriving at mutual understanding, tasting bliss. The engulfment in amorous flames and attendant transports, exquisitely detailed. The tireless circumvention of obstacles, external and internal, in order to *finally* frame a gorgeous woman's face with one's fingers, kiss her like there's no tomorrow, unite in upwellings of joy.

Were there any bored, lonely, isolated beauties thirsting for adventure, rapture and daring, in the town where I was marooned? Not as far as I could determine: girls with an abundance of spirit fled the town following high school and seldom returned, it lacking in opportunities for their personalities to blossom. So I continued reading of love and picturing the beauties I had no doubt I'd get to know and undergo soul-altering experiences with in the not-too-distant future, after returning to Manhattan. In the meantime, as the weeks advanced and spring arrived, I was becoming increasingly overwrought—enmeshed in a fevered, irritated and jittery, state—on account of harboring desires for which there was no immediate outlet.

By way of illustration of my overwrought condition consider my excursions into town, necessitated by procurement of provisions. If I happened to glimpse a woman from the corner of my eye—such that she was little more than a blurred outline—she'd instantly, so to speak, leap into my head and overpower my imagination: the indistinct image in my peripheral vision would become a vivid picture of a ravishing beauty of electric presence with fire and hunger swirling in her eyes. I'd become tense, experience a sort of anticipatory punch—swirl of nerves—in the pit of my stomach, crackle with yearning and become giddy, tremble head to toe. But then I'd turn to gaze at the woman straight-on and perceive she bore little resemblance to the one I'd pictured and all hope of calming myself, escaping stress, would vanish. I'd be standing there, still trembling, with only my arousal for company—arousal that, having no other place to go, would angrily churn in my belly, flare in my bloodstream, strand me in sensations of loneliness and desolation.

IV.

The change came swiftly, during an unseasonably warm spell commencing early April, when the temperature stopped just short of eighty for over three weeks and the remaining snow vanished in a flash and my blood began, as it were, leaping skywards during my strolls—dizzying me with intimations of summer's lushness and vitality, half-blinding me to the fact the landscape, aside from evergreens, was primarily beige and grey, still dormant. It was on one of these warm nights after having spent the afternoon reading on the pocket of sand at shoreline with nothing on, allowing the sun to kiss and stimulate the whole of my skin since I can't recall when, and also after having been without sleep for nearly two days, that I passed from relishing my imagination's representations to being persecuted by them. Bluntly stated, my imagination began conjuring forth unsettling images and notions—engulfing me in outright panic—and there was little I could do to stop it. It's one thing to recreationally ride one's imagination to appealing unfamiliar places, use it to introduce novelty and wonder into one's life, add exhilarating nuances to aspiration, all the while remaining fundamentally grounded. It's quite another thing when one's imagination, unexpectedly unfettered from one's will and unmindful of one's well-being, commences to distort perspective, abolish the boundary between fancy and fact, displace actuality.

But to return to the night in question, after I'd been in the sun all afternoon and was unable to sleep despite being *excessively* sleep-deprived: it was while reading Byron's *Manfred* in bed that I became convinced the overhead lamp's bright light upon the book's pages was dangerous—convinced the pages were staring back at me with hostile intent. Listen: the brightness on the pages seemed to be humming with energy—palpable, agitated, volatile energy—and leaping at my eyes, slamming said energy into the center of my head, transferring it to my nerves—streaming it throughout me, saturating my senses. I detected hissing in my ears, prickles in my skin; the tips of my fingers and toes were tingling, vaguely stinging; an oppressive electric sensation gripped my chest, as if my flaring nerves were rushing in unison towards my heart. Then my imagination turned against me in earnest—compelled me to recall a medical article I'd read, unsuspecting it could haunt me. The article dealt with epilepsy and, among other things, stated epileptics may experience seizures as a consequence of staring at brightness, be it sunlight reflected on water or a strobe's pulses or fire's flames. *Visual representations of combustion are able to spark nervous combustion, cause deadly neurological storms, overtax sanity!* is the phrase my nefarious imagination placed in my thoughts, adding, *Beware! Hissing ears and tingling skin are telltale warnings! Danger's nigh!*

Never mind there's no history of epilepsy in my family and I've never had a hint of a seizure: no sooner did I dwell upon the phenomenon of brightness inducing seizures than I was fearful of focusing upon the words before me, the black ink of which was making the white of the pages brighter—more sinister—via contrast. Holding the book further away, as distant from my eyes as would allow the words to remain legible, contriving to look at them obliquely with my head turned slightly sideways, was of no assistance: I imagined bright light was on the point of slamming into my eyes with such force it would inundate my forehead with buzzing vibrations, jolt me senseless—blur vision, render me deaf. So convinced did I become a seizure was imminent I dropped the book as if it was on fire, sprang from the bed, began frantically pacing from room to room, dashing up and down the halls and stairs. While seeking to shake off overexcitement via physical exertion I continued dwelling upon the nature of seizure-triggers despite myself, became more convinced I was in danger of falling thrashing to the floor, foaming at the mouth.

"So insanely naive I've been—pompous, hubristic—and there's no excuse!" I recall informing myself. "Reveling in isolation, stoking my imagination with insomnia and too much reading—intentionally inducing vivid waking dreams! Yearning nonstop, unnecessarily flaying myself, when there's virtually no chance of finding a girlfriend here—either they're too young or raising kids, understandable in a rural town. Now I find I've accumulated overmuch unspent energy and the lack of an outlet for this energy's forcing it to take matters into its own hands! Place a lid on a heating pot and it'll boil over! Why would it be different with people? A seizure's the means by which my energy will boil over, achieve equilibrium—there's no escaping laws of nature!"

Suddenly the mansion's walls were rushing at me, smothering me, apprehension surging—I fled to outdoors firmly believing I could drop to the floor, thrash and bite my tongue and scream, at any moment: it might be too late to reverse onset of the seizure but I was going to do my best. It was near midnight, I was hastening towards forests near shoreline—surely unspoiled nature and sea-breeze, thunder of surf, would soothe me—rescue me. Over a mile from the mansion was a particularly dense forest, perhaps old-growth, with a clearing yards from shore—waves slamming into larger than average rocks, spinning the air into salt-mist. Before reaching that forest I happened upon the town cemetery—I'd likely already known it was there, even if I'm unable to confirm. Through a wrought iron archway I perceived rows of tombstones, many dating from the nineteenth century and earlier, among trees and shrubs on a gently ascending landscaped slope. I found myself wondering, despite a note of caution in underlying emotion, how many beauties of bygone days (when young people were settling and building the town, instead of exiting it to chase their dreams, fulfill ambition, elsewhere) lay in the graves before me—found myself entering the cemetery, strolling among the tombstones and reading the names there-upon in the ghostly amber light of evenly placed lamps.

My reading of tombstone-names alarmed me but I didn't feel it was safe to cease doing so, as such was distraction from my greater fear of suffering a seizure. I hadn't advanced very far before I halted before a tombstone that stood out due to its height and elaborate gingerbread flourishes, read engraved thereupon, *Clarissa Maye Nighting: The Sky Rains Tears at Loss of Your Wellspring Eyes. 1869-1896.* How I wish I'd never encountered that epitaph! No sooner did I read it than I was fashioning an appealing version of the deceased Clarissa in my mind's eye: fine-textured auburn hair, closer to red than brown, spilling in rippling waves two-thirds of the way to her waist; flawless tan complexion of a woman enamored of the sun and swimming in the sea; petite but feisty and daring, hungry for un-common experiences, unwilling to settle for easy contentment; her stride sprightly, effortlessly graceful. Clarissa was both care-free as a little girl and mature beyond her years: naturally disposed to blitheness, but extremely willful, possessed of readiness of wit, occasionally a mournful quality about her. Clarissa's voice surprised those hearing it for the first time, as it didn't appear to match her petite frame—was readily audible above others in crowded rooms, although she never spoke louder than anyone else—girly on the one hand, as expected, but echoing sultry depths on the other—sometimes infinitely tender, other times gleefully guttural. And Clarissa's epitaph rightly paid tribute to her *wellspring* eyes! Her eyes were dark brown ablaze with an ardent disposition's silver light, perpetually reflecting pinwheel-ing moods—sometimes as if on the point of conveying secrets tantalizingly just outside of understanding, primal pre-civiliza-tion realms. But Clarissa wasn't rebellious, since rebellion im-plies discontent—she couldn't be happier she'd been born. When

Clarissa gazed upon someone and smiled that person felt as if heaven was smiling upon them, and she had many suitors—was the region's most sought-after beauty—but was disinclined to marry. Clarissa's favorite pastime was wandering the shoreline alone.

Clarissa's appearance and personality crystallized in my mind's eye instantaneously, in the amount of time it takes to blink, and there was no erasing it thereafter—no stopping it from banishing all else from my awareness, bringing about troubling flutters in my heart. But who was I to complain? Terror of succumbing to a seizure was gone, courtesy of Clarissa monopolizing my attention. I was vaguely aware of being in the cemetery, fleeing fear outdoors—impressions of breeze, silhouettes of trees against lamplight, occasionally intruding upon consciousness, causing me to pause, blankly stare, even if I was unsure why. Mostly I saw Clarissa's silver-suffused eyes gazing into mine—heard her breathy voice intoning affectionate words—felt the race of my pulse. The moment Clarissa's name and epitaph leapt into my fancy I was immersed in sensory commotion no other woman had inspired.

I don't recall returning to the mansion: my gaze was too turned inward on Clarissa's picture for alterations in scenery to attract notice—surroundings were a stream's blurred surface. My only confirmable recollections of the remainder of that night concern fruitless attempts to sleep soundly after finding my way back to bed. I was in urgent need of sleep, having been without it for over two days, but closing my eyes only caused Clarissa's picture to blaze with greater clarity, along with wonder, excitement, and fear. I'd turn onto my left side, flip onto my right side, attempt to sleep on my back: all to no avail. Did I really believe repositioning my body would quench the fireworks in my veins? It had become blustery outside, as is frequently the case in coastal towns, and I'd opened windows to allow the ocean wind to whip about the room and cool and calm me but my nerves were still every bit as agitated, my skin slick with sweat. The elements were unable to counteract the combustion within me, stop my senses from flaring in response to Clarissa's piercing eyes and beguiling voice.

Did I manage to obtain some sleep, even if it was assuredly not sound sleep? I have no idea. Clarissa's picture was aglow on the same mental screen where dreams unfold, so how can I be expected to know if I slept, since all I saw was Clarissa regardless of whether my eyes were open or shut? I dreamed of Clarissa unceasingly and these dreams shot hot electricity up and down my spine, whipped it to the top of my head and tips of my toes; on account of these dreams I was tense and ablaze in every discernable portion of my body, muscles strained, and the situation was intensifying. I'd already been frayed and afraid before Clarissa took up residence in my imagination and churned up my feelings and now my uneasiness was leading me to detect echoes in the air, the suddenly shadowy menacing air, that were as unidentifiable as they were disturbing. I was beginning to believe that if I didn't soon find a means of escape from my ignited body, achieve some measure of satiation, I'd be in danger of irreversibly losing my reason.

V.

I started to feel as stymied by the Maine town as much as, if not more than, I'd felt stymied by the Manhattan apartment. What a nefarious trap the town was, baited with false promises of rejuvenation! I'd travelled to the town in good faith, persuaded proximity to nature would bring balance and serenity into my life—heal my spirit, restore self-esteem, reassure me I was in charge of my destiny, steady happiness within reach. What I'd encountered instead was dearth of opportunities to preoccupy myself with anything besides gyrations of the imagination; and what I'd discovered is that living in gyrations of the imagination, while initially beguiling, ultimately exposes one to overmuch yearning, turns one's body into a neurological conflagration from which there's seemingly no refuge—suddenly reality's open to interpretation, nothing fixed or reassuring, all points of reference gone, sunny days turning pitch black. I needed to exit the town before involuntary fascination with a dead woman led to a dangerous amount of desperation—I'd been miserable in the Manhattan apartment, but hadn't invented phantoms, feared seizures and insanity. Conflict's focal point in the Manhattan apartment had been external—far worse to be attacked from within!

Needing to exit the town was one thing, ability to do so was another. I was already too entangled in Clarissa's spell to consistently focus on the necessity of escape, much less formulate actionable plans. Visualizations of Clarissa undermined comprehension of the precariousness of my situation—intervals of clarity were increasingly rare and brief. How gaze outside an inner storm that's displacing all else, orient oneself in unaltered perceptions? How fully grasp one's in danger when the danger's becoming the beginning and end of the perceptible world, eroding all conception of stability? The first night of fruitlessly seeking to sleep soundly after reading Clarissa's name on the tombstone swiftly spun into the next day and the next day swiftly spun into the next night. During this interval I infrequently exited the bed, ate little and exercised less, which, coupled with my lack of sleep and inability to sleep, increased absorption in my imagination's separate world. With each passing hour Clarissa's hold upon me gained ground and I was little better than a leaf caught in a swift stream's current.

The second night after encountering Clarissa in the cemetery I was still writhing in bed, sleep elusive, as her beautiful visage and wild eyes and sweet sensual voice continued to blaze in my mind's eye, echo in my ears, engulf me in icy heat. I recall biting pillows, ripping silk, until down was spilling about and airborne, clinging to my sweat-drenched skin—recall rubbing ice cubes up and down my legs, over my belly and chest and neck and face, in further futile efforts to calm myself. When I closed my eyes Clarissa's picture flared, jolted me, with greater insistence, seemingly singeing my skin from the inside. Where did the air begin and my skin, boundary of my body, end? I began to believe it might be a matter of hours before my senses were overtaxed to the degree they'd scatter my thoughts into nonsensical noise, transform my imagination's pictures into shattered white light: if I didn't manage to sleep I'd surely be torn from what little grasp of logic remained! Attempting to think was a *physical* ordeal, fraught with stabs in my nerves, stinging heat radiating. When I managed to fight through inner tumult—place myself in my surroundings, clarify thinking—what greeted me? My ears were buzzing—temples throbbing—pulse racing—heart hammering my breastbone—muscles strained, pained. If one's blessed with equanimity one has no reason to realize how inextricably intertwined mind and body are, but nonstop stress stabs it home.

VI.

My final recollection of confirmable surroundings, accuracy of the hour, as I thrashed in bed is of the nightstand clock's scarlet digits at 12:27 AM: I'm fairly sure I was unable to gaze outside accelerating inner tumult thereafter. My chest constricted, pulse surged, vision blurred! I believe I heard myself intone (possibly aloud, but more likely in my head), *Please, for God's sake, please!*

All I want to do is sleep! as tears of desperation welled, swept away depth perception. Electricity as of needles stabbing from within tore through me—froze me limb to limb, immobilized me on the mattress, steel slabs seemingly pressed to my chest; for no discernable reason I believed I was spinning into a dark whirlpool in the lower center of my forehead, at my third eye—the room's dimensions dissolved, ceiling and floor falling away! It occurred to me ability to formulate thought—all conception of rationality, the very building-blocks of my personality—would be drawn into the whirlpool's blackness and I'd soon be staring empty-eyed at nothing whatsoever, and doing so for the remainder of my days. So much for salvation in the countryside, I'd never known such terror—an irreversible psychic implosion was possible! A split-second mental picture of me splintering inward in a fireball of overstimulation—being engulfed in blinding silver light, razed to the roots of my nerves, permanently blacked out—effectively blinded me, erased the room and sensation of myself in my skin, and... Well, no sooner did I firmly believe a violent seizure was unavoidable—utterly surrender, resign myself to defeat—than exhaustion overtook me and I fell asleep.

It makes sense that sleep spared me inner collapse the instant I abandoned hope of escape, right? I'd endured multiple shocks, my faculties no longer able to sustain waking consciousness. Are we not equipped with physiological defenses? Has not our life-force evolved to step in of its own accord, shield us from ourselves, when faced with dangerous distress-levels? It's plausible we're fitted with biological safety switches—fuse boxes—calibrated to shut down precariously stimulated senses, frenzied imaginations, threats of imminent mental breakdown—flight into sleep's survival. Be that as it may, one might suppose that, considering I hadn't *verifiably* slept in nearly three days, I fell into a deep dreamless sleep. Not so. I dreamed, as follows:

160

I'm awake in bed, delightedly dwelling on the beauty—sweet visage, cascading hair, spirited grace—of the departed Clarissa. I'm gasping at the lively light in her eyes, tingling to the sultry music of her voice—can't stop hearing her intone tender words—can't stop yearning to show her how much those words mean to me, take her in my arms, kiss her. At times she seems close and touchable—at times I upwell inside as if I'm truly about to wrap my arms around her—but she remains unobtainable, restricted to the realm of sight and sound, and my yearning sears and I begin to feel as if I'm surrounded by approaching flames. *If only Clarissa were still among the living!* I cry aloud and, as I do so, wonder if there might be a living Clarissa in town, who'll bless me with reciprocal attraction, bring bliss into my life. Is it possible? Then the ocean wind's whooshing outside the windows, intermittently rattling them. The wind grows stronger, hisses and wails, and I'm listening intently, without comprehending why. Is it only the wind I hear? At first I'm unsure, then sharper sounds are discernable—sounds that wind alone would seemingly be unable to make. Or is it that the wind's gusting in the gutters' narrow troughs, hitting higher notes, becoming shrill? Or that the wind's knocking over the metal jugs on the deck, clanging them together? I listen more intently, apprehensively, not twitching an inch—suddenly start, as a new idea occurs to me. Is it true? Are the mystery sounds cries? I redouble my efforts to separate the wind's whoosh from the mystery sounds, identify the latter... Oh, there *are* cries piercing the wind—rising and falling, reverberating! Are the cries those of cats, nighttime birds—meowling, screeching? Perhaps a raccoon's fending off an aggressive dog, or a coyote's attacking prey? No! The cries are human! They're cries for help! Whose cries are they? Soon as I pose the question I know they're Clarissa's cries! Yes, it's *Clarissa's* voice, as familiar to me as mine! Clarissa's a radiant living woman, just as I've pictured her! Why is Clarissa crying for help? She's suffered a seizure, fallen into a paralysis-inducing trance—been mistaken for dead, buried overhastily! She's awakened from her trance, ascertained her predicament, is frantically shrieking with her remaining strength! It's only I, attuned to Clarissa as only a true soul-mate can be, who's able to hear her screams pierce layers of soil, and knows she's frenziedly pounding the lid of her prison, writhing wildly! I see Clarissa's terrified face—torn burial clothing, battered bloodied hands! Clarissa's hair isn't swishing in sea-breeze—she's not gazing upon expansive sky: she's thrashing in a casket's blackness, gasping for vanishing air! How dig through six feet of soil fast enough to save her, when there's not enough time to alert people and reach the cemetery before oxygen's gone? I believed Clarissa was dead and now realize she's alive, but fated to die because I failed to realize she'd been misdiagnosed! Then I'm aware of gasping for breath, arms flailing, chest constricting—aware of kicking blankets to the floor, leaping to my feet, dazedly stumbling—eyesight blurring, hearing fading.

I next recollect being restrained, particularly at my shoulders, arms, waist—the more I resist the greater the restraint. Have I, upon exiting the bed, stumbled into the heavy fabric of the ceiling-to-floor curtains framing the largest window, become entangled, wrapped like a mummy? Am I twisting the wrong way, winding myself tighter in the folds while seeking to escape? How else explain why it's increasingly difficult to move? The curtains seem to possess movement independent of mine, as if they're actively pulling at me instead of passively enclosing me. How so? In glancing about to understand I discover no drapery's obstructing vision—that steady wind's upon my skin—I feel and smell salt-mist. Am I gazing out the window? Have I opened the window? How can the curtains enclose me while allowing me to see? Am I only entwined below the neck? But why, then, are the curtains continuing to yank at me when I've ceased resisting? There's too much contradiction and I'm afraid! Why am I afraid? Because, upon shaking my head and opening my eyes wider, I discover I'm not in the bedroom, or even the mansion, but outside with—somehow—most of the town visible below me.

It's unusual for dreams to realistically convey sensation of touch, as in the *extremely* vivid tugs at me seeming to stretch my skin, strain my joints. Suddenly my right bicep's squeezed and yanked at, and I'm twisting my arm every which way, seeking to shake free, yelling! Soon as I yell strident voices, surprisingly nearby, are audible and I'm whipping my head towards them—agitated silhouettes are coming into focus, acquiring faces: drapery was never restraining me, it's three men! Why are strangers handling me roughly, shouting? Have I offended them? Then my knuckles strike an unyielding surface—pain's jolt is unmistakably authentic! It's no dream, I'm awake!

Sunrise was nigh, scarlet-gold shimmering across the sky and on rooftops, igniting the Atlantic's surf. I was in a circular enclosure well above ground, higher than winter's skeletal treetops—in place of walls was iron railing slightly over a yard high—vertical beams, curling inward and spaced a few feet apart, supported the roof's inverted cup. Clearly my knuckles had struck one of the beams while I struggled against the men—the latter, toolbelts at their waists, were steering me towards a stairwell below a large bell. A bell? Soon as I perceived the bell I knew I was in the belltower of the nineteenth century church! Then I became aware of the meaning, instead of merely the tone, of the men's words—they spoke of the shame of throwing a young life away, vowed I'd be led, willing or not, to safety—one of them declared I wasn't going to die on their watch. *What?* Apparently I was asking questions with glances—a man emphatically pointed at the railing, shaking his hand: my bathrobe was snagged in its spikes, flapping in the wind! On the railing's opposite side, where barely over a foot of surface area was between it and a plunge to earth, were my slippers! I glanced at myself: I was unclothed except for boxers, goose-bumped, shivering!

It was the shock of the chilly air, extent of my shivering, that enabled me to finally understood I'd fled the mansion in bathrobe and slippers, too disoriented to dress, and wandered into town, ascended the belltower's spiraling stairs—done so in the belief that, although it wasn't possible to exhume Clarissa quick enough to save her, there was nevertheless a backdoor... Backdoor? Oh, no! I'd persuaded myself it was possible to unite with Clarissa in death if I acted immediately—otherwise she'd reach the next world before I could join her and we'd be forever apart! I'd come to the belltower to fling myself off, intending to unite with Clarissa in perpetuity—been on the railing's opposite side, absorbed in extricating my arms from the snagged nightgown's sleeves, until yanked from the brink by construction workers.

Sudden awareness of the degree of my delusion—outright terror of myself—was hampering breathing, tearing at my chest, blurring sights and sounds—I went limp in someone's arms. The final moment of consciousness I recall is Clarissa Maye Nighting's visage reappearing in my mind's eye—superimposed upon a moldering skull.

The Urban Primeval

S teve and I were seated in a burgundy plush velvet booth at a popular Upper East Side restaurant on a Tuesday evening. Placed in high spirits by salmon dinners and German beer, a fresh pitcher of which had been set on our table, we were animatedly conversing. What I best remember from our conversation, and feel is worth recounting, is what follows.

"Take a look at this cutie," I said, indicating the petite brunette who'd just dashed up to the restaurant's proprietor, he seated nearby (we being in the back of the restaurant) with a laptop. "Decked out fluffy in lavender and pink, looking inno-cent-little-girl with ponytailed hair."

"She's a beauty, all right," agreed Steve, "and, like many beau-ties, is practiced in the art of persuasion—her sweet-as-pie, vague-ly alarmed, expression and the way she's nervously, and very charmingly, twisting a foot against the floor is pure persuasion. Now she glances at her foot, now she uplifts her eyes and hits the boss full-on with a honeyed look of apology. If a look like that doesn't soften him, he isn't human—the minx already knows she's home-free." He was referring to the matter being discussed, of which we could catch a few words, as well as deduce from body language: the woman was late for her shift as a hostess.

"Right, he's let her off the hook, even if he's acting as if he hasn't—drawing it out with a rote lecture. And he's right to let her off the hook, she's the perfect hostess—tactful and charming, gorgeous, does wonders for the atmosphere—hiring her's a savvy business move and he knows it. Her eyes alone ought to entitle her to late arrivals."

"A blue-eyed brunette," Steve observed as if half to himself, an abstracted look overspreading his face.

"What? You're getting dazed like a schoolboy, as if you haven't had dozens of escapades with darlings galore?" I teased.

"She reminds me of someone," he said, disregarding my teasing. "An authentically dangerous darling of infinite charm and unbridled wildness alike—a truly disturbed woman, absolutely unpredictable, at the mercy of elemental proddings, who plunged me into blinding periods of fear, no exaggeration..." He trailed off, again appearing abstracted.

"Why fake vulnerability, put on an unhinged-by-a-relationship-gone-sour act, for me? Save it for a sentiment-addict with a luscious behind."

"We've known each other a long time, so I needn't snow you with a cynicism routine, act like I'm immune to disorientation where women are concerned, always dictating the terms and triumphing," he responded, regarding me with unaccustomed seriousness. "I'm hardly invulnerable—no man worth his salt will ever be. Fool around with a number of women and the law of averages will ensure one meets up with one who'll thoroughly toss one off-balance, bring on previously unknown levels of stress. The shallow response is that it's damaging to the ego—the healthy response is that it's an opportunity to grow, of which there can never be enough. I was involved with a woman who flipped me inside out to the marrow of my bones, effectively altered reality, ego be damned. I'm not talking about a commonplace, purely situational and worldly, scare of the pregnancy or matrimonial variety—any readily comprehensible scare rooted in societal convention. I'm talking about being swept into blind panic, emotionally scattered to the winds, fearing for my sanity and life. I'm talking about a woman's susceptibility to heightened distress, frightful tumult, lying dormant within her, zero indication of its presence behind the placidity of her demeanor, and then appearing from out of the blue for no ascertainable reason—leading me to wonder if my senses are deceiving me, perceptions a mirage—suddenly nothing I thought I knew seeming to be of any use, the emotional equivalent of being slammed against shoreline rocks by high surf. I don't mean the typical antics of a woman who's fighting for a lasting relationship, trying every which way to bring me to heel: such behavior's to be expected, no big deal. I mean wild animals that lurk inside petite darlings and might be driven to knife me in my sleep!" He paused, took a deep breath, appeared to be gathering his thoughts; then, audibly exhaling and placing palms on the table, fingers spread, "Want to hear a story?"

"You know I enjoy hearing your stories," I grinned.

"It's not that kind of story," he frowned. "Nowhere near."

"I know it won't be all about frolic this time—it's just that I couldn't help recalling the others."

"Forget the others and, truth be told, they're partly flimflam anyway—all about me being constantly in control of the situation, as if any guy ever is. This one's about the situation spinning completely *out* of control, sanity hanging in the balance—the understanding civilization's a lie, security an illusion, rationality relative, predictability a joke—that nothing can shield one from the utter indifference of the elemental."; then, smiling, "All right, so I'm playing it up—well, *maybe*... What it's *probably* about is a wildcat who lived inside a kitten and proved to me I'm an idiot when I begin to believe I have a clue as to what's going to happen in my life next. You decide."

"I'm all ears," I said, raising my glass.

———————◄O►———————

"I won't dwell on how we met," Steve began, "nor will I use her real name—I'll call her Christelle, because it's a name as angelic and tailor-made for a beauty as her real one. Christelle was five feet five inches tall, a size two, had blue eyes and long wavy pitch black hair—bore a general resemblance to this woman. *(He glances towards the hostess.)* And not to subtract from this woman (she's gorgeous), but Christelle was extraordinarily beautiful and her beauty was matched by her magnetic energy—men and women alike, as if they'd fallen under hypnosis, would frequently pause on the sidewalk, interrupt whatever they were doing, and admire Christelle—even grade-school-age kids would stare gape-mouthed, I'd never seen anything like it. There were several occasions when guys became dazed, apparently forgetting what constitutes appropriate behavior, outright losing it as far as blatant staring goes, as if they'd been invaded by an outside force—staring, stammering, unable to function. Like the time we were renting skis and the guy fitting her skis literally froze, couldn't speak, and we needed to request assistance from someone else. Christelle was in her late twenties but easily passed for a teenager, albeit a sophisticated-beyond-her-years teenager. The blithe little girl quality of her ready smile, bouncy cheerfulness of her movements, mellisonant tones of her voice... At first encounter Christelle appeared to be innocent, sheltered, and naive, but such was an illusion. I've never known a woman more whip-smart and perceptive, possessed of a more varied and precise vocabulary, and she was never put out of countenance by *anything*—she had no prejudices whatsoever, didn't know the meaning of fear. Long story short: the moment I met Christelle I forgot other women existed.

"There was an initial friendship period of nearly two months, something I'm unaccustomed to—the extent of my attraction to Christelle was such that I found myself treading extremely carefully, there was far more at stake than a good time. Christelle was suddenly a mystery to solve—a person to come to terms with, go through a rite of passage with—and I had no choice. Like, one day I'm minding my own business, happily flowing along, indulging in fun and frolic, and the next I'm yanked aside and assigned a mission, yearning twisting tight in my guts. I was by no means certain we'd become more than friends—we became so close as friends I was half-ashamed to thirst to be more than friends, began to view such as a violation of trust. Hey, I was questioning my responses to her—sometimes even laughing at them, informing myself I'd regressed to schoolboy stage, having a crush on a teacher. Christelle was as bright and sensitive as she was beautiful and charming and getting to know as much as possible about her meant the world to me. I'm sure we came as close to trading our life stories as two people can. I told Christelle things I've never told anyone else.

"I call it our friendship period, but we were (as we agreed afterwards) determinedly chasing each other the while, even if discreetly—never openly admitting it, daring to venture too much at once. Lingering glances of admiration, both overt and stolen—the joining of our hands on the slightest pretext, with much interplay of fingers—hello and goodbye kisses that wanted to be something more but always stood down—enchanting restraint, thrilling caution, sustained and built upon for weeks. Then, almost overnight, I began becoming restive and uneasy if a day went by without seeing or speaking to Christelle—was accompanied at all times, including in my dreams, by the picture of her face. The most seemingly inconsequential things she did or said began to haunt me shortly after we were apart, bring about sensations of delight and misery alike, somehow simultaneously. The bliss I experienced when recollecting the lilt of her voice or leap of light in her eyes or indefinable sweetness that hovered about her lips, and the distress I experienced because she was no longer beside me, is something I'll never be able to adequately convey."

"Sounds like you're falling for Christelle all over again," I broke in. "You're supposed to tell of her wildness, not get side-tracked into descriptions of initial attraction and courtship."

"Point taken—I'm seeking to set up the story but zigzagging," he smiled. "One memory suggests another and I succumb to the whirl. I'll summarize. Christelle's personality as I understood it early on was a mixture of childlike insouciance, effortless charm, sharp intelligence, unwavering honesty. Her appearance was that of a precocious teenager, although she was a decade older. She..."

"So you've said," I broke in again, theatrically glancing at my watch and yawning.

"Do you want to hear this or not?"

"I want to hear a straightforward story of a beauty gone berserk, not the flip-flopping of someone who's still under her spell."

"Christelle was special," Steve responded, becoming reflective again, "but I'm over her. There were over three desolate months of post-relationship listlessness and inertia, when nothing could spark my interest, inspire feeling—misery and depression would've been preferable to the emptiness—but it's over."

"Sure it's over," I teased, tossing a wadded-up napkin at his head. "That's why you're getting too distracted to tell the tale you said you'd tell."

"I'm aware of how it looks," he said, throwing the napkin back. "The more I say it's over the more it looks like it isn't, even if it is. But forget that! No more courtship details, I'll jump ahead. All I'll say before beginning the story proper is that following intimacy new aspects of a woman's personality are revealed and that in Christelle's case these revelations were heaven on earth—first of all, intensification of her admirable qualities, a degree of tenderness and trust able to leave me speechless with awe; second, pronounced mania for role-play games and skill in devising them, such that I was never aware of anything she wouldn't do—no balking whatsoever; and, lastly, occasional inclination to sit on the terrace for hours, gaze at the view, even though a Manhattan view was nothing new to her, since she grew up with a view of Central Park at greater height. There was, however, one exception to the wonderful things. Christelle started being late—very late, as in over an hour—for virtually everything and you know how I hate to wait."

"Beauties have a different conception of time," I interjected. "It's as if they're genetically disposed to disregard the clock—it really is as if they can't help it. They sometimes miss flights."

"In Christelle's case disregard of the clock's a gross understatement—she redefined disregard of the clock, placed it center stage. When I'd ask her to explain why she was late she had such a guileless way of doing so, apparently oblivious of anything being amiss, that I couldn't help but smile. She once gigglingly waved her nails in my face after arriving around an hour late and said she'd been painting sparkles on them, done trial and error to get them just right for me—all stated in the most blithesome voice, with the sweetest look in her eyes. It was impossible to be annoyed, especially when she wrapped her arms around me, squealed with delight, kissed me for all she was worth.

"As the weeks went by, though, Christelle's propensity to lateness became more pronounced—over an hour late started to be over two hours late and then closer to three—and it became less easy to find her excuses charming. Still, I did my best to suppress displeasure, and, having said that, will admit I didn't always succeed. It was the sole source of discord between us. The futility of remonstration began to annoy me more than the offense. How could Christelle continue to be late—*extremely* late—when she knew I was unhappy about it?

"The final bit of preliminary information is that about a couple weeks before my story proper Christelle turned up at my door over three hours late. No longer able or willing to conceal irritation, I demanded an explanation in a sharp tone—the first time I'd addressed her that way. 'The wait's to whet your appetite,' she replied matter-of-factly, not batting an eye, as if describing the weather. 'If you're going to be angry when I appear in all my glory, after I've taken special care to be pretty for you, then you're saying to me you're not worthy and I ought to go home.' Far from offering an apology, she looked at me challengingly. Perhaps three tense seconds passed until it dawned on me that she had, indeed, outdone herself in transforming herself into a vision of bliss. I won't go into details but elegance was balanced with suggestiveness and she was as resplendent as a freshly unfurled flower at dawn. Moments later I took her in my arms and she was giggling, hungrily pressing herself against me. We ended by, as always, passing a heavenly night, replete with games she liked to play, and a pillow fight. So that's the closest we came to quarreling before the night I'm going to describe—which means we'd *never* quarreled before the night I'm going to describe and I was all the more unprepared for what occurred."

"Sounds like Christelle has a very high opinion of herself," I laughed. "Not worthy? That's classic—truly a beauty being a beauty."

"Right, I'd like to think only a drop dead gorgeous cutie could come up with a priceless answer like that—a drab wouldn't dare unless excessively deluded. And Christelle's answer was dead-on accurate—in all her glory couldn't have been more true. In retrospect being annoyed was shoddy, three hours late or not. Christelle spent those hours thinking about me, dressing to please me—she always made the wait more than worthwhile and shame on me for adopting that sharp tone. It doesn't matter that dolling herself up was unnecessary, especially her obsession with her nails—she was a dream come true at all times. And having said that, I'll also say I could never be involved with a non-fashion-conscious woman. It's more than appreciating the delicious things they deck themselves out in, ways they present themselves—it's mostly about their pride and verve, sensibility and disposition. Women who dress well love well because when they dress well they're thinking about love."

"Right," I agreed, "if a woman doesn't keep abreast of fashion, enjoy dressing up and doing her make-up and showing up other women, she's not a real woman. Or at least not one I'd ever want to..."

"All right," Steve cut me off, slapping the table. "We agree real women fuss over their appearance—that if they don't, we avoid them like the plague. Let's move on, I want to tell the story—introduction's over! Here's the tale of the awakening of the wildcat in the kitten—likely the most unsettling night I've lived through."

"On a cold Saturday late afternoon in mid-March Christelle, after we've been an item for over two months with zilch friction aside from the fleeting amount occasioned by her lateness, arrives at my apartment over four hours after the arranged time. The moment I open the door she emphatically crisscrosses her hands, hisses in a menacing tone (one she's never so much as hinted at adopting before), 'Shush, dammit! I don't want to hear it!,' and stomps past me without our customary greeting-kiss (kisses that generally last minutes, and we often wind up slipping to the floor); then, whipping about to face me with a glare, she adds with a snarl, 'I'm going to freshen up, if that's all right with your highness!,' and dashes to the bathroom, slamming the door.

"*Surely I need to pinch myself awake—how can this be happening in the real world?* springs into my head as dread grips my chest—as a sense of loneliness envelops me, freezes my nerves. I couldn't be more surprised if the moon escaped earth's gravity, spiraled off into space. My first impulse is to advance to the bathroom, ask Christelle why she's angry. Instants later I think the better of it, deciding she needs breathing room. The most upsetting aspect of her behavior is there's no precedent for it—she's never been remotely peevish. I'm soon pacing in the living area, racking my brains to ascertain why she's incensed.

"I have more time to wonder what's wrong than I want. Christelle's in no hurry to exit the bathroom and the longer she remains within it the greater my agitation. There's an uneasy, twisting-in-my-belly, sensation, as of prescience—subconscious perception—of an inescapable night of turmoil. The ceiling and floor seem to be descending and rising to meet in the middle—the air's seemingly being mashed against my eyes—the glare Christelle flung at me's blazing in my mind's eye, knifing my spine. She finally emerges from the bathroom nearly an hour later and a certain amount of annoyance is intermingled with my uneasiness.

I'm intent on asking her why she feels it's a good idea to alarm me for no reason I know of but come to a dead stop—the ability to speak is strangled in my throat. Why? Because she's still glaring at me hard, as if I've done an unpardonable thing—because her mouth's twisted into mockery and contempt—because every sinew of her body's projecting unadulterated rage—because it's as if she's, I kid you not, been carried towards a separate plane of existence by the intensity of her anger.

"Need I say I never imagined my sweetheart capable of glowering at me as if wanting me dead? And would you believe it? While this hell's happening Christelle's surely as radiant and alluring as any woman's been since the dawn of time. She's wearing a skimpy semi-transparent aquamarine negligee with ermine fringe and silver open-toed heels—nothing else, aside from bangles on her wrists. Her raven black hair's cascading about her shoulders, heightening via contrast her flawless lily-white complexion. She's wiped her face clear of makeup and none's needed. Heat of emotion's investing her with luster no makeup will come close to matching. Christelle's eyes might be none too friendly, throwing knifes, but they're nevertheless radiant with silver-inflected sapphire light, as stirring as the brightest stars on a pitch black night. Despite the obvious, it's tough to believe my darling's annoyed!

"Yeah, what would *you* do if a half-naked woman, delectable as any ever born, crowning example of our species—the light of an overhead lamp sliding about her litheness, accentuating her incomparable curves—was a couple yards away and you'd already spent incandescent fun-filled nights with her? Suffice to say I'm soon oblivious Christelle's infuriated. After all, she's dressed for love—uninhibitedly advertising her attributes, thrusting out her chest, shaking her hair, extending a leg! So what if she's throwing knives with her eyes, in thrall to an unsettling mood? Certainly her moodiness will pass and she'll be her customary sweet-dispo-sitioned self, right? Certainly I'll be able to caress and kiss away her anger, right? I want to clasp Christelle tight, submerge myself in her soft skin, gaze into her eyes, kiss her for all I'm worth, and this want chases all else from awareness, blurs reason! Blind to obvious—non desire-distorted—perception, I step towards her with open arms.

"'Are you insane?' she shrieks, jumping back, flailing her arms, kicking at the air between us; but then, annoyed at hav-ing retreated, she takes several rapid hissing breaths, squares her shoulders, stomps up to me. 'What I want from you, *loverboy*,' she screams, derisively spitting out the last word, 'is for you to fetch me a bottle of Scotch, and no dawdling! Do it *now*, or this bitch will be on you like a cat on a mouse!'

"*I've stepped into a nightmare!* I hear myself think as Chris-telle's enraged face looms inches from mine and her rapid breath scatters heat about my neck and cheeks. It dawns on me, in a split-second burst, that she's in a place where rationality's fantasy and all's justified in her eyes—that she's acting upon impulses with zero grounding in logic and the oncoming night's going to be fraught with danger the likes of which I have no experience of—and there's little I can do about it. It's as if a nefarious being, born of thin air, has taken possession of Christelle's personality and is forcing her to obey *its* commands. Where does that leave me?—where's *my* personality, what good is my will? If Chris-telle's reason has been overrun by dark primal forces and is no longer calling the shots what's the likelihood of calming her any-time soon? So that's what whips through my thoughts, alarms me to the core of my being, but do I act accordingly? I'm unable to wholly cast my pride aside! 'Christelle, I don't appreciate being ordered about as if I'm a pathetic lackey, insulted and threatened," I inform her. 'What's gotten into you? Is the Christelle I know and love here today? I'm confused.'

"'Fine,' she responds quietly but acerbically, with a sharp flash of her eyes. 'I'll be going home soon as I gather my things, hope it's not too inconvenient for you to wait—I don't want to be a bother.' Curtsying mockingly, she about-faces, stomps into the bathroom again, and slams the door.

"*She'll gather her things and be gone? Not likely—there's too much of an air of unfinished business*, I think as I recommence pacing in the living area and the flash of Christelle's eyes—bright as sunlight striking steel, the very picture of sardonic defiance—lingers in my vision. And do I want her to be gone? I never have before—time spent with Christelle's always been a life-sustaining gift. Would you believe it? I'm reassured by the thought there's undoubtedly unfinished business and angry women are seldom inclined to exit before making scenes. Not that I'm looking forward to a scene, mind you, but I'm hoping she'll emerge from the bathroom disinclined to leave. If there's some unpleasant back-and-forth involved, so be it, I'll deal with it, am eager to calm her—I want her to stay and be a sweetheart again, I've been looking forward to tonight for three days. But this new and frightening, enraged without discernable cause, version of Christelle: who knows what she's capable of? Who knows what the creature that's invaded her mind and body is plotting and will compel her to do? I also catch myself wondering, *Why this sudden interest in Scotch? Is my sweetheart an alcoholic and, if so, how could she have concealed it for so long? I've never seen alcohol in her apartment, or smelled it on her breath. What's going...?*"

"If alcohol's the source of Christelle's disturbance," I interrupted, "why are you wasting my time? Nothing's more typical than substance abuse. Nothing's mysterious and wild about someone getting crazy because they're craving another dose of whatever. So much for possession by primal forces, nefarious creatures appropriating her will. Just another boring booze drama, happening in households nationwide."

"You know me better than that," Steve countered, impatiently cleaving the air with his hand. "Don't worry, it's not about alcohol. Do me the honor of listening—you'll see."

"OK, I'm listening—I haven't stopped listening."

"OK, then. I'm still pacing in the living area, awaiting a possible infuriated female exit-tantrum, hoping the exit won't materialize and happy resolution will be achieved, when banging—as of the door being kicked, objects being thrown—issues from the bathroom. There's also shouted commentary, punctuated with an abundance of uncharacteristic cursing, the gist of which is that I possess many less than admirable qualities she shouldn't be expected to put up with. I'm thinking: *So the fiend that's altered my girlfriend's temperament has given her a new vocabulary! Will the fiend be content with raining abuse upon me and bashing around in my bathroom or will a dose of up-close confrontation be called for? Certainly my darling will feel she needs to taunt me to my face! But, hopefully, she'll soon tire of it and shrug her shoulders apologetically and embrace me, eager to be kind. Mostly, I need to act like I believe she's right in all she says while, at the same time, not inviting additional rancor by being too much of a doormat—not the easiest balance to strike. Yes, keep my mouth shut without overtly cowering and allow her to rail until she's spent. With any luck, the Christelle I know and love will reappear and want to cuddle.*

"Ordinarily, as in the case of every other woman who's been troublesome in my place, I'd want Christelle gone—I prefer tranquility to tumult, am disinclined to put up with tantrums. Well, until today, that is. Because this is darling Christelle, who's never been anything but an angelic sweetheart and I want more of the same. Sure, present events are pointing towards the opposite of

a sweet outcome, but... OK, so I'm being irrational! I'm not resolving to get her out the door soon as I can, as I generally do with
tantrum-tossers. And I've no intention of doing the shut-her-out
thing to teach her a lesson either, avoiding communication for a
few days—avoiding everywhere I might run into her, not answering the phone, ignoring the inevitable slew of apologetic messages
and texts—waiting for her to feel lonely, start to worry I might
be fed up and finished, before I get back in touch. I'm absolutely
not doing that with Christelle! Naively or not, I refuse to believe
she needs to be trained via avoidance tactics. I'm prepared to do
whatever's necessary to help her exorcise her demons—the bliss
we've experienced thus far, on every night we've hooked up, *must*
continue."

"You foreswore the avoidance routine?" I asked. "That speaks
volumes."

"I resolved to calm Christelle, even if numerous signs pointed to it being extremely difficult, if not impossible—I had no
choice."

"Highly courageous," I smiled. "How long did it take for
you to exorcise her demons? Was she soon on her knees kissing
your hands, begging for forgiveness, eager to be unwaveringly
obedient?"

"Your sarcasm's all too justified," Steve responded, smiling
wryly. "Preparing myself for tantrums, spewing of venom, was
laughably naive. Christelle emerges from the bathroom not blazing with anger but with tears streaming down her cheeks, an
expression of utmost misery on her face. 'Please—*please!*—get
the Scotch for me, Steven!' she pleads while glancing about in
a haphazard skitter-scatter manner, as if recoiling from untold
horrors.

"Dealing with an angry woman's straightforward—one
squares one's shoulders, listens, presents one's side without as-

signing blame, resumes listening, accord's generally within reach. Dealing with tears, distress, misery, terror is something else altogether, and who knows what's within reach, how it will end? The floor's instantly torn from under me—disbelief, pity, disorientation, fear erupt in my breast. Sure, I know ready-to-wear tears are one of the most effective weapons in a woman's arsenal—summoned whenever she feels they'll compel a male to behave the way she wishes him to behave; but there's nothing put-on about Christelle's tears, no falsity in her pain. It doesn't matter that her distress is greatly disproportionate to the situation and makes no sense—all that matters is the authenticity of her distress. It's as if she's at war with inner demons and has seized upon my disinclination to obtain the Scotch as a means by which to fight the war. Like it or not, I've been conscripted into Christelle's inner demon war—cast in the role of external reference point. Her eyes are unlike any I've seen! There's dismay and disequilibrium and vertigo in them; glimpses of ghastly things are swirling in them; there's—dare I say it?—madness in them.

"'Christelle, I'm sorry—sorry beyond measure,' I say without hesitation, tenderly and quietly. 'I was wrong and apologize. I'm going to get the Scotch for you, OK? I'm going to get it now.' But then a thought causes me to pause before I've half-turned towards the door: *Should I leave her alone? Is she safe with herself?*

"'Go, damn you!' she shrieks, frantically gesticulating at the door. 'Why are you mean to me?'; then, as she starts slowly shaking her head, abstractedly pulling at her hair, 'You're always telling me you like my hair and you play with it all the time so I guess you're telling the truth. Why don't I just tear it out and hand it over? Would that please you? Want me to tear my hair out so you can have it without having me? Want a dead part of me so you don't have to be with living me? Huh?' Curtsying in mocking fashion again, with a poisonous smile, she kneels and claws at the floor; then, springing upright and saluting, "Yes, I very much want to please you, Sir! If you want me to die, I'll die!'

"*Where is this coming from? How can sweet Christelle be saying such things, have these ideas?* I'm thinking, thoroughly aghast. Not daring to step towards her, I say, still very softly, 'Christelle, why are you speaking of dying? How can you possibly think I'd want harm to come to you? I'll do anything to protect you. Please, darling...'

"'Don't you darling me!" she cuts in with a scream, becoming absolutely still, facing me with livid eyes. "You don't *ever* get to call me darling again, do you hear?' Then she literally wilts to the floor, grasping her temples, collapses in a heap—I'm instantly kneeling beside her, cradling her head in my lap, softly stroking her forehead, saying, 'Christelle, I'm so sorry and will do anything you want me to do. I'll make things right any way I can. I love you so much.'

"Rob, I kid you not. I'd rather endure any other hell on earth than see a woman's pain again—hear it again—as I saw and heard it then. Christelle's eyes were wide open but glassy, unseeing—her lips were moving but uttering moans instead of words—her face was an ashen mask, one of her legs was twitching, the other immobile. I felt as if I was paralyzed, even while stroking her forehead and speaking.

"Then I hear, 'Why are you still here, if you'll do *anything* for me?' Christelle yanks herself from my lap, backs away on hands and knees, glares. 'Was it all a lie, what you said? You say you love me but you won't budge! Won't run a little errand! Is a bottle of Scotch too much to ask? Is one lousy bottle something you *won't* do, even though you said you'll do anything? You say you love me and it's a lie! A filthy lie!'

"'Christelle, I...'

"'Go, before I claw your lying eyes out!' she breaks in with a shriek. 'Why won't you go? Why do you hate me? Why do you treat me like trash? What have I done? God help me!' Overcome with sobs again, she covers her eyes with her hands, lunges forward onto her elbows, slips to her side, curls up in a ball with her back to me, twitching and trembling.

"'You've been an absolute angel, Christelle—my best blessing!' I can't help but exclaim. 'How can you not know that's how I feel about you? Treat you like—like what you said? I couldn't do that in a thousand millenniums, I'd rather die! Honey, I so want...' I trail off on account of the way she's lifting a profusely shaking arm off the floor, pointing at the door. Again I'm frozen, torn between heeding her request—hope of bringing this hell to an end—and staying to watch over her, prevent possible self-harm. Her distress is such that it's literally wobbling the air, infusing it with blurry zigzagging light—seeming to fold the room's dimensions in on themselves. Will obtaining the Scotch restore sweetness to her eyes? Could it be that easy? Then I hear sounds issuing from Christelle's mouth that I can only compare to the spine-chilling howling of a fatally injured dog, struck by a car, I once heard on Houston Street. I'm immediately alongside her, gently touching her shoulder—whereupon she flips onto her back, frantically waves my hand away, fastens her eyes upon me, pleads, 'Please!'

"The mournful, outright terrified, tone in which she pleads 'Please!' jolts me to my feet. 'I'll be right back with your Scotch, Christelle,' I say, my voice nearly breaking. 'I'm going now and will be right back, OK? I won't be long, the liquor store's across the street. Don't worry.'

"Christelle isn't going to be close to calm until I obtain the Scotch—my sole purpose at this moment is to do so. I doubt anyone's sprinted to the elevator so fast; I'm sure I set the all-time record for a roundtrip to the liquor store from my building. What greets me when I return? Christelle, unclothed and sobbing loud, is seated on the floor with her back against the couch, absently combing her hair with her fingers. Behind her, a sizeable section of the couch is sparkling silver-white, which confounds me—I'm doing a double-take. Then I realize the sparkles are splintered glass—the glass is that of the picture window, behind and above the couch, that was intact minutes ago. Open space, jagged at its edges, is where the window once was. Before I have time to react to the smashed window Christelle falls silent, fairly strangles her sobs—gives me a poisonous look, states in a flatness of tone that chills me to the marrow of my bones, 'I wanted to kill myself.'

"It's as if the air's unzipping, opening wide—allowing a sanity-straining realm, governed by incomprehensible rules, to rush into the room, swirl safety and rationality aside. The feel of myself in my body's already different—I'm seeking to align with unfamiliar muscular tension, rediscover how to move—I'm trembling to the core of my being and also, or so it seems, immobile as a statue. My gaze whips behind Christelle out the gaping hole of the smashed window into the dark expanses above the blurred buildings in the distance and it's as if I'm being yanked into those distances, exiled to frigid winter. Awhile later I'm gazing into Christelle's distant glazed eyes as flaring nerves stab at my chest, one of my arms spasmodically twitching to the right. I'm setting the bottle of Scotch on the dining table, or so I believe—turns out I tilt it too far and it smacks lengthwise onto the table, rolls off and hits the carpet, bounces to my ankle, shoots throbbing pain up my shin. Instants later I'm watching one of Christelle's hands snatch a shard of glass from the couch, bring it near her throat—far too steady and resolute is the movement of her hand. 'This is what you want, isn't it?' her voice intones very slowly, in the same unsettling flatness of tone. 'You'd like this, wouldn't you?' she continues, making a cutting movement with the glass. 'You'd be off the hook if I was dead.'

"'No, Christelle!' I yell, springing towards her.

"'Don't you dare come over here!' she shrieks, making an emphatic halt-gesture with one hand while pressing the glass to her throat with the other. 'You stay put or I'll slash and it won't be pretty!'

"I dead-stop a few yards away, near enough to discern the glass is pressed against her throat firmly enough to indent the smooth-ness of her skin, gingerly enough to not puncture—slightly more pressure combined with motion and blood will flow. 'Christelle,' I plead, 'how can you do this? You're so bright and beautiful—an angel I'm lucky to be with, I thank God every day for the miracle of you! Don't you know I love you? Please put it down, Christelle! I'll do whatever you want to make things right.'

"'Love me?' she scoffs, contemptuously tossing the glass back on the couch. 'You say you love me but you hurt me! You refuse to do a tiny thing, make a fuss and get pompous and mean, and only do it when I'm dying inside, like you want to push my buttons to feel that way first! When you see I might get that way you should stand down and give a little! But it's a big joke I was in a sani-tarium once, isn't it? If I've had problems that suits you just fine because then you get to puff yourself up and pity poor pathetic me!' Before I can respond, she seizes her temples with both hands and screams, 'Aaaaahhhh!' while rising to her knees, thrashing her head side to side, her hair whipping about; then, abruptly falling silent, brushing her hair from her face and fastening her eyes on me, she says in the flat tone, 'Better be careful, I won't be your dumping ground—you're not using me as somewhere to put bad emotions.'

"'But I never knew about a sanitarium, Christelle, and it's my understanding a sanitarium's a wellness resort, similar to a spa,' I say as the walls of my apartment seem to slide up and down and whirl around and trade places—as the overhead lamp becomes blindingly bright, somehow saturates the room with a sinister sheen. "You're the healthiest person I know, glow with vitality and good cheer. How...?'

"'How what?' she interrupts with a hiss, slapping her thighs hard enough for reddish hand-prints to appear. 'You're wondering how I've been unbalanced, in need of help? Why don't you just come out with it and say I've been in a loony bin? Yeah, go ahead! Trot out judgmental slop and say I'm nuts, like other weasels! All scared baby-men! So scared! Way in over their heads, crashing me to earth all the time when I didn't deserve it! It's so easy to pass judgment, try to restrict me! Cowardly is as cowardly does! Always scared of me being me!'

"The smashed window's before me—shards of glass are on the couch, dustings of glass are on the carpet—glittering, stabbing at my eyes. I've never felt more torn from my foundations, aflail. *My sweetheart's been treated for mental illness?* I'm thinking. *Others were scared and hurt her? She's afraid I might do likewise? What's real?* Then I hear myself say, 'Christelle, I could *never* judge you, want to restrict you in any way! How can you think so? I love and admire you, am honored and thankful you're in my life, bringing bliss to me every day! With all due respect, your imagination's running away with you.'

"'Do you know how sad and mad it makes me when you say I'm imagining things, as if I'd make things up? I'm not a liar, Steven!' she yells, springing to her feet, stepping close. 'You insult and doubt and demean me, like the others! It's always me who's crazy, never them! There's more to a relationship than mean accusations, and more to a relationship than running away because I'm not always going be a pushover! Are you going to run away too? Am I a curse for you?'

"'Christelle, you're the darling of my dreams, stunning on every level—certainly you know I feel that way about you!' I say, reeling at her words and tone—my legs are rubber, spatial perception's twisting sideways and upside down—my body might as well be suspended midair. 'I could *never* insult you, such would be the same as tearing out my heart! Please, Christelle!' Her eyes are fastened onto my face with such intensity they're slamming electricity under my skin.

"What I'm next aware of is an ear-splitting shriek as Christelle's palm whacks one of my ears, stings burst in my head, violent light erupts in my eyes. 'Think you can flatter your way out of this?—think you can play me, like I'm beyond stupid?' she asks, her voice seething with malice; then, as she tentatively steps away, her voice becoming incredulous, distressed, 'My God! You just want to tear me apart and laugh, don't you? What have I done? Why do you want to beat me down? You're so used to manipulating people, getting your way—you just don't care!' Instants later she's backed into the corner left of the couch, wedged herself between the wall and the built-in cabinet atop which the octagonal terrarium sits, but not in fear. As highlighted by the terrarium's fluorescent light, her expression's that of a cornered cat, resolved to pounce and fight. "Think you're getting any sleep tonight? Dream on! You're going to be kept up until tomorrow night at least, that's a *promise*! Don't try to pressure me, control me! I'm done with men who think they can turn me into a shoe-licking fool! Won't be licking your shoes, Steven! You won't see dirt on my tongue!'

"I'm still smarting from the whack of Christelle's hand, harder than her petite frame would indicate—temples throbbing, vision semi-blurred, shaking to my heels. A cold gust whips through the vanished window's opening and I'm shivering, wondering why winter's invading my apartment and I'm at the mercy of the uncaring elements. Unreal! Christelle's anger, my smashed window, the havoc of this night! She's always been a darling angel, eager to love and be loved! So why is she tight in every sinew, radiating rage—her eyes ablaze as if I've threatened to kill her mother? I'm not sure what I'm doing or why—I turn my back to her, stroll towards... Well, *where*? How escape?

"Seconds later I hear screaming—seconds after that I hear, 'I have a present for you!' and one of my forearms is on fire. 'Like it?' she snarls, having scraped me with a wrist-full of bangles. 'Thanks infinitely for the trinkets! I *adore* shoddy bribery, being bought off with dreck!' (As an aside, the bangles are 90% sterling silver, sleek of design—I gave them to her a month ago—she flung herself into my arms at the time, cried, 'I'm in love!,' joyfully kissing them, giggling.) Then she's bolting for the kitchen, yelling, 'Thanks *so* much for making me feel lowly and useless and dead! What a *priceless* treat, I'm forever in your...' She breaks off on account of a loud bang, yelps, 'Well, that's a thing!'

"When I reach the kitchen the microwave's on the floor, its housing dented, glass front smashed. Christelle's standing with her back to the sink on the kitchen's opposite side—in her hand's a steak knife, seized from the cutlery set, its blade pointing straight up—she's trembling head to toe, deathly pale of visage, staring fixedly at the floor. It's as if all's happening in slow-motion—I'm somehow both hyper-alert and dazed—the light's as sharp as it's blurred—I ought to be astonished but evidently have reached the point where I'm too emotionally battered to register astonishment. I've come to a dead stop, fearful of triggering Christelle—unsure why she's holding the knife, what her intentions are, or if she's aware of having intentions. She's shaking the knife abstractedly, as if semi-aware of clutching it. I'm on the point of speaking, am enunciating the first syllable, when she starts—whips her eyes at mine, shrieks, 'Here—*here!* Take this knife—*take it!*—and do what you want to do and *kill* me! I *so* want you to be happy, don't want to burden you anymore! It'll be an easy way out for you!'

"The woman before me is the same Christelle in appearance, breathtakingly beautiful, but it's not Christelle I see in her eyes—nothing's as harrowing as a loved one who's turned maniacal, especially when there's no discernable reason for such. 'Put the knife down, Christelle!' I hear myself yell. 'Just drop it! Someone's going to...'

"'Get hurt?' she cuts in with a snarl; then, immediately—frighteningly—absent in her look, staring at the ceiling, twirling the knife in her fingers, such that it's wobbling, and in the emotionally drained tone, 'Maybe...sometimes I get prickly all over...nettle leaves, they sting...nettle stings and needles! Who cares if I die? You won't care at first, or later, or in a dream in the morning! Bad wings fly through my veins but I'm just a silly girl!'

"'I'm aware of being gripped by dread due to Christelle's disjointed raving, but am more aware of the wobblings of the knife, opportunity to liberate it from her less than firm hold. No sooner do I lunge forward, intending to slap her wrist, send the knife flying away from her, than she—quick and agile as a cat—seats herself on the counter, shouts, 'Ha!' and slams the knife onto it, such that it's knocked from her hand, whirls onto the floor, skids into the smashed microwave, stops.

"I'm directly in front of her—seize her, hoist her over a shoulder, carry her from the kitchen—I want her away from all knives, and it's insanely surreal such is a concern! Christelle's reaching under my shirt, raking her nails across my back, thrashing and kicking with all her might—cursing, hissing, spitting—I hear, 'What are you going to do to me? You're not going to win because I don't care what you do, aren't afraid to die! Let the dark wings fly through my veins! Let the smothered morning come! Let the dead sun kill the sky!'

"*What am I going to do?* Slashing nails and pained wailing so different from the Christelle I love and thought I knew—rationality's dead, I have no clue what I'm going to do! The minutes seemingly last an hour and racing through my head's the idea of a night of tumult that lasts a week. Despite myself, I'm suddenly persuaded there's no limit as to what Christelle's capable of—I'm envisioning slashed throats, a leap from the terrace, my bed on fire! I'm berating myself for failing to detect Christelle's unstable, allowing tonight's events to unfold—racking my brains to recall indications, finding none—her instability's appeared, in full bloom, from out of nowhere! Reality's arbitrary—I'm a ghost instead of flesh and blood—the sky's under the floor! And then, as shrieks burst from Christelle's throat, it hits me: *No need to get lost in a wilderness to be at the mercy of the elements, unpredictable indifferent nature, feel backed up against a wall by the naked need to survive—the wilderness lives inside us and can seize ahold of us at any time, rip us from the illusion of security! The walls of my apartment, doorman downstairs, notion of shelter, safety? Pure fantasy! I'm on the Upper East Side, surrounded by cityscape, but it's a lie! We can surround ourselves with civilization, revel in the miracle of technology, and what does it avail us? It's a flimsy veneer, false sanctuary! It's nothing that will assist us when we find ourselves at the mercy of ourselves! Hiding behind locked doors won't keep our primal heritage at bay!*

"Not to imply sequential thought's possible while dealing with a clawing screaming writhing Christelle—the above monologue occurs in what I can best describe as an instantaneous mental picture. As far as confirmable perceptions go, I'm blankly staring at unsorted mail on the coffee table—readjusting my hold on Christelle to avoid dropping her."

189

"Makes sense," I responded. "It's one of those split-second insights thousands of words won't do justice. Words can't wrap themselves around what's instantly clear via emotional intuition."

"Exactly, but on with the story. I'm at the coffee table to the couch's right, starting to shake on account of Christelle's nonstop twisting and jerking—seeking to safely ease her to the carpet. 'So just go ahead and throw me down, have fun!' I hear in a shrill tone. 'I made the glass-bed, make me sleep on it, get diced up—I'm not afraid to bleed as the bad wings' flap, get dark! Let blood rain! My snakeskin booties are over there and I'm a skinned snake—pretty snakeskin booties, shearling, leather, alpaca, angora—gutted animals and a dead me too!'

"'No harm's coming to you on my watch, Christelle,' I respond, hastening from the couch towards my bed in the alcove. 'It's beyond me why you of all people, springtime personified, can want to...'

"'Is this springtime enough?' she interrupts with a hiss, twisting one of my ears, attempting to bite my right arm's bicep.

'Why, for Christ's sake?' I yell, alongside the bed now, a hand on her forehead to keep her teeth away from me.

"'Because I'm bleak under a dying sun, where sere forests rot, withered leaves whirl, storm wings tracing death-patterns on the earth-facing sides of clouds! I'm not afraid! Do with me whatever! Get the knife and gut me up, rip out my heart! I know you want to!'

"'That's so utterly ridiculous I feel stupid answering—please wake up and turn into Christelle again, I miss her,' I respond, dipping sideways and down, easing her onto the mattress—swiftly straddling her thighs, pinning her wrists. 'Jesus, Christelle! How can you think I could harm you? The idea's lunacy and I'm quite frankly getting fed up!' I'm aware of bending close to her eyes, gazing into them from inches away, as I speak. 'Why are you doing this? What bad thing have I done?—why won't you tell me? I don't deserve this, I know it and know *you* know it! I'm scratched and banged up, my window's smashed, microwave's trashed! Why have you bloodied my arms with bangles I gave you out of love and admiration, and that you said you adore? I'm not the one raising hell with no explanation—*you* are! Why won't you talk to me? Why won't you quiet down? I don't know where Christelle's gone but she's nowhere near here! I love the real Christelle very much but there's a fake Christelle in her place and I don't like her one bit! The Christelle that's here is mean and cruel and I don't know her, and don't want to!'

"'Steven, don't you think we've had enough?' Christelle suddenly says, quietly and softly and tenderly, lips trembling. 'Please let me go—I'll be good.' Just like that she says it and becomes limp in every limb, ceases to struggle—just like that her eyes become extraordinarily kind. The Christelle I know so well and love more is gazing at me again—the sweetness of the light in her eyes immediately dispelling my panic and fear. In place of tension-saturated air, splintered light, grating claustrophobia is evenly illuminated clarity. It's as if a suffocating veil's been unwrapped from my face. It's as if I've been washed ashore after being shipwrecked in a storm-tossed sea—I feel solid ground under my feet but am unable to wholly believe it's real. What flashes into my thoughts is something along the lines of, *Christelle's herself again, thank God, but will it last? Dare I believe her, trust her? One of Christelle's many praiseworthy qualities is she never lies—resorting to trickery and subterfuge isn't in her nature, or so I've always had reason to believe. But after today's events, as incredible to me as the sun turning black, do I really believe I know her? More to the point: what if the demons seize her again—the demons that truly seem to exist independent of her will? Can she be said to be able to answer for* their *behavior? Should I release her or not? How long do I wait?*

"The contrast between the strife of seconds ago and tranquility of now's borderline hallucinatory—equanimity's overspreading Christelle's visage, her eyes are contentedly closed, and it's verging on ridiculous to continue restraining her. As for the demons returning: what choice do I have but to overlook the chance, even if the suddenness of their exit's causing me to wonder if they'll return with equal suddenness? I can't pin Christelle all night—what I most want's an end to the nightmare. So I release my hold, sit on knees beside her—she's a limp doll indeed, settling into the softness of the mattress as if too spent to so much as rise to hands and knees, or so at least I'm hoping.

"Within two minutes Christelle stirs enough to place her head on my lap—is hesitantly smiling, combing her hair with shaking fingers, regarding me with apologetic, hopeful, loving eyes—as angelic in aspect as it's possible for a woman to be. But how can tonight's events not be unsettling me through and through? The thought of possible additional conflict's keeping me apprehensive, forcing me to be on guard. So I gently suggest she might wish to return home. 'Please don't ask me to do that, Steven,' she half-whispers, her voice quavering, a frightened look clouding her face. 'I'd be so lonely, cry all night and day.'

"'But why do you want to stay?' I can't help but persist, still very gently. I know Christelle won't be leaving but wish to compel her to speak in order to better assess her frame of mind, determine as best I can if her sweetness is likely to last.

"'Because I love you and being with you is the same as breathing—I can't go home, am scared to be alone,' Christelle answers, clinging to me with worried eyes, cheeks quivering. Before I can respond she slips off my lap and rises to her knees, embraces me softly—soon we're lying alongside each other face-to-face.

"Ummmm—so nice, sweetie—thank you,' she intones, trembling against me, winding a leg about my legs, slinging an arm over my shoulder, closing her eyes.

"I'm caressing her forehead, uncertain what to do. You've been in my apartment but I'll reiterate that, since it's an alcove studio, I'm able to see a great deal of it from the bed even though it's larger than most one bedrooms—meaning I'm glancing at the glass shards on the couch and the jagged edges of the smashed window's frame while recalling the brandished knife, venomous tones of Christelle's voice, rage in her eyes. How reconcile these things with the picture of innocence alongside me? *"Damn her! I think. She raises holy hell over I've no idea what—smashes my window, holds glass to her throat, waves a knife, gashes me with her nails—and here she's snuggling as if we've been deliriously happy lovebirds all day, with no explanation as to why she turned manic—why sending me to get a bottle of Scotch (that she hasn't so much as glanced at) was important. The difference between who she is now and who she was minutes ago scares the daylights out of me, it's as if reality's rules have been rewritten! How can I know she won't spring awake any second, again afflicted by whatever awful things lurk in her blood? The intensity of her fury, what she's already done, leaves little to the imagination—I don't dare shut my eyes as long as she's here. The shattered window... Could she get riled up and nuts enough to slash me with a piece of it, or with the knife? Probably not but can I completely discount the possibility? I can picture it now: gashed and thrashing, the sheets running red with my blood! A sanitarium, that loony bin crack? What's going on? Her ravings about bad wings and dead suns and me wanting to hurt her were either genuinely outside of sane or she was putting me on! And why would she put me on in such an extreme manner? I'd love to persuade myself today's a one-off and Christelle will be her sweet self again going forward but how can I?*

"Unable not to become annoyed at the sight of Christelle blissfully oblivious while I'm worried and hurting on account of her behavior I shake her awake, sit upright, scoot a couple feet away, say, 'How can you rest easy after what you've put me through, ignore what you've done? This is the last thing I imagined I'd ever say to you but today you seem downright evil. And now you have the nerve to look surprised, which reinforces what I just said. Well, guess what? I'm disinclined to pretend all's peachy when it's not! You've smashed my window—waved a knife like a deranged lunatic, placed us in danger—scratched me, tried to bite my arm—and now you expect me to let you stay in my bed? How charming! You go berserk, turn into a maniac I don't know and don't want to know, then say you'll be good and I'm supposed to smile and forget about the window and bangle-gashes and all else! Going berserk and then acting like all's sweet suits you just fine, doesn't it? It must be nice to have no conscience, sweep atrocious behavior under the rug! I've only wanted to love and protect you and share the best things in my life with you, would sooner die than be an obstacle to your happiness, so why blame me for what ails you, fling your lunacy in my face? Your personal doormat, eager to be trodden upon: is that what you think of me? You think you can vandalize my place and attack me and then decide to be good and all's suddenly like it never happened? Do you really expect me to pretend you've been a darling when you've been mauling me? Take a look at these scratches and cuts! *(I place my forearms in front of her eyes.)* Believe it or not, they're real and sting like hell! You really expect me to blot them out of mind? Is forgiveness on demand, no matter what awful things you've done, your idea of a relationship? If an abusive relationship's what you're after, count me out—sickness doesn't appeal to me! How can you expect me to believe you when you say you'll be good? Given what you've done, trusting you would be insane! Guess why my clothes are still on and staying on? It's because I dare not get comfortable while you're here! I've seen a lot of things I haven't seen before and don't want to see again! I want you out of here *now*! Gather your things and go demonize someone else!'

By the time I finish speaking I've exited the bed, am on my knees on the floor and have pulled Christelle over half off the mattress, she on her back, such that if I were to let go of her she'd fall to the floor. I have no intention of letting go but jiggle my arms to emphasize I could. 'Steven, please, I...I only want to sleep beside you,' she pleads, looking authentically terrified. 'I'm sorry I...' she trails off, quietly sobbing while gingerly—very gingerly—nestling her head against my chest. 'I'll be good,' she resumes, barely audible. 'I only want to be with you—I love you, Steven. I'll die of loneliness if I go home.'

"My gaze briefly darts from Christelle's eyes to the smashed window—a steady breeze, punctuated by gusts sharp enough to flutter the edges of the bed's blankets, chill my cheeks and hands, is blowing through the space previously occupied by the window. Despite the sight of the absent window and feel of the breeze (which aptly sum up my incredulity concerning today's chaos), I'm not only unable to continue to be annoyed, I find myself ashamed of having become so. How fragile Christelle is now, as she gazes at me with imploring eyes—heart-meltingly absent of guile, pristine as an alpine stream. She's brought strife into my life but what's uppermost in my mind is appreciation of her wonderful qualities, how special she is. The sweet light in her eyes affords me glimpses of deathless joy—suddenly all worry's a joke and I'm grounded and fearless, as if there's no unexpected situation I won't be able to handle with ease—difficulties become trivialities. I've never been this close to anyone and now, regardless of what Christelle's put me through, am aware healing energy's radiating from her lovely lissome body, slipping under my skin, shimmering in my nerves and blood. It's while reminding myself how blessed I am to have become involved with Christelle—how much she's altered my life for the better—how much happiness and fun and freedom she's brought to me—that I gently reposition her in the center of the bed, slip a pillow under her head. When I tell her I'll return after having a bite to eat she whispers 'I love you, Steven,' her face flushing with joy.

"It's not until entering the kitchen that I realize how splintered to bits I am—it's as if a desolate arctic expanse is in my veins and nerves and I'm being slammed up against inner walls I didn't know were there, separated from the sensation of myself in my body—it's tough to orient myself, the very feel of objects in my hand is blurred. I open the refrigerator, reach for the carafe of filtered water—my hand shakes so uncontrollably I have trouble grasping the handle, am obliged to wrap both hands around the carafe's middle, and, once I do so, nearly drop it—the floor's seesawing, ceiling and walls tilting. As I attempt to pour water into a glass, hands shaking, most of it spills onto the counter, then the floor—my gaze is following the falling water, I feel I'm nearly sinking to my knees. Afterwards I'm cramming lox into my mouth above the sink—the sink's bright white enamel's pulsing in out of focus—a slab of lox escapes my fingers, falls into the brightness, turns blood red. When I reach for the lox, intending to toss it in the trash, it's writhing on the enamel, oscillating like light reflected on a swift stream's surface, and I'm unable to ascertain its location, repeatedly reach for what isn't there. When I kneel to sponge the water off the floor I wind up rolling onto my right side, curling into fetal position—lie there for I've no idea how long, vaguely aware of profusely shivering.

"The following thoughts jolt me from dazedness: *How can I be sprawled on the floor, unguarded and unaware, as long as*

Christelle's here? I'm on sentry duty, need to keep watch! She appears to be exhausted but how do I know it'll last? She appears to be her sweet loving self again but how do I know what's real? If anyone had told me my darling would go ballistic, raise holy hell, scream for Scotch, bash in windows and wave knives, I would've thought them wildly deluded, which only goes to show how naive it would be to assume additional strife isn't in store. I'd dearly love to sleep, but it's a fool's option. And the night's still young—morning's almost half a day away.

"I flog myself from the floor because an inescapable all-nighter, fraught with who knows what variety of stress, is ahead of me. I resume eating, but differently; instead of reaching for whatever first catches my eye and cramming it into my mouth, I determine in advance what to eat, arrange salad ingredients on the counter with utensils and a large and small bowl—such is a means of reaching for a sliver of certainty, reacquainting myself with ability to choose what occurs in my world. I dice the vegetables—tomato, cucumber, onion, red pepper, zucchini—after which I combine them in the large bowl with a can of sockeye salmon. That done, I mix olive oil, coconut vinegar, lemon juice, and kelp granules in the small bowl, add it to the large bowl, stir. I'm reassured by my ability to execute these tasks—I'm no longer shaking, coordination's returned—and I've never savored a meal more than this one: it's as if it's my first serving of succulent nutritious food after surviving on bread and water for weeks. While eating I'm dwelling upon Christelle's laudable qualities—her beauty, charm, intelligence, sense of humor, love of play—how she flips her hands about while speaking, the excited aquamarine of her eyes, stirring electricity of her touch.

"But there's also the smashed microwave a couple yards away, right?—I envision Christelle holding the knife again, hear her yelling I should take it from her, stab her—her eyes scattered, unseeing. Of course Christelle's behavior scares me to death, the more so because I still can't think of a viable reason for it, aside from the one she alluded to, a sanitarium stay. But is mental illness possible? Christelle's posture alone's the very picture of health, her demeanor predominately serene. Does her energy occasionally build up, become unstable, scramble for an outlet—surge towards primal places? After all, civilization's but a hubristic attempt to erect facades between ourselves and nature, suppress uninhibited emotion—always doomed to fail. Technological wonders or not, we're still elemental inside, and it occurs to me Christelle's upheaval has carried me outside the society-sanctioned comfort zone in which I've enclosed myself, liberated me from my habitual world. Untamed nature's forceful in my apartment, in tumult's lingering reverberations and the wind whooshing through the smashed window, reaching the kitchen, fluttering my shirttail—bringing with it thoughts of the immeasurable sky and vastness of the universe and miracle of existence. I'm picturing our ancestors bringing down megafauna with spears, feasting near fires that keep saber-toothed cats at a safe distance, their eyes ablaze—precariousness, survival opportunities, triumph, joy. By the time I've finished the salad I'm laughing at the notion of being hoodwinked by civilization, robbed of precious experiences.

"Not only am I no longer shivering when I exit the kitchen, I remove my clothes to relish the wind on my skin as it picks up speed, gusts increasingly frequent and sustained. Advancing to meet the wind at its point of entry, I gaze at the view and my senses feel so fresh and electric it's almost as if I'm seeing it for the first time. What a beautiful city! Blocks of buildings, myriad rows of glowing windows, shooting skyward beyond my terrace's swishing evergreens; and the diffused light, honey-amber, which permeates the whole, seems to illuminate the air from within itself; nor to forget the unbroken electric hum, simultaneously soothing and blood-stirring. Above are the stars, Orion among them, that are bright enough to pierce Manhattan's light, and beyond them is unending blackness and I blow a kiss to the whole—delight in the miracle of being alive amidst the expanses. My skin's goose-bumped, tingling—I'm passing my cold hands about my midriff and chest and neck, thrilling to the chill, arching my back to get my nerves to flow: it's as if the sparkles racing up and down my spine are merging with the twinkle of the stars and endlessness of the sky, suggesting places that'll forever elude thought. I'm hyperventilating, stretching, firing up my muscles, flinging myself into yoga balance-postures—wrapping into eagle, unwinding to tree, tilting forward to warrior three, lowering to right hand and left knee in spinal balance—wind up on my back in front of the couch, just outside the dusting of glass, gazing at the sky as wind continues swishing over me: it's as if I'm floating above the floor, fleshly boundaries dissolving.

"By the time I'm in bed alongside Christelle I'm more appreciative of her than I've ever been, which is saying a great deal. She's undeniably special—she's an elementally restive spirit prone to impulses that predate civilization, represent the authentic state of affairs from the perspective of nature and existence. Mental illness? The term's often a self-serving invention of society, excuse to categorize, judge, exclude. In Christelle's case it's accentuated sanity—such is how I view the matter, no one's convincing me otherwise. Civilization's agenda is to domesticate us, debilitate us—channel our perceptions, muddle our thoughts, hobble our imaginations—we're conditioned from birth to serve its ends, not those of nature—not those of life. Asleep beside me is a woman who can metamorphose into a wild creature, be as changeable and uncontainable as the wind, go into the other-world—the subsurface-world—the fountains-of-life-world. Tonight's events have convinced me that, as easily as someone might awaken thirsty for a glass of water, Christelle could awaken under the influence of another onslaught of unrest and, instead of becoming uneasy, I'm cherishing the majesty and unpredictability of life—it's as if I'm safe in a place where civilization's unable to dupe me into accepting substandard versions of well-being.

"It's immaterial that I dare not sleep. I no longer wish to sleep, as such would be abandonment of wonderment. I place a pillow against the headboard, sit upright with my back to it, peer into the city-light-suffused dimness of my apartment, listen to the night-sounds, my nerves shimmering. Several times I find myself elaborating upon what sprang into my head when I was carrying a storming Christelle out of the kitchen, as for instance: *Civilization's a tenuous monument to human vanity that carries no weight in the eyes of existence, is no more able to subdue nature than the sun can be caught in a net. Think of the thousands of generations of our species born when we were too busy living to conceive of erecting permanent settlements—a period when life was instinct and survival and every moment of optimum health was savored to the hilt. Civilization's an extremely recent aberration and has no lasting hold upon us—the expanses of non-civilization-muddled time are our true heritage and have made us who we are today. Civilization retreats when extremity of emotion overwhelms us—delirium carries us untold generations back in time and links us to the primal, blessed be. Our species hasn't changed in tens of thousands of years, only surrounded ourselves with scenery that fosters the myth of being masters of our destinies, as if the said myth's anything but worthless ego-stroking, narcissism—we're still the same untamed creatures at heart and at the mercy of the whims of the elements, thank God! Our far-off ancestors were alert for danger, vibrantly alive with vigilance, every waking moment because they lived amidst wild animals that could attack at any time. Where are the wild animals now? They're lurking inside us—hunting us from within ourselves. Here I am, not scanning the darkness for wild animals but watching and waiting in the event they reawaken in my sweetheart, plunge me into depth-dredging upheaval, strain sanity. Who says we can't experience the identical uncertainty our species did fifty thousand years ago when faced with the utter indifference of glorious nature, be the richer for it? The stars seen by those alive at the dawn of our species are the stars we see now—we're equally vulnerable below those stars, surrounded by the unsympathetic unknown, and the more we realize it the stronger and happier we'll be.*

"Several times I exit the bed to stand before the missing window, savor the winter wind's touch, seemingly turning transparent before the stars and darkness. It's an unexpected vacation—society's claims upon me cease to exist, the notion of employment at a law firm's absurd. After being emotionally and physically and mentally knocked about earlier, dragged into intervals of thought-annihilating strife, seeming to nearly lose the ability to feel myself in my body—faced with threats of suicide and violence, dealing with a brandished knife, bloodied by my sweetheart's nails, wondering if she was disturbed enough to swan-dive off the terrace, set fires, God only knows what... It's that harrowing experience, by tearing me from the illusion of security—forcing me to question my perceptions, wonder if they're telling the truth—which makes liberation from society's grip, however temporary, possible. By the time the sun's splashing tangerine across the sky (love that my place faces east), I'm sure I'm as joyously electric as I'll ever be. Infinite gratitude sweet, bright, storm-tossed, darling-of-nature Christelle!

"It's the first day Christelle brings tumult into our relationship but not the last. She's her sweet blithe self again for over a month, going out of her way to demonstrate affection, including ceasing to be late for our meetings, but her unrest returns. I'm not saying I looked forward to renewed tumult, such would be insane, but will say that when tumult returned I was compelled to dredge my depths ever deeper for the ability to endure, discovered fortitude I didn't know I had—felt curiously renewed afterwards, transported to the appreciation-of-life's-mystery place. Once the storming passed Christelle's embraces were nothing short of otherworldly—she'd intensify herself, get trembly and electric, seize me firmly, lovingly heatedly writhe and rub—inspire yearning I'd never known, shimmer my very soul. But nothing I say will do our relationship justice, I don't expect others to understand stress multiplied joy—accelerated emotional motion's as uplifting as enlightening. Christelle and I were together for nearly two years, the most fulfilling of my life—she'll forever be in my fondest thoughts and my heart can't help but skip a beat when I think of her, which is every day. I grew by leaps and bounds as a person in Christelle's company and owe her great deal. She's the yardstick by which I measure other women and I still experience bouts of loneliness—jabs of desolation—in the dead of night because we're no longer together. And please don't ask why we're no longer together—that's between Christelle and myself. But enough.

"Although," Steve hastened to resume, "I should mention that, because Christelle and I parted ways over two years before I met you, I've told the story in hindsight and spun it. I didn't mean to imply I was overlooking Christelle's distress in the interest of going to primal places. Simply put, I *extracted* positive feelings from the chaos of that night, and the others, to remain as balanced as possible. I did my best to prevent such nights from occurring—was alert for signs of disturbance, sought to calm her in advance. Christelle's the love of my life."

"No need to qualify," I said. "It's clear you'd never want Christelle to be distressed—you found ways to deal with regrettable events, extract positivity. You faithfully stayed with her instead of bailing."

"Stay with her is right—I did all I could, she's..." Steve trailed off, absently waving at the air, glancing away; then, meeting my eyes again, "Rob, I've told you so much, might as well add that Christelle joined the Peace Corps, was assigned to an Ivory Coast village. She could no longer endure New York, regular society in general—was annoyed at herself for succumbing to disturbances, determined to put a stop to it—goodhearted to the marrow of her bones, and as caught off-guard and disoriented and upset by her storms as I was. Last I heard, two Christmases ago from her mother, she joined St. Gertrude's Benedictine Convent in Idaho, is spearheading charitable work, ensuring people in need are provided with quality medical care, have access to healthy food. She's found serenity and I'm happy for her. God bless Christelle."

"You're lucky to have a love of your life—I'm still looking. I haven't met a woman the next one couldn't emotionally erase. I mean, I remember all of them—am grateful to all of them—adore all of them—but none have uprooted me *way* inside, shown me a new world."

"Don't worry, you'll find the love of your life," he smiled. "No man who's looking escapes that responsibility. Nature's in charge."

"Sure hope inescapable natural forces are in charge and deliver."

"It'll happen, and possibly when you're completely off-guard," Steve said, raising his glass. "Love's waiting to flip rationality upside-down, thrill you more than you've imagined possible. But enough of life-altering loves! And not to imply picking up women's a lighthearted matter—finding a darling's never a given and I wouldn't want it any other way, love the chase and challenge. Have you caught our hostess' name? It's Alessandra. How delightfully *that* trips off the tongue!"

"I've often wondered about names, as in whether the genetic makeup of parents influence what they name their offspring. In my humble opinion there's a better than eighty percent chance a woman named Alessandra's a spirited beauty and that might be because her mother's a spirited beauty as well. Names likely influence destinies."

"Easy assumption when a gorgeous spirited Alessandra's in front of you," he laughed. "But, sure, assumptions are made about people based on their names before they're seen, same as titles for books before they're read. But that's a discussion for another time, and if Alessandra had a less appealing name I wouldn't care. What a swirly floating-over-the-floor stride she has—could easily be a dancer between gigs."

"Heading out, Steve—don't want to obstruct. And time to go anyway—have a ghastly 8:00 AM meeting, west coast time-difference."

"Appreciate the gesture, Rob," Steve said, reaching for his wallet. "She's working and it's not like I can draw her aside for long, but encouraging hints have been dropped. She's untied her ponytail, let her hair fall free, fluffed and swished it, then tied it again and then untied it again, two-handedly flicked it behind her shoulders while looking straight at me, lifting her chest, eyes lusciously focused, and treated me to downturned-eyes smiles. She's flushed slightly while fiddling nearby, adjusting place settings where no adjustment's needed, dusting with a napkin where there's no dust. Can't wait to speak to her."

"I noticed," I smiled, grabbing the check, gesturing for him to put his money away. "You've been hinting and flirting each other up and waiting for me to get lost."; then, standing and extending my hand, "Dinner's on me, no discussion—goodnight, Steve."

"Goodnight, Rob," he said, shaking my hand. "Next one's on me, hopefully not so far in the future—two months is too long."

"Way too long," I said, turning to pay at the bar.

Love on Glass

Wednesday, April 20, 2022

My life's been stolen from me again. I imagined I'd over-come this propensity to become lost in another despite myself—imagined I'd mastered my will, become a united person unto myself—but was deluded. A warm sunny spring day, and I was heading to a patch of woods at The Lake's edge in The Ram-ble in Central Park a couple hours before due at work—softly lapping water soothes, as do birdsongs, wind-rustled leaves. But then *she* stepped into the sunlight from a building on Madison Avenue and all was swathed in shadows. The swooning again, as if the sidewalk's tilting and spinning and the gutter's a chasm into which I'm about to fall—suddenly I'm struggling to remain standing while blurred of vision, nauseous, alarmed. I called the office, announced I was suddenly sick, not caring if I was believed.

Her name's Clarissa and she resides in the building she exited. I know courtesy of the doorman, obligingly calling out, "Have a nice day, Clarissa, the city's scheduled to inspect your terrace today," myself near enough to hear. She responded with, "Thank you, Louis, as always, for being proactive and have a nice day as well," enabling me to hear the spine-caressing witchery of her voice. It *was* a nice day, Clarissa, until you crossed my path and, like a black cat, presaged of stress to come. Clarissa's graceful and poised and aloof like a cat, as were the others; and svelte and gorgeous, with a sultry voice, as were the others: beauty's a stab in the nerves, envelopment in vertigo, gasping for breath. Such cascades of raven black hair Clarissa has, beguilingly swishing; and such deep dark eyes, in which lightning-flashes lurk; and such an unblemished complexion, like milk—a curtain of milk. What do the contours of Clarissa's visage conceal? Hunger and recklessness are what they conceal, and that's the trouble: hunger leapt from Clarissa's eyes, charged the air, electrified my breast, ensnared me in attraction's net, reawakened *my* hunger—hunger best allowed to remain dormant.

So I've thrashed about gasping, clawing the sheets—nerves seeming to singe my skin—throughout the night (it's presently a couple hours after dawn), with the picture of Clarissa's visage ablaze in my mind's eye. I've been compelled to commence this journal in an attempt to understand why a beauty's able to seize me by the roots of my nerves, flip my priorities upside down. Stability's impossible until I come to terms with Clarissa—I haven't asked to be upended; and who knows if the coming-to-terms will remain within safe boundaries? I shudder at the possibility of brushing safety aside, being swindled by hunger into committing inexcusable crimes. Is it self-discovery or self-destruction? I'm uneasy before the chasm within me—the darkness that Clarissa, by simply existing, has forced me to acknowledge. I sincerely desire to be a well-adjusted law-abiding citizen, happy example of society's beneficial influence—truly want conformity to be my god. So why are there aspects of myself I dread confronting? Why won't unrest leave me be?

Thursday, April 21, 2022

I was diagonally opposite Clarissa's building this morning, a quarter block north, keeping an eye on its entrance, awaiting her appearance, while pretending to be absorbed in net-surfing my phone. She appeared at 10:26 and I followed. She owns a hair salon six blocks away and works Wednesday through Saturday, eleven to five, information obtained from her salon's website. The salon's window affords a clear view of its interior all day, two large trees conveniently blocking sunlight's glare. She was alone after closing for nearly an hour, busy on a laptop—another instance of fate being against me. I always pray the amount of obstruction between myself and a new beauty, something as simple as her having no set routine, will be great enough to delay an approach long enough for attraction to dissipate.

I'm not sure why I'm suggesting the possibility of escape from unwanted attraction when I've never managed such an escape and tend to think I never will, as my nefarious subconscious may be at work, only selecting accessible beauties, reading indications I'm unable to articulate. Inner leeway, lessening of tension, is fantasy when desire churns. The unknown's beckoning again, I don't know what I'm capable of and don't want to know—a new beauty dissolves the sky.

I know it's futile to flee to Central Park, seek relief in open space, but fall in with false hope anyway, wind up on my back on the Great Lawn—all horizons cram close, the air dims, smothers vision—I'm digging shoulders and hips into the lawn, writhing. The grass stains on my clothes afterwards, pressed deep into the fabric, betray the extent of my fear—access to Clarissa's distressingly obstruction-free. An encounter's inevitable, escape's impossible—I can no more relax than as if standing on a crumbling cliff's edge, vertigo choking.

Friday, April 22, 2022

I passed close to Clarissa on the sidewalk this afternoon, as she was strolling to Dean & DeLuca for lunch, and briefly caught her eye—my spine instantly shimmering, veins inundated with heat—electric numbness, a sense of buoyancy, engulfing me—I was as if disembodied in the space of air between us, lifted aloft on the breeze. Although Clarissa's still a stranger, she's the most important person in my life—the beginning and end of my present world, sole means of reclaiming quietude of mind. Silvery darkness, as piercing as sunlight's glare on steel, is in Clarissa's eyes—clear indication of suppressed inclinations to experience sensations strong and strange and frightful enough to tear every trace of thought from her head. Clarissa's capable of yanking aside the curtain—civilization's onslaught of distraction—that shields the majority from apprehending the utter indifference of the universe to their existence and is therefore susceptible to urges to explore the boundary between life and death. Clarissa may not be aware of harboring such urges but I perceive them in her as surely as I perceive whether there are the clouds in the sky—she can no more conceal herself from me than I can stop myself from revealing myself to her.

The brilliance of the stars against the blackness of a moonless night—the impressions of precariousness and transience that tingle one's nerves—the awareness of the unsolvable mystery of existence, why and how we're on earth, that contrarily sweeps one towards euphoria, multiplies appreciation of life: Clarissa's eyes have the identical effect on me and I'll not be at ease until she blazes in my embrace.

Saturday, April 23, 2022

This morning I was near Clarissa's salon before opening time, awaiting her appearance, and when I spotted her half a block away strolled towards her, intent upon swimming in the light of her eyes again. Yesterday our eyes only met obliquely—today I was determined to meet her glance head-on and hint at my fondness for her, entice her into becoming curious concerning me. Our eyes not only met head-on but from a few feet away, giving me additional time to make an impression: Clarissa smiled, even flushed slightly, and I smiled in turn. I slowed my pace, made as if to speak—a greeting was fluttering on tongue's tip; at the last moment, just as we were about to pass one another, I intentionally glanced away, as if involuntarily shy. Our first mutual acknowledgement of one another, heightened by its wordlessness, couldn't have transpired more vividly. The sweet lines of Clarissa's smile are now united with the lightning light of her eyes in the picture that's ever more insistently monopolizing my mind's eye, quickening my blood and hunger. How rich with promise of delirium-to-come is Clarissa's smile! I'm thoroughly under Clarissa's spell—tense and agitated day and night, in the grip of waking dreams in which she's the undisputed queen, sleeping fitfully at best, night blurring with day—but that doesn't mean I won't remain self-possessed enough to effectively pursue her, give her to understand she was right to gift me with a sweet glance and smile. I'm never more adept at pursuit, charming and tactful and bold, than when a beauty's displaced my blood with the wild world within her and I'm hungering for release. Granted, slipping into pursuit-mode's sometimes scary, as there's no set way to go about it and it's often as if I'm on autopilot—it's not easy to feel at ease if rationality seems useless, an outside force guiding me.

But I need to set this aside, orient myself, apply myself—hunger's waves gather swiftly, froth at the edges of awareness, threaten to drown awareness—the window for carefully considered action's frequently small, emotion churning me under—out the door I go!

Monday, April 25, 2022

A first and only date: such is how it's always been with a beauty who's seized and unsettled me, abolished sound sleep—such is how it was with Clarissa. Early Saturday afternoon I approached the window of her salon. I was resolved to catch and hold her eye with minimal show of shyness but had to play it just right, be respectfully interested instead of intrusively so—as if our brief exchange of smiles on the sidewalk earlier, when we each wished to speak but refrained, had unexpectedly made a lasting impression and set my emotions in motion, inspired me to gather my courage, return to investigate. I have a great deal of experience in placing my beauties at ease and it's not difficult to convey admiration—such admiration couldn't be more sincere. My beauties know it takes courage to approach them and it's up to me to encourage them to be gracious. I know I'll be thought of as a gentleman instead of a questionable individual as long as I'm religiously deferential, hesitant even while focused upon the goal—never must too much insistence be in the foreground but always must it be clear I'm oblivious of every other woman on earth. I'm always extraordinarily polite, even while consumed by yearning that puts me in mind of a thousand needles stabbing me under my skin—I'd never gain access to a beauty if I wasn't able to channel hunger into exemplary behavior. And who could count how many spontaneous encounters occur between strangers in Manhattan every day? Attraction-magnetism strikes from out of the blue, mutual inclinations are unexpectedly detected, and strangers fly into each other's arms without overmuch thinking involved, trusting all will be well. It's my responsibility to communicate all will be well, inspire my beauties to trust me, enable nature to take its course.

Clarissa felt me observing her before she glanced up and saw me: there was flutter-twitching, ever so subtle, of the smooth softness of her cheeks, gentle disturbance in the lines of her otherwise placid expression—curiosity, a trace of wondering delight, came into her eyes: when she glanced up she was already smiling. Gazing into Clarissa's eyes is like gazing into a shimmering whirlpool, puts me in mind of the wellsprings of creation, and there's a sensation of transparency, giddy surge of electricity—energy, benign disorientation, joy. Clarissa bestowed an appreciative and kindly look upon me, then downturned her eyes, blushed—I could feel her tingling with hope and anticipation identical to mine. I never cease to be amazed at the manner in which the nerves communicate subsurfacely—in which emotions sympathetically align as a consequence of an exchanged glance and one instantly *knows*. Clarissa was clearly pleased that I found her pleasing. She was cutting a customer's hair—a good thing. I was able to strongly suggest I'd be returning later—prepare her in advance—with a look and smile before as-if-very-reluctantly turning to depart, not wishing to be a distraction at the wrong time, interrupt her work. Nor did I neglect to cast her an over-the-shoulder glance, as if I couldn't help myself, while strolling away.

When I returned to Clarissa's salon shortly before five, softly tapping on the door's glass before stepping within, she wasn't surprised and didn't act coy—I can still see the forthright flush of delight, as blood-stirring a gift as any man could hope to receive, overspread her face. I'd already heard the melodious lilt of her voice—as close to auditory candy as a voice can be, reverberant with emotion and intelligence—on Wednesday, when she spoke with the doorman; but how infinitely more elevating to be addressed directly, her voice modulated and softened and sensuous in my favor, as the sweetest of smiles graced her face. Our conversation was as effortlessly flowing as thrilling—getting acquainted's often facilitated more by vocal inflection than words, or so it seemed on Saturday. Nor to omit mentioning the brief pauses, Clarissa's trembling glances saturating the silence, raining shimmers down my back. And I was treated to Clarissa's giggle for the first time—sweet pings of blitheness prancing up and down my spine.

I never physically touch my beauties before they touch me, not the slightest tap of their elbow or shoulder—always allow them to choose when the touch-boundary's to be breached, as I wish to communicate I wait for behavioral cues, presume nothing—it's for them to set boundaries, determine what's acceptable, so they feel safe—crowding a woman is counterproductive, allowing her leeway better yields positive results. Inside of two minutes, moved by my observation that her hair was a good advertisement for her salon, she leading by example, Clarissa grabbed my shoulder, warmly squeezed. Less than five minutes later she two-handedly seized my right forearm in response to my dinner invitation, fingers stroking. As we strolled to the restaurant, freshly planted flowers scenting the air, they occupying the soil at the bases of the trees, spring warmth and a slight breeze accelerating sensation, Clarissa playfully rubbed against me—I grasped her waist, turned her towards me, briefly kissed her—her exclamation of delight gave me the go-ahead to steer her into a doorway, press her to the wall, resume kissing. It's magic when a beauty grants permission to do what couldn't be done moments before—time swirls, surroundings blur.

Candlelit dinner in the sushi restaurant with plush velvet burgundy booths and walls of mirrors, suggestive of a dance club—the brass tabletop blurrily reflected Clarissa's beauty, heightened to otherworldliness by her warm regard, as she faced me. Within two minutes we were clasping hands, rubbing knees, her eyes brightening, and I was whirling towards a frame of mind apart from societal restrictions, where nothing dreamed of wouldn't be dared.

I've no idea why nature's allowed humans to invent vanity and civilization, create false realities, suppose themselves special. It's a given civilization won't last but a blip of time in earth's history, count for anything in the eyes of existence, and laughable anyone could believe otherwise. When I'm tense before one of my beauties, attraction rising, I travel back in time to pre-civilization, when the sole rule was survival, each instant alive a gift, vulnerability multiplying appreciation. I only need a first date for arousal to scorch me to my bones, revise interpretation of reality, reveal civilization to be a one-dimensional sham. Clarissa and I gathered a wave, vanquished caution.

Clarissa's a lonely beauty, as were those before her. Only lonely beauties are able to uproot me from my accustomed life, stir me to action—I'm adept at spotting them, including among large crowds, whether I wish to be or not—the cast of their nerves, tone of their posture, calls out to me. They're not lonely because no man wants to bed them—every man with a pulse wants to bed them—but because few men are able to emotionally engage their hidden places, bring their buried inclinations to light, and they won't settle for anything less—will never bow to external pressure, agree to socially-sanctioned relationships, are more rebellious than they imagine. Unresponsive to overtures of those who limit themselves to safety-zone emotions that yield predictable outcomes, shut out the unknown, they can't help but warm to the manner in which I slip under their skin with the urgency of my need. Their interest is awakened by intimation of danger, and when danger's accompanied by unfeigned respect, impeccable manners... Well, I'm never more charming than when a beauty's bewitched me! Failure to rope in a beauty isn't an option, and this isn't ego, stupid pride—necessity strips one of ego, puts one in one's place.

It was when Clarissa and I exited the restaurant arm-in-arm and her voice acquired additional sultriness, playfulness, verve—surrounded me on all sides, as if emanating from the air—that I knew desire's escalation was as unstoppable as a river plunging over a cliff. There was no escaping what I'd set in motion, we were as good as fated to pass a vivid, and possibly frightful, night together—I was both shuttering and tingled dizzy, euphoric. At one point we passed near a high wide window as a street lamp's light was striking, appearing to shatter, it. Clarissa's reflection was captured by the window, the symmetry of her figure and grace of her gestures splintered in the light. I gasped at the sight—every muscle of my body coiled tight—the pictures swarming my imagination were of Clarissa and I making love on broken glass.

I took Clarissa, as I did the others, to the East End Avenue basement apartment opposite Carl Schurz Park, its sidewalk-level windows facing east—sunlight floods the apartment, flows through the intruder-proof grating, from dawn until late morning—direct sunlight in Manhattan's worth ounces of gold. The day I glimpsed Clarissa and understood pursuit of her was inescapable I went to the East End apartment, opened the windows to dispel mustiness, stocked the refrigerator, dusted and swept, placed current periodicals on the coffee table—turned on faucets, flushed rust-tint from the water. Why risk alarming Clarissa, arousing suspicion, by taking her anywhere pervaded with indications of disuse? I hadn't been in the East End apartment for over seven months, the last time a beauty hijacked my will. I'm always very cautious, and then some—it's foolish, as well as tacky, to assume consummation's a given—and, thus far, caution's paid off: I've never had a beauty panic and bolt on me, relegate me to unfulfillment. Much care goes into setting the stage for encounters—nonconsummation would be living death.

(I'm aware I've contradicted myself. As in that I'm confident of success with regard to coming to an understanding with my beauties but never take success for granted. I can't have it both ways, or can I? Relationships, regardless of how brief, are emotionally multi-dimensional, subject to alterations of mood swift as shifts of wind. My relationships with my beauties, undeniably brief, consist of what transpires between first glimpse of them and parting ways after consummation. I might wish to escape compulsion to pursue them at the onset—chafe at being abducted from my life, forced to cast customary priorities aside, heed desire's demands—but that doesn't mean I'll continue wishing to escape. Always, pursuit of my beauties becomes the sole all-consuming aim of my existence—a state of mind and body I wholeheartedly embrace, as nothing equals the amount of immersion and urgency, each moment indelibly impressed upon memory. Always, my initial fear of indulging the danger-flaunting aspects of my personality becomes joy at inability to stand pat emotionally, avoid the unknown's pull, cease hungering to explore the boundary between life and death—fear's strangulation, predictability's paralysis. I've stated failing to rope in a beauty isn't an option, but in practice I'm not close to being self-assured at all times, such would be imbecilic as well as limiting—uncertainty of consummation's no small part of what makes pursuing my beauties fulfilling. Consummation's never assured—I must *earn* it. I must be deferential while focused upon the goal to the exclusion of all else—always endeavor to anticipate possible obstruction, disarm the vicissitudes of chance. After all, I *am* pursuing highly intelligent, finicky, feisty, moody women! The moment I assume consummation's a given's the moment I'll lose the requisite urgency, likely arouse a beauty's pride, chase her away. I dread the possibility at all times and such dread gives me an additional advantage, since it increases attention to detail. And, besides, it's just plain *beautiful* to be knocked about by inescapable compulsion, the outcome a mystery.)

Minutes after Clarissa and I entered the East End Avenue apartment we were cuddling on the couch, one of her legs slung over my lap, the chandelier's amber light flowing about us—her hair fluffy and electric in my fingers. Her voice, whispering ardently, shivered me to my bones. No hesitation, wariness, distrust was in Clarissa's manner.

A first slide of my hand up a beauty's leg under her dress is euphoria stolen from heaven—when Clarissa gasped responsively, clasped me tighter, I knew I'd soon be springing my surprise on her. As I kissed her while pulling her hemline to her waist pictures of shards of glass glimmered in my mind's eye. The sensation of stroking Clarissa's thighs, electrically tensing, meshed with the motion of her tongue as I spun into the light of her eyes—her sighs ignited my spine as her stomach pulsed against mine, her breathing deeper. The room dipped up and down slowly as I lifted Clarissa's dress over her head—she unclasping her brassiere, shaking its straps from her shoulders. She removed my clothes so swiftly it's as if they were never there.

"Clarissa, I'd like to watch you set the mirror alight, so that it wishes it could spring to life and hug you as I can," I said, leading her across the room. The mirror—four feet high by three wide, loosely leaning against the wall—was aglow with the chande-lier's amber. For several minutes I regarded our reflections as we swayed in unison—lightly tapping her along her midriff, rubbing legs, fluffing her hair. How hypnotic Clarissa was, her visage bright with the amber light! Then our reflections whipped to-wards facing the ceiling, briefly, as I seized the string glued to the mirror's base and yanked it from the wall, scampered out of range with Clarissa in tow—the mirror crashing to the hardwood, our reflections splintering. Clarissa, with a cry, sprang back further.

"Please don't be alarmed, Clarissa," I hastened to say, grasp-ing her hands, facing her. "The falling mirror's a ritual with me and I've practiced ahead of time, know how glass of this type of mirror scatters and how fast to move away, and I made sure your back was to the mirror before breaking it, my safety standards are of the highest order. If at any point you feel uncomfortable, for any reason, say so and I'll stop immediately and we'll decide how to continue, or not to continue at all—your word's law. We'll do this together, step by step—what you feel, I'll feel—I won't take us anywhere you don't want to go. Trust me, I'll be care-ful—I'm always careful." I eased Clarissa—ravishing wild-eyed svelte Clarissa—towards the floor and subsequently adjacent to the shimmering shards of shattered mirror while caressing her, whispering soothing words. "Clarissa sweetheart, here we go—easy now, so easy—we're taking it easy, as if lying on a down comforter." The lily white of Clarissa's skin was milk poured on the floor, a living river of milk—silver mirror-dust floated near, caught the chandelier's light, turned golden—I alchemized into vapor, became an electric ghost, as I gently pressed her against the floor, fell into the flares of her eyes.

I don't know how I get away with convincing my beauties to participate in my smashing-of-mirrors ritual, by all rights I shouldn't, although... Well, loneliness is a catalyst—I don't lie to

218

them, promise anything beyond a first and last night. Of course lies can be told via omission, but am I to blame if assumptions are made? I'm made how I'm made. Who's responsible for their personality, impulses?

Tuesday, April 26, 2022

Resuming from yesterday, and I'm not sure why I'm troubling to detail an encounter, I've never done so before. Do I wish to relive the encounter or forestall future encounters, or both, perhaps liberate myself from the necessity? I've no idea and like that I don't.

I said, "Clarissa, you're the beginning and end of my world—strong, beautiful, regal—and I thank you. Trust me, I'll be as careful as if we're walking a tightrope—I'll see to it we float on air. Maybe there'll be minor mirror-cuts but they're trivial compared to the contentment we'll experience—I know what I'm doing and hope you believe I do."

I knew my lonely beauty was more than merely indifferent to cheap and easy means of satiation: she was inherently isolated from them, literally incapable of selling her yearnings short for the sake of "fitting in." I knew she'd never thought to question why she was alone, simply accepting it as so and perhaps coming around to preferring it to be so, as she was thus spared temptation to waste time on pursuits that would yield boredom at best. I knew she was happy and balanced before I met her, because she'd never met anyone able to show her greater gratification via accentuation and celebration of her uniqueness was possible. I knew she was fundamentally unaware of the vital shadow-world within her, because none before me had set about conjuring it to the surface, for her to recognize and revel in. I sympathized with and admired and needed Clarissa—needed her to assist me

219

in approaching, and then reeling away from, a gateway to death. Clarissa and I were of like disposition, in the sense of hungering for expansion of possibility's boundaries, being willing to toy with death in order to reaffirm our love of life. Danger's a reliable means of overhauling one's senses, overcoming delusion, strengthening one's bond with life. All is contradiction: what appears to be obvious, as in that safety and security guarantee contentment, isn't so—existence doesn't abide preconceived notions as to what fulfillment consists of—civilization's a lie.

I reached behind Clarissa's head, gathered shards of glass in my hand, formed a fist: hard heat stung my palm and fingers, shot up my arm, but I was too caught up in the scampering of Clarissa's fingers, twisting of her body—the semi-alarmed, as if undecided, tone of her moaning—her invigorating tension, as of suspension between surrender and recoil—to fully register the pain, believe it real. Nor was I afraid when blood dribbled from my hand onto the milk of her chest.

Blood's red and skin's white, drenched in amber, undulated seemingly up against my eyes, as if seen through a magnifying glass held close, as I caressed Clarissa and myself with my handful of glass—oh, but softly, so softly! I barely scraped the surface of, took care not to gouge, our glistening skin. Bloodletting's an art—only a safe amount, erring on the side of caution, and no more. And yet, what a surge in the nerve-stream it is when I have life and death at my fingertips! The understanding I could cut deeper, open deadly wounds, end a beauty's heartbeat as well as my own, causes me to, so to speak, black out inside, vanish from in front of myself: I obliterate thought via immersion in the unthinkable, leave mental and emotional detritus behind. All the useless strangling stray thoughts and the impressions and moods associated with them that cling to me as an unavoidable consequence of existing apart from nature in so-called civilization is what I rid myself of when thrilling to a beauty's electric tautness during a shattered-mirror-ritual. I love and respect life—worship vitality, well-being, undying desire. I worshipped the life in Clarissa, every spark of vivacity in her veins, and wouldn't have done wrong by her for all the beatitude in heaven.

I continued cutting the two of us for perhaps five minutes, unabatedly kissing the red lines on Clarissa's otherwise unviolated litheness, although time was a blur—as it always is—and it may have been nearer to ten minutes, or more. I stress again the cuts were shallow, respectful of safe boundaries—enough for red streaks to appear but not pool into droplets and run. Clarissa's eyes were wide and wild more with wonder than fear, and her fear was waning on account of my caresses and compliments, hushed admiration—I was doing my utmost to dissuade her from delaying progression towards the point at which we'd deliciously shudder in response to apprehension of where life ends and death begins. I tasted blood's metallic bitterness when I kissed the shards of glass in my hand, before flinging them across the floor, clattering and sparkling as they spread out, struck the wall.

Lovemaking's a face-off with death, fraught with peril, for those of us who hum with more vitality than our customary lives allow us to expend. Is it our fault we're on the outside of convention looking in, unable to value what social norms encourage us to value, and lack of an outlet leads to accumulation of disequilibrium, disquietude? There are too many awakenings in the dead of night when I'm longing for quietude, desperate to escape being stung, and sometimes I lose comprehension of what constitutes self-preservation. I don't want to cut myself and beautiful women with glass—such an act repels me as much as it would anyone who treasures life. But some people, knowingly or unknowingly, live for when they're badgered into falling in line with their inner tides and undertows, complying with the pull of their deepest chasms, being swept outside thought. I'm one of them and Clarissa's another and we couldn't help but unite in necessity to reach a state where cessation of life's a convincingly imagined possibility. Clarissa, her eyes alight, clasped me tight and licked blood from my lips as I took her. The blood of our wounds blended—my sliced hand spreading additional blood with each caress—as we set about swooning.

Enrapt by our slippery skin rubbing on skin, a perception-intensifying drug if there ever was one, I was pressing myself harder against Clarissa—nearby scattered glass glittering bright as stars on a black night—as if it were possible to submerge myself in her bloodstream, exchange places, observe myself through her starshine eyes, deathlessly animated. Certainly exertion was straining our glass-cuts—stretching them, tearing them wider open! How much longer would the cuts remain within safe boundaries, avoid nearing where they'd drain off enough blood to weaken us? I'd exercised due restraint, mindful of mortality's limitations, when cutting us but now the red lines of those cuts, formerly little more than a playful cat's light scratches, were freely flowing red, soaking us as thoroughly as a blistering day's sweat. Or were they?—it's possible the clinging sticky warmth *was* harmless sweat, my imagination racing. I was gazing into the dazzling silver, beckoning depths, of Clarissa's eyes—awash with tingles at the same time identifiable physical discomfort, hints of pain, commenced. We were, indeed, seriously aggravating our wounds—dangerously bedazzled by desire, oblivious of possible life-endangering consequences! The universe is immeasurable and likewise is desire—the stars blaze in the night and desire blazes in our depths—I live for the moments when desire erases memory. It's all about surrendering the ability to consciously act, trusting that veering towards blind impulsiveness will turn out well, no one harmed.

Clarissa's urgent caresses, rippling musculature, radiant visage, arousal-slurred voice... Well, it was as if I partially believed I was dreaming, floating above the floor! Then I was rolling onto my back, pulling Clarissa along—she was atop me undulating, shoving at my shoulders, licking my chin. I continued rolling until she was below me again—rolled us partially over the shattered mirror, at the edge of its spill-pattern—and subsequently onto the Persian, its multicolors announcing softness and safety; then I was kissing her fervently enough to bruise my lips on her teeth, blood's taste on my tongue anew. Glints of smashed mirror were clinging to our shoulders and elsewhere, some wet with red, but I was lifted outside the sting, indifferent to discomfort. Arousal's anesthesia—forceful emotions deaden pain—Clarissa and I were rebelling against pain's barrier, expanding experience. Speculations as to what leads to serenity are illusory, futile—fulfillment can't be reduced to formulas—surefire routes to happiness are fantasy. Civilization-mandated behavior, commonly known as law and order, will never tame life, count for anything in the eyes of existence, and I find such extremely comforting—civilization's an infection.

Occasionally my beauties recoil, seek to halt our doings—occasionally I must sweet-talk them, demonstrate the tenderness welling within me is such that I'm near fainting with the force of it—occasionally much time's expended maneuvering them into wanting what I want as much as I do. Initial disquietude's a sane reaction, as there isn't a chance a woman's expecting mirrors to be smashed, but Clarissa was special, her disquietude quickly gone. What's more enthralling than a ravishing woman writhing with happy abandon on the floor?—delightedly twisting her head side to side, fearless and trusting? I couldn't help but continue stimulating Clarissa, disregard the chance of unattended wounds causing us to faint, or worse. Indulgence in flirting-with-death activities isn't for the faint of heart! Are some people afraid of losing life because they've never truly tasted of life? I long to reach states where I'm too joyful at being alive to be capable of worrying about losing life, as if abundance of positive emotion's perpetual—brushing awareness of precariousness aside's cathartic. Doesn't matter if I'm stroking ego here, flattering myself—nothing's illusory about the mirror-cuts, I've bled copious amounts! I'd like to believe life's a storm-tossed sea and those who remain ashore, afraid to brave the waves, will always be nearer to death than the fearless ones, but perhaps I'm merely blindly seeking to avoid tedium, swindling myself. As I can't stress enough, I've never sought to fall under a beauty's spell—am no more able to shake off their influence than leaves are able to escape being ripped from branches by driving rain, battered to the ground.

As stated, this is the first time I've sought to describe what it is to fall under a beauty's spell, be emotionally abducted from my customary routine. Maybe by rationalizing the situation, overthinking it to death, I'll kill my urges? But hope frequently makes fools of us.

Wednesday, April 27, 2022

At one point Clarissa and I were seated on the Persian, stomachs pressed together, our breathing increasingly deeper. The blood of our wounds was upon our arms, thighs, chests, shoulders, throats, faces—having mostly been smeared there—but I was blind to its implications health-wise, even while discerning it in the chandelier's light. I recall that shortly thereafter a dance of light, vivid as sunlight striking droplets of dew at dawn, came into Clarissa's eyes, electrified me to the top of my head. I heard myself announce, "Clarissa, you're the wildest darling ever born!" as I licked her neck, spun us sideways onto our sides on the Persian again—stretched lengthwise, legs intertwined, Clarissa slurring half-whispered words, her gaze and touch sparkling me from the inside out. There's *always* an interval during which I'm too dizzily excited to be alert for danger, the extent to which we're bleeding—fresh wounds are readily agitated, may evolve from nonthreatening to concerning—abandon while bleeding heightens elation and I've no say in the degree to which such clouds judgment. Flatly stated, it's impossible to assess safety-status, monitor blood-flow, during advanced arousal and thus far I haven't become sufficiently alarmed in hindsight to be dissuaded from repeating the experience. Braving danger's a means of remaining vibrant—what I dread most is losing verve, being bested by fear. Ha! Do I authentically wish to escape obsession's hold, or will obsession-fueled elation always be too addictive? Such is my personality's duality.

How is it nighttime flashes by seemingly rapid as lightning-strikes, whereas daytime plods along slow as fog in a soggy windless valley? Surprisingly soon—and, perhaps, just in time—the sun was flinging red-orange through the slats of the half-closed venetian blinds, streaking over Clarissa and I lying side by side on our backs. It was the sun's heat on my cheeks, glare in my eyes, that brought me around to full consciousness. As to whether I'd been semi-awake and dazed or authentically dozing I cannot say. Whatever the case, I found myself initially disinclined to stir, as I was as exhausted as serene. It's a badge of honor to feel shattered on the one hand, inundated with uplifting buoyancy on the other—soothing tingles counterbalancing the impression of being too used up to trouble to twitch a finger. More minutes of lying alongside Clarissa passed, the sun's brightness and heat keeping me conscious. When I did stir—having willed myself to do so, without immediately comprehending why—there was difficulty in righting myself to hands and knees and assisting Clarissa with the same, compelling her to crawl with me to the couch. Once seated on the couch we fell against one another and I was aware of wishing to sleep but fought it off. Gently shaking Clarissa, I announced it would be in our best interest to guard against succumbing to sleep—a statement I supported by drawing her attention to the blood on us, adding there was no telling how much we'd lost. "Remember the mirror?" I inquired, indicating the scattered silver on the hardwood outside the Persian.

Examination of our wounds revealed that, although some were sticky, not having had ample opportunity to dry, none were actively bleeding. So I led Clarissa to the kitchen, where we fortified ourselves with my "energy mix"—coconut milk, raw yogurt, blueberries, spirulina, fresh ginger, whey protein, filtered water. Then we gently sponged each other with olive oil soap in the shower, dried off, applied diluted tea tree oil to our wounds—we looked like we'd spent the night in a room crowded with annoyed cats. As Clarissa and I turned about before the bathroom mirror, observing ourselves from all angles, uneasiness tightened my stomach. I was wondering if I'd carry my smashed-mirror ritual too far someday, while also marveling at how there wasn't one deep cut. Then I recalled that after rolling us away from the splintered mirror onto the Persian I'd wiped off the glass clinging to our skin with a wet washcloth—the washcloth in the bowl of water placed nearby in advance. I was reassured by the recollection but wondering if I'd always be capable of exercising due caution, remaining true to advance precaution. Excitement blurs thought, undermines ability to gauge proximity of danger, as in possibly of losing too much blood to manage to rise from the floor, and there's the chance of mistaking false safety for authentic safety. Or should I say it becomes questionable as to whether I'm *consciously* gauging proximity of danger? I'd like to think subconscious awareness strictly enforces self-preservation, ensures my beauties and I emerge well within safety's parameters—I love life and absolutely do not wish to be responsible for losing it, and hopefully such governs every aspect of my behavior, consciously or subconsciously. I'm not sure I want spirited beauties to cease roping me in, even if I profess otherwise—indulgence of one's mist-enshrouded realms, outside thought's compass, is more apt to yield transformative experiences.

To outward appearances, reflected in the bathroom mirror, I was drained in every nerve—jittery in my gestures, unsteady of step, shivering—but in my innermost realms I was extraordinarily calm, aware of having been swirled free of unwanted thought-noise, sensory clamor. Outward appearances often deceive—trembling may indicate leaping-out-of-one's-skin elation, life-force inundation. Springtime's restiveness, when viewed and judged from the perspective of convention, can appear to border on agonizing when it's a heady onrush of jubilation. Outlines of nearby objects were soft and harmonious, and the air was as crystalline and rich with depth as after an all-night storm. Clarissa's beauty, seen through my rejuvenated eyes, was as gut-punchingly otherworldly as if glimpsed in a rapture-drenched dream. The symmetry of her countenance and swish of her hair—delicacy of her hands, curl of her shoulders and back! She was jittery with energy, eyes beaming diamond-fire brightness. I may have been thrashed to the marrow of my bones, semi-aching in seemingly every sinew, but excitation was racing up my spine, radiating to my fingertips. I may have been unable to sustain an even stride, twice obliged to flatten palms against walls to steady myself, cease wobbling, but felt as if I was spreading to the expanses of the sun-blasted sky outside the windows. I've climbed Kilimanjaro, gritted my teeth against high-altitude nausea and thumping headaches, each step seeming like fifty, long enough to attain the summit. I've surfed ten-foot-crosswind-roiled waves, avoided injury on razor sharp coral—skied forty-five plus degree slopes, staying fast enough to avoid a spill; and none of these endeavors approach the sense of accomplishment and thrill of pursuing a beauty and rolling bleeding on glass with her, returning to my senses used up and euphoric at dawn. The most extreme experience available to me occurs two blocks from my primary residence and how wonderful, and humbling, that is.

We applied bandages, loose-fitting enough to facilitate breathing, to a handful of wounds, assisting each other as needed. My beauties have thus far been fairly playful during the bandaging interval, very willing to kiss—an indication I've done my job as far as keeping them calm goes—showering together, soaping one another, works wonders. Traumatizing a woman's inexcusable—I'd sooner die.

Upon returning to the living room, examining the amount of blood on the Persian, Clarissa and I couldn't help but exchange amazed glances—there may have been a trace of worry in our eyes but we were also tacitly congratulating one another, reveling in our daring and abandon. "We're going to be the craziest happiest couple," Clarissa smiled, rubbing her head of undried hair against my shoulder. It's when she spoke those words—words which anticipated future meetings, an evolving relationship—that I commenced to emerge from the spell I'd fallen under at first sight of her. Unwilling to outright lie or more subtly lead her on via reciprocal caresses, and also hesitant to reveal we wouldn't be seeing each other again, I couldn't avoid becoming noticeably uncomfortable. It wasn't long before she raised her head from my shoulder and sought my eyes, inquired, "What's wrong, honey?"

My beauties never react favorably when informed we've spent a first and only night together and need to part ways for our own good, since there may emerge an instance when our chemistry carries us too near danger for us to correct the matter in time—additional nights of shattered mirrors could compromise sane perception, carry us towards a point of no return. I've dealt with a great deal of recrimination, rage, threats, thrown objects, sobbing, pleading, accusations of unconscionably leading them on. Many have assured me they trust me implicitly, are fearless in my arms, and won't lose heart and turn tail and bail, however daunting our activities, which is precisely the problem—they're overlooking the fact real danger's lurking, and that I don't trust myself to consistently keep us safe, as I owe it to them to do. My beauties will allow me every liberty, so long as I'm taking such liberties in their company—the moment I wish to be solitary they want me to regret it and suffer. But I'm not complaining—merely observing.

Many beauties have asked, directly or obliquely, how I could be so unfeeling as to pursue them only to reverse direction the morning after, renege on implied intention of continuing to see them—cursed me for not leaving them be if all I was going to do was instill false hope. Of course there's no acceptable response. Announcing I came under their spell and pursued them despite myself isn't anything a man with a trace of tact would do. I do my best to slip out of their lives as quickly as I slipped into them, and agree with whatever they say concerning my shortcomings—aside from stressing we need to part ways I never contradict them. A beauty once announced she knew I loved her, in my own way, which is true. I *do* love these women, insomuch as I *dare*—I don't see how prolonged association could steer clear of disaster. Some rivers rush over cliffs, shatter into spray on rocks below, and that's how I feel about allowing attraction to these women to flow unchecked.

Thursday, April 28, 2022

I returned to the office today. Falling under a beauty's spell is officially a vacation, as indicated by the billing number I enter into timesheets. Coworkers inquired about my vacation and I stated I went to an unforgettably incandescent place, not wholly a lie.

Clarissa refused to accept we were parting ways—refused to put her clothes on, exit the apartment—yelled I'd have to drag her naked into the street and she'd raise holy hell every step of the way, make a public spectacle. Having dealt with suchlike drama before—knowing words are worthless, attempts to argue a joke—I shrugged my shoulders and walked towards the door, informing her the apartment wasn't my primary residence and she could stay all week if she wished—whatever she chose to do, I wouldn't be returning. To her threat to inflict damage on the apartment (which I've also heard before) I responded, "If you feel you need to trash the place then by all means do so, I know I deserve it and am sorry for deserving it." I wanted to tell Clarissa how much she meant to me, assure her parting ways was extremely difficult and I'd be stabbed by regret—tell her how special she was—but of course such would've led to additional drama, since my actions contradicted the words. When I ascended the steps to the sidewalk, unable to shut the door because Clarissa was at my heels, she apologized for threatening to mistreat my apartment, assured me she could never wish to cause me grief, and burst into tears. She'd rapidly slipped into her dress, one of its shoulder-straps off-kilter, hem uneven—was following me barefoot, not having had time to put on her socks and boots—seconds later I was yanking my wrists from her grip on the sidewalk, willing myself to ignore her protests, blot out her beauty (such expressive eyes, and the tone of her voice, tugging at me!)—dashing westwards, returning home: it's one of the most desolate intervals I've endured in my life. If only Clarissa could know how dearly I wish it were possible for me to continue knowing her! If only she could know how the energy of her presence, caress of her gaze, every luscious line of her radiant countenance, won't cease haunting me anytime soon! It tears me apart that fleeing only succeeds if it's done without explanation.

Clarissa's as near to being my dispositional double as anyone will be, and as breathtaking as flamboyants in Puerto Rican forests, but I'll be true to mutual safety and never see her again, as with the others—it would be highly irresponsible to see her again. When it comes to first and only encounters with my beauties my record's spotless: I've remained safety-conscious, ensured we steer clear of too much loss of blood. I'm proud I've thus far resisted second encounters: arousal's a tricky beast, adept at birthing delusion, sabotaging judgment, and I can't help but fear the urge to greet another day will someday pale beside the temptation to view death as a door on an amount of rebirth I've never known—begin to believe a fatal bloodbath's a means by which to attain undying serenity. Urges to get away with rashly defying death thrill me almost as much as they chill me and I dare not risk putting them to the test. Sunsets in Puerto Rico, stunningly violet and scarlet, tempt me to stay in the waves, surf until after dark, but prudence dictates I come ashore along with everyone else, their sanity keeping me sane.

My beauties monopolize my imagination for weeks after we part—their vibrancy, expressive gaze, tingle-inducing caresses, moans and sighs lingering in my nerves—propelling me into sweat-drenched nights, insomnia stalking me. I occasionally succumb to weakness—wish to backtrack, seek out a beauty's company and apologize, declare I've made a mistake. Or succumb to rationalization—inform myself I've built an emotional foundation and a beauty's comfortable with me, undaunted by my bloodletting ritual—that I'll be able to see her again, add on danger without alarming her. Well, I don't believe dying in a gorgeous woman's company is glamorous or assigns one special privileges in the afterlife—romanticization of death's for dupes. And yet hunger births greater hunger and greater hunger births life-endangering rashness—a second night with a beauty's scary tempting at times.

I don't wish to die of anything but natural causes after living a long fruitful life, unbroken self-sufficiency and becoming a centenarian's the goal—life's a gift, I set my sights high! I also know it's a dangerous game I'm playing, am wary of being swept into frames of mind where I'll feel it's acceptable to risk making the glass-cuts deep enough to be authentically threatening, our lives perhaps draining away while I'm oblivious it's happening—temptation to multiply danger's the greatest danger of all. I've never seriously injured one of my beauties nor myself and, God willing, never will. I'm comforted by my first and only date rule, which I've never violated and don't intend to violate.

Friday, April 29, 2022

I welcome office regularity at first, fairly cling to the tedium of my duties—am grateful I'm able to do so, as such indicates I've remained in touch with the safe predictable world. I'm never more personable and efficient at work than after fleeing from a beauty, eluding obsession's pull. But contentment with regularity's fleeting—unrest accumulates, and unbridled sweep of emotion's a drug wilder than any other.

Balancing an outward appearance of what's considered normalcy with nerve-straining yearnings, obsession's pull... How many are like me? Society insists upon maintenance of appearances, suppression of impulsiveness, which means nothing to one's churning depths. We no longer hunt our food—merely obtain it with resources earned in artificial environments, nature nowhere evident. Some coworkers complain about office politics and I wish Is could care. I'd like to be challenged at work, feel it's something besides a joke—it's just too easy, infuriatingly predictable, and therefore more engaging outlets are needed. It's only a matter of time until another beauty seizes me by my bloodstream.

It's obvious detailing an encounter with a beauty, attempting to plumb my depths, ascertain my motives and what spurs me, won't prevent future occurrences—the only thing I've accomplished by jotting in a journal is demonstrating hope of escape's delusional.

And so goodbye!

The Departure

Chapter I

J ulian spent a good part of his time in an apartment perpetually saturated with a sunset's red. For when the sun vanished a
blazing streetlamp took its place, continued passing light through
the scarlet curtains and bathing the rooms in his favorite color.
Blood red lamps were seldom turned off. He drank a great deal
of tea, often added liquor to the tea, constantly paced back and
forth, in circles like a convict, thought and thought and thought.
He would visualize fantastic scenes, wander imagined landscapes
where the ordinary senses were little respected.

He strolled through fields of wildflowers and ferns which
flailingly thrashed despite the windless air. The ferns were luminous light green dipped in cottony down. Every flower was
the slash of an impressionist's brush, resembled red, orange, and
blue tearings of cloth. Thistle tufts spiraled skyward, suggested
glass wool. Cardinal feathers danced in whirlpool patterns, were
flames without a fire. Multicolors were vibrant and slurred, un-
restrained, bursting out.

Or he would find himself astray in vast forests, preoccupied
with the rustling of the leaves while surrounded by darkness and
gloom. Sometimes the leaves would hiss like rushing water and

he would begin to believe a river was flowing through the upper canopies, raise his eyes to behold the pearly sides of fish darting through shifting blue green. He would fear the river would fall onto and drown him.

Often he thought of Hölderlin:

For misfortune is hard
To endure, but fortune even harder.

With the lines in mind he would envision himself wandering a treeless tundra, utterly exposed to the elements, unsheltered. He fed on buds and berries, on roots he clawed from the cold soil with his hands. When lightning slashed the sky he flattened himself in the grey grass, gusts whipping rain at his back. He was pale and dewy when he awakened at dawn, heated and eager to trudge the entire day, fan an inner fire into white hot flames. He felt engaged in a stirring struggle, an elevating fight, was often ecstatic, rapt with sensations of limitlessness.

When his trek through the tundra neared its end he felt a fear which made him bold, led him to stand on the highest hills during storms, raise his arms. He wished to attract the lightning, be blasted from the face of the earth—lest he reach civilization, be invited to food-laden tables, regaled with friendship and wine. Lest he lose his nakedness, sacred exposure to the elemental's indifference. Lest he lose the aspiration of being more than earthbound, the conviction of being destined for a more encompassing realm. Lest he be plowed under with plenty, pampered and cared for until his thoughts and nerves lost their edge, gained a bourgeois stupor. Lest his sensibility degenerate into that of overweight animals, slushy flab. Lest he be swindled from his unobstructed relationship with the untamed.

Shall we say Julian was infatuated with being high strung? Shall we say he found such indispensable for launching into the imaginative flights he thrilled to? Shall we say his drinking of tea and liquor, uninterrupted pacing, and self-confinement was an intentional cultivation of hysteria?

Yet when Julian's excitement reached the point at which it became unmanageable, placed him in mind of an irritatingly high musical note, one tremulous, shuddering, threatening to splinter into shrill cackles he would bolt from the apartment as if rabid dogs were snapping at his heels. He would pace about the city as if hunted by an enemy which was *everything*.

The sun would strike the plate glass, strike the steel, breed a screaming brightness, silver glares. Luminous spiderwebs and gold dust shimmerings would saturate the air. The swirling dresses of the women would be blue and purple flashes, mingle with the yellow and copper slashes of their flickering jewels, their belts and sashes, resemble a spinning kaleidoscope of multicolored flowers. The men would seem to be jerky automations, accumulations of angular threats. Every face would hold a pair of dark electric marbles, black pearls near to bursting.

The sun would heat him to a frenzy—until he came to lack a will of his own, be a hyper-impressionable creature yanked about by sensation, rendered helpless as tufts in the wind. The gleams and swiftness would increasingly dazzle Julian's eyes, assault them, prod them, stimulate them. He would find himself engaged in the gathering of images, hunting of what he called flashes—special moments when his senses seemed to be personified by, combined in a given object or angle of vision. It was when an observation required the use of *all* his faculties at once.

Perchance he turns a corner, clashes eyes with a woman turning the same one from its opposite side—and the tone, the cute shrewdness of her gaze rips his depths outward, flips him inside out. How is it an uprush of emotion seems to float in the air between her and himself, first obscure, then transform her appearance? How is it her visage becomes hauntingly familiar, resembles those he envisions during waking dreams, insomnia fueled nights? How is it her visage contains a hint of, a faint suggestion of childhood's ghostly joys, most daring wishes, bears a resemblance to a nameless something he feels he understood before he was born? Each gathered image would feel like a gem blazing in the center of his chest.

When Julian was alone indoors afterwards it sometimes happened that one of the images would, so to speak, burst into flames and engulf him, become stinging impatience, a variety of blind, for its own sake, objectless *ambition* which he would struggle to distance himself from, embody in thought, cage in a logical sequence of premises yielding an explanation easy to bear. Should he fail to do so the image would accompany him with the persistence of a double, a second consciousness, place him in mind of a guardian ghost or interfering daimon.

One afternoon Julian, apparently inclined to arbitrarily preoccupy himself felt it would be desirable to acquire a silver ring, a simple band without ornamentation. He raced about town searching, visited many jewelry stores—they only carried platinum and gold—many boutiques—their rings had stones. Several places volunteered to make the band. He informed them he could find one faster.

Julian never found a silver band and did not care, as finding one was not the object of his search. The search was the object of his search, as he was happily absorbed, time seemingly suspended. The colorfully stocked jewelry cases gratified his eyes, as did the stunning women attending them. When the women bent forward to locate an item in a case their hair would flop on the glass counters, enticingly coil. Their perfume would fill his mouth like candy, lead him to seek a confectioner and purchase gumdrops before finding another jeweler. So readily he would become sidetracked, lead to indulge impulses almost not his.

At one point while chasing the ring he glanced within a curio shop's window, spied a plaster statue of Venus. Instantly it was endowed with the ethereal presence of Botticelli's graces, became an entranced angel. He continued walking and was not disturbed, the angel seemingly out of mind. That night the angel returned. There was faint quivering in Julian's breast which gradually became crackling heat scraping at him such that he imagined a fetus somersaulting inside him, battering him from within, impatient to be born. But the moment Julian feared an attack, pictured himself thrashing on the floor under a seizure's influence the disturbance softened, became smooth and thick and warm, was the sensation of spirals coiling into pulsing points, shrieking disks of white. Hot slender fingers seemed to enter his nerve-stream, electric snakes were slithering through his veins.

Out of internal turmoil was birthed a sensation of motionless motion, of elevation and weightlessness. Two currents seemed to be meeting head on, slowing one another, creating an eddy, serenity. He felt a yolky bubble expanding within him, felt its membrane pressing against the inner side of his skin and passing through it into the air, becoming a clear sphere the center of which he was.

Between his eyes and the sphere's boundary was luminous pale green mist in which he beheld a tall and slender golden haired woman descending spiraling ivory steps. About her wisped violet flecks. Her delicate, unusually radiant fingers slid down a handrail of chrome. Her silvery gown bent the surrounding light into wild curves, erased itself in places to become blinding glares. Her skin was pearly white, was softness concealing a steely fire. Her eyes were blazing sapphires.

She was simultaneously two beings. One was indicated by her body—its harmonious curves, seemingly half-entranced movements. The other was indicated by the force, the ruthless fire which possessed and directed her body, preyed upon it, brought about her aloofness, paraded mystery, the threatening.

How is it something inhabited her which seemed to resent earthly existence, which had a way of spitting invisible sparks, radiating quiet fury? How is it a seething phantom seemed to surround and inundate her, turn her severe, untouchable, cold? How is it the child in her was chained—and with it her very real kindliness of disposition, natural generosity of spirit? How was it possible for her to at once reach out and reject? How had she attained to intimate aloofness?

It was not easy for Julian to regard the woman as an image. Her appearance and manner were hauntingly familiar, somehow suggested someone he had known throughout his life. She was somehow more corporeal than any woman he had encountered in the flesh, tantalizingly close while unattainable.

Julian was captivated by the way the woman's gaze never seemed to wholly depart from her eyes, by the way she appeared to be peering into realms between herself and anything she was facing, realms invisible to him. She appeared to be surrounded by mirrors which reflected glances she intended for her surroundings back to her, as if she was compelled to perceptually be a world unto herself.

The vision of the woman gradually vanished, was consumed by a fuzzy white glare such that sparkles were dancing within Julian's eyes. He paced about his bedroom in an abstracted, mildly drunken manner, was only aware of being pleasingly unaware of immediate surroundings. When he reacquired regular awareness he found himself gazing into a mirror above a dresser.

The bedroom seemed to have more than doubled in brightness and tufts of light were suspended between Julian and his reflection, resembled frazzled cotton balls. Lingering like a thick perfume was the mood and music of his afternoon, his drifting from store to store, dazed pursuit of a ring. He recalled the jewelry cases and their ravishing attendants, saw building fronts and busy sidewalks twisting in bright bronze haze, was filled with the same unnamable longing, expectant turn of mind which had accompanied him through the streets, saturated and sanctified all, transformed even urban litter, cans and candy wrappers into crystal beams.

While Julian regarded his reflection in the mirror, was seeking to separate it from the light's effects, the golden haired woman returned, approached in the form of a glimmering gold phantom. She encircled his reflection as a starfish encircles a clam, seemed to pry it open, and what he saw in the mirror was a blinding, steadily increasing glare. He lost awareness of his body, felt like dissipating electric vapor.

The following morning Julian awakened with the impression of being watched, of being among people who wished him harm. He sensed omnipresent opposition, felt the very air had gained weight, was pushing down upon and seeking to stoop him over. Were not his bedroom's walls itching to slam together, crush him?

Julian bolted from his apartment seeking relief in open spaces, vigorously walking haphazardly. To no avail: the quick steps, the angular gestures of people on their way to work filled him with terror. Every person seemed off balance, dangerously tottering. He feared being slammed into, knocked down. He imagined himself sprawled on the pavement with an arm extended, imagined a stray foot crushing his hand. He held his hands to his chest to shield them, formed fists, was ready to lash out, explode. In everyone's eyes he read an accusation.

Julian's panic became the need to flee the city. But the thought of boarding a plane, bus, or train and having to conceal desperation, sit still and be polite filled him with dread. He loathed the idea of being cooped up in boxes with stagnant air and cramped seating. With rage which seemed to please him he dwelled on the chance of being seated next to an endlessly chattering bore. The more he wished to flee the more he distrusted every means of doing so. It was not until he passed near a wooded park and was reminded of the countless uplifting hours he had spent in meadows and forests that it occurred to him to walk. He immediately lost his abstracted air and set about exiting the city on foot, absent of inclination to bid farewell to anyone or anything, only attached to his compulsion to depart.

Chapter II

Julian was walking across a forest clearing as if placed on wheels and rolled, dreamily regarded the trees as if they were moving and not he, as if they were designs on softly rippling tapestry. He was but distantly aware of breathing, felt no distinct sensations, was absorbed in a somnambulistic frame of mind. Nearby objects were faraway, ungraspable, seemed to either lie underneath a layer of water or be composed of colored water which could at any moment change form or flow away. His surroundings resembled reflections on melting glass.

He was overcome with the limpness of a wet rag doll and allowed his body to sway, sank to the ground. He curled his hands into claws and combed the grass, tossed adjacent stones aside, reclined on his back and wriggled until the earth's irregularities were avoided, placed his legs between a fern and patch of daisies, turned his palms up, sighed. These preparations were executed as if he was a rubber toy with wires within it, a toy positioned by unseen hands.

Above him foliage swayed, blurred, blended with clouds tending towards greyish olive green. Shifting patches of sky between the clouds were a blue so blazing he could not decide whether the clouds or sky were in the foreground. The wind's whispers added to Julian's sense of half-presence, of vaguely floating. Trembling blades of grass caressed his cheeks and he closed his eyes, pictured the city he had fled. It was located in a flat windswept grey expanse, utterly alone, no vegetation visible. Its buildings were dwarfed by a storming sky, were blank motionless rectangles below twists and swirls. The anxious people, intimidating when he was among them, were spastic twitches haphazardly scampering. The traffic noise, formerly grating, knifing his ears was muted by hissing gusts.

The more Julian sought to recall the particulars of the city the more he realized his recollections were hazy with dreamy indifference, languor. Try as he might vividness eluded him. Already the city was melting, dissolving, disappearing from concerns and imaginings alike. Emotionally faraway were his wanderings through decorative gardens in the dead of night, through rectangular beds of blue lupines alive with the motion of flames, groves of mimosa trees coated in liquid moon, silences rich with an echo's echo, unchartable depths. Faraway were the wanderings through alleys carpeted in oil, littered with glinting glass, smothered in dirty leaden vapors, the odor of gas station restrooms, rotting upholstery.

All that remained of the city, the sole part of it he thrilled to was *her*—always was a part of her inscrutable, outside thought, as a person perceived so vividly her details became indistinct, impossible to wholly encompass. She was the daughter of contradiction, a union of opposites. She embodied both prebirth's darkness and the promise of an idyllic after-death. She was someone haunting him he needed to flee and someone summoning him he needed to pursue. He was alive to her softly twisting under his skin, erasing the tickling of the wind trembled blades of grass with caresses from within. She seemed to be dancing about him. Eventually he slipped into a dreamless yet fretful sleep, hazily aware of inwardly grinding.

Julian awakened before sunrise surrounded by shadows. To the tree trunks he ascribed undulations, a sinister manner of twisting—and imagined them creeping towards him, stealthily stalking him, becoming murderers. Closer and closer they came. His hands trembled, started flopping about. His chest throbbed, was painful, as if about to explode. He wished he could bridle his imagination and cease scaring himself but could not: an irrationally contrary impulse was compelling him to continue. Only when he thought of an ax tearing into his throat, pictured himself prostrate and convulsing, gurgling blood was he able to jerk his head away, vigorously shake it as if by so doing he would empty it of those images. He felt he was being shoved deep within himself and bound, almost feared he would be unable to reemerge. Sensation went blank: an interval of waking consciousness vanished, he had no idea how many seconds or minutes were unaccounted for.

When Julian regained his senses he found himself reliving a vivid night. It was past midnight and he was in the attic of his grandmother's house. Outside was thunder crashing. Lightning flashes silvered the glossy wood walls and rafters, inundated the attic with shifting white. He was perusing old photographs, particularly those of a great-aunt, a woman whose startling beauty was undimmed by yellowed black and white, whose eyes could still cast spells, a woman whose will had not been inferior to her appearance, who had become disenchanted with America and returned to Europe early on. The storm became more violent and rattled the windows such that their glass seemed near to breaking, birthed a pleasant apprehension, enveloped him in a fog of unformulated thoughts, gentle confusion, warm mistiness. His surroundings seemed conjured from thin air, verging on immaterial. He advanced to the attic's trapdoor like an automation, descended the ladder, walked the length of the hall suffused with dim amber light and exited the house, sat on the front porch steps, wind dashing rain into his eyes.

Rain slammed onto the street and sidewalk, sharply recoiled, hissed. Gusts convulsed the boughs of maples and evergreens lining the street, sounded like a shrieking conflagration. He visualized a fire growing furious beneath steady blasts of air, conceived of a fire growing so hot it no longer needed to be fanned, conceived of one sustained by its own intensity. What if such a fire overreached itself, craved fuel not found in this world? What if such a fire became so insatiable it surged clear of this world, entered another realm in which it could locate nourishment, achieve repose? What if someone was in thrall to such a fire, a physiological, a within the nervous system fire and sought to encourage its hunger? What if someone mastered the discipline of concentrating and focusing such a fire, guiding it towards a blaze self-sustained, unquenchable, undiluted? Are there people equipped with sensibilities which find this world's limitations unendurable and systematically hound them from it, compel them to seek another? Gold is heated to enable it to separate itself from the ore, shed impurities.

Julian was seized with an urge to remove his shirt, lie on the sidewalk with his chest exposed to the lightning and icy wind. It was unnecessary for him to stir from the porch to experience sensations of being thus exposed, feel frosty needles pierce his chest, seethe with terror of gazing into crackling white, with the thought lightning might thrust down, blast his body to darkness. The more he feared the lightning the more he cultivated the lightning within himself, acquired electric nerves which longed to escape his skin, leap into the lightning, pulse and strike.

When the recollection faded Julian held fast to the sensations it inspired, was overcome with knifing desire to resume his journey, cease losing time. Despite the difficulty of discerning outlines in pre-dawn he was able to walk rapidly without encountering obstructions, injuring himself, and like a migrating bird he could not help but be always pointed in his destination's direction. Instead of seeing his way through the shadows and trees with his eyes he somehow echolocated his way. The trees emitted a presence which he sensed without needing to touch them.

Chapter III

Julian had emerged from the forest shortly after sunrise and was on an unfrequented dirt road. It was past noon, the sun was ablaze in a cloudless sky and he had not taken a breather, had not had anything to eat or drink—and appeared none the worse, was rapidly striding, bursting with enthusiasm, elated. It was as if privation was his sustenance. The thought of resting, of a cool drink, of a plate of food was distasteful, something Julian associated with boredom, with dull, indifferent, mindless plodding, with puppet mannered academics debating logic in whitewashed rooms, with thick throated raucous women, fumbling clumsy triple chinned men—and with emphatic stomps in the dirt, with a surge of fury he imagined himself smashing through a mirror on which annoying people quivered, scattering it in all directions, crushing its shards underfoot, rendering them dust.

Dust devils whipped up and down the road, churned amber haze skyward which was rendered three-dimensional, made golden by lively sunbeams. Often he perceived *her* lithe outlines twisting in place of the dust, felt she was dancing nearby, enticing him to join her, change substance and flow. In the center of his gaze were writhing pictures of her he supposed were drilling deeper into his soul. He envisioned himself drenched in silvery sweat, surrounded by pearly light—and felt his cheeks were melting, that he was constituted of soft wax. He believed he could flow free from whatever prison he was placed in, escape all chains.

But Julian was not entirely flowing free: the city he was heading for, the woman he was to meet, the act he was going to perform—he did not seek them half as much as they sought him. He was little different than a scrap of steel under the influence of an electromagnet, could not help but hasten on his journey. Sometimes he felt enveloped, contained in something too small, pressed flat against a wall that was on all sides of him. He would compare himself to steam in a pressure cooker, flowers coated with shellac, feel he was wrapped in wet leather ribbons. At other times it occurred to him he no longer had a definable personality, that he was on his way to becoming a field of energy, stripped of thought, immune to pain.

Often he could not conceive of beginnings and ends, was only conscious of continuity, felt he was riding a swift wave's crest. He thought of the wave as an expression of joy on the part of nature, associated with the alteration Dionysus wrought in the Thracian women, their transformation from weavers into maenads, from staid wives into unleashed celebrants. He imagined hillsides of luminous emerald grass grazed upon by milk bloated goats, strewn with stones bleeding honey, frolicked upon by semen soaked satyrs and nymphs. He thought of winds sweeping through fern choked bogs, playing melodies on pussy willow limbs, of autumn forests, trees of flickering gold, of bewitching murmurs, the welling of amethyst hued springs, thought of the wave as blending them all.

At one point Julian found himself at the railing in the center of a bridge, gazed down the length of the sparkling river it spanned, envisioned himself dashing over a desolate alpine plateau. His clothes flailed like flags in whipping gusts, were near to tearing. His hair was yanking at his scalp, blown into his eyes. The air was clear, gleamed in places like glass. Jagged peaks of ice and stone came into view, appeared to float in purplish grey haze. And he continued running although he was nearing a precipice. And when he raced over its edge his coattails became wings, his feet shed their shoes and were talons. His clothes vanished and his body became transparent. He was a diamond eagle intercepting sunbeams, inundated with golden flashes while soaring towards phosphorescence drifting above.

When the vision vanished Julian was gazing at, almost felt attacked by the river below—so fiery were the flickerings on its surface, aggressive were the churnings of its blue. The bridge seemed to spin, rise and fall, pitch from side to side, behaved like a boat on choppy water. Did he not feel gust whipped spray slapping his cheeks as surf surged over the stern? Was he not knocked to his knees, nearly pounded through the deck? Did he not raise himself drunkenly, race for the bank wobbling like a lopsided top, collapse in the road like a straw dummy? Were his arms and legs not as if made of rubber as he crawled from the road into a patch of grass, came face to face with a cluster of violets? Did the petals of the violets not lose their pliability, come to resemble sapphires? Did the sapphires not acquire a light like that which hums in an enraptured woman's eyes? And having the eyes, was Julian not led to construct the remainder of such a woman's visage, led to believe she was pressing close to him, heating his cheeks, licking his lips? Did he not feel himself becoming as shapeless as breeze stirred vapor, vulnerable and soft? Did he not feel he was a pool of lotion into which his surroundings were plunging? Was he not supposing himself sinking into sweet warm mucous, approaching a blindingly bright void? Was he not semi-delirious?

Yet Julian caught hold of himself shortly thereafter, leapt upright smiling and resumed walking. He perhaps would have walked until dawn had he not happened to glance at a pond hours later, perceive the moon's shattered reflection on its rippling surface which reminded him of a city at night, reminded him of his destination. He had not forgotten his goal, his goal would not allow him to forget, but suddenly he was under the impression that he had, was stabbed by urgent nerves. He pictured his destination's multicolored streets—the neon, bright tubes of red and green, the streetlamps, quivering gold disks, the headlights of traffic, swift silver squiggles. He was seized with knifing impatience to be there, to be immersed in metropolitan scents, voices, light, and warmth, to be strolling those streets, be in the vicinity of safety, vicinity of her.

But the instant Julian was itching to break into a run and reach his destination sooner the senselessness of such, his insufficiency overwhelmed and disgusted him. Why was it not possible for an instant arrival to occur, why was the thought of doing something not identical to the doing, why was a wish not action in itself? Why must he be imprisoned in a body, why could his flesh not dissolve, allow him to live in his wishes, his dreams? Why could he not stroll among his visions, caress and frolic with the images he was endlessly conjuring forth? The fact that such was outside his abilities made him tense with a silent scream. With fury he flung himself on the ground in a field, as if seeking to sink into the earth.

Julian's exhausted body did not allow him to rise—and for well over an hour his blazing nerves, cerebral energy refused him sleep. It could be said he was experiencing the limits to which flesh and spirit, muscles and emotions could be pushed. It could also be said that instead of sleeping he lapsed into something of a catatonic state, underwent a comatose shutting down of his faculties.

The following sunrise, though, Julian awakened in a peaceable, not far from blithe mood, resumed the journey as if out for a soothing scenic hike. Clumps of goldenrods seductively swayed in the breeze, resembled ostrich feathers dyed yellow, filled the air with pollen, an amber mist. Butterflies fluttered among them, often alighted and uncoiled their tongues to sip nectar. He paused to observe a spicebush swallowtail, admired its iridescent green hindwings with edges more delicate and detailed than the finest lace. He encountered a putrefied rabbit carcass and managed to avoid noticing the unpleasant smell—so absorbed was he in watching the bright red and black burying beetles scurry across it. Nor did he fail to hear the goldfinches as they darted from thistle to thistle, socialized and fed.

Such was his serenity Julian was saddened when the dirt road fed into a busy paved one like a tributary into a river. The traffic made him uneasy—and he almost felt he was strolling through a noisy factory or near jackhammers. Yet when a man stopped to offer a ride he declined. He had an innate resistance to assistance.

Julian was not on the highway for long. He noted a shopping mall was not far and quickened his pace—as he was anxious to eat and phone for a taxi. Signs announced the mall was newly dedicated and he entered through mirrored glass doors framed in brass, found himself face to face with an escalator's gleaming steel teeth. As it lifted him upward his eyes were assailed by rows of lights mounted in the white ceiling, filled with ribbony patterns suggestive of luminous worms.

Upon reaching the third and top level he found himself facing a restaurant's entrance flanked by elevated disks of burgundy glass with water racing over their edges into copper bowls of water swirling amidst shimmering white stones. A woman in a scarlet dress seated him facing windows framed in decorative scarlet curtains and with flowerboxes overflowing with red roses at their base. The seat backs, napkins, and lampshades matched the curtains—and he found his eyes wandering among them, yanked about by magnetic red while also watching people in multicolors mill about on the white tiles outside the windows, rose blossom perfume permeating the air. It seemed to him he was sliding forward across his table, near to spilling over its far side and spreading over the floor.

A svelte woman in a pleated emerald and gold skirt and white blouse with a pearl barrette gleaming amidst jet black curls sat slightly to Julian's right facing left in profile at the windows and he turned oblivious of all else. With delicate tapered fingers the woman drew her hair away from a pale, a hauntingly austere face. Luminous silver haze hovered about her, prevented Julian from discerning her as clearly as he wished, being assured qualities he assigned to her were not inventions of his imagination, representations of his wishes. And the more he sought to penetrate the haze with his gaze the more he found himself sensing instead of seeing, the more he became a seismograph measuring tremors, the humming of coiled nerves. She was motionless with an almost defiant, an intimidating inner tightness. From her perfectly erect spine, absolutely still thighs flowed an energy to which he responded by contracting, growing taut.

It was increasingly difficult for Julian to see through the windows. Their glass resembled sheets of melting paraffin and the people on the other side were advancing and receding grey gold shadows surrounded by bright copper undulations, scarlet dripping throughout. Then the windows—or at least the interplay of light upon them—crept forward and engulfed the woman such that she seemed nearly indistinguishable from flickering reflections on a shimmering pool's surface. When the pool began churning, became a foamy swirl she—or at least her reflection—appeared to be flailing within a funnel, steadily disappearing.

While absorbed in the distortions Julian allowed himself to slide forward on his elbows, knocked his glass of water to the floor. The shattering glass seared his ears, distracted him such that he reobtained more straightforward perceptions, was allowed to realize the woman was still immobile, radiating energy. She was even threatening. Was he not suddenly aware of a sly, a subtle fire, could he not feel slippery flames lapping against him? Were the flames not patiently seeking to dart inside and devour, turn his moist interior into dry blackness? Was he not wishing to increase his density, become as still and fireproof as stone? Was he not tight with panic to the point of pain, animated with the need to reach open expanses, shake the woman from awareness and dare to breathe deeply, feel safe?

Julian abruptly rose, tossed more than enough money on the table and fled the restaurant, was soon among the crowd on the white tiles outside the windows. He passed the display windows of clothing stores, noticed the mannequins wore silky dresses similar to those of the women strolling near him. The mannequins were elegantly posed, possessed the imposing silence of wax figures, their lively lifelessness, suggestion of sinister intentions, an ability to reach for energy in hidden depths and use it to menace those with flesh and blood, and also as if dipped in luminous darkness, surrounded by the tone of a firefly night.

Julian and the others were reflected upon the windows, appeared as formless phantoms, shadows in whirlwinds, shapeless mist. The dance of reflections on the glass made the mannequins on its other side seem to move, gesticulate and shift their weight from leg to leg. Before long he found himself believing the mannequins were walking with him, even regarded the reflections as equals, as people as real as the flesh and blood ones. Did he not flinch from the glass if a reflection suddenly moved swiftly or changed hue? Was he not leery of the higher placed mannequins, afraid one might miss a step and crash through the class?

When Julian stepped onto a down escalator, observed an elevator rising on the opposite wall the reflections and mannequins vanished. The elevator was a glass cylinder encircled at base and top by tiny white lights, its interior suffused with an olive amber glow which made the people within seem suspended in cloudy liquid, made him think of cadavers in a vat of formaldehyde. Upon reaching ground level he paused to watch a bubbling pool below a slanted mirror, its top nearer to him than its base. The pool was illuminated by red and violet floodlights and the coins littering its bottom resembled gems being shattered by invisible mallets, reminded him of crumpled razorblades. In the mirror the pool's rippling water became pulsing patterns which suggested screaming faces, scowling theatrical masks. He visualized demons swarming about him, heard growling hisses and winced at the thought of cold claws sinking into his skin. From the corner of his eye he spied a payphone and made a beeline for it upon spinning back to awareness it was essential to summon a taxi. Afterwards he dialed a number he knew by heart.

Julian awaited the taxi at the mall's main entrance. To his left and mirrored in the building's glass were rows of spouting water resembling wind agitated poplars. A fine mist was alighting upon his cheeks and he was picturing waterfalls, bottomless gorges, and haze enshrouded mountains when the taxi appeared. The driver was surprised and delighted that Julian's destination was hours away.

Chapter IV

Julian was dropped off downtown in a major city minutes before eleven, was irritated by the glare and spaciousness of the unexpectedly deserted streets. It occurred to him the streetlamps were spotlights, the sidewalk a stage. He felt watched from behind multitudes of windows, was compelled to escape, go backstage. He entered a street dimmer and narrower than the primary ones and subsequently entered streets increasingly darker and haphazard, increasingly featuring sudden turns and suggestions of dead ends. He surrendered to unpredictability and allowed the streets to dictate his direction, behaved like a drunk in a funhouse of mirrors, one who does not consciously care if he locates the exit but who, by simply nudging against walls and advancing where they vanish, exits quicker than the non-intoxicated overly confident individual who overthinks the predicament, who wildly taps in every direction at once only to wind up spinning in circles and succumbing to flustered frustration. Julian was amped up but indifferently, strolling as if blown about. Within the less frequented streets he encountered tattered remains of ancient newspapers and heaps of damp trash. To them he added thoughts of slimy dungeons, musty cellars, soundless caverns, muddy crawlspaces. He wondered what it would feel like to be buried alive, surrounded by wormy soil and found the resulting sense of desolation, the melancholy which deadened his limbs like an opiate curiously pleasant.

Julian reentered streets similar to those he had fled, streets starkly illuminated, straight and wide. But he was no longer uneasy in them. It seemed to him the streetlamps were less bright than initially supposed, that their light was muted by yellowed glass. Was a fine dust not suffusing the air, semi-obscuring specific features, swathing them in veils of auburn haze? An iridescently garbed woman approached. Was her black hair not streaked with luminosity? Was her skin not incandescent? Was she not nearly dashing? Did she not resemble a trembly ghost, seem blown towards him? Was her mouth not uncomfortably open, stiff with a cry lost in wailing wind? When he turned to regard her after she passed him did she not resemble silken drapery ripped from its rungs, haphazardly tumbling?

Windows with their blinds drawn aroused Julian's curiosity. From muted light and indistinct silhouettes he constructed restless boys and girls. The boys were slender and supple, had soft, pale, silky complexions, had hair which was long and fine and blond. Their expressions were radiant, their eyes blazing brown. The girls were similar to the boys, equally lithe and soft and aglow, were as swift and graceful as trout swishing their tails and flashing their silvery sides in clear brooks. Their light blue hair reached below their waists, their bright eyes resembled spinning pearls. The boys and girls frolicked among velvet pillows which they tore to shreds, transformed into clouds of floating down. Or they would entangle each other in satin blankets while humming haunting melodies. They splashed mirrors with oil and danced before them, thrilled to their liquidy reflections. So real to Julian were these imaginings he began to feel a warm breath upon his cheeks, began to feel airy hands massaging his shoulders and back. And did he not hear playful whisperings, the mellifluence of a doting woman's voice?

Julian entered a tavern through a door he lifted from the ground in a narrow alleyway, descended a spiral of stairs as if he was a regular although he could not recall having been there.

Blue white smoke undulated in rusty light, resembled swimming jellyfish. A lamp behind the bar radiated blood red which struck the goblets hanging upside down over the counter, ricocheted among them, sparkled and spun. At the busy barmaid's back fluorescence illuminated shelves of liquor, leading the bottles to gleam in an unfriendly manner. Disturbed profiles leaned against rustic wood walls, a hostile electricity was in the air. People appeared wound up, had the mannerisms of jittery robots, seemingly communicated by abruptly nodding and jerking their heads, examining each other's faces. When Julian glanced above the gathering he perceived the entertainment.

On an elevated stage with her back to black curtains was a light bendingly beautiful folksinger. Undulating about her were streamlets of turquoise mist. At her feet was a plush burgundy carpet upon which her long pale blue gown swished. Her gown seemed held together with incandescence and air, as if it were an angel's shimmering mantle. She was strumming a medieval melody, one suggestive of dusky cloister corridors, illicit trysts. When she commenced singing her soft slyly metallic voice danced deliciously indefinable tickles up and down Julian's spine, whipped throughout him under his skin, caused him to picture dancing needle tips, compelled him to draw increasingly deeper breaths, rise and fall on tiptoes.

When the folksinger approached the song's conclusion her expression altered, abandoning steely professionalism and becoming softer, shot through with moist white light, as if anointed with coconut oil. She strummed more vigorously, launched towards the climax, intensified her delivery, emphatically crossed her legs and pressed them together, vibrated, pulsed, squirmed. Then a rapid succession of resonant screams with her chest thrust forward and right arm raised and she splayed her legs wide, seemed about to rise, was filled with upward motion, feeding on the audience's energy as heat raced up Julian's legs.

Although the audience had served as the singer's launching pad Julian felt she became independent of it, was soaring free—such was the contrast between her upward movement and the crowd's agitated back and forth. Julian sensed he was soaring along with the singer, matching her emotions with his. Tingling surrounded his eyes and flowed over his forehead, made it easy for him to imagine his face becoming radiant, expression blurred. The singer became increasingly obscure, was eventually a bright shadow losing outlines, spreading out, and it was as if the blood in Julian's feet and forehead was trading places, as if the floor was quivering jelly. He began walking while only vaguely conscious of such, came near to believing the ground was moving as he stood still and soon found himself outside in the primary streets. Neon's fading glow merged with sunrise's purple and red, matched his sensation of inundation by gently breaking waves.

As the singer's voice lingered in memory Julian reflected on the freedom of music, its ability to pass untraceably by. One moment melodies are constructing intricate designs, saturating the atmosphere with fluted towers and exotic gardens and multicolors, the next they are gone, leaving one with the impression of fullness, with a longing to pursue the indefinable. Julian was consumed by such longing, felt summoned by the rising sun's brilliance, by the graceful breaking of red waves upon orange clouds. He watched the interplay of sunrise colors so intently he came to believe he was on an equal footing, suspended above the sidewalk and able to float among them. He aimlessly strolled for another hour.

Upon locating a hotel Julian requested a room with dark curtains, arranged for a one o'clock wakeup call and two taxis, one there and the other at a residential address. He entered his room holding his breath, approached the bed as if someone was asleep beneath the blankets, had the expression of a child approaching a stranger. He was hesitant alongside the bed, behaved as if expecting the blankets to abruptly shift. Finally he became limp as a doll and fell onto the mattress.

Chapter V

At a quarter to three Julian was on a porch with morning glory vines entangled in its curlicue grating. Before he lifted his hand to knock a beautiful woman in an indigo gown opened the door. Julia was tall and slender, her outlines dancing in afternoon's light, of unblemished complexion below which waves of emotion surged. Her blue eyes beamed silver light. Wordlessly they stepped into each other's arms, kissing as if deprived for years. Julian pressed against Julia's warm cushiony chest, felt half submerged, her fingers scampering over his face and through his hair as perception of time's passage vanished, her breath heating his cheeks, sighs electric. When the taxi arrived they climbed within as one.

Sunset was commencing when Julian and Julia exited the taxi at a mid-nineteenth century mansion converted into a hotel in the country. Its red brick exterior was smothered in ivy, the leaves of which gently flapped, rose and fell in waves in light breeze, seemed flowing from the gargoyle populated roof to the ground. They had reserved the largest unit in the least frequented wing and ascended stairs, strolled to the end of a burgundy carpeted hallway. Shortly after they stepped within the front room pitchers of matcha tea, bottles of cognac, a platter of beluga and condiments, and strawberries and crème fraîche arrived.

The lights were off and sunset's colors streamed into the room, immersed all in undulation, bright patches invading velvety dimness, solidity rendered vaporous. Ghostly movements held their attention until Julian's hand, apparently with a will of its own, skittered up a wall, located the chandelier's switch and flicked it on. Abrupt materialization of sharp outlines, reduction of movement in the brightness, took them aback and they regarded the stillness with a slight terror. Julian hastened across the room and yanked the terrace door open—and with relief they observed the billowing of the burgundy curtains as ribbons of sunset's kaleidoscope writhed on the terrace's polished marble. Motion absorbed by Julian's eyes became the sensation of being tickled under his skin by swirling fluffs of down. He thrilled to the wind's music, thought of drunken strolls through groves of swaying mimosa trees, fields of rustling wildflowers, thought of sailboats softly pitching in quiet bays. A gust suddenly thrust the curtains towards them, as if about to rip the drapery rod from the wall, and Julian and Julia could not stop laughing.

They raced about turning on all lights and igniting clusters of decorative candles they arranged on the mantlepiece and floor, shutting the terrace door lest a gust quench them or fan a blaze, spread fire. The rooms became almost unbearably bright, were saturated with shimmering rivulets of silver and amber and white, acquired a suspended in space aura as of an amphitheater illuminated by a full moon. The effect was heightened by two floor to ceiling mirrors opposite one another on the dining area's walls. Between the mirrors was the dining table on which their beverages and victuals had been placed. The chandelier above the table resembled airy rings of sparkling opals, showers of pale lavender flares. The mirrors reflected what was reflected in each other and their exchange of brightness bred wavery depths, crystal pools blurred by surface agitation, dancing light.

The urge to strip couches of their cushions and toss them on the long wide mahogany dining table seized them simultaneously, crisp glances exchanged, they transferring the beverage and food trays to high back dining chairs. Then they were on the table, toasting one another with tea and cognac, feeding each other strawberries while caressing one another under their clothes, Julian thrilling to Julia's supple curves, his hands traveling higher within her gown while her hands massaged him under his shirt, localized sensation blurring expansively as if his body was an upwelling spring or tropical sea's ebb and flow, and he was picturing his fleshly presence flowing from his reach as if seeking a limitless realm.

Julian and Julia assisted one another undressing, windmilling their clothes overhead before releasing, watching them flutter to the floor and were rolling among the cushions, joking about proximity of the table's edges, risk of tumbling off while squeezing and licking and play biting each other's attributes, Julian particularly relishing Julia's swishing whispering blond curls, gushing sighs. One moment his skin would be mildly irritated, prickly and tight and the next soothed, relaxed and unwinding as if doused with warm lotion, slipperiness. Julian felt flipped inside out and joined to the air when Julia rubbed against him.

They spooned more matcha powder into their tea, were chasing an on-edge frayed nerves sensation then countering with cognac shots, clasping one another ever insatiably—as if seeking to surrender their personalities, unite identities—glances and gestures displaced words, vocalization was gasps and sighs, gratitude was trills and moans. Julian and Julia were smearing each other with caviar and cream then licking it off laughing, the cushions becoming soaked and soiled, noisily smushy. The ceiling appeared to descend, resembled a fountain's softly settling mist shot through with brightness. Was the chandelier spinning?

They were painting one another with caviar with their tongues—waggling their tongues at the mirrors, amused at the swaths of dark indigo on their paleness. A crystal mini-bowl of shredded greens tumbled to the floor, bounced instead of shattering, scattering the greens. Julian and Julia were mashing strawberries on the table, flinging their scarlet at the emerald of the greens and adding ivory cream, watching the colors combine and reflect the chandelier's gleams and candles' flames. Within seemingly a split minute they were amidst the slippery colors on the floor, quaffing more tea and cognac, throwing caviar and condiments at the mirrors, rolling about hysterically, hugging each other tighter.

At dawn's approach they separated and circled about the rooms, their eyes almost painfully sensitive to brightness and perceiving solidity as liquids. So refined had sensation become it was difficult for them to distinguish steamy air from sweat slicked skin. Like dandelion tufts they felt the density and undulation, the sensuousness of the air. Their hearing was pronounced, such that they detected a whirring as of hummingbirds. Was the whirring not amplifying, becoming steel brushes on cymbals? And was it originating from within or without them? Was it associated with their sudden stepping towards one another, radiant glances exchanged at arm's length between the mirrors? Did it have anything to do with the joy flooding them at sight of the mirrors looming like pools of mercury behind them, sight of one another steadily engulfed by silver incandescence?

They gasped as tingles surged up their spines, spreading to their fingertips, electrically numbing—and silently put their clothes on and strolled to the terrace and descended its winding stairs, entered a meadow dew dusted, flower brightened, wind swished. They did not speak, as their thoughts were each other's, their wills one will. Neither was the master, both were mastered by their united urge. They were as irreversible, spontaneous, and serene as an upwelling spring.

They laughed like children oblivious of the concept of death. And they tossed back radiant faces, inhaled the morning mist, gazed into one another's blissfully blazing eyes, embraced, and slowly backed away. As Julia stood amidst the swaying flowers, her hair waterfalling and rippling, Julian raised a pistol, shot her in the chest. As he watched her—a luminous swirl of silver and aquamarine—tumble towards the ground he fired a second shot into the side of his head.

Bonus Story: Why Waste English Setters on Dog Shows?

Gratefully dedicated to undisciplined dogs
and the people who love them.

———◆○◆———

Steven to Angie & Ella
Sent: Sunday, August 28, 2010 10:47 PM

Miffed, my darlings? You ought to be. What girls worth their frilly underthings—that every man with a pulse wants to peel off—put up with being stood up? All the same, I ask for understanding.

OK, I bailed on our Pierre brunch after making the reservation, but ask yourselves: how often do I fail to show up after setting a meeting up and talking it up? I can count the total for the year on one finger. Is it my fault Byron, one of my oldest friends who I—at most—see every other year, chose today to swing through town on a drive to Cape Cod from Cape Hatteras? I'd say that qualifies as extenuating circumstances.

As to why I didn't bring Byron along so you could meet him: he had his dog Zuke with him and Zuke couldn't be left unsupervised in my apartment. There's no telling what would've been chewed beyond recognition or ripped to shreds.

Zuke's an English Setter—one of the wildest, most spirited, bouncing-off-the-walls-with-energy breeds; and, at eleven months, is in the prime of exuberant disregardful-of-authority puppyhood. Full grown size-wise, still a puppy disposition-wise—perfect combination for maximum riot. Turn your back on him for a second in my apartment, and he's mauling a pillow or chomping on electrical cords or overturning the trash. So that's why you didn't meet Byron and we went to Central Park with Zuke instead.

Yes, an English Setter: slender, swift of movement, graceful of bearing, a breed not often seen in this country outside of dog shows. As for dog shows, the contract Byron signed with the breeder stipulates that he show Zuke. Will he do so? Here's his take on the subject:

"I shell out fourteen hundred for Zuke and the breeder has the gall to inform me I'm to hit the dog show circuit with him! Free advertising's what she's after, as when his pedigree's announced—not to mention I'd be *working* for her without reimbursement, like some sort of whipped sucker. But having botched it with breeders in the past and been turned down due to being honest and naive, declaring I had neither the time nor inclination to go anywhere near dog shows, I was prepared and trotted out a barrage of fake enthusiasm, assured her I was looking forward to showing Zuke, winning prizes; said I intended to hand him over to an obedience school—named the school, well-known in the industry. Still, she was suspicious—subjected me to a borderline interrogation. So I dropped more names and locations of trainers, demonstrated familiarity with American Kennel Club applications, policies, etiquette—was very well-informed, as I'd anticipated invasive questioning, studied the literature. Finally, she swallowed my act and agreed to the sale.

"Christ! Forcing an English Setter, bred for hunting, to endure dog show circuit transport cages is *abuse*! Handing an English Setter over to spirit-breaking parasites at obedience schools is something I couldn't be paid anything to do! All I want is a lively pet, who's loved and appreciated and treated like royalty! Anything wrong with that?

"All the training rigmarole, dog shows... Follow the money, it's an obscenely lucrative industry! The breeder thinks she's going to enlist me in publicizing her business, at the expense of Zuke's well-being! Screw her! And what's she, located in Vancouver, going to do about it when she discovers I duped her, attempt to confiscate Zuke? Hello publicity nightmare if she attempts it! Zuke's going to remain free-spirited and out of control and race like a maniac through fields and up and down the beach to his heart's content and she can drop dead!"

Enough preliminary, sweethearts. By way of seeking to make amends for missing our brunch-date (again, I nearly never do!), I'll entertain you with our Zuke-in-Central-Park adventure. Because, hey, you adore gloriously free-spirited dogs as much as I do.

Once we cross Madison at 85th Street, Central Park's trees are visible at block's end and Zuke's excitedly whiffing the air—inhaling nature's heady scents, tugging at the leash as if possessed, half-dragging me down the sidewalk. I alternate hanging on with my left and right hands and both arms are tired by the time I release Zuke behind the Met after crossing the Drive—it's a privilege to be entrusted with holding the leash, connected to a magnificent dog's strength and energy. Drunk with freedom after being cooped up in Byron's car and my apartment, Zuke bolts towards Cleopatra's Needle, darting every which way.

An English Setter racing free's an uplifting sight. Zuke's on permanent overdrive, easily swifter than any other dog in the park, able to sharply switch direction with minimal loss of speed. He buzzes other dogs, compels them to chase him, but none can come close to catching up. English Setters are pranksters, I admire them unreservedly.

Another trait of English Setters is they love people, are social butterflies, relish attention. Zuke greets people by rearing up on his hind legs, placing his front paws on their chests, often rather abruptly. He's simply saying "Hello!" and is as harmless as a baby but some people don't comprehend and become discomfited, apprehensive. It's amusing to watch Zuke jolt people from their thoughts, force interaction upon them: one moment they're in their private worlds, the next they're compelled to deal with an exuberant—leaping, sniffing, licking—creature that, even if domesticated, has a foot in the wild kingdom.

Byron and I play catch with a Frisbee under the ancient oaks near Cleo's Needle, sun dappling through their sky-obscuring canopies, innumerable songbirds vocalizing, as Zuke races between us leaping and snapping in ineffectual attempts to seize the disk gliding just above his reach—finally, half out of his mind, he barks in protest, squarely facing Byron. So Byron tosses the Frisbee to Zuke and, upon snatching it, he's delirious with delight—capers about in such zigzag angles of abrupt switches of direction it's amazing he remains upright. Then we're chasing Zuke to snatch the Frisbee and he's teasing us in turn—crouching on the lawn, permitting us to approach, only to dash yards away soon as our hands are inches from his mouth.

"Zuke's really charged up," Byron grins. "Let's go over there." He gestures towards the densely populated Great Lawn.

We're shortly entering the Great Lawn via its nearest gate. (Feigning ignorance of the no-dogs rule—if anyone calls us on it we won't argue, let's see if it happens.) And, hey, a populated expanse of lawn's Zuke's ideal playground, be a shame to deprive him of it. He forgets about playing keep-away, indifferently drops the Frisbee—madly dashes across picnic blankets, pausing here and there to say hello to people, be praised, petted—nuzzles and licks some of those who respond enthusiastically. Softball games are being played and Zuke interrupts two of them. In the first instance bounds into the batter's box and, in a demonstration of affection, places his paws on the catcher's knees. In the second instance fields a base hit and dashes in circles with the ball, the defensive players flinging their arms up in futility, batter laughingly trotting home, then going to first base because it's not a home run.

It's then, darlings, that I'm rewarded with transcendent moments—as when the truly unexpected suddenly reveals itself to be a plausible and existing reality of which one's the cause and beneficiary. I'm as if hovering outside my body, gazing upon the scene from a distance: Zuke, softball in his mouth, is racing like a maniac while both teams' players take turns halfheartedly chasing him; Byron and I, making a show of attempting to catch Zuke and leash him, are shrieking "Zuke! Zuke!" at the top of our lungs. We're causing a great deal of commotion on this previously peaceful afternoon and many of those nearby have whipped their heads in our direction, and guess what? No one's lecturing us, cursing us, even though we're blatantly violating Central Park's rules regarding where and when dogs are allowed to be unleashed.

It needs to be experienced to be believed: despite dashing around and shouting and clearly sharing responsibility for the commotion, I'm enveloped in sensations of security. How so? Because I understand that, as long as Byron and I pretend to try to catch Zuke while dispensing profuse apologies, announcing he got away from us and ran through the gate, no one will voice opposition. *How do two adult men get away with sowing chaos in a public place? All they need is a spirited dog.*

I'm thoroughly relishing the situation: many people are highly amused, laughing; others are watching with interest, or no readily discernable expression; a small percentage are exhibiting traces of annoyance. Am I worried concerning the latter? Not a bit. They dare not voice annoyance because then they'd be branded as dog-haters and incur the contempt of the majority. (Is it too far-fetched to suggest that dog-haters, especially in the eyes of people who frequent parks, are situated towards the bottom of the totem pole, somewhere in the vicinity of snitches, telemarketers, and neglectful nannies?) Nor does it hurt that Zuke's a poster child for canine cuteness: wide trusting vaguely sad eyes, long floppy ears, soft sleek tri-colored coat, a grown puppy romping without a care in the world. As I overhear one woman say: "Such a pretty puppy-wuppy! I could hug him all day!"

Deeming it time to return the softball, Byron tosses the Frisbee to Zuke: he drops the softball to seize the Frisbee and a player scoops up the softball. The players, jovial fellows, shout things such as, "Hey Zuke, we could use you on our team!," "Gold Glove fielding, Zuke!," and "Now we have a spitball!"

We've created a disturbance on the Great Lawn for over five minutes—good fun, but unwise to push it. Tolerance for a madly romping dog, no matter how cute and friendly, won't last forever, especially since the Great Lawn's officially a dog-free zone. So Byron and I exit and head towards Belvedere Castle, Zuke following close, we immediately leashing him.

And that, Angie and Ella, was our secret all along: as long as we chased Zuke, he was going to dash from our grasp, customary in a game of tag. I like to think of it as our covert canine and human agreement: Zuke disrupts gatherings of picnickers, sunbathers, ballplayers and we count on him to avoid us while pretending to try to catch him. We've the option of ending the game at any time, simply by turning about and heading for the exit, whereupon Zuke will dutifully follow.

Additional adventures are forthcoming, we alternately releasing and leashing Zuke—when we're near the Drives, or children's play areas, he's leashed. We always make a point of rather theatrically leashing him following his romps, to give credence to our apologies for his having "escaped." But I'm not taking it for granted I'll always get away with allowing dogs to romp in many of Central Park's forbidden spots—luck had a lot to do with it. Unleashing Zuke and racing around yelling the way we did happened spontaneously, we were simply drunk with it.

In Bethesda Tunnel Zuke demonstrates his hunting skills: suddenly freezes and stares, apparently mesmerized; then a swift dash, and—presto—he's grabbing a bag dangling from a man's hand, giving it a sharp tug: out tumbles a roasted chicken. Zuke wastes no time in seizing the chicken and racing towards The Mall. Quite breathtaking.

"Jesus Christ!" the man yells, glancing about to see who's responsible for the nefarious chicken-snatching beast.

"Zuke!" we're screaming at the top of our lungs—the tunnel very effectively amplifies and echoes our yelling.

The man glances at us for a couple instants, then towards the end of the tunnel, where Zuke's devouring his prize at the base of the stairs leading to The Mall—upon his face is a mix of being none too pleased and amused despite himself. Before the man can speak, we're approaching and apologizing profusely, offering forty dollars for the inconvenience, adding one of us will happily go buy him a new chicken at the store advertised on the bag, within a fifteen-minute walk.

"Aw hell, I can get another bird for a lot cheaper than that and do it myself—lots of places to get one on the way home, it's not like you guys stole it," the man answers, refusing the money and the errand. He makes it clear the offer of recompense is recompense enough. "What kind of dog is that, anyway?" he asks, gesturing in Zuke's direction.

"An English Setter."

"Hunting dog, right?"

"Too much of a hunting dog for the city I think," says Byron, apologizing with his eyes. "He's a country dog and doesn't know any better, shouldn't be snatching grocery bags."

"He sure as hell knows what he's doing!" the man declares, smiling broadly. "That bird was out of this bag and over there in seconds! It's worth a bird to see that and blessings on Zuke! I'm glad he's enjoying it! And he's still got his nuts! Good for you! Don't neuter him!"

"Dead horses will fly to Mars before my dog gets neutered," responds Byron heatedly, no longer ill at ease, Zuke's thievery having been dismissed. "Break his spirit? Steal his manhood? Where do people come off assuming they've a right to make those decisions?"

"Neutering's criminal!" the man fairly shouts. "Had a dog awhile back—Black Lab, feisty and smart, bundle of energy. I took off on business, convention in Atlanta. The first wife goes off and hauls him to the vet, gets his nuts cut off while I'm gone! Brando wasn't the same after. Spark missing from his eyes—he got lazy, wasn't as quick and bright. Sometimes I thought he was asking 'Why?' when he looked at me—it was like he was wondering how I could let him be savaged. And I sure asked the wife why! Guess why? Because some bought and paid for toady of a journalist on TV said it was beneficial! She was always glued to the tube, mistaking blather for gospel truth! No one easier to hoodwink than the first wife! Once a beauty pageant winner, but with low mileage! As scatterbrained as she was unable to keep her looks, and with her bedroom skills flagging as fast! She's been swapped for one who ruts like a rabbit *and* has a head on her shoulders."

"Yeah, just because I have a dog I'm expected to blindly buy into pro-neutering propaganda! Dogs haven't chosen to be born into our civilization, so the least we can do is be kind to them, refuse to mutilate them. Neutering dogs suggests they solely exist for our pleasure, are toys to be manipulated by us, which is disgusting. It's not like I'm going to irresponsibly allow Zuke to go around knocking up other dogs, add to overpopulation of unwanted dogs in the shelters, but the control-freak zombified loonies don't care. They say neutering's in a dog's best interest, as if being robbed of sex-drive will make a dog happier. What they *really* mean is it makes dogs more submissive—easier to train to do stupid tricks that reflect more on the vanity of humans than anything that's good for dogs. They get a dog because they want a creature to boss around. They want to show off in front of others of their ilk, say 'Watch Rover roll over! Watch Rover heel!' They're controlling despotic creeps who victimize animals because they need to feel superior, excusing it as concern for the animals' welfare."

"Damn right!" says the man, pumping a fist. "It's disgraceful what's commonly accepted to do to a dog, and I don't see the pro-neutering people rushing out to sterilize themselves, so where do they come off doing it to dogs? Responsible dog owners let a dog be a dog, accept them and love them as is. Not those scaredy-cat twits who want them to be stupid and lazy, like my stupid first wife! Dogs *ought* to steal chickens and raise a ruckus! To hell with those that disagree!"

As if on cue, chicken-thief Zuke trots up to us; not only is he inapprehensive of the man from whom he's filched the chicken, he greets him enthusiastically, placing his front paws on his chest.

"You're a good boy, aren't you, Zuke?" says the man, caressing Zuke behind his ears, petting him. "Such a *good* dog!"

We part from the man the best of friends and continue on our merry roving tour through The Mall (after cleaning up remnants of the chicken) and thence to The Pond via a winding route, leaving bustle and fluster and laughter in our wake, Zuke unleashed at least half the time. Towards journey's end I'm near delirious with the license to carry on that Zuke's antics are making possible. When he's loose I'm screaming his name like a maniac, dashing about like a ten-year-old. Zuke has transferred a portion of his freedom to make a spectacle of himself to me and I'm savoring every moment. Thanks to our frequent yelling of Zuke's name, it's possibly engraved upon the memories of dozens of people.

Alas, the waking dream's over too soon: we exit the park at 59th and 5th and Zuke's leashed going forward; no longer surrounded by open spaces, he immediately settles down. We stroll back to my place, chat for a couple more hours over a salmon dinner, of which Zuke gets a hefty portion, then say our goodbyes. Byron resumes his journey to his ex-girlfriend's Cape Cod place—meaning they've placed their "ex" status on hold, are revisiting steady-relationship experiences. Who knows? Maybe Byron and Lisa will eventually stop informing themselves these meetings are one-offs (these so-called one-offs keep adding up!) and full-out surrender, possibly marry? But I digress.

So, dearest ones, there's my excuse for bailing on our brunch-date and why I ask for special consideration, something you know I nearly never do. And although Zuke had a huge hand in keeping me away from you, I think you ought to think kindly of him and send sweet thoughts his way. I owe Zuke much gratitude for placing my NYC self in touch with the animal world—I'm still humming with it, have zilch wish to turn in as early as I ought to, be well-rested for tomorrow's new-client tour, and the slideshow presentation, and lunch at Smith & Wollensky's that'll likely last until evening. (Lunches are the worst sort of emotionally draining *work*, since we need to balance lightheartedness with professionalism, neither be too serious nor too carefree.)

Sowing a bit of chaos in Central Park in plain view of hundreds and getting away with it—three Central Park employees, that we know of, even looked the other way, bless them—lifts fun to wildest heights, and more: it's shown me the sorry degree to which constraint's infiltrated my life, accompanies me everywhere, subconsciously and otherwise—understanding the enemy better enables me to deal with the enemy, test and extend boundaries. Being in on the capers of a spirited dog's rejuvenating, therapeutic, instructional. And, hey, has romping with a dog ever motivated anyone to chuck their job, sell their co-op, relocate to an inexpensive foreign country, live free of obligation henceforth? But don't worry, it's just idle speculation—I'm not chucking everything, taking off anytime soon. NYC's too much fun.

Why do we love dogs, easily bond with them? It's not only that dogs are blind to our shortcomings, unselfishly offer affection and devotion, it's that we travel back to unrecorded history with them, when the first wild dogs approached us, inquisitively, and we tossed them scraps, and they wound up accompanying us on hunts, assisting us on hunts, providing companionship in the face of unpitying nature. It's miraculous how we bonded with dogs and that they trust us, and they turn us into better people. Dogs exist in our civilization without being fully of it and remind us of our authentic ancestry, when we lived unencumbered in emotional expression, non-splintered in our heads. Countless generations preceded us and our present state of civilization-engendered emasculation's an aberration, encompasses a minuscule amount of human history. How can we not want dogs among us, when they temporarily liberate us—gift us with glimpses of what we once were, when human freedom was boundless, vanity nonexistent?

I'm totally disinclined to sleep, only want to continue riding today's euphoria—can't stop seeing Zuke's tricolor coat flashing in the sun! Will have to brave tomorrow sleep-deprived, even if the stakes are high, new client introductions, urgency to put on a show. But we all know it's far from the first time I've gone there, since it's usually the two of you who irresponsibly—ha ha!—fire me up too much to sleep!

Good fun and goodnight, sweethearts!

Love,

Steve

About the Author

Robert Scott Leyse has lived illegally in Paris; worked as a New York cab driver on the night shift; slacked galore at the U.S. Geological Survey and corporate law and pharmaceutical advertising firms (while valued by his employers); taken a belly dance class in Green Bay, Wisconsin; nearly slid to his death on loose gravel above a sea cliff in his hometown of San Francisco (nails bloodied by digging into the dirt saved his life); and the most incandescent yoga class he's had was on a SUP during a storm in Condado Lagoon, Puerto Rico. He eats insects and drinks blood, but can't be paid to eat potato chips or cake.